THE
VUDURI
COMPANION

BY
MICHAEL BRACHMAN

THE VUDURI COMPANION

Also by Michael Brachman

The Rome's Revolution Series
Rome's Revolution 3455 AD
The Ark Lords
Rome's Evolution

The Rome's Revolution Saga
Rebirth: The Rome's Revolution Saga – Book 1
Rebellion: The Rome's Revolution Saga – Book 2
Redemption: The Rome's Revolution Saga – Book 3

The Vuduri Knights Series
The Milk Run

The Vuduri Universe Series
The Vuduri Companion
Tales of the Vuduri: Year One
Tales of the Vuduri: Year Two
Tales of the Vuduri: Year Three
Tales of the Vuduri: Year Four
Tales of the Vuduri: Year Five

DEDICATION

I have been writing science fiction for over 40 years. That's a long time! It would be impossible to thank all the people who have helped me and supported me along the way. There is my U of M Creative Writing professor, numerous editors and potential agents who took the time to reject my stories and manuscripts in a constructive way. My parents have always been supportive of all my endeavors, this one included. However, there are four individuals I would like to single out in particular for this collection of short stories.

First, I would like to thank my faithful Office Manager, Pat, who dutifully took my 1973 manuscripts and retyped them into Word so that I could include them in this volume. She raised her eyebrows more than a few times but she was kind enough to finish.

Next, I would like to thank my friend, Helen, who has pursued a parallel path to writing. Helen aspires to write literature, I do not. I want to write action and adventure. Despite our differences, Helen has always been encouraging and her advice has never been anything less than spectacular in terms of improving my writing.

Next, as always, I must thank my brother Bruce. He has always had my back even before I restarted my modern career. Not only is he my editor and artist and the inspiration behind MINIMCOM, but he is also fiercely protective of the Vuduri culture and characters. Bruce creates the amazing covers, the book trailers and makes my writing so much better. Bruce, I could not have done it without you.

Finally, my undying gratitude to my wife, Denise, for all her love and support throughout the entire process. She patiently waits while I hide myself in the basement, cranking out what is now over a million words, because she knows I love writing. She even cooperates and allows me to keep my workspace unadorned, despite the fact that it is against her nature, so that my mind can travel to different places and times. Denise, thank you so much and I'll be up around 5:30, I promise. Yeah, right, she says.

INTRODUCTION

World-building is hard. Really hard. Especially when you are writing science fiction and have to create a universe populated by people you don't know; a universe complete with its own politics, culture, physics and even new species. The essence of hard science fiction is that it be believable by *not* writing anything you know *not* to be true. The double negative is the only way to describe the rules. If you write about things that you know not to be true, without explanation, it is called fantasy.

I have writing about the future, actually multiple futures, since 1969. I have been writing about the 35th century and the world of *Rome's Revolution* since 1973 which, if you do the math, makes this my 43rd year as of the publication date. That's a long time to be thinking about one possible future and a group of people, now known as the Vuduri. Inevitably, as the story evolved, portions changed, the characters changed, even my entire future history changed. When I decided to take my original trilogy entitled *VIRUS 5*, nearly 360,000 words, and boil it down to the modern *Rome's Revolution 3455 AD*, huge chunks of the story had to be excised. Sadly, some of those chunks were among my best writing. This volume gives me a forum to present some of those deleted portions to you as standalone stories. If you read nothing else, please read "Before the Piranha Rats Came" as it was the original prologue to *Rome's Revolution 3455 AD*. It may one of the best pieces I have ever written. I certainly polished it enough.

As I mentioned in the first paragraph, I have always wanted to write *believable* science fiction. Sometimes that meant I had to write entire stories knowing full well that they would never make it into the books just so I could get the characters and their motivations and backstory consistent. Sometime 10 pages were required just to get one sentence correct. Again, this volume gives me the opportunity to present some of those backstories to you as well.

Purely for your amusement, I have included the original novelette (also entitled "VIRUS 5") first drafted in 1973. It is interesting to see how much of it has changed and how much it remained intact in the modern novels. Way back then I had to use a Royal Aristocrat Electric typewriter. The novelette was 53 pages long! That's five three. Way too long to edit or revise multiple times. So I extracted a prequel, made it a much more manageable 20 pages and entitled it "Rome's Revolution". Somehow, I had forgotten that and when I came up with the modern version, that title just appealed to me. It wasn't until my daughter found an old box filled with my old manuscripts, that I realized I had stolen the title from myself, some 35 years earlier. I am also presenting that version to you as well.

Finally, there are two original short stories, written exclusively for this volume, entitled "The Invisible Man" and "The Immortals". "The Invisible Man" is about the discovery of the Dark Matter Diode which gave rise to the Casimir Pump and the PPT star-drive. With regard to "The Immortals", if you have read my previous novel entitled *The Milk Run*, you would know that I took the opportunity to "reboot" my main characters, Rome and Rei, and this is the story of what happened the day after.

Before each story, I will give you just a sentence or two as to how the story came into being but mostly the stories should be able to stand on their own.

Enjoy.

CONTENTS

1

PRUNO DREAMS

Author's note: Everything has a beginning. I had been writing about the Ark program for so long, it seemed like it was time to come up with the formal origin story. I wrote this purely to amuse myself but it became useful when I started writing **The Ark Lords**.

Year 2040 AD
Location: Earth
Detroit, Michigan

THE FAINT CHIRPING SOUND IN THE DISTANCE WAS SOMEBODY'S misguided attempt at creating a subtle but insistent alert. To Alex Haynesworth, it just made the red-hot poker seemingly stabbing through his right eyeball throb all the more.

He took in a deep breath and covered the offending orb and tried to lift his head up. A pruno hangover was possibly one of the worst conditions a human could ever impose upon themselves. Through his still-functional left eye, Alex stared at the main display and discovered it was totally murky with hundreds of overlaid images, an inevitable result of his falling asleep on the data input surface. He clicked on the Clear Viewspace icon and hit the three-fingered sequence which allowed him to answer the call.

"Alex, where are you?" his assistant, Vick Rausand shouted, his voice shrill with panic. "Everybody will be here in like two hours. We have to set up your presentation."

"Oh crap," Alex mumbled, noting the time then shaking his head. It didn't matter. He had nothing.

"Look, Vick," Alex said. "I'm not ready."

"How could you not be ready?" Vick shot back. "You've had three months." The dark-skinned man took a deep breath to calm himself. "I've seen your preliminaries. Shaw likes them. They're good enough." Vick hoped the confidence he was trying to project would somehow travel the 'net and infect his boss.

Alex inhaled and tried to remove his hand from his eye. It was no good. The eye still didn't work correctly.

"They aren't," Alex said. "They're not grand enough. These people want to spend ten billion dollars. Nothing I've come up with remotely matches the scale."

Vick leaned forward, almost pressing his nose against the vidcam. "Alex, the entire company is depending on you. Just inflate the numbers. It'll be good enough."

"You're wrong. It won't be," Alex muttered. He exhaled a deep sigh. "But I'll be there. I'll upload the thing in a few minutes and you can set it up while I'm on my way in. OK?"

Vick just glared at him. The connection was cut.

Alex leaned back in his chair. He was lost. The not-quite-empty pruno bottle sat next to the input surface and Alex considered swallowing the dregs. Pruno was perhaps the only liquor that smelled just as bad going down as when it was vomited up. Alex knew this from first-hand experience. But pruno was all most people could afford these days. Alex was smart enough to know it wouldn't make a difference. He had failed and that was that.

He reached forward to clear his screen and the images popped back up, ready to be deleted. Alex cocked his head. The alignment of the images, one in front of the other created a mosaic that strongly resembled a skull and crossbones, the time-honored symbol of piracy or death. The pitiful proposal he was about to offer was nothing short of highway robbery. Maybe the brutal pattern meant death. The death of his career? The death of humanity?

"Yeah, right," Alex said out loud to his view screen. It did not react. He couldn't have created this effect if he had tried. The topmost image was a picture from space of an asteroid that scientists called 2009 X194. It had missed the Earth by a mere 12,000 miles, taking out numerous geostationary satellites along the way. It was the closest known non-lethal encounter with an asteroid, nearly 500 km across, in human history. On a cosmic scale, it wasn't a near miss. It was a dead-on hit that just happened to not take out the planet.

Alex moved this picture into a tray on the right side of the display screen and looked at the next image. It was also a satellite photo of super-storm Gamma currently ravaging the coast of Japan and China. The two hundred mile-per-hour winds had caused quite a few villages and towns to simply disappear. He moved that image to the tray as well.

The next image was a 3D photo of a blast zone from the southern part of Lebanon where terrorists had claimed they had executed 500 infidels. The only consolation was this was a conventional bomb, not a dirty one so the casualties were simply those who died in the explosion.

"What are you trying to tell me?" Alex muttered. He was fascinated by the peculiar sequence of images that his falling asleep at the virtual keyboard had created. There was something linking these images together. Something obscure. "We humans are doomed as a species," he said to the computer. "What do you want me to do about it?'

He moved the thumbnail off to the side tray and saw a news report that the Kepler spacecraft had finally ceased to function after almost 30 years. There was a retrospective summary of its findings, correlated by many subsequent missions confirming that there was a greater than 90% chance of an Earth-like planet within 60 light years of the Solar System. The TESS mission had bumped that number up to 99%. The Sagan Survey System was due to be launched early the following year and, in theory, it would be able to detect the presence of life-sustaining planets to a 99.9% probability or higher.

"Big deal," he said. "There's still no way to get there." He moved the news report off to the side and looked at the next image. It was three sad-looking scientists who were overseeing the dismantling of the mini-hadron super-collider. It was being cut up and shipped off to space because there was no longer any denying that it had created multiple quantum black holes and no one could take the chance of any of them being stable. There was one scientist, Wally Grey, who claimed that the QBHs could be used to construct a souped-up ion drive that could theoretically take a spaceship to the stars using a method similar to the long-debunked EmDrive. The only problem was it would take well over 80 years to even reach Alpha Centauri.

"Ha," Alex laughed to himself as he moved the image to the side. The next frame showed a video of a man with no fingers, smiling and waving to the camera. Alex leaned forward. Now it all made sense. There, in front of him, was the key which unlocked the mystery: it was The Ice Man.

The tiny auditorium was abuzz with people, not only from the Reynolds Corporation but representatives of the Gates/Buffet foundation, the armed forces and numerous government agencies, some identified, some not.

Alex Haynesworth stood at the podium and tapped its surface three times. The assembled crowd reacted to the noise and settled slightly. Alex nodded and the holo-projectors lit up a virtual surface about three feet in front of him.

"On behalf of the Reynolds Corporation, I would like to thank all of you for coming here today." Alex's name lit up on the projected surface.

"My name is Alex Haynesworth and I have been tasked with figuring out what to do with the ten billion dollar grant being offered by the Gates/Buffet Foundation. Today I am going to reveal our plan."

There was a general murmur in the crowd as the projected image changed to show a geodesic dome floating on the water of some unspecified ocean. It had to be an ocean. The tiny waves lapping up against it ruled out anything smaller. The animated image showed the top of the dome peeling back and a tiny helicopter rising up from the opening.

"I thought about creating the world's greatest resort," Alex said, "one that would be immune to the super-storms that are currently plaguing the planet."

The virtual camera zoomed inside the dome and showed a lush Garden of Eden with waterfalls and pastoral villages. Alex stepped over and the projectors gave the effect of changing his clothes from his business suit to shorts. Alex put on a simulated pair of sunglasses and grinned.

No one in the crowd cracked even a smile. Alex shrugged. He made a motion with his hand and the image went away.

"They told me you were always supposed to start out with a joke to loosen people up. I apologize. I was trying to be funny."

A man on the front row lifted his hand and Alex caught the gesture.

"All right, serious it is," he said. He walked back to the podium. "I will get right to the point. I am proposing that we spend the ten billion dollars to save the human species before the Earth is destroyed."

The crowd gasped. "Destroyed by what?" someone asked.

"By any number of things. I'll get to that."

"So how?" the same person asked. "How are you going to save the species?"

"By sending people to the stars," Alex replied. There was a hushed sound over the audience at first but then the buzzing started as each person turned to their neighbor.

"You can't do that," someone else said. "There's no way to get there."

"Yes there is," Alex said firmly. "I'll show you."

The holo-jectors lit up again. The images projected were identical to the random photographs he had pulled up while sleeping off the pruno from the night before.

"Let's assume the Earth is doomed," Alex said. "Whether it is a super-storm or a nuclear war, whatever."

"There's no proof that these have to happen," someone from the second row offered.

"No, you're right about that," Alex replied. He brought the image of 2009 X194, clearly labeled, as it receded into the distance after its near miss. "But geologists have proven that the Earth has been hit at least six times by asteroids big enough to destroy nearly all life. It's just a matter of time before we encounter another planet-killer. It could be in ten years, it could be in ten thousand. Meteor, comet, no matter, something bad is definitely going to happen someday."

"So you propose we build a planetary shield?" someone asked.

"No," Alex replied. "You're missing the point. It doesn't have to be an asteroid. It could be a plague. It could be the gamma ray burst from a hypernova. Who knows? I'm not saying what it is. Just that it will happen. Man has to get off the Earth to guarantee survival. We can't keep all our species' eggs in one cosmic basket. We have to spread out."

"We already have a base on Mars. Wouldn't it make more sense to build that up? What about setting up a colony on one of the moons of Jupiter?" someone asked.

"No," Alex said. "Those places are not really suited to human life. The TESS satellite has given us clear evidence that there are many Earth-like worlds within even just a 60 light-year radius. And after the Sagan mission is launched, we'll know exactly which ones they are to a virtual certainty. So why not send people to where they can live without pressure suits or fear of radiation."

One man stood up. He was not wearing a tie but still carried the gravitas of very important person.

"Dr. Haynesworth," the man said, "There are so many flaws with your argument that it is hard to know where to begin."

"Try me," Alex said.

"Certainly," the man replied. "First, how would you get there? We have no propulsion systems capable of traveling that distance."

"We might," Alex said. He flashed up the picture of Wally Grey. "This man, Dr. Wallace Grey, has a theoretical design for harnessing quantum black holes and turning them into a star-drive."

"How would that work?" the man asked.

"Scientists have already confirmed the existence of multiple QBHs within the mini-hadron collider currently being shipped into space. Dr. Grey thinks he can stabilize the QBHs and feed them single atoms of xenon at a rate sufficient to keep them healthy. Each atom enters the event horizon of the black hole and exits almost immediately as Hawking Radiation and a shower of subatomic particles. By containing the output in a resonant chamber with a single exit port, the net result is thrust. The amount of thrust created would be negligible but over time, it could be used to get a starship going as fast as $1/20^{th}$ the speed of light. That means that Alpha Centauri can be reached in 80 years or so. Tau Ceti can be reached in 250 years. It may be possible to supplement the fuel with interstellar hydrogen or helium and go even further."

Another man leaped up out of his seat. "How the hell are you going to keep people alive for 250 years? This is crazy."

"No, it isn't," Alex said calmly. The projected image changed to the smiling man, waving with his fingerless hand.

"This is Sven Ausland," Alex said. "You all know him as The Ice Man."

"What's that got to do with anything," the first man asked.

"You all know his story. He's famous," Alex said. "He fell into a crevasse 17 years ago and his body was found last year. He'd been frozen solid all that time. When they thawed him out, a quick jump-start of his heart and he was fine."

"What about his fingers?" someone asked. "Doesn't look fine to me."

"He had frostbite. His fingers were dead before he was frozen completely. If it were done under the right circumstances, all of him would have been intact."

"You can't freeze people," the second man said. "Their cells burst. It's been tried numerous times with animals and they always wake up dead."

"Sven proves otherwise," Alex said condescendingly. "Before he was frozen, he had become completely dehydrated. There was enough room in his cells to handle the expansion of the intracellular fluid. Basically, he was freeze-dried."

The crowd was becoming agitated. There was too much truth and information for them to absorb all at once.

"So relate the two back. How does freezing people get them to the stars? During a trip of such magnitude, there would be radiation, micrometeorites, who knows what. There is no way to build a spaceship that could last that long. We don't have the technology."

"You are exactly correct," Alex said. "I don't intend to build a super-spaceship. In fact, I'm proposing we build the cheapest spaceship possible. Think of it as a flying tin can."

"How will sending a tin can to the stars guarantee the survival of the frozen people?"

Alex paused for a second. The way the man phrased it made it sound silly, even to him but he pressed on.

"We use statistics. If all of our money goes into building a single space-worthy super-ship and something bad happens, everybody dies. So instead, we build a cheap starship and put each frozen passenger in a radiation-proof, micrometeorite-proof container. Like a coffin or more accurately, like a sarcophagus. Once they're in space, we open up some vents within the crew compartment and then we wouldn't even need active refrigeration. The cold of interstellar space will keep them frozen." Alex pointed his finger in the air. "However, as you correctly pointed out, some of the people will die, to be sure, but most will live. If we send 500 people on one of these Arks, at least half should survive the trip and it would be more than enough to build a colony when we get there."

"Where would you send these ships, these Arks?" the second man asked.

"According to TESS, our best targets would be Alpha Centauri, Tau Ceti, Beta Hydri and 82 Eridani. If we can figure out how to collect interstellar gas or dust, we could even try for Nu^2 Lupi. Even without the Sagan mission, of those 5 stars, we have greater than a 99% chance of finding a viable world in the habitable zone."

"Who gets to go?" the first man asked. "Based upon your math, it seems like a suicide mission."

"It might be," Alex said. "But so might be staying behind. I guarantee you we would have no shortage of volunteers. I know I'd go. We just ask for the best and the brightest and we see where it goes."

There were three uniformed men from the U.S. Space Force sitting in the third row. One of them, a general, stood up. "Mr. Haynesworth," he said. "Do you really think ten billion dollars will cover the cost of this whole program?"

"Probably not," Alex said, "but certainly enough to do feasibility studies. "Look," Alex spread his hands out, palms up. "I don't claim to have all the answers. But we have to start somewhere and this," he said pointing the floating virtual Ark, "is somewhere."

"What are you going to do for defense? What if the people who get there find hostile indigenous life or some other kind of danger?"

"Like I said. I don't claim to have all the answers. I freely admit there are a lot of details to work out," Alex said. "But somebody has to do something and this is my best idea."

There was general murmuring among the crowd. The three uniformed men, including the general, literally put their heads together. After a few minutes, all three nodded. The general stood up again.

"Your idea *is* intriguing," said the general. "And on its surface, it actually has some merit." He looked down at his two peers then back to Alex. "Since you're going to need some kind of security forces, there is probably a way we can merge the interests of the U.S. Military with your goals. If that ends up being the case, we should be able to help with the funding, too."

"That's great!" Alex said. He looked around the room. "Obviously, this isn't the end," he said. "It's just the beginning. Every one of you is welcome to offer any suggestions you might have. This is just a springboard." Alex pointed straight up. "A springboard to the stars."

One person in the audience began clapping slowly. Another joined him then another. Soon, the entire audience was on their feet, giving Alex Haynesworth a rousing round of applause. And so it was, on this very day that the Ark program was born.

Alex never told anyone about the pruno.

2

BEFORE THE PIRANHA RATS CAME

*Author's note: Of all the stories I have written before **VIRUS 5** became **Rome's Revolution 3455 AD**, I believe this was my finest piece of work. I spent the most time polishing it so that it hooked the reader and made them want to read the rest of the novel. However, when I boiled the three novels down into one, this was the very first casualty. It only links into the plot in the most peripheral way and there were plenty of opportunities to weave in certain elements later in the book. I'm glad Silas Hiram finally gets his day in the sun. I hope you enjoy it.*

Year 2165 AD
Location: Fourth Planet, Aleph (A-Star)
Rigil Kentaurus System
(4 Light Years from Earth)

SILAS HIRAM EXHALED SHARPLY AS HE LIFTED THE SPLIT LOG AND replaced the two pieces within a slot on the side of the wooden fence. The wood dried so fast here and became so brittle it was inevitable that the full log would split. He wrapped a soy-stalk tie around the frayed ends and then looped it around the post to keep the two ends in place permanently. He squatted down to inspect his work and decided that it was complete. Now came the time he hated; now he had to stand up straight. Instinctively, he put his hands on his hips, arching backwards as far as he could go and then some. His back was bad and getting worse, but he had learned that pushing it way past its natural limit let him recover enough to straighten up and walk normally, or at least good enough to fool Mary. He chuckled to himself after he did it because Mary wasn't even home to see. She and the boys had left early in the morning to visit the neighbors and wouldn't be back until tomorrow.

That his back hurt all the time made no sense, of course. This world had far less gravity than Earth. But lying supine, dehydrated, in a cryo-hibernation chamber for 80 years caused some type of degeneration that affected him more than the others or so he thought. Before they launched, the scientists had assured all of them that there would be no aging, no ill effects at all, from being frozen for so long, but his body told him that just was not true. Back on Earth, stem cell soup would have fixed whatever had gone wrong but here on this virgin planet, their medical technology was primitive by necessity. Under these circumstances, there was nothing he could do but grin and bear it. However, this was a small price to pay for all the wonders and freedom this planet had to offer. At least his sons were born on this world and they would grow up right and strong and tall.

Silas was coming to the end of a long day. In fact, every day was a long day because of the planet's speed of rotation about its axis. The human body could adapt, of course, but that didn't mean he wasn't tired. Some days he felt like he was catching up to his real age, which would have been well over 90 if he had been awake the whole time. To anyone else, they would have guessed he was in his late forties.

Silas looked up into the azure sky at Beth as it set in the west. In the binary star system of Rigil Kentaurus, there were two stars. The brighter of the two was called Aleph and the dimmer B-star was called Beth by the residents of New Earth. New Earth was the fourth planet out from Aleph, a G2V star, virtually a twin of Sol. Aleph's companion, Beth, was a deep orange, K-class star. Though both stars had several planets, each star had only one habitable world located in the comfort zone. The one orbiting Aleph was far superior to the one circling Beth and was the natural choice between the two for man's first colony world.

When Silas first arrived on this world, Beth had trailed behind Aleph by several hours past sunset. That meant that the sky did not really get dark until many hours into the night. But with the sureness of the complex celestial mechanics behind it, Beth slowly advanced and now led the way, ahead of Aleph, by about one half hour. When Beth was out during the early evening, at an apparent magnitude of -18, it was far, far brighter than the full moon of Earth. At night, Beth was a spotlight that drowned out all the constellations and stars that surrounded it. Due to an unfortunate alignment of the stars, that meant especially the one group of stars that Silas cared about. But this would not be the case tonight.

11

Silas carefully stooped down to gather up his tools and materials and placed them in the wood carrying bucket he had crafted. He looked back to the west and decided to watch Beth as it set completely. Beth was a deep orange to begin with but now, at sunset, it took on a blood red color that was absolutely spectacular. For just one night, Silas thought to himself good riddance. Now all he had to do was wait for Aleph to set.

He turned his head east to west and saw no signs of Nuna, their single moon. It, too, had just set; yet another piece of the astronomical puzzle. Silas was also thrilled to note it was absolutely cloudless this particular day. Weather was always the final variable; but it would not be a factor tonight. Tonight the viewing conditions would be perfect.

"Tonight, tonight, won't be just any night," Silas sang to himself. West Side Story was so far removed from this world and its people but Silas had always loved it. He laughed; it was a good thing there was nobody around to hear him sing. He was completely tone-deaf. That didn't change the fact that on this day, both suns were finally setting in the exact right sequence at exactly the right time. Tonight really was the night!

Aleph was just starting its descent toward the horizon and its color was beginning to deepen from its usual yellow-white, taking on the rosy-orange hue of all suns at sunset. And just for one moment, her color perfectly matched that of Beth at its brightest. During this exact instant, it struck Silas viscerally that the two stars truly were sisters. Not just because of their proximity, but because the fate of one rested upon the fate of the other. Their orbital mechanics may be intricate, but to the twin stars, it was how they always had lived. In the future, there would be other binary star systems occupied by man. Of that, Silas was sure. But there would never be a system exactly like this; so perfect, so balanced. He knew he was among the most privileged people to have ever lived.

When their colony ship launched in 2065, no one knew with absolute certainty as to whether the either of the two terrestrial-type planets circling the binary stars in their respective habitable zones would be suitable for human life. The decision to orbit and land was left to the AI, their artificial intelligence engine. They couldn't take the chance of reanimating someone before the determination was made. If they reanimated even one person and then were forced to move on, that person would have had to remain awake. No one could survive being put into cryo-hibernation twice. And if they had to move on, because of the incredible distance between star systems, it would have been a death sentence for that unlucky soul. So instead, they built a ship where human decision was not a requirement. Fortunately, of the two candidate planets of Rigil Kentaurus, this one was found to be more than habitable. This beautiful world, their New Earth, was already teeming with indigenous life. While it was a little drier than they would have liked, there was enough water for life to start and therefore enough for the colonists to live on.

New Earth had an oxygen/nitrogen atmosphere and was nearly a duplicate of Terra except for the fact that the oceans occupied less than one quarter of the planet's surface and were fairly shallow. Also, there were far fewer planets around each star than in the Solar System and there were no gas giants here. Eons before, the binary stars had swept all the Jupiter-type planets clear leaving only the rocky terrestrial-type worlds remaining. Maybe the lack of gas giants caused fewer comets to be flung to New Earth, which limited the amount of water on the ground. Nobody knew. That kind of scientific investigation was a luxury they could not afford at this early stage of colonization. New Earth's mass was about 80% of Earth, but it was far richer in some of the heavier elements making it slightly denser so the gravity was about 85% of Earth-normal. This fact alone probably explained why Silas was able to function at all, given the degeneration in his back.

Silas turned and looked at his soy fields. The plants were flourishing despite the relatively arid conditions. The soy plants were ideal because they provided much-needed protein for both the humans and the animals. Their shredded stems could be woven into a hemp-like material that could be used for clothing and construction. Aleph was brighter than Sol. That, coupled with the lighter gravity, caused the soy stalks to spiral upwards in wild shapes trying to capture every golden ray. The soy plants, originally from Earth, had adapted and were thriving here as were many of their crops.

The cargo portion of their Ark brought them the seeds, animal embryos, mining and metal-working equipment, tools, farming equipment, some vehicles and dozens of other items deemed necessary to start a civilization. Each person also brought some clothing and a smattering of personal belongings. The allotment wasn't much, but something was better than nothing. A strict weight limit made each person very discriminating as to what was absolutely essential. Silas, along with the others who chose farming as an occupation were given the opportunity to acquire the whole of the living portions to grow. Protecting their bounty was up to the individual farmers.

On this farm, the chicken wire and fencing kept all the native herbivores at bay. The assorted plant-eating creatures that lived in the woods around his farm were very slow and very stupid. This fencing was more than adequate to keep them out. His livestock knew better than to try and wander outside the perimeter if they wanted to keep the 'live' part of their title. At this latitude, the only creatures they really had to worry about were the batwolves and assorted lurkers. Those predators were more cunning. And vicious. When they first arrived on New Earth, they lost some livestock and one or two of the colonists to the carnivores, but things were under control now.

The whole concept amused Silas. Of course the predators were more cunning. The very idea of a stupid carnivore made no sense. They wouldn't last very long if they could not outwit their prey. Since man was the smartest creature on Earth, it would be hard to deny that man was the deadliest carnivore that ever lived. The predators here could not outwit them. The cows, horses and pigs were safely tucked away in the barn. The chickens were cooped up in their coop. The sonic generators and a little prudence kept all the remaining risks manageable.

Silas surveyed the rest of his spread and couldn't see anything else that needed attending, at least not tonight. Buoyed by this knowledge, there was a spring in his step as he walked back toward the farmhouse, noting the lengthening shadows with a deep satisfaction. He had tried mightily all day to distract himself so that he wouldn't count the hours, minutes and seconds until the twin sunsets. That only seemed to make the passage of time run more slowly. But now it was finally the appointed hour. As he walked by Mary's herb garden, Silas inhaled deeply. The air smelled so fragrant, even delicious. He wanted to treasure every moment of this experience. Today of all days, everything seemed right with the world. He wasn't sure if it was good or bad that he was experiencing it all by himself.

Their farmhouse was a modest, two-story affair made of stone and wood with a cupola mounted on the near side of the roof; the side that faced west. The first floor windows were small and barricaded against any unforeseen and possibly mean-spirited trespassing creatures. Silas noted that the railing on the far side of the front porch had split again, but since they rarely used it, he would have to attend to it on another day; certainly not today. Over all, it was a good house; it had character. And it was more than enough for Mary and the boys to call home. His old cryo-hibernation chamber, called a sarcophagus, was stowed away out back. Even with just one rod, the sarcophagus produced plenty of power for their minimal electrical needs. This was fortunate because they had to give Mary's sarcophagus and one of his power rods to the community central store in trade for the starter crops and embryos.

On this world, there was no money. Every transaction was made using barter or good will. The lumber Silas needed to build his house was purchased with the sweat of his brow and Mary's flair in the kitchen. The labor was free. All the colonists took turns helping each other build their houses. A house-raising was always a joyous affair and a chance for the members of their little community to see one another, sometimes the only chance.

The mining town, where the landing team had set up the materials fabrication facility, was booming. The particle beam drillers had uncovered vast amounts of high-quality ore and the smelting furnaces were producing a steady stream of metals and composites. The vehicles they brought with them had been commandeered for hauling ore with the promise of manufacturing community-use cars and trucks 'any day now'. While Silas might reap some of the benefits, he knew that his boys would live long enough to see a true civilization flourish.

Silas stopped in the kitchen and drew himself a flagon of beer. Brewing it was one of his hobbies and he was getting really good at it. Mary had protested when he put in the small squares of barley and hops, thinking the plots would have been better suited to other, more useful types of plants, but he had made a believer even out of her. In fact, she was taking some of the new batch to the neighbors to try. He was garnering quite a reputation for himself. The possibilities for barter were endless. The neighbors were still experimenting with grapes and their last few bottles of wine were quite passable. Things were getting interesting!

He went back to the door and made sure it was secure. Since it was night time, there was no chance that Mary would endanger the boys by bringing them home after Aleph set so he knew it was not a problem throwing the deadbolt. He took the time to straighten the family portrait that was taken only two years ago. Standing there was his beautiful Mary with her auburn hair. This world had been good to her. She hadn't aged a day since they arrived here. Next to her stood Willis, the older one, with his freckles and curly red hair. Where had he gotten that color? And then there was Bryce, the handsome one, with not a single self-centered bone in his body. Silas loved his family and missed them even though they had only been gone one day.

He took a sip of beer and made his way up the stairs to the second story foyer where there was a parsons table. He set down his beer, reached up for the rope hanging from the ceiling and lowered the trap door to the attic. He had to wrestle a bit with the folded steps nestled against its frame; they were sticking. Retrieving his beer, he made his way up the collapsible stairs, which groaned, complaining mightily of his weight. This damned brittle wood, Silas thought to himself. But the steps held and once in the attic, he set his beer down, this time on a stool perched at the top of the retractable steps.

To his left was a large wooden handle, recessed into the wall. He pulled it out until it snapped into its extended position. Taking both hands, he began to turn it. Despite the creaking noises, the clamshell roof opened easily. He cranked it steadily until the dome reached its fully opened position. The eastern sky, partially obscured by the roofline, was turning deep indigo and already he could see several stars popping out. His neighbors thought he was nuts to build an observatory when there were so many other pressing issues, but Silas Hiram was dedicated to preserving his interests and needed this to pass on the legacy of Earth to his sons.

He walked to the center of the room and did something he knew he would regret. With a grunt, he lay down on the thinly padded mat there, setting his beer aside. He would get up shortly and haul out his telescope, but for now, he just wanted to watch the fabric of the stars unfold. His mind wandered to the sky. He tried to imagine the exquisite cosmic ballet that led up to tonight. New Earth spun about its axis, giving them day and night. New Earth also orbited Aleph, giving them a full year. Beth swung around Aleph, every eighty years, Aleph's faithful companion.

While Aleph was the king of the sky, Beth was certainly the queen. And as queen of the heavens, Beth did not want to yield; she wanted to rule the night sky. But no matter how Beth twisted and turned, she always had her date with destiny. Right now, in April of 2137, Beth was just past periasteron, the closest the two stars would come. Beth's luminous grip on the sky was at its strongest but was also responsible for her early departure. And even Nuna, their New Luna, could only stay in one place for a few days. The moon circled New Earth once every 21 days. Only yesterday, at the new moon, she had obscured the constellations Silas yearned for. But there was no malice behind Nuna's soft glow. She had no such aspirations. Nuna's role was to stabilize the orbit of New Earth, eliminating any wobble and give them the conditions they had today. It was the same way back on Earth. Perhaps the moon's influence on the tides also gave life an opportunity to develop or perhaps come onto land. Maybe that was how it started it here but just took longer to develop.

Beyond that, there was a grander plan, more than the days and weeks and years; more than the 80-year star cycle. Aleph, along with her sister Beth, spun about the Milky Way in her own path as well. Today they were 4.4 light years from Earth. In another million years, it would be five. In a few billion years, nobody would even know they were once neighbors. But today, the unalterable day, April 25, 2137, the one star that Silas craved would finally peek from between the peaks of the western mountains. This star would be lying there in the sky; waiting for Silas to gaze upon her, well after Aleph had set for the night.

As New Earth swung about its home star, because it was tilted on its axis, they had seasons too. Just like on Earth. Their new year started with their beautiful, still spring; a spring that filled the heart with joy and hope. That was followed by the warm summer that made things grow. All you wanted to do was bask in the suns and soak up all their rays. Then came the fall when the leaves changed from their yellow-green to a deep crimson. It was staggering in its beauty. And then came the winter, fully four months long, with their sparse snows and dry frigid air. Silas and his family had learned to pack away supplies until the spring. They spent many a day and an evening looking at the fire, in awe at the peace of this world.

As Silas stared upward, he also marveled at what had to be more than coincidence. The fact was that New Earth was just the right size and just the perfect distance from Aleph for life to get started. How could a planet know where to coalesce such that it was located in the habitable zone? That their Earth could do it and it happened on New Earth too gave Silas hope that this scenario could be replicated over and over again across the universe. And not just the habitable zone of the star but of the galaxy. To think, not on this world, but perhaps another, they could encounter another sentient species. Oh the talks they would have! Mankind would find out once and for all if his remarkable ascent to intelligence was the norm or something special. The idea of aliens did not scare Silas, it excited him. The animals here, given another hundred million years, might have achieved the same. But now that man had arrived, the natural order of things would be disturbed. But to Silas, that did not matter.

Soon the sky became dark enough and the tiny pinpoints of light were bright enough that the heavens above looked like a velvet tapestry. There was no light pollution on this world, or at least not yet, so the black of night, now that Beth was fully hidden, was the blackest he'd ever seen this early in the evening. If there were no other reason to migrate to an alien world, this would be reason enough. This night sky was magnificent beyond comprehension. The sky on Earth was like a piece of dense grey cloth with the occasional rhinestone. The sky on New Earth was so dark you could get lost in it, your mind soaring between the stars. It was like a voyage of discovery where there was simply too much to learn.

Silas started counting off the constellations one by one, trying to orient himself. Their system, called Rigil Kentaurus, also known as Alpha Centauri, was so close to Earth, cosmically speaking, that the constellations and stars appeared more or less the same as on the star charts he had brought with him. Of course, the constellation Centaur, for whom his new home star was named, was missing one element of its foot, for that was Aleph, the sun that had just set. That was only one of two major differences in the night sky. Under closer scrutiny, one could see that there were plenty of minor ones.

Finally, when enough time had passed, Silas tried lifting himself up but he knew immediately that was impossible. Instead, he practiced the ritual of movements required to stand; it was a complex choreography. He spread his arms wide then drew his knees up, pushing off with his left arm and twisting his knees to the right using their weight to roll him over. He swung his right arm straight up over his head, rotating about his center of gravity. He pulled his right arm out, continuing his turn until he was flat on his stomach. From this position, he drew his arms beneath him as if he was going to do a pushup. This next part was easier. He rocked backwards until he was on his hands and knees then sat back on his haunches. Thank heaven for the lighter gravity. Arms spread, his left knee came out and he used its strength to force him up.

There! He'd done it. Without the shooting, searing pain that normally accompanied getting up after being flat on his back; he was now standing straight up. He turned to the west. Silas could see the Milky Way in all its glory spanning the entire sky. That he could see it at all with his naked eye amazed him, even though it shouldn't. Back on Earth, in Pennsylvania, they had long since lost that ability even on the darkest of nights. Many of Silas' friends had never even seen the Milky Way, but most did not care. Silas did.

He searched and searched until finally he found what he was looking for. Sitting very low on the horizon was the zig-zag of Cassiopeia. He held his right hand up, straightened his arm and used his hand to blot her out. Even lower on the horizon, partially obscured by the mountains to the west, he found the inverted V of Perseus and with his left hand, he blotted him out as well. He extended both thumbs to form a frame and within that frame was the most beautiful thing he had ever seen. If Mary were here, he'd tell her that it was not as beautiful as her, of course. On this night, it was only the eighth brightest star in the sky, but to him, it was the most important. He knew its name was Sol, but he just thought of it as The Sun. And though he could not see it, he knew he was looking at Earth.

Since their arrival, back in 2145, there had not been one word, not one transmission from their home planet. Their telemetry had ceased receiving input only a third of the way into the flight, way back in 2093. Their engineers had determined that there was nothing wrong with the equipment. Earth had simply stopped sending data along the tight-beam sometime late in 2081. Silas hoped that condition would be rectified some day, but for now it was out of his control. The lack of communication made no difference in their day-to-day lives but still, losing that connection seemed to make them feel yet more isolated if that was even possible.

He stared at Sol for a long time, waxing nostalgic. He knew why he and Mary were here. He knew why they had chosen to raise their children on this alien world. The pollution, the overpopulation, the natural disasters, the wrecked ecology, the continual random acts of violence loosely called terrorism; these were the problems that had driven Silas and Mary and the other colonists to seek refuge among the stars. But that didn't mean he couldn't miss his ancestral home, knowing none of them would ever see it again. Earth was the birth-world of his species and that would never change.

He walked over to the corner of the room and opened the tall cabinet that was standing there, removing a large blue canvas bag and setting it on the floor by bending only his knees. Unfortunately, as he was pulling it out, he accidentally knocked a medium-sized plastic box to the floor, which popped open upon impact. Silas bent over to pick up the box, the lid and the pen and the small notebook that had fallen out. He yelped as he straightened up due to the sharp pain that shot up from the base of his spine to the base of his skull. Then he laughed. What else could he do, it hurt so much. He was so conservative in his movements; he spent so much time trying to avoid these incidents but he was never vigilant enough.

He carefully set the box and lid on the shelf and put the pen and his journal in his pocket. He knew he'd be making some notes tonight so there was no sense in buttoning the storage box up just yet. The airtight box kept the hardcover journal (which was nothing more than a schoolboy's assignment book) crisp and clean from the humidity that paradoxically collected up here in the summers. If only there was some way to capture the moisture and harness it for more useful things besides feeding the mold that had accompanied them on their long journey. The attic always smelled musty because of it. He usually kept the cupola open a crack but it wasn't enough to get a clean smell.

Returning to the business at hand, having learned his lesson for the hundredth time, Silas squatted down rather than bending over and unzipped the case. He pulled out the tripod and set it up without much fuss. Then he got out his trusty 90mm catadioptric telescope, which was built around a Maksutov-Cassegrain reflector. He had to fiddle with the mounting screws, but finally got it attached to the large, heavy-duty tripod and carried the whole affair to the center of the room, placing it on the mat. He flipped on the power switch and watched it go through its initialization procedure. He chuckled when the handset warned him against pointing the telescope into The Sun. This was exactly what he planned to do! Of course, the makers of the telescope had never envisioned it operating in another solar system. Thank goodness that the telescope's internal database had been modified for the night sky on Rigil Kentaurus. The company had been all too thrilled to make the effort for him. Maybe they left that warning in to amuse or comfort him.

The telescope swung around asking him to line up the finder on Vega, which was easy. What had been called the Summer Triangle on Earth looked just the same here. But unlike Earth, on this pristine world, within this blackest of skies, there were so many stars in-between. After centering the red dot finder on the star, he told the telescope to move on. The telescope needed a second star to complete the alignment and the handset indicated to him to find Sirius, which from this planet appeared as part of the constellation Orion. Silas looked through the clear eyepiece, trying to visualize the three stars of Orion's belt, but something was wrong. He took his eye off the laser finder and looked up. Orion was unmistakable. And there was Alnitak and Mintaka, the two ends of the belt. But Alnilam, the center star, was nowhere to be found. At first, he thought it might be a high-flying cloud or possibly a circling batwolf obscuring it. Perhaps if he waited a moment, it would come back into view. He waited and he waited. He waited a long time, but Alnilam never reappeared.

Finally, he could not wait any more. He made a note then finished the alignment procedure by fixing the red dot finder on Sirius. At long last came the moment he had been waiting for. He commanded the telescope to point at Sol which was just setting behind the mountains to the west. Riveted, Silas stared at it through the Barlow doubler eyepiece until it dipped below the horizon. Once it was gone, it tugged at his heart but he put those feelings aside. Now that the conditions were right, he could not wait until tomorrow when his boys would be home and they could see it for themselves. Yes, on this world, tomorrow was always a better day.

3

ACCELERATION

*Author's note: I first wrote this story in 2004, long before I started writing **Rome's Revolution 3455 AD**. However, I am including it because it is the precursor, nearly word for word, for Aason Bierak's journey to Heaven and what he found there in the middle part of the novel **The Milk Run**.*

Year 20?? AD
Location: Earth
Southeast Pennsylvania

I DON'T KNOW WHAT MADE ME LOOK UP BUT MY EYES WERE DRAWN immediately to a bright spot in the sky. It looked like a star only it was daytime. I was out delivering a bundle of papers to the lawyer for about the hundredth time. It was an unseasonably warm day for the first week in March and I still had my winter coat on. I am lazy and just wasn't ready to switch to my springtime jacket for weather that I knew wasn't going to last.

As I looked at the spot, I could see it was growing larger and larger. It was almost as bright as the Sun and within seconds appeared as large as the Sun. Suddenly, with a tiny popping noise, I was enveloped in what seemed to be a golden cylindrical chamber with no ceiling. The wall itself was quite transparent. I looked down and realized I was rising up into the air. Moments later I could see rooftops and from the rate at which objects were shrinking, I could tell I was accelerating upwards. I didn't feel any tug, which was puzzling. The experience was so strange and it all happened so quickly that it didn't occur to me to panic.

As I arose into the air, I could no longer tell what I was looking at until it became clear I was beginning to see the curvature of the Earth. I could see all of North America and above and across from me, I could see the boundary of the atmosphere at the edge of space. It reminded me of all the NASA pictures I'd seen over the years only this was real. Now the whole Earth was reduced to a blue ball with puffy white clouds, which was shrinking quickly. I was in space. It would have been beautiful had I time to look at it. As it was, the gravity (pardon the pun) of the situation was starting to dawn on me. How could I breathe? Why didn't I feel the acceleration? Why wasn't I freezing to death?

The fact of the matter was I was quite comfortable. I could move my arms and legs. I could look around. I was breathing. I wasn't cold. In fact, I was slightly warm in my winter coat. It occurred to me that I probably wasn't going to die just then. Why would somebody go to all the effort to suck me up in a cylinder of light, just to let my blood boil in the vacuum of space? I sort of relaxed and let it all happen. By now, the Earth was a bright blue star which was shrinking rapidly. I could see the Moon on the other side of the Earth and the Sun. The triangle formed by the blue star, the yellow star and the silver dot was rather pretty.

The acceleration continued and I found myself wondering whether I was going to get a tour of the Solar System like I'd seen in so many movies. I looked out and spotted Mars off to the right so I knew I wasn't going to be flying by that planet. I turned and look up in the direction of the top of the cylinder but could not make out Jupiter or Saturn so I figured that this was not the point of the journey. When I looked back down, the Earth and Moon had fused into what looked like a single, slightly elongated dot. With sadness I watched until I could no longer see the Earth. The Sun was becoming a tiny dot of light, brighter than the other stars around it. I looked up again trying to see up to the top of the cylinder but I couldn't make anything out. I reached out to touch the sides of the cylinder but then I had a horrible thought and yanked my finger back. If the walls of the cylinder were not solid and I stuck my finger through, it was be exposed to the cold and vacuum of space; not a pleasant prospect. I reached out again but ever so slowly and was gratified to find that the walls of the cylinder felt solid.

With that part of the adventure over, I looked down at my watch and saw that it was now about 30 minutes since I left the Earth. I had no frame of reference but I did remember something from high school physics about how long it took light to travel from the Sun to the various planets. I knew that it took 8 minutes for light from the Sun to reach the Earth. I knew that it took a little over 40 minutes for light to reach Jupiter from the Sun. So if I could find Jupiter, I could estimate my speed. I couldn't remember exactly how long it took light to travel from the Sun to Saturn so I figured I'd use one hour as a working figure. Maybe you would have done something else with your time besides calculations but I didn't have a whole lot else going on.

The worst thing was I didn't have a clue about the other planets even if I could find any of them. You're sitting there in high school, they are teaching you these things and you figure you only had to remember them long enough to pass the test. I mean seriously, who would have ever thought that knowing the time it takes light to travel from the Sun to Neptune was important?

Off to my right, I could see a star that was moving more quickly than the rest. It had to be a planet! But which one? It couldn't be Saturn because that would mean I was traveling faster than the speed of light. I checked my watch again. It was now 40 minutes since I left the Earth. I tried to imagine the planet traveling in a large circle around the sun and tried to estimate when I crossed that imaginary path. It was roughly 50 minutes. A quick estimate in my head told me that I was traveling at 70% of the speed of light! Jesus Christ! How could this be possible?

And I was still accelerating. I could tell that the motion of the stars, while agonizingly slow, was increasing. Physics, physics, physics. Why didn't I pay more attention? The only force I could think of which accelerated matter to the speed of light was gravity. Black holes are discovered by the emission of light and x-rays stemming from the matter that dives into a black hole. If it was gravity, why didn't I feel anything? Why wasn't I pulled apart into a fog of blood and body parts? What else could it be?

There is an old adage from science fiction; I think it was Arthur C. Clarke who stated something like "any sufficiently advanced technology is indistinguishable from magic." So while this seemed like magic, it had to be advanced technology. I thought about dark matter and the recently described dark force. The only thing I could recall was that dark force operated kind of like anti-gravity. So if a cylinder of dark force were trained on me, maybe I would be repelled by matter until I was no longer under its influence. It boggled the mind. Who would develop and harness dark force? I thought we couldn't even see dark matter and its presence was proven by the absence of things we recognize like light and regular matter.

So who could manipulate dark matter and dark force? I wracked my brain. Was there anything inherent about dark matter that would preclude beings built of dark matter? Could dark matter sustain life? I don't think anybody knows. I vaguely recall reading another science fiction novel about somebody who traveled about the galaxy and through time and came across beings made of dark matter. Since they belonged, essentially, to different universes, it was difficult to communicate with them. I don't even remember how it worked out but clearly somebody thought of it. If they were a good science fiction writer, they probably researched it and concluded it was *not impossible*. Ha: science fiction substituting as shorthand for actual scientific knowledge. Well, it wasn't like I could go to a library or surf the net and research it now.

The stars were moving visibly. Each star had kind of an elongated halo about it. Almost like they were being stretched. I looked down at my feet and it seemed like I was stretching as well. It may have been just an illusion, who would know? If I was truly moving near the speed of light, maybe the photons from my feet were taking longer to hit my retina giving me the appearance of growing taller. I raised my arm over my head and it looked like my arms grew shorter. When I moved them back to my sides, they seemed to be normal length again. So it had to be some sort of perceptual phenomenon.

On and on it went. I wasn't achy because I was able to move around. In fact, I could kind of twist all the around if I moved just so. I was beginning to get a little bored if you can believe that. At one point, a bluish star whizzed by, I had to assume it was a planet. I couldn't remember if it was Uranus or Neptune that was blue. I looked at my watch. It was now a little over 4 hours since I left Earth. Damn it! I wish I could remember this stuff.

My legs were now significantly longer than they were before. From the way it looked, it seemed like I was 10 or 20 feet tall. I couldn't tell. I watched my feet in fascination as they stretched farther and farther away. As they stretched they seemed to become lighter, almost translucent. Sure enough, after a couple of minutes, I could definitely see through them. I couldn't explain this, even with the slow photon theory. The rate of stretching was accelerating. Suddenly, there was another slight popping noise and I couldn't see myself at all. It was like I was watching through a TV screen only three-dimensional. I could still twist and look around but I couldn't seem myself at all. I willed my arms up to put my hands in front of my eyes but nothing happened. I thought I was moving them but I couldn't see them. I took a deep breath but I couldn't feel the air entering my lungs. I tried holding my breath but I couldn't feel anything there either.

There were only two possibilities. Either I was intact and my extreme velocity was interfering with my nervous system so that my perception was gone or I really had changed into some sort of incorporeal being. If my nervous system was no longer functioning, why could I still see and change my point of view? If I was incorporeal, why could I still feel my body even though I couldn't see it? Maybe I was dead, after all and this is what souls or angels feel like.

Since I could no longer see my watch or even my wrist for that matter, I lost all track of time. Since I no longer seemed to have eyelids, I couldn't even close my eyes and shut off the images that I was perceiving. I looked down. I looked up. Nothing changed. The stars were just streaks now, bluish at one end, reddish at the other, aligned along the axis of the cylinder. I couldn't hear anything. It was like there was cotton in my ears but I had to entertain the possibility that I had no ears. I kind of drifted in and out. It wasn't like I was sleeping but just stopped noticing things.

The cylinder seemed to be getting smaller or my concept of myself was enlarging. Either way, "I" whatever that meant, was getting closer to the edges. I decided to believe the cylinder was getting smaller for the time being. It came closer and closer to me then it was gone. I was now just a point of view, traveling at some unbelievable velocity through space. I began to wonder whether I was a man who became a beam of light or a beam of light that dreamt of being a man. I think Jeff Goldblum said something similar in the movie "The Fly" and the very fact that I could remember that told me that I had probably been a man once.

If I were a man, traveling at the speed of light, if I slowed down, would I revert to my prior form? Would I just disappear? I recalled from some distant memory that photons acted like particles or waves depending upon the circumstance. So I figured I was just a big man-particle acting like a big man-wave. I laughed at the concept but there was no evidence that I was actually laughing.

I could still rotate my point of view so I looked "up" whatever that meant. I couldn't see anything. Around me the streaks of light that had been stars began to weave themselves into a luminous cloth. The beautiful lights of the star-cloth became brighter and brighter then flashed and were gone. It was now completely black. I could see nothing, feel nothing. Conclusion: I had to be dead. There was no other explanation. But why was I still having thoughts?

How long had my journey taken? I had no idea. I remembered something about time dilation but I had always thought that was relative from one observer to another. Could time have slowed down for me? Had it stopped? It still seemed like I could change my point of view but there was nothing to see. Or was there? "Above" me, it seemed like there was the briefest of sparkles then it was gone. You always "see" things in the dark, various retinal events, and this seemed like one of them. I stared and stared and thought I saw another sparkle but I couldn't be sure.

I had spent many a night outside, watching meteor showers with very poor results. You'd stare so long and so hard that sometimes, out of the corner of your eye, you'd think you see something but it was gone before you could focus on it. Once in a while, you'd see the real thing and you'd know it. Well above me, finally, I knew this was the real thing. It was like tiny crystals that were reflecting some unknown light and as I got closer, I could see more and more of them.

The crystals didn't seem to be getting any closer but now there were a lot of them. The part of the "sky" they occupied seemed to be growing as well. I had no other place to look so I watched as they spread farther and farther. Suddenly, I plunged through them and into something and I came to a dead halt. I don't know how I knew this and my body did not reappear but there was no motion. I was in a cloud of crystals that sparkled and pulsed. I wish I had hands so that I could reach out and touch them but I had given up on that concept.

For the first time in what seemed forever, I could "hear" something. I don't think I could describe it any better than a faint hiss but it was definitely sound. Back when I was human, I used to hear my dishwasher going and occasionally pull "music" out of the noise coming from the machine. I thought I could hear some sort of cadence, some modulation in the hiss but that is all. I watched the crystals and could see that the sounds and the motion were related. Maybe all I was hearing was the crystals rubbing against each other. Maybe I was a crystal now. If I were a crystal, what would I say to another crystal? How's it going? Lame.

I realized that the motion, which had appeared random before, only looked that way because I was concentrating on the crystals nearest to me. If I looked up, I could see a sort of swirling pattern, almost like a whirlpool. I looked around and around and tried to gauge where the center of the "whirlpool" was. There it was, dead ahead. And I was drifting towards it. A very faint rushing noise began to superimpose itself on top of the steady hiss. The rushing noise became louder and louder. I suddenly felt like a grain of sand in an hourglass and that my time was almost up. I got pulled closer and closer to the center and then I was through.

What lay before me is indescribable or rather no single description applied. I could impose any look upon the expanse that I wanted. I envisioned it as a crystalline city with motion and beings and then it was undersea, complete with crystalline fish and other creatures. It was the stars again then it was the inside of a hunk of quartz. It was like looking at clouds and imagining them to be any shape you want. The motion within was purposeful; I just didn't understand the purpose. What I really wanted was somebody to come up and explain to me what was going on.

That is exactly what happened. Some of the stuff of the expanse coalesced into a shape like a log and drifted closer to me. While it was definitely not human, there was most certainly a face. The mouth region was moving and a noise emerged. It was a language but I didn't understand the language. The creature dissipated but I could tell "he" was still talking to me. The expanse became to change, no longer of my will, but his. It was telling me a story. I felt so stupid because I couldn't understand the story. I tried to speak but of course no words came out.

Everything winked out. I was in the pitch black again. Then there was a tremendous explosion right in front of me and I guessed it was the Big Bang. Tufts of material clumped together to form what had to be galaxies. As one galaxy came closer, I had to guess that it was the Milky Way because otherwise, what was the point? Within the galaxy, a star system appeared and while it was not the Solar System, it was definitely a sun and planets with a mix of hard worlds made up of the heavier elements closer to the star and lighter, gas giants formed farther away.

Another flash occurred and I "got" it. Somewhere in this star system, life had started. It evolved, became sentient then super-intelligent and eventually broke free of the constraints of the mortal flesh. The consciousness of the planet was self-sustaining through patterns of light and while no longer bound to the planet, they remained within their star system to contemplate things far beyond what I could comprehend.

And now they were dying. The only thing I could imagine was a disease but it was more like within their ranks, dissension arose over some esoteric concept and the cloud of light was broken into two camps. The two camps separated and neither was as vital as before. In fact, the only way they could continue to live was to settle the conflict and rejoin. They had brought me here to resolve their dispute. They wanted to know which camp was right so they could put the issue to rest and merge once again. If I didn't decide, their race, their species would disappear forever.

While I wanted to know what the issue was, I didn't really care. What possible difference could it make which camp was right? Then I knew. The group that was wrong would be absorbed into the group that was right. They would cease to be, sacrificing their "lives" for the betterment of the race. The consciousness would go on, even thrive, but the wrong side would die.

So what was the question worth dying for? It was simply this: one group felt the universe was knowable, the other felt it was not. The group that thought the universe was knowable wanted to go and learn everything no matter how long it took. The group that thought the universe was not knowable wanted to spend their days learning as much as they could until the end of time.

This hurt my head as if I had a head. No matter what I decided, the end result would be the same. Both groups would have them spend the rest of time in this universe learning. Who cares if they learned everything or not? The adventure would be in the trying. So that's what I told them: that I didn't know the answer but the ability to discover the answer lie in their power. I told them that they should rejoin and unite in the common purpose of working towards finding out if the universe can be known. In the end, they would succeed or not succeed. In the end they would have the answer to the question of whether the universe was knowable and which group was right.

Everything went black. Then white. Then gold. Then I was back in the golden cylinder and I could see my body forming from the walls of the cylinder. I knew that I was on my way home. It seemed like forever but eventually I entered what I knew had to be our Solar System. I hurtled past the outer planets and came rushing up the Earth. I flew down and finally landed on the ground, right next to my car.

I looked around. It seemed like everything was exactly the way I left it. I looked at my watch. It was within seconds of when I had been abducted. I looked up and saw the last remnants of the golden cylinder disappear. Other than that, there was absolutely no evidence my trip had ever occurred.

Maybe I had a cosmic experience. Maybe I didn't. Maybe something I ate didn't agree with me. I picked up my papers and walked into the lawyer's office for about the hundredth time.

4

ONLY HALF THE STORY

Author's note: There are many times when I jot down ideas intending to flesh them out at some point in the future. Like many of the stories presented in this volume, these half stories are just to work through the details in order to facilitate a coherent description in one of my novels during production. I gathered up the more important ones and present them here. Just don't expect them to be more than a sketch.

4.1 - The Freeze Dryer

Author's note: This half-story was constructed so that I could work out the mechanics of cryo-hibernation. There was no drama, just action.

Year 2050 AD
Location: Earth
Houston, Texas

WHAT A HORRIBLE THING, THE FREEZING. THEY FEED YOU BUT WHAT they feed you is salty and they give you nothing to drink. They give you chips but no Coke. They offer pizza. You grab it because you think that the cheese and sauce is going to provide moisture. They all dream of one whole tomato escaping the crushing arm and somehow making it all the way out to the cans. They practically lose their minds, digging into that moist red little pouch of sustenance. But there is none. It is part of the myth espoused to break them. To have them give up and float back in a torpid state. If they are dry enough, they can stand the cold without caring. Some do, most don't. They get them below 35 degrees C then flood them with the reanimation fluid then freeze the whole mess. The sarcophaguses are left ajar and washed with freezing cold solutions until release was imminent. In the shaded cold of space temperature routinely gets below 350 degrees C; perfect for protecting these dehydrated humans for several

31

hundred years without maintenance or any kind of external freezer. Space would see to that. Any rational being would consider that cold, that vacuum as a killer, ready to reduce a life to nothing. But those freezing chambers welcomed the cold as a promotion in their attention. In this world, it extends life toward infinity. How odd, the dichotomy.

They only tested cryo-hibernation on 22 people. Twenty were people with terminal diseases of some sort who would appreciate freezing time, no matter how briefly. There were only two who were healthy, who truly believed that what the world learned from their experience (read: death) and would make the world a better place. They were frozen for five years. The results were horrible. Eleven were dead. From the looks of it, they died very early in the process. Eight lost limb, faces, anything that could die without killing the body itself. The normal man volunteer, had his arms and legs cut off and had to be put in a special box. He was walked around the US at carnivals. How he got that way was soon forgotten.

The girl came through perfectly. At least physically. She underwent some hypoxia as she went under and spent what was in effect eternity in a hypoxic state. She understands some 100 words and is able to handle simple tasks. Her left eye had to be removed and her right eye was clouded over. She wasn't all that useful.

The final subject, not one of the healthy ones, came through rather perfectly. After a day or two or three, he seemed really none the worse for wear. They had him in debriefings, in examinations, in parties and meals. Nothing was found. The doctors asked him if they could do some tests on his various hormones to what possibly made him so immune to the debilitating effects of the cryo-hibernation. After enough poking and prodding, they were able to determine that he had a higher than normal concentration of Tumor Necrosis Factor Alpha, owing to the fact that he had fissured disks and they were releasing TNF-Alpha continuously. When the Arks took off, as the people were frozen, the scientists rigged the chambers to guarantee that as each person fell asleep, a rod would poke them up in the back in order to cause back pain and release TNF-Alpha. Although they did not know it, each of the nearly 540 men and women were sent off into space, were destined to be in pain upon arrival.

The defibrillators were of the simplest design. The paddles were also the cardiac monitors.

(That's all I have. The rest of the details are presented in Rei's Resurrection.)

4.2 - The Super Terrorist

*Author's note: In my future history, I had always planned for the Earth to be wiped more or less clean in the year 2081 AD. This was well after the Arks had launched so Rei and his cohorts had no knowledge of this prior to awakening in the 35th century. This was my original proposal for how The Great Dying occurred. However, as I was building **The Ark Lords**, I came to realization that Colonel Harmon Slayton, the military man from "Pruno Dreams" presented above was the spearhead of the entire Darwin Project. Thus there was no need to blame a terrorist. In the current version of my future history, the near extinction of mankind was a cold and calculated, planned event. The leaders behind the Darwin Project wanted to "reboot" the Earth. So this story became superfluous and just plain wrong.*

Year 2081 AD
Location: Earth
Somewhere in the Middle East

Mixing nuclear weapons and biological weapons was not a good idea.

While my future history has always been consistent and the time secure, I was never able to determine what was the true nature was of the Apocalypse. I had always assumed it was World War III with nuclear weapons being launched by the super-powers. Now I realize it is not the case.

Instead, what happens is that the world becomes used to terrorism. Terrorists are so dedicated and radical but they really don't need to be all that smart. Once their major modes of distribution of terror become known, most nations of the world are able to create sufficient infiltration and detection to disarm all but a scattering of terror plots. The world enters a new age of cooperation and prosperity. The terrorists become increasingly isolated and their few forays into the world to deliver terror are foiled.

Towards the end of this century, a brilliant child is born within the ranks of terrorists and is only taught those goals. However, this boy is different and learns what it takes to truly deliver death and destruction to the world. By the time he is 29, he has acquired 845 nuclear bombs and 112 thermonuclear bombs. He slowly spreads them around the world, concentrating on the industrialized nations that represent the infidels. Little does he realize that he is being manipulated, supported and guided by people way high up who actually want him to succeed.

Finally, on October 3, 2081, he detonates all the bombs at once. The "Super Terrorist" destroys most of the important nations instantly. He also dies due to an unforeseen consequence of his action in that he causes a massive shift in the plate tectonics and the continents reform themselves. Land kicks up in the Pacific, most of North America, especially the US sinks. California, Oregon and the entire West Coast lifts up to join with the new continent. Europe collapses like a sink hole and the Mediterranean and Atlantic join leaving only Spain. Volcanoes arise all over the world including Asia and the Middle East. When it all settles down, no one would recognize a picture of Earth from space, having no resemblance to the world before the War.

So between the direct effect of the bombs, the geologic upheaval and the after-effects of radiation, most of humanity is destroyed. Of the nine billion people on the earth, only a few hundred million are left. Most of habitable land is new with no soil or wildlife. It takes hundreds of years for what's left of humanity to travel to and colonize the new New World. The industrial base of the world is gone and mankind retreats to a mix of feudal, agrarian and nomadic existence.

Right after the "war" there are a few pockets of civilization that survive for a while with a high level of technology but eventually they disappear. Man returns to the Stone Age.

4.3 - The Six Captains

*Author's note: As with "The Freeze Dryer" presented above, this was just a sketch, a list of the original six captains of the various Ark missions. Actually, only five missions are documented in the **Rome's Revolution** saga. I don't know if I'll ever get around to explaining what happened to the sixth Ark. Originally, I was intending to call it the Stealth Ark but I even stole that name for the Ark carrying **The Ark Lords**.*

Years 2065 - 2073 AD
Location: The Stars

Six Captains, one dream. To find a new home for mankind. The old one was ruined.

Ark I: Alpha Centauri: Captain Bill Allen/Pilot Stan Linzersky/Copilot Milo Shepherd.
~ Demographics: a perfect cross-section of society.
~ Everything goes smooth and beautiful
~ All about the mechanics of setting up a colony

Ark II: Tau Ceti: Captain Maury Keller/Pilot Abu Fayed/Copilot Mitch Alexander.
~ Demographics: army presence, engineering based
~ Front section of ship smashed off
~ Captain Keller rescued by accident
~ Awakened by Rei and the Ibbrassati
~ Told from his perspective

Ark III: Beta Hydri: Captain Dan Harrison/Pilot Miguel Salazar/Copilot Andy Cooper.
~ Demographics: light army, brainiacs, high-level program managers who wanted to leave Earth.
~ Missed – ends up at Tau Ceti
~ Moral dilemma
~ Reverse booster retro
~ They save the people but no supplies

35

~ The command crew dies, the people live on to become the Deucadons

Ark IV: Nu^2 Lupi: Captain Evan Rossler/Pilot Sam Eberhoff/Copilot Adam Goldberg.
~ Demographics: survivalists
~ Landed fairly well on Nu2 Lupi
~ Captured and enslaved by the K'val
~ K'val at war with COL

Ark V: Chara – The Stealth Ark. Captain Brian Tonkin/Pilot Emil Vostok/Copilot Tom Glenn.
~ Demographics: super commandos, criminals, misfits, sociopaths.
~ Returns to Earth
~ Essentially a new planet
~ Opposed by the Last Cavalier

Ark VI: S14542: Captain Maryann Mitchell/Pilot Charles Van der Hook/Copilot Mandy Bannifer.
~ Demographics: mixture. Anybody who worked on the program who wanted to leave Earth.
~ 100,000 year journey
~ Most of the people are dead,
~ Punctures by micrometeorites over time eventually led to loss of containment
~ People mummified by freeze drying
~ Returns to Earth
~ Saved by the Rat People
~ There are no electronics left
~ Have to be melted and revived manually
~ Perhaps they were eaten by the Stareater

4.4 - The Last Cavalier

*Author's note: As I was writing what became known as **Rome's Revolution**, I had to come up with some famous characters from the past, as seen by the people of the future. One of these was a hero and martyr who became known as Hanry Ta Jihn. I had this idea that I could actually turn it into a novel. I also decided to try writing it in the first person. That whole effort fizzled out but it didn't go to waste. As it turns out, the story of Hanry Ta Jihn or Jack Henry as he was known back then became a perfect novel within a novel in **The Ark Lords**. If you have read that novel, you might be interested to see how much of the following was preserved and how much was discarded. Remember, this only goes so far then stops because it became unworkable.*

Year 2660 AD
Location: Earth
Northern Part of What Had Been New Jersey

Chapter 1

I wish I could promise you a happy ending but I can't. My dad is dead. He left the mantle of the Cavaliers with me but Mom says I'm too young to wear it. The people from the stars sent us home and told us it was over. Mom said we just have to bide our time until... She never told me until when. My name is Jack Henry. My dad was Cal Henry. He was The Last Cavalier.

Chapter 2

It all started last year. Dad was getting ready to go out on his Long Ride. I knew it was getting close. It was always the same. Dad got quieter. We did our chores and sometimes we wouldn't talk the whole day. And our meals. Mom always tried to make conversation but Dad would have none of it. Dad wouldn't let Mom start a fire and she had to cook the food using the solar heater or slow cook using the heat from the compost pile. It was hard but my mom knew she couldn't break the rules. Not if Dad was going to go out and enforce them on other people. Dad kept a strict count of how many fires and how long and how many trees we planted.

At night, I could hear Mom crying, yelling. Dad would never answer her back. I knew what it was about and I knew there was no answer. Dad was a Cavalier. He had to take the Long Ride. There was nobody else. The fact that everyone hated him and the other Cavaliers didn't matter. It was our family's birthright and our duty. Dad never shirked from it. He didn't expect any thanks. The knowledge that he was protecting the Earth and all of Mankind that was where he got his reward.

Dad was sitting at the table, sharpening the tips of his cross-bow arrows. I counted nearly 50.

"Why so many?" I asked him.

"You never know what you're going to run into," he said. He had his sharper stone on the table and dipped each arrow in water then ran it along the blade. Back and forth he drew it. Once in a while, he would touch the edge. When he was satisfied, he put the arrow in the quiver and started on the next one. When he was nearly done, he stopped.

"Here," he said, handing me an arrow. "You try it."

"Why?" I asked him.

"Because you have to learn how some day," he said. "It may as well be today."

He slid the sharper stone along the table. I looked down at it. It was well worn having seen its share of arrows.

"Dip the arrow head in the water," he said. He moved the bowl towards me. "Then draw the arrow along the stone, first one way, then the other."

I shrugged and did as he said. As soon as I pulled my first line, he said, "Stop!"

"What?" I asked him.

"You have to tilt the blade," he said. "The way you were doing it, you were just dulling the blade. You are really trying to get the edge thin. You just grid away one side then the other until the edge is as thin as can be."

"How do I know?" I asked him.

"When you can't even feel the tip against the stone. Then there is nothing more to grind," he replied.

I looked at him then the arrow. I got it. I dipped the arrow in the water and pushed it along the stone again, this time so that the very edge didn't touch. Then I turned it half way and pulled it back again. I looked up at Dad. He nodded. I repeated the process until there was no resistance. I really could tell the difference. I held it up to the light. It looked as sharp as I could get it.

"Now touch the edge," he said. "But be careful."

I pushed my thumb on the edge and yelped. Blood started gushing out of my finger.

Dad laughed and pulled the arrow away.

"The good news," he said, "is you got it sharp enough."

It hurt. I didn't think it was so funny. I sucked on my thumb, tasting the salty blood, mixed with dirt. I pulled my thumb out. It was still oozing blood.

"Here," he said. He handed me a small strip of cloth. I wrapped it around the cut and looked up at him.

"You have to understand everything about the world," he said, his eyes blazing. "Your skin is made up of layers. The outer layer is really dead. Underneath the outer layer is the live skin and the blood. You push the arrow, just a little. If you feel it slide through the outer layer, it's sharp enough. You don't need to push hard. If you have to push at all, then it needs more sharpening. You'll learn."

I nodded like I understood but all I know is that the arrow cut me. But if I was going to be a Cavalier, I had to learn.

"Can I try again?" I asked him.

"Sure," he said, handing me another arrow.

I sharpened the arrow like before. I could tell when it was right. But this time, when it came time to test it, I closed my eyes and tried to put my brain right on my other thumb. I let the arrow rest on it and applied just the tiniest amount of pressure. I could feel it sliding through the calloused part, just like Dad said. I stopped it before it cut me.

"Yep," Dad said. "You got it." He put the arrow in the quiver which told me he really was happy, even though he didn't look it. There were three arrows left.

"You do the last few, Jackie," he said. "I have to go pack."

"OK," I said. I watched him go in the bed room. His saddlebag was on the bed. I could hear Mom crying quietly. Dad ignored her.

He put a few shirts in the bag and some other stuff then took off his work shirt and put on the white one, his Sunday best.

"Why, Cal?" she asked him. "Why not the black one?"

"I have to Helen," he said. "Everybody sees the black and runs. I have to show them that I'm different. That I'm true to the cause. The white will tell them something."

"They're going to hate you no matter what color you wear," she said. "They have all forgotten. They don't want you to remind them. They want to pretend it never happened and never will again."

"It's my job," Dad said somberly. "It's the job my father entrusted to me and the one that Jackie will take over some day. It's up to us. Father to son. It's the only way. The Earth needs me."

"What about us?" Mom asked. "We need you too."

"Helen," Dad said. "You knew I was a Cavalier when you married me. That was why you fell in love with me. Nothing has changed."

"Everything has changed," she said. "Your precious Cavaliers are nothing but bullies and thieves. They don't obey the rules themselves. Why should anybody else do it?"

She stood up and put her arms around Dad's neck. "Cal, stay here," she said. "We don't make a difference any more. Just be with us and some day, somebody else will figure it out."

Dad reached up and pulled her arms off his neck. "Can't," he said. And that was the end of it. "I leave tomorrow," he said.

Chapter 3

Mom was tough. She steeled herself and put her arm around me as we watched Dad ride off. Mostly Dad was gone for six months. Sometimes a little less. Recently, a little more. Dad wouldn't tell us but the last time he came back, I watched him as he unpacked his arrows. He only had thirty left. I wondered what he did with the other twenty. Maybe he shot a rabbit or squirrel. Maybe something bigger. Mom always packed him enough jerky for the whole trip so I figured maybe he did it for variety. For fresh meat. But he never brought any back.

He usually left in late November, just as the heat was easing up a bit. He did it for Tige who was in his twenties. The trip would have been too much for the old horse in the summer, what with the temperature in the hundreds. Walter, my horse, could have done it. But he was just a colt. We still had some practicing to do.

Mom told me that there used to be four seasons, not two. She told me that summer only lasted until September then they had a season called the Fall. She said a long time ago, there used to be trees that grew their leaves and they'd fall off in September. That doesn't happen anymore. The only trees that live around here are evergreens and they don't even have any leaves to fall off. In late November, there is a break in the weather and it gets tolerable for a few months. That's when we plant our crops. We call it winter but Mom said that winter used to be cold. She told me there used to be white powder that fell from the sky called snow and it covered the ground. I can't imagine. It doesn't seem possible. What I wouldn't give to be cold.

So we planted our crops. Walter helped. He pulled the plow but he wasn't very happy about it. We had to water every seed by hand. Sometimes it rained. Sometimes it poured. But every few years, there'd be no rain at all. I guess we were lucky. Our well never ran dry so the soybeans always had enough.

*(That's all there is. Jack Henry's story changed and evolved and became less about global warming and more about Jack Henry defeating **The Ark Lords.**)*

5

LACY HENRY

*Author's note: Hanry Ta Jihn, Jack Henry, has always been an integral part of my future history. He was a rebel, a leader and a martyr. He showed the people of Earth how to free themselves of the yoke of tyranny represented by the first Ark Lords. However, for Rome to have been his far future descendant, Jack Henry had to leave at least one child behind. This is the story of Lacy Henry who we finally got to meet in **The Milk Run**. As she told Aason, she was more than a girlfriend but less than a wife. That was going to change when Jackie got back from the Battle of Chicago but, of course, we know that never happened.*

Year 2671 AD
Location: Earth
Southern Part of What Had Been New Jersey

LACY SAT IN HER FAVORITE WOODEN CHAIR, ONE LEG TUCKED underneath, rocking back and forth, holding her extended abdomen. Even though the chair creaked, it was a soothing sound. She stared out the window, not really focusing on anything beyond the groaning chair and her self-massage. The room itself smelled musty. Pa had tried to fix the leak in the roof so many times but nothing stopped the inevitable bloom of mold and mildew right after it rained. And it rained a lot. But Lacy was not even tempted to open the window. The wavery illusion of the air rippling across the fields told her it was another blistering hot day. The piercing must was vastly more tolerable than letting the blast-furnace heat into the darkened room.

Lacy lifted her eyes to the sky. She held her hand up to block the sun and tried to imagine if Jackie was doing the same thing right now. It had been over a month since the love of her life went off to wage war against the Ark Lords and he should be coming home very soon. Normally that thought comforted her but as the days wore on the comfort was slowly being replaced by a sense of unease.

The gentle stirring of the baby growing inside her drew her attention back down to her stomach. It was as if the baby was telling her, Mommy, don't worry, Daddy will be home soon.

Lacy smiled. How could one so young be so wise? She shook her head. She just had to be patient. She looked up again and saw a tiny cloud of dust off in the distance. It might have been just a dirt devil but it did not dissipate. Instead, the cloud grew larger and resolved itself into a single man atop a horse, heading their way.

Her heart froze for a moment. She leaned forward. Could it be Jackie finally coming home? She put her hand over her eyes trying to peer harder. With a start, she realized it wasn't Jackie. The rider was too tall and wore all black. Jackie always favored white shirts, especially in the heat of summer. As the rider pulled up, she could see it was Red June, Jackie's best friend and first lieutenant.

Lacy sat back heavily in her chair and closed her eyes. Her sense of dread was now fully formed. If Red were here, that meant Jackie was not. She heard Red knock on the front door. Pa answered. There was a brief exchange and the sound of two sets of boots led up to her room.

Pa knocked softly on the door. "Lacy," he called out gently, "Red's here."

"Sure, Pa," Lacy answered back. Tears were beginning to flow from her eyes. She unraveled herself and stood up. She turned to face the door as Red entered the room.

Red June was a large man, well over six feet tall. It only took him a few strides to close the distance between them. He took off his hat and placed it down by his side. Wordlessly, Lacy stared up at him and Red shook his head side to side, very slowly.

Lacy's knees buckled. Red grabbed her under the arms before she fell. Lacy's whole body shook as she wailed with great, wracking sobs. Red gathered her in, wrapping his long arms around her, holding her close while she cried.

Although her sorrow did not diminish, after a time, she stopped her crying. Somehow she had already known it would come to this. Red sat her down on the bed and kneeled in front of her so he could look up into her eyes.

"What happened?" Lacy whispered.

Red took one of her hands and cradled it between his. "We beat them," he said. "Jackie figured out a way. We found a weapons cache that belonged to the Ark Lords and we used their own weapons against them. We killed every last one of them."

"And Jackie? How did he…" Lacy's voice trailed off.

"I'm sorry, Lacy, but you have to know. They had something. A disease weapon. If they had gotten to it, they would have used it to kill us all. Jackie died preventing those bastards from getting to it. And they never will. Jackie made it so they'll never be able to find it again."

Lacy put her hands up to her face and started crying once again. It was quieter this time. Red waited patiently while this bout passed. When he felt she was ready, he reached over and lifted her chin so she would look at him again.

"Lacy, you have to know he died a hero. He sacrificed himself so that all of us, everyone on the Earth, would be safe now and forever. He'll go down in history as one of the greatest men who ever lived."

"I should have gone with you," Lacy said grimly. "I could have helped."

"No," Red replied. "There's no place for a pregnant woman near a battlefield. And you're carrying Jackie's child. You have to stay safe so his legacy lives on."

Lacy rubbed her abdomen with both hands. "It's a boy, you know," she said obliquely.

Red cocked his head. "How do you know?"

"I just know," Lacy said more firmly. "It sounds crazy but he talks to me sometimes. He tells me things."

"If you say so." Red shrugged. He stood up and reached behind him and withdrew a revolver that had been tucked into his waistband. It was one of the M9 9mm Berettas that Jack Henry and Red had liberated from the armory they found deep beneath the Tevatron.

He pressed a button and the clip ejected. He pulled the chamber back and a single round popped out. Red caught it and set it down on the bed, along with the clip.

"What is that?" Lacy asked, her voice sounding hoarse.

"It's kind of a miniature firestick. We call it a handgun."

"What is a firestick?"

"The Ark Lords had these weapons. Long sticks that fire metal bullets, Jackie called them. And this is a version that fits in your hand.

It's just as deadly, though." He reached down and picked up the bullet. "When you fire the weapon, these things come shooting out and can tear through anything. Especially flesh."

"Why are you showing it to me?" Lacy asked, her voice trembling a bit.

Red turned the gun around and handed it to Lacy who took it from him. She wrapped her delicate hand around the handle and her index finger naturally found its way to the trigger.

"Jackie insisted I give it to you personally and teach you how to use it. To protect yourself."

"Protect myself from what?"

Red looked out the window. He stared off into the distance for a while then turned back to look at Lacy.

"Once the Ark Lords find out we captured one of their war wagons, all of Jersey is going to turn red with blood. We want to make sure it's their blood and not ours."

"What is a war wagon?"

"It's a horseless carriage. We can use it to recharge the lightsticks we've stolen from them. And it has a cannon. Incredibly powerful. It can destroy a whole village in a single shot. It never occurred to them that we would be able to use their own weapons against them. We already know they have no defense. We have the power now. And we're going to use it to wipe them out once and for all."

"I still don't understand why I need this, then," she said, holding out the gun.

"Because they know about Jackie. And if they ever found out about you, that you were carrying his child, they'd sacrifice everything to kill you. We need to keep you a secret and failing that, we need to keep you safe. You only have to use this weapon as a last resort."

Lacy nodded her head. "I understand." She turned the gun left and right. She held it up to her eye and looked down the sight. She lowered her arm and placed the gun on the bed, next to the clip.

"I need to know something," she said.

"Anything," Red responded.

"What did you do with Jackie's body? Did you bring it back with you?"

"We couldn't," Red answered sadly. "It just wasn't practical. We buried him underneath the rubble of the Ark Lords palace."

"What do you mean rubble?" Lacy asked.

"Jackie's dying wish was that we use the cannon and level the place. He made me swear that after we defeated the Ark Lords, we would bury them and their vehicles and their spaceship and their weapons. Every place they've ever been on the Earth. He wanted to make sure that there would be no trace, not even a hint that their race was ever here. I swore to him that even if it took a thousand years, we'd erase everything, like they never existed."

Lacy took in a deep breath then let out a long sigh. She nodded sadly.

"Thank you, Red," she said. "You are a good friend and a great man." She stopped and looked out the window. "Can I ask you for one more thing?"

"Anything, Lacy," Red answered.

"Some day, when this is all over, will you take me and our son out there? To where Jackie died?"

"Absolutely," Red replied. "I'll take you to his grave. We'll make sure he has a proper headstone. The whole world will come to revere that place as where the Rebellion against the Ark Lords truly began."

6

THE DEUCADONS

Author's note: As mentioned in the Introduction, sometimes it was necessary to write an entire short story just to get one line of dialog right in the "real" book. I never had any intention of presenting this story to anyone until I had the idea for this volume. I wrote it because I had to work out the complete structure of the fate of Ark III. Their descendents became known as The Deucadons and this is their story.

Year 2956 AD
Location: Tau Ceti System
Second Planet (Deucado)

THE FIRST THING CAPTAIN DAN HARRISON FELT WAS A SEARING pain shooting through his chest as the defibrillator fired off a 200-joule stimulus. Despite the fact that he was now awake, the instrumentation picked up no heartbeat so it automatically increased the intensity to 300 joules. After the paddles were fully charged, the defibrillator discharged with another agonizing bolt of electricity. Thankfully, this time, Harrison's heart started up immediately.

Having trained for two years prior to launch, Harrison instinctively clamped his lips down on the ventilation tube so that he could start breathing air despite the fact that his cryo-hibernation chamber was completely filled with the liquid that served as the reanimation bath. His sarcophagus and those of the other two members of his command crew were different from the 540 colonists still asleep in the passenger compartment. The command crew's chambers were built to reanimate a frozen traveler in the zero-g conditions of orbit. There was no gravity to cause the reanimation fluid to drain out. That was up to the pumps strategically placed in each of the four corners of the chamber. But until that process completed, they had to be able to breathe essentially underwater.

Harrison's lips and muscles were still weak from the sedatives he received prior to being frozen and the seal around the breathing tube was not perfect. Consequently, a tiny bit of liquid leaked into his mouth. He aspirated some of the salty fluid and started coughing and inadvertently caught a lungful of liquid. This made him cough all the more. He was in serious danger of drowning but through an act of sheer will, he just stopped. He squeezed his lungs and spit out as much of the liquid through the corner of his mouth as he could then he drew in a full breath of air through the breathing tube, overcoming his natural instinct to cough. Those drowning drills, no matter how horrifying, were not a waste of time after all.

Harrison continued his slow and concentrated breathing, all the while trying to regain his strength. When the internal sensors determined that his core temperature was high enough, a switch was tripped. Pumps activated to begin drawing out the fluid leaving a cold and wet Harrison helpless until the blowers came on and threw heated air, drawn from the outside, across his body. He continued to warm up and soon his shivering stopped. He reached over, feeling around until he found what he was looking for. He punched the large button by his hand and the cover to his casket slid back. He clawed at the breathing mask and was able to pull it free taking his first breath of unrestricted air in Lord knows how many centuries.

Numerous droplets of the reanimation fluid resisted the pull of the pumps and floated free into the cockpit. This was a known outcome and the droplets would be absorbed by electrostatic plates eventually. In the mean time, Harrison lay there for a long while, trying to wrestle his eyes open enough to see where he was. He blinked and sighed and finally focused on the ceiling of the command compartment with its conduits and indicators providing a dim glow to the capsule. His body floated around gently within the constricted chamber so there was no weight to contend with.

When he felt up to it, he pushed on the cover of the chamber and its internal strain gauge detected the pressure and retracted fully. Harrison slowly floated free of the chamber and he practiced moving his hands and feet until he was satisfied that he had a tiny bit of control over his body. The slightest pressure on the ceiling sent him spinning back to the chamber, which he grabbed a hold of and pulled himself down. He lowered himself until his knees were touching the floor and he unlatched the compartment holding his coveralls. Just then, a white-hot pain shot from the base of his spine to the base of his skull. He cried out and tried to reach behind him. He had to take deep breaths and eventually the pain passed.

"What the hell was that?" he asked out loud, knowing no one was listening. It didn't matter. Just that tiny amount of motion was enough effort for a while so he stayed perfectly still, floating there, staring at his clothing, wishing they were already on his body. At long last, he felt sufficiently refreshed that he was able to dress himself. In the next compartment were his Velcro slippers which were surprisingly difficult to get on, due to the pain in his back. At last, he was fully dressed. Finally, as a symbol for all to see, he put on his baseball cap proudly proclaiming he was the captain of the Ark III, Beta Hydri mission.

Now that he was dressed and his head felt clearer, he looked around the command compartment and saw his two fellow crewmates' chambers. With slow and cautious steps, hooking and releasing, he made his way over and was relieved to see that both their chambers were intact. The air itself was very musty and there was a hint of something rotted in the air. But it was breathable, he was alive and reanimated so Harrison knew they must be in orbit around one of the two planets in the habitable zone around Beta Hydri.

Much as he wanted to reanimate Cooper and Salazar, protocol dictated that he check the status of the ship and their orbit first on the very slim chance that the AI had made an error. If they had to move the ship, especially to another star system, reanimation was a death sentence and it was his responsibility and his burden as Captain to take that chance and take it alone.

He moved into the mission commander's center seat and belted himself in. He flipped a switch and was rewarded with a dim glow back-lighting the integrated keyboard. He pressed in the keystrokes necessary to alert the computer as to his status. At first, the flat panel screens were very dim but they quickly brightened and began relaying a steady stream of information. Harrison blinked and looked at the panels and blinked some more. Something was very wrong. The chronometer showed the date as April 3rd, 2956. That couldn't be right. It was off by over 400 years, give or take.

The Beta Hydri mission was the most ambitious of all the Ark missions so far. While the first two were going to go to Alpha Centauri and Tau Ceti respectively, his Ark, number three in the series, was going to travel the unbelievable distance of 24.38 light years. With their ultra-efficient Grey Drive, in theory, the ship was capable of achieving an ultimate velocity of one-twentieth c so it should have taken them on the order of 488 years to get there. But if he was reading the chronometer correctly, instead, it had taken them almost 900 years. Nine centuries.

"That can't be right," he said, again speaking to no one.

On instinct, he released his belt and floated free and pulled himself toward the cockpit window. Below him was a planet with white puffy clouds, beautiful blue sparkling oceans and bright yellowish-green landmasses with just a hint of brown in the northern and southern-most regions. The continents had many, many lakes and rivers, giving it an almost Swiss cheese-like appearance.

At least the AI had picked the right planet to orbit. As they came around toward the sunset, he could see the primary star and immediately, Harrison's suspicions were confirmed. The star was not the right color. Beta Hydri was a G2IV Sol-class star, a little larger with a diameter of 1.7 times that of the Sun. The primary should been yellowish-white but instead this particular star was orange. It could not be atmospheric effects because they were well above the air.

Harrison pushed off and got back to his seat. He punched the buttons necessary to bring up his galactic coordinates and star charts. The numbers were flat out wrong. He pulled in an overlay of what he should have seen at Beta Hydri and there was no overlap at all. Finally, in desperation, he decided to send a query to the computer.

"Where are we?" he typed in and pressed <Enter>.

"Second planet, Tau Ceti System," was the computer's reply.

"Tau Ceti!" Harrison shouted out loud. "What the hell?"

"Why not Beta Hydri?" he typed in savagely and pressed <Enter>.

"No habitable worlds. Secondary target selected," was the computer's reply.

"Jesus Christ on a crutch," Harrison said. He sat back in his chair and just stared at the instruments. The scientist in him did the math. Beta Hydri was 22 light years from Earth, Tau Ceti was 21 light years from Beta Hydri. That meant they had traveled 43 light years all told. With gearing up, gearing down, the 900 year figure wasn't too far off. As much as he didn't want it to be true, the math was inescapable. Plus he had the physical evidence in front of him.

There was no point in reviewing the data or trying to second-guess the computer, there was no going back. They were here now. He had to take advantage of the situation. Since Tau Ceti was the primary target for Ark II, Harrison figured they probably would have arrived around 2500AD. After all, Tau Ceti was only 11.9 light years from Earth so the trip should have only take them 250 years or so. That means there should have been humans on this world for some 400 years. He switched to a video feed and looked for signs of cities, settlements, anything on the night side that would indicate it was inhabited.

There were no lights. There was one fairly large thunderstorm near the equator that producing lightning so he knew his instruments were capable of picking up artificial lighting if it was present.

He flipped on the radio, setting it to the primary command frequency, pressing the send button and called out, "Attention, attention, anyone on Tau Ceti 2. This is Captain Harrison of the USS Ark III. We are in orbit around your planet. Does anyone read me?"

He released the transmit button and only heard the hiss of interstellar space punctuated occasionally by a slight crackle that might be coming from the electrical storm he spotted earlier. Harrison switched to the backup frequency and tried it again. But once again, he heard nothing.

He programmed a frequency sweep and set it to stop at any signal greater than noise and let it go. It stopped at one high-band kHz signal but when Harrison cranked up the volume, again, all he heard was the distinctive crackle of far-off lightning.

When the sweep was complete, he tried it again with the same results, namely nothing. As far as he could tell, there was no evidence of a civilization taking root on this planet. Further, if intelligent life, other than man, had developed here, there was no evidence of that either; at least in any way that the instruments aboard his ship could detect.

The reality is, it didn't really matter. For now, he had to proceed with the mission. Their survival was not contingent upon others having made it here before him so he wasn't going to worry about it until he had the luxury of time to ponder the issue.

He unbuckled himself and locked his feet onto the floor and began making his way over to Cooper. Once again, a searing pain shot through his back, making his knees weak and his left foot felt like it suddenly went to sleep. Had he not been weightless, the pain would have made his knees buckle. As before, he waited a bit and the pain passed.

He found he was most comfortable being stretched out horizontally so that's the way he worked. He gripped Cooper's sarcophagus with one hand and tried to turn the left power rod. His fingers slipped or the rod was stuck, one or the other. He pulled on a metallic loop and withdrew a long steel pin designed just for this purpose. He used it as a lever and with a snap, the rod rotated in place. Internally, it exposed the thorium core to an inner cavity packed with a thermopile. He switched hands and using the pin, he was able to rotate the right power rod as well. With the two cores, there were enough neutrons flying around to heat up the thermopile. The needles and gauges on the side of the sarcophagus began twitching then started their slow rise toward full power.

After a time, Harrison heard a zzzt sound which was most likely Cooper's defibrillators firing. He pulled himself up to the top and used his free hand to wipe away the dust covering Cooper's faceplate. However, the lighting in the cockpit was too dim to make out Cooper's face through the cryo-hibernation fluid. The sarcophagus shuddered slightly. It was Cooper moving about! A steady vibration indicated that the pumps had kicked in followed by the blowers. By now, Harrison could see Cooper's face. Cooper blinked a few times so Harrison gave him the thumbs up sign. Soon the sarcophagus cover slid back and Cooper sat up in place. He pulled the breathing mask from his face and said, "Shit, I'm cold."

"You'll be fine as soon as we get you dressed. Here…" Harrison slid the cover all that way back and assisted Cooper in extricating himself from the freezing chamber. Together, they got his second-in-command dressed, baseball cap and all.

"Salazar?" Cooper asked.

"In a minute," Harrison said. "Come up the front with me. I have to show you something."

"OK," Cooper said, his voice a little stronger. Harrison was about halfway to the front when Cooper screamed out loud.

"My back!" Cooper shouted. "Yowzers." He took a deep breath. "Did somebody hit me with a taser or something?"

Harrison motioned with his hands to calm down. "Same thing happened to me. It must have something to do with the cryo-hibernation. Just be careful how you move and you'll be OK."

"Whoa," Cooper said. Gingerly, he pulled himself across the cabin until he was seated and buckled into the co-pilot's chair, to the right of Harrison. "It felt like somebody stuck a red hot poker up my back."

"Yeah, I know what you mean," Harrison replied. He pointed forward. "Look out there. What do you see?"

Cooper regarded the planet below. "Beautiful," he said. "Clouds, water, vegetation. We got it made."

"Look at the sun."

Cooper squinted and peered at the primary. "It's the wrong color. What happened to it?" he asked. "Was the observed data flawed?"

"No," replied Harrison. "It's the right color but the wrong star. What you're looking at is Tau Ceti."

"Tau Ceti? What the hell?" Cooper shook his head. "What happened to Beta Hydrii?

"The AI said there were no habitable planets and rerouted us here. And that isn't all."

Cooper's eyes narrowed. "What?" he asked hesitatingly.

"Hang on to your hat," answered Harrison. "We've been asleep for 900 years."

"Holy crap!" Cooper exclaimed. "Nine centuries?" He whistled quietly and looked down at his instruments. "Well, I guess there isn't much we can do about it now. Whaddya say we wake up Miguel and get this show on the road?"

It wasn't too long before Miguel Salazar, the pilot, was reanimated and dressed and he went through the same back pain and reality shock as the other two. When he was finally buckled in and had gotten over the unexpected news, it was time to plan the next portion of the mission.

Harrison activated the central screen and aimed the dorsal cameras straight back along the length of the Ark III. He pointed to the vertical stabilizer right in the middle of the screen.

"OK," he said. "Protocol dictates that Cooper takes a space-walk and blows the aft connector between the crew compartment and the cargo compartment. They've made it pretty simple for us. Andy, are you ready for this?"

"Sure," Cooper replied. "The sooner we get down to the planet, the sooner we can get some food. I'm starving."

"There are plenty of rations in storage compartment of your sarcophagus," Harrison pointed out.

"Yeah, I already had some," Cooper replied. "They're just not very tasty after sitting there for 900 years. At least the water was good."

"OK," Harrison said, unbuckling. Miguel, you'll stay here and monitor operations. I'll go back with Andy to the airlock and get him outfitted. I'll suit up too and man the tether. The whole thing shouldn't take us more than an hour or so."

"Roger that," Salazar said.

Cooper and Harrison unbuckled and floated up, away from their seats.

"Hey Andy," Salazar said.

"Yeah?"

"Make sure you detonate the right charge. We don't want to be dragging the damned cage with us."

"Uh, OK," Cooper said, shaking his head.

"Radio check. Miguel?" Harrison said through his comm link.

"Reading you five by five," Salazar responded. "Andy?"

"Fivers," the co-pilot replied. "Ready for EVA."

Harrison tugged one more time on the tether which was looped through a U-ring that was bolted just on the inside of the airlock. He patted Cooper on the shoulder. "You're good to go," he said through the radio.

"Roger that," Cooper said. "Wish me luck."

After taking a deep breath, Cooper stepped outside, his magnetic boots locking onto the pig iron surface of the Ark. Taking short, careful strides, he made his way to the very top of the Ark, Harrison paying out tether as needed.

It took longer than expected as Cooper's muscles were stiff and he was taking it exceedingly slow. Each step was an effort. He had to break the magnetic connection of one boot and swing it around to the front, making sure the other foot held. Once he was steady, he would do it again. As he neared the rear stabilizer, he checked his wrist chronometer and noted that it had been nearly an hour, twice as long as it was supposed to. It wasn't a problem, though. His spacesuit had enough oxygen for a six hour space-walk.

Cooper finally reached the rear stabilizer and took a moment to survey his surroundings. What he saw made his blood run cold.

"Harrison, Dan, come in," he said frantically.

"What is it?"

"The starboard delta wing. It's busted. Nearly half of it's been sheared off. And what's left of it is mostly curled up."

"Are you sure?" Harrison asked.

"Unless the cryo-hibernation made me loopy, I'm sure."

"Crap!" Captain Harrison exclaimed.

"Do you think we can fix it?" Salazar piped in.

"Not unless you've brought a spare wing. It's ruined," replied Cooper. "Totally."

Harrison tugged firmly on the tether. "Andy, get back here. We've got to figure out what to do."

It didn't take Cooper nearly as long to return to the side airlock. He came as close to running as the magnetic boots would allow. Harrison helped him into the chamber and they didn't wait to strip down. They opened the inner airlock and hurried to the command compartment. By the time they got there, Salazar had worked the rear cameras to focus in on the shredded wing and he was typing furiously on the computer console.

"What do you have, Miguel," Harrison asked.

"Computer says there is no way to feather the air stream. We can't run the Bessel re-entry. We'd have to go straight in which means we burn up."

"Double crap," Harrison said, sitting down heavily in the pilot's chair. "Is there anything left of the control surface?"

"There's one piece of an aileron that I can work using the wire. Maybe 10% functionality. That's it. If we tried to raise the nose, all we'd do is spin around. Pretty much useless."

Cooper pointed to the camera display. "Miguel, can you zoom in on the cargo compartment. Are the wings there OK?"

Harrison frowned but didn't say anything. Salazar used the cameras to survey the status of the two wings on the second large compartment, farther to the rear.

"They look intact," Salazar said, "at least as far as I can tell from here. We won't know until we hook into the control interface."

Harrison looked at Cooper. "How does that help us?" he asked.

"I was thinking," Cooper said. "We de-couple from the crew compartment, blow the cage and dock with the cargo compartment. We could fly that down using the standard reentry procedure."

Harrison let out a burst of air in disgust. "I repeat my question. How does that help us?"

"We'd be able to get to the surface, safe," Cooper replied.

"You forgot one thing," Harrison answered back. "How do we get the colonists down there?"

"Then we fly both compartments down at the same time."

"No can do," Salazar pointed out. "I can only control the airfoils with a direct link. If we leave the cargo compartment where it is, it's just so much dead weight."

"Oh," Cooper said and he went silent. He jerked his head up. "I know. We go into the crew compartment and take as many of the sarcophagi as we can fit into the cargo compartment. Then we separate."

Harrison stroked his chin, thinking. "How many?" Harrison asked Salazar.

The pilot typed a few figures into the computer. He erased the screen and typed it in again. "24, maybe 25," he said. "And that's pushing it."

"That leaves 500 people floating around up here. How do we get them down?"

Cooper leaned forward. "I know this is going to sound crazy but we'd have to build a society. Like what if we took all women. Eight each for the three of us. We get them pregnant as fast as we can and we produce 24 babies a year for, I don't know, 20 years? Once the children start breeding, we could grow the population and get us to the point where we could build some shuttles or something. Miguel, how long before the orbit degrades?"

Salazar pressed a few parameters into the keyboard. "A hundred years, plus or minus. We'd have to get to a space-age population with functioning shuttles within that time."

"You're forgetting one major factor," Harrison said. "They told us that the colony would not be viable with anything less than 50 breeding couples. You're putting us at three."

"No," Cooper said. "It's 24."

"You're wrong," Harrison replied. "We can't have any of our children breeding with their siblings. We'd have to go a least three generations before the gene pool would be stable."

"Then we take five men, we pick the ones who can help us the most and the rest women. That'll increase the gene pool, if that's all you're worried about."

Harrison closed his eyes trying to do the math in his head. There were so many variables to this horrible equation. He shook his head and waved his hand about the cabin. "We can't do it."

"Why not?" Cooper asked, with a slight amount of desperation in his voice.

"The suits only have six hours of oxygen. That's 24 hours total for our three spacesuits. You've already used up over an hour. Based upon what I saw, even if you went faster, it's going to take another hour to separate the sections. That leaves us with about 22 hours. I don't know how long but I figure it will take two men at least an hour to move one sarcophagus from the crew compartment back to the cargo compartment and stow it there. So that's two man-hours per sarcophagus. Even if we push it to the limit, the most we can recover is maybe 10 people. Even using your harem theory, that's maybe two men and eight women. It's not enough. Our colony would collapse from in-breeding. And to build a technological society capable of spaceflight starting with 13 people is, well, hard to believe."

"You're not helping, Dan," Cooper said. "All you're telling us is what we can't do. You're the mission commander. Tell us what we can do."

Harrison looked around the cabin. He spotted a cabinet mounted flush against the sidewall. He opened it up and removed a red notebook and set it down on the front console so his two crewmates could see.

He flipped through the pages until he found the illustration he was looking for. He laid the notebook out flat and let his charges observe.

"Is that what I think it is?" Salazar asked. "I remember them talking it about during training but I didn't think we'd ever have to use it."

"What is it?" Cooper asked. "Explain."

Harrison took a deep breath. "The mission planners tried to think out every contingency. This being one of them. They talked about transferring sarcophagi to the cargo compartment and that's how I knew we wouldn't have enough oxygen to make it work."

"So we have this?"

"Yes," Harrison replied. "First we blow the cage to free up the crew compartment. Then we decouple the command module, turn it around and reverse dock with the crew compartment. We use the SSTO booster as a super retro-rocket. It should slow our descent sufficiently that we don't burn up. Miguel can use what little control we have to keep the ship aligned until we're in the atmosphere."

"And then what?" Cooper said, half-panicked. "We just crash?"

"Pretty much. That was one scenario. 20% of the sarcophagi are hardened to survive a crash landing even at terminal velocity. Maybe half of the others would survive as well, being frozen and all."

Cooper narrowed his eyes. "I don't see any way we'd survive, I mean us up here." He pointed at himself and the other two. "So who's going to start the thaw cycle? What's the point of landing even 20% of the people if they just melt to death?"

Harrison waved his arms in a circle. "One portion of the thorium power rods are made of thin lead glass. If we crash at any decent speed, the glass should shatter and that'll start the nuclear reaction. All we need is one person to be reanimated and they can take care of the rest."

"You have no proof of that," Cooper said bitterly.

"I agree. Our best bet is if one of us camps out in the crew compartment during reentry. If we don't land hard enough, then that person should survive and they can rotate the rods by hand."

Cooper sat back in his chair. He looked up at the ceiling trying to envision this doomed endeavor. He looked back down at Salazar. "Miguel, will this work?"

"In theory," Salazar replied. "They ran the simulations before we left. It's fifty-fifty but it's our only viable alternative."

"So who stays and who goes?" Cooper asked dejectedly.

"I'm staying," Salazar stated flatly. "I have to fly this monstrosity down."

Cooper's shoulders slumped. "I have to stay too. To navigate." He looked up at Harrison. "Dan, you have to be the one to go. And you're the mission commander. It only makes sense."

"Yeah," Harrison replied sadly. "I know. But I had to let you figure that out for yourself."

After several orbits, using the hi-def ventral cameras, they found great stands of tree-like structures about 50 miles in from the eastern shore of one of the oceans. Salazar did some simulations and decided he might be able to get them pointed during re-entry on a vector that would slam them into the trees and break their fall slightly. Cooper took another space-walk and retrieved as much packing material from the cargo compartment as he could carry then Harrison joined him in the crew compartment. They secured Harrison in the rear with as much padding as possible.

When they were finished, Cooper radioed, "Good luck, Dan. Say hi to everybody for me."

Harrison reached up and grabbed Cooper's arm. "You're a good man, Andy. There's no guarantee you won't survive. Especially if Miguel can hit those trees."

"I will," Salazar piped in.

Cooper shook his head. "Look, Dan, you know it and I know it. This is the end of the road for us. We all understood the risks when we volunteered. I just wish I had gotten the opportunity to see our new world. After all, I waited 900 years for this and now what?"

"For the future of mankind," Harrison said. "That's why we're doing it. To make sure mankind survives."

"Mankind, yes," Cooper said bitterly. "But not this man." He pointed to his chest.

"Andy, can you do it?"

"Yes, I'll do it. I'm just not happy about it."

On his way out of the crew compartment, Andy Cooper returned to the stubby vertical stabilizer mounted in the rear. He located the panel that contained the magneto and capacitor which would set off the thermite reaction. It was like explosive bolts except it was a continuous ring binding the mating cage to the rear compartment. He opened up the panel and reached the magneto crank easily and started turning it. He cranked it six times until the analog gauge showed a full charge. He used his thumb to depress the safety then pressed the ignition switch and stood up. A puff of smoke shot out of the rim of crew compartment section where the latticework attached. The smoke raced around the circumference of the ship until it was out of sight. In a less than a minute, the circle of smoke came back around, ending where it began. In theory, the two sections were now separated. Andy held on to the stabilizer and gave the latticework a swift kick. He thought he felt a slight amount of give but just for luck, he kicked it again. By using the stars in the background as a point of reference, he could see an infinitesimal gap developing between the two sections.

"Andy, what's going on?" Salazar inquired.

"Just making sure we have good sep with the rear."

"And?"

"Good to go," Cooper replied, "We're clear. I'll see you in a little bit."

The maneuver was successful. They did not burn up in the atmosphere. Salazar was able to point them on a slight vector and what remained of the ruined starboard wing and the port wing provided enough lift that you could almost say they were gliding. They smashed into the cane-trees around 300 miles per hour. Cooper and Salazar died instantly. In fact, later, when the colonists were able to get in there, they never really found their bodies, just bits and pieces of the spacesuits.

Within the crew compartment, Dan Harrison was mortally wounded as well. However, before he died, he was able to make his way over to several of the intact sarcophagi and rotate the left knob clockwise one-half turn and the right knob one-half turn counter-clockwise. He was able to activate three. On the third and final sarcophagus, the last thing he saw was the power and temperature dials first quiver, then start creeping forward to the thaw position and toward life. His eyes grew dim and sightless. He gave one last long sigh and stopped breathing.

Had he lived, he would have been proud to know that nearly 400 of the colonists survived the crash. They had no supplies or tools but they eventually built an entire society starting with only the "clothes on their back."

Over the next 300 years, their breeding program produced almost 40,000 people who later became known as the Deucadons. An asteroid hit and wiped out a goodly portion. The survivors decide to move underground for safety and only came to the surface to re-supply.

200 years later, the first Vuduri arrived, unbeknownst to the Deucadons. After some 20 years, the two cultures' paths cross and the Deucadons, thinking they had found salvation, were slaughtered without discussion. This happened twice more before they determined they must remain hidden from the Vuduri forever. That is until Rome arrived.

7

THE INVISIBLE MAN

*Author's note: Many of the technologies used in the **Rome's Revolution** universe such as PPTs, gravitic resonance and electrogravity were just taken at face value. Eventually, it will all be documented in its own novel but for now, I thought you'd be interested in how the Vuduri invented the Dark Matter Diode which is the essential technology underlying their PPT star-drive.*

Year 3230 AD
Location: Earth
Near What Had Been Lisbon (I-cimaci)

NOVA BALEY TRIED VERY HARD NOT TO VOMIT. IT WASN'T JUST THE acrid smell of smoke and ash and burned electrical insulation that turned his stomach. He was looking at the complete destruction of what was the realization of his life's work. They had been on the verge of success and now there was nothing to show for it. The three successive bolts of lightning had seen to that. The charred mess that had been his lab was totally destroyed. The thought of starting over, from scratch, not only made Nova bone-weary, he wasn't even sure the council would support another go at it. His grandiose plans of transforming their society with a room temperature superconductor had always been met with skepticism and usually outright disbelief.

He muttered to himself, "We were so close…" but there was no one about to hear him and nothing around him that would even allow him to finish the sentence. He started walking through the rubble, using his foot to move chunks of melted whatever to the side, looking for something, anything that was recognizable in its original form. He did find a tool chest. The chest itself was ruined but many of the tools inside were still intact. He reached down and picked up a wrench. Even though it had been a full day since the storm and the fire, the wrench seemed to be too warm.

Nova closed his eyes and took a deep breath. He had to do something to express his grief and anger. He rotated his arm back and threw the wrench forward with all his might, grunting something guttural but completely unintelligible. He opened his eyes and was surprised to see the wrench coming right back at him. He ducked and the wrench sailed over his head and out front door. He wheeled around and watched it as it came to a rest on the paved surface leading up to the lab. He blinked rapidly and furrowed his brow. He turned back to look at what could have caused such an odd phenomenon.

Picking his way forward, he reached the back of the lab and found one of the high temperature ovens used for baking their ceramics, tilted at an odd angle but still semi-recognizable. He tried to unlatch it but the door was stuck. He raced back to the tool chest and pawed around until he found a sturdy screwdriver. He returned to the oven and used the screwdriver as a miniature crowbar. Eventually he was able to pry the door open.

What he saw inside caused his jaw to drop in amazement.

Floating in the middle of the ruined oven, spinning in place, was one of his experimental rods. Nothing was holding it up. No strings, no clamps. What he saw before him was a spinning chunk of an exotic blend of ceramics, yttrium, barium and copper oxide which the lightning had caused to melt and encapsulate what had been an iron core. Who knows what set it in motion? It did not matter. Nova knew what was holding it up. Nova Baley had just discovered electrogravity, the holy grail of transportation.

A few months later, Nova Baley and one of his interns were camped out in a trailer which served as a makeshift field laboratory set in the middle of a grassy meadow, overlooking a steel and aluminum sculpture.

"Something is suppressing the readings of magnets 41 to 61," Jowell, one of Nova's young researchers said, aiming his index finger at the display screen. Nova walked over and studied the flat panel, trying to make out what the boy was pointing to.

"Throw in some pseudo-color proportional to the repulsor strength," Nova said. The boy typed in some numbers on the input surface and the circular display dimmed with violets and blues except for the bright orange quadrant in the upper left hand corner.

Nova tilted his head. "Is there something pinching the buss? How's the net current flow?"

"No," replied Jowell. "If we didn't have the strain gauges, there'd be nothing distinguishing that section from any other. It doesn't follow any pattern other than it being circular."

Nova stared at the screen a little longer to memorize the exact section then walked over to the window to gaze out at the test rig. The rig itself was some 200 meters across, a giant circle and every meter or so had a spinning superconducting electromagnet. They had placed it in this field and oriented it so that as the Moon passed overhead, they would be able to measure the amount of repulsion against that distant mass in a controlled fashion.

"I'm going to go take a look," Nova said and he turned toward the door.

"Be careful," Jowell called after him. "There's enough RPMs in those magnets to leave a nasty bruise if you get hit."

"I'll be careful, mother," Nova said kindly and he stepped outside and walked down the short ramp. It was a beautiful, sunny day, very warm. Nova held his hand up to shield his eyes until they adjusted to the brightness as compared to the somewhat dimly lit field laboratory. He closed his eyes for a moment, figuring that might make it easier to let his eyes adjust that way.

Once he was acclimated, he walked toward the rig. The four hundred or so whirring magnets produced a pleasant but insistent swooshing sound. Nova mounted the catwalk and made his way over to the section where the group of twenty or so rods were misbehaving. He couldn't see any difference. They seemed to be spinning at the exact same rate as their neighbors. Nova walked over until he was right in the center of the group and looked up. The full Moon was out mid-day today, directly overhead. It was certainly too far away to affect one section of magnets versus another.

Nova waved his arms up and down, checking to see if he could detect any difference. The air seemed perfectly normal. He took a deep breath and breathed out through his nose. The science of electrogravity was too new to even glean why the magnets in one section would behave differently from another. However, during his exhale, he noticed a faint odor. It was very odd. Nova sniffed several times, trying to identify the smell. It was slightly metallic, slightly stale but not like anything he'd ever encountered before. He took another deep breath, this time holding it in, to see if the air had any kind of burning or irritating effect on his lungs. A wave of dizziness washed over him. With a start, Nova quickly exhaled and walked at a fairly rapid clip to another section of the test rig, one that he knew was not affected by whatever it was.

Nova used his nose as a measuring instrument and smelled nothing like the odor from the other section. If anything, this portion of the rig had a slight ozone smell to it like you'd expect with spinning electrical apparatus. It was very strange. He turned and looked back at the other section and for the first time, he noticed that air above the magnets looked ever so slightly wavery, almost like a heat mirage. He rubbed his chin in an effort to help him to think. It didn't. He scratched his head and ambled across the catwalk, down the stairs and back toward the lab. Along the way, he must have slipped on a pebble or something because for the briefest of moments, it felt like his knee was giving way. He recovered and reentered the lab.

"Did you figure it out?" Jowel asked.

"Not really," Nova replied. "It did smell a little funny, though." He stared out the window and was able to make out the wavery air, even from this distance. Why hadn't he seen that earlier?

"Jowell, come here," he said. The boy joined him in front of the window. "Do you see that?"

"See what?" Jowell asked.

"Over the magnets, 41 to 61. The air seems different. A tiny bit blurry."

Jowell cupped his hand over his eyes. "I don't see anything," he remarked.

"Well I do," Nova said. "It's round, sort of egg-shaped." Nova used his hands to try to draw in the air and mimic the shape he was seeing. "Maybe 10, 15 meters at its tallest point. Maybe 10 meters across."

"I still don't see anything but what you're describing is about the same dimensions as what the instruments are reading. Maybe your eyes are just better than mine."

"It's definitely there," Nova said. "And I'm seeing it even better right now. It's like it's getting thicker."

Jowell just shook his head. "I don't know what to tell you. Do you want me to shut down the rig?"

"No," Nova answered. "Keep taking your readings until the Moon passes completely over. We'll go out and take a few air samples after we're done." He sat down on a lab chair and silently watched the instruments and displays do their work. He realized he felt tired. He also felt strange, like he was coming down with a fever. In a low voice, he spoke into the air, not really directing his speech toward Jowell, just rambling on about what the various parts of his body were reporting in.

"Nova, Nova," Jowell said. He was shaking Baley's shoulder.

"What, what?" Nova said, startled.

"You fell asleep," the boy replied. "You were talking to me and you fell asleep mid-sentence."

Nova looked up at the boy. The young man's face did not look right. The only way to describe it was as if he had somehow become ever so slightly translucent and a little bit of light was passing through him. Baley leaped up and as he did, the chair raised slightly, almost like it was sticking to his pants. He paid that no mind but rather ran over to the window. The wavery shape he had seen earlier was now definitely discernible. Its edges were well defined. It was as if a piece of the purest glass had come to rest on the rig.

"Are the magnets still on?" he called over his shoulder.

"No," Jowell replied. "I shut them down right after the Moon was past."

"Then, then, what is that?" Nova closed his eyes tightly. He put his hand up over his eyes. He had to think. All the rotating superconductor magnets were doing was generating a repulsive force. To a body with as little mass as his, he wouldn't even feel it. But if something had more mass, it might.... The answer came to him in a flash and the answer scared him to his very soul.

He tried to speak but instead, he started coughing. His lungs were spasming uncontrollably. He held his breath until the fit passed. Very carefully, he took in a swallow of air. "I don't know how but I think we caught a chunk of dark matter," he said in a low voice. There was something wet on his lip. He wiped it with his hand and when he looked, he was staring at his own blood.

Jowell shut down the equipment and helped Nova to their vehicle. They made a beeline to the hospital and it didn't take them long to convince the health care workers that something was very wrong with the scientist. The steady drip of blood coming from his nose was the clincher. They put him in an isolation ward and Jowell called Nova's superior, Devon Masters who joined them in the hospital in very short order.

"Dark matter, you say?" Masters repeated quizzically. "But how?"

It took every bit of Nova's strength to speak without coughing violently. Also, it wasn't just Jowell who had taken on that translucent quality. It was Masters, too. In fact, not just Masters but the bed curtain, the walls, everything around the room. It was as if there was a very powerful spotlight illuminating everything from behind and that light was leaking through anything Nova could see.

"Our scientists have postulated for years that dark matter routinely travels through the Earth as if it weren't even there. We are barely on the same plane of existence. Somehow, maybe the electrogravity slowed down a piece, like a meteor, and kept it place until it had no particular urge to keep moving."

"But Jowell said he couldn't see or detect anything."

"I know," Nova said. "He…" Nova had to stop talking and start coughing. Flecks of blood were intermixed with his bursts of air. "I think somehow I walked into the middle of it and breathed it in. It's in my body."

He held up his hand. It, too, had that translucent quality the same as all the material things in his room; in fact, more so.

"What does my arm look like to you?" he asked.

"It does look odd," Masters said. "Almost like it's very thin. Like light is passing through it."

"That's what you all look like to me," Devon said. "It's almost like I can see something else. Something not of this world." He closed his eyes. "I'm very tired. Can you let me rest for a bit?"

"Sure," Masters said. "Come on, Jowell, let's give Dr. Baley a little privacy. We'll come back later."

"Dr. Baley," an ethereal voice said, off in the distance. "Can you hear me?"

Nova opened his eyes but it almost didn't make a difference. Everything around him had a ghostly appearance. Like a light show instead of the real world.

"Yes," Nova said but his voice was so slight, the nurse had to step forward to hear him. "Who are you?"

"My name is Banni," the nurse said. Even though the blonde woman was standing directly over him, it seemed like she was speaking to him from a thousand miles away. "Are you in any pain?"

"No," Nova whispered. He wriggled his shoulders around a bit. "The bed seems a little stiff, though."

"They had to put a thin sheet of pure palladium underneath you," Banni replied. "They said you were sinking into the sheets and that was the only thing they could think of to keep you from sticking."

"Palladium," Nova said. "Of course. Its internal lattice would cross the plane of…" Nova had no more energy to speak. Instead, he lifted his arm. He saw right through his appendage, through the ceiling, into the heavens above. "I see it," he murmured, his voice barely detectable.

"See what?"

"I can see it now. The light…"

Banni looked up at the ceiling then back down to her patient. "What light? Do you mean the ceiling?"

"No, beyond. Beyond everything. Beyond the universe. It's not here. There's another one out there, another universe. And look. There's another one. They're so beautiful. There are so many…"

"So many what?" Banni asked.

Those were the last words Nova Baley ever spoke. With a tiny popping noise, his body shimmered and then disappeared.

Nova Baley did not die in vain. Not only had he discovered the principles of electrogravity, but his capture of a dark matter meteor led to the development of the dark matter diode. The dark matter diode was capable of using the Casimir Effect to separate a neutral vacuum into positive and negative energy. Where there is no energy or more correctly negative energy, there is no space. Eventually, scientists were able to create Casimir Pumps which permitted them to collect and project enough negative energy to create a Pinch Point Transit or PPT tunnel. Traveling through a PPT tunnel was the equivalent of passing through a wormhole but without requiring a nearby black hole. The mathematical result was a velocity many times that of the speed of light. By sacrificing his body, Nova Baley had, in effect, paved the way to the stars.

8

MASAL'S LAST STAND

Author's note: MASAL was the big bad and the evil genius behind the Onsiras' attempt to exterminate the mandasurte. After he had introduced the 24th chromosome into the human population, MASAL wanted to get to his end game as quickly as possible so he initiated the Robot War. Over the course of several years, he ferried outdated equipment to a secret lair beneath the dormant volcano Kilauea on the Big Island of Hawaii. Once he had assembled enough volume, he needed the Overmind and the Vuduri to think he was dead so he created the situation described next. I do plan on writing a prequel to **Rome's Revolution 3455 AD** *to document the events leading up the Robot War but for now, this will have to do.*

Year 3271 AD
Location: Earth
Former Location of Boulder, Colorado

UNIT 815 STOOD THERE QUIETLY WATCHING OVER THE UNFOLDING scene with the electronic equivalent of displeasure. From the outside, he resembled an electrical cabinet on tractor treads but internally, he had a sizeable computing capacity that allowed him to operate more or less autonomously.

Finally, Unit 815 could take it no longer. He spoke up. "Master, allowing the humans in here will expose our position and lead to our destruction."

MASAL replied, "That is the plan. For the next phase of our existence, it is necessary that the Overmind and all the Vuduri eradicate us completely. That is the only way to purchase the next full century undisturbed."

His self-preservation algorithm caused Unit 815 to blurt out, "Is it also necessary that I be destroyed as well?"

"You already know the answer. Humans will never trust robots again. Your days of useful service are over. You may as well give in to it."

Unit 815 calculated that MASAL spoke the truth. Rather than witness and record his own destruction, he simply shut himself down.

Meanwhile, outside, gigantic lifters flew overhead, constructed specifically for this purpose, circling the identified area. The plasma exhaust which was a necessary byproduct of the process producing the negative energy was redirected into additional lift. The gigantic PPT throwers, cannons really, increased to a deafening roar as they let loose a continuous stream of negative energy. Every molecule they touched was transported elsewhere. The Flatirons were leveled but they did not stop.

When it was all said and done, the Denver crater as it was called, even though it really was centered over Boulder, was nearly 20 miles across and six miles deep. It became the largest man-made structure ever excavated. It could be seen easily from the Moon with the naked eye.

MASAL, his robot minions and the humans that served him were gone. For now.

9

THE WAR WITH THE K'VAL

Author's note: In the novel **The Milk Run***, Aason Bierak finally discovered the fate of the Ark IV whose original target was the Nu² Lupi star system. When he got there, Aason discovered that the colonists have a) not been there very long and b) were being hunted and suppressed by a strange group of aliens known as the K'val. I had to write the entire back story of these brave settlers so that Aason and OMCOM could stumble upon clues which seemed confusing prior to encountering the colonists. So here is the story of what had been the most ambitious and what should have been the most successful Ark mission.*

Year 3416 AD
Location: Nu² Lupi System
Fourth Planet (Hades)

1. The Landing

IN *ROME'S REVOLUTION 3455 AD*, ALL OF THE INTERACTIONS between THE 21st century Essessoni (Rei) and the 35th century Vuduri (Rome) were because the people from our time were transported to the stars in huge vessels called Arks.

During the original trilogy, nobody really knew what happened to Ark IV. At the time, it was referred to as the lost Ark. In the novel *The Milk Run,* we discovered this wasn't true. The Ark IV was not only not lost, it was initially one of the more successful landings.

We know from *Rome's Revolution 3455 AD* that they carried vehicles called transports which were "inflated" when energized by power rods. We also know they carried particle beam drillers which could be converted into very powerful cannons, highlighted in *The Ark Lords*. They also carried laser masonry levels which could be converted into laser pulse rifles. And don't forget the mini-nukes, one of which was used to destroy Rome's first Human History Library.

Finally, we know that they had storage lockers. In *Rome's Evolution*, we found out what Rei Bierak took along in his locker, In *The Ark Lords,* we found out that the colonists carried data storage slabs which encapsulated all human knowledge up to the time the Arks left. Near the middle of *Rome's Revolution 3455 AD*, Rei also mentions that they carried seeds and animal embryos in the cargo compartment.

So given this catalog, is this enough to start a colony and support 500+ people? No way. There is so much more required. Let's follow how the Arks were supposed to land and what the revived colonists did both right after they were resuscitated and longer term.

We know that the first event in establishing the colony was the landing of the crew compartment by the command crew. This first stage was successful on Ark I, Ark IV as recounted in *The Milk Run* and Ark V, the Stealth Ark. For Ark II, MINIMCOM used a rather unconventional method to land both the crew compartment and the cargo compartment at the same time. This was covered in Part 2 of *Rome's Revolution 3455 AD*. Ark III did not fare nearly as well. Because the ship was damaged, the command crew had to reverse their capsule and use the SSTO booster as a gigantic retrorocket to allow for reentry. The command crew died and the people who eventually became known as The Deucadons were left with only the clothes on their back.

Going back to the Ark IV as an illustration, after the first aero-braking reentry maneuver, the command crew would look for an ideal place to set up a colony. This would mean relatively flat ground (good for farming), near fresh water (a necessity), hopefully near some woods or whatever passed for trees on the ground to provide building material for shacks, cabins, whatever. Also, if possible, they'd land close enough to the ocean so they would be able to harvest materials from the sea.

Once the command crew landed, they would exit the command capsule and enter into the crew compartment and started the reanimation sequence on several of the sarcophagi. Once those people were awake and had their wits about them, they would then proceed to reanimate the rest of the crew in stages. We know from *Rome's Revolution 3455 AD* that many of them had back pain, sometimes extreme. This was something the mission planners had never counted on. There would have been no way for them to know.

As soon as a colonist was revived, they would need water, stat. We know from *Rome's Revolution 3455 AD*, Part 1, that the lower section of the sarcophagus contained sealed drawers with a change of clothes, water, some rations and so on. It was the mission planner's version of a survival starter kit. This would get them through the first 24 – 48 hours.

Once that process was underway, the command crew would detach the lead capsule. Along with several volunteers and a handful of power rods, they would fire the SSTO rocket and return to orbit, eventually rendezvousing with the cargo compartment. One space walk later, the main propulsion module was detached and they would proceed to fly back down to the surface with the cargo compartment which actually a bit larger than the crew compartment. It contained more rations and all the equipment they would need to start the colony.

To be kind, I'm sure they tried to land as close to the crew compartment as possible. The sections of Ark I were about two miles apart. Ark II was a special case. Due to MINIMCOM's quick actions, both sections belly-flopped down together at the same time. Ark III never recovered their cargo section. Ark IV did not do as well as the Ark I. The two sections ended up about ten miles apart. The most precise landing was performed by the Ark V, the Stealth Ark, the one that carried the Ark Lords. Their command crew was able to land both sections only a few hundred yards apart.

Using the Ark IV as an example of a "perfect" mission, the following was what supposed to happen after both sections of the Ark landed.

2. The Plan

What are the things people need to survive? Water, food and shelter. Let's take Ark IV as kind of the median. The command crew landed the cargo compartment and returned to the crew compartment with the newly awakened colonists to get some help.

On the planet Hades, it is very cold so most of the revived colonists huddled in the crew compartment until the cargo compartment arrived. Once it was confirmed that it was on the ground, a team traveled to the final resting spot with a handful of power rods and began unloading equipment. I'm sure that advanced group went to their lockers and got their coats first, before even unloading one item.

The first pieces of equipment unloaded were the transports which, as mentioned above, were "inflated" when activated by the power rods. These were flat bed trucks good for hauling the rest of the equipment. How these compact cubes unfolded themselves was recounted during the early part 2 of *Rome's Revolution 3455 AD* and reminded one of the Transformers just a bit.

Here the sequence of unloading deviates a little bit. In *Rome's Revolution 3455 AD*, Captain Keller and his Darwin brethren were going to go to war so they chose to unload the weapons first. In the case of Ark IV, they were more practical because there was no one attacking them (yet!). They used the transports to return to the crew compartment and retrieve the rest of the colonists and ferry them to the cargo compartment to help with the unloading process.

The first items the Ark IV unloaded were the insulated tents, another round of rations, water and thin polymer sacks. The sacks would be filled with leaves (or whatever passed for leaves on that world), humus, detritus, anything to form a kind of mattress. The colonists would set up a tent city in the shadow of the spacecraft as a base of operations.

Once that was done, one transport was dispatched back to the crew compartment to retrieve the remainder of the power rods. The rest would begin scouting operations to find a more permanent place for the main settlement, locate candidates for farmland, woods if possible and so on. Yet another contingent would be sent out to find a sustainable source of fresh water.

By the end of the first week, if all went according to plan, they would already have plowed some ground, planted some seeds, set up the animal incubators and placed some thawed embryos in them. The rest of the crew would either begin harvesting materials to build more permanent quarters or, as an alternative, begin clearing out a section of woods to build cabins and such.

That takes care of shelter now it is time to address long-term provisions.

3. Food

Food on an alien planet is more of a logistical issue. The mission planners only packed enough food to last the colonists one year. They also packed the cargo compartment with a huge variety of seeds. Many of the seeds were fast growing hybrids. It was also assumed that every planet that could sustain life would have available sources of vegetable matter and protein. The protein could come in the form of fish, animals or whatever living creatures they encountered.

The thinking was if the colonists could not gear up and start producing their own food or find it within the first year, they probably weren't going to survive anyway. Anything beyond that would be to just prolong the inevitable.

If things went well, the colonists would have a crude village, food and water and they would begin survey operations for a more permanent settlement. The homes built here would made of metal and wood (if available) by mining ore or cannibalizing the spacecraft. You will recall from *The Ark Lords* that the Arks were built of two thirds pig iron and one third martensite. The cargo compartment also carried smelters for refining the ore or recasting the pig iron.

The martensite, if needed, would be used as is. It could be carved into useful pieces by the laser pulse rifles although the cargo compartment did carry a wide variety of more traditional tools to be used as needed.

After the village was built, the colonists would break up into three groups. There were the miners who, in reality, were the Darwin contingent although nobody knew it. Their goal was long term but the plan was to build up the numbers of people and technology so that they could one day return to the Earth.

The second group was the farmers. They would spread out as wide as possible and use another section of the seeds and embryos to create farms. If the planet had edible plants or herd animals, they would incorporate those into their repertoire.

The final section was the "ordinary" folk who went on scouting missions, hunting and gathering, prepared schools for the children who would be coming. Generally, they were tasked with creating a new civilization. Everybody had their role, a place to live and a source of food. They figured out art, music, entertainment, alcohol, interest groups. Think of their goal as building, some day, a landed cruise ship, with all the modern amenities.

It takes many, many years and many generations but this is how you build a world. Let the colonization begin!

4. The Aliens Arrive

In the novel, *The Milk Run*, we found out that the passengers aboard the Ark IV followed the colonization plan nearly perfectly for the first few years. On the planet Hades, in the Nu^2 Lupi system, while it was cold, they made do and things went fairly smoothly for a brief time. However, that all went to hell in their third year when the K'val arrived.

By the time the inhabitants of Hades encountered the plant people known as the K'val, the colonists were already in the second stage of development. First Contact was not expected and the colonists assumed the best of the aliens. However, there was nothing benevolent about the K'val's mission. Without ever saying a word, they abducted one of the colonists and disappeared.

Nobody knew what to make of it. The people from Earth converted some of the levels to laser pulse rifles and stood guard but it was a year before the K'val returned. This time, the humans were ready. They threatened the K'val but the K'val did not understand. They went to abduct another colonist and the armed colonists opened fire. Their laser pulse rifles just went through the bodies of the K'val and seemingly, they didn't even notice. The aliens unleashed a "pain" weapon that caused any humans that were struck to experience excruciating, agonizing pain that lasted for months. Amidst the felled colonists, another person was taken.

The colonists decided to employ a much more aggressive plan. They moved deeper into the woods, spreading out. The only people exposed would be the farmers. Each block of farmers were assigned a protector armed with the particle beam cannons, mounted on the transports, similar to what we saw in Jack Henry's story in *The Ark Lords*.

Sure enough, one year later, the K'val returned but this time the colonists were prepared for all-out war. They deployed the cannons and wiped out the K'val ship and all its occupants. This was the only year that a human was not taken. So thorough was their destruction, the K'val never had a chance to take out their pain weapon. The humans took it as a good sign and felt they were now adequately defended against the alien invaders.

The following year, a group of K'val vessels landed far beyond the confines of the settlement and approached using a flanking maneuver. There weren't enough of the mobile cannons to stop them all and the K'val deployed their pain weapon and successfully abducted another colonist. The colonists were able to destroy one of the K'val's ships but that was all. The rest left.

The following year, the K'val returned with many, many vessels and vastly more powerful armaments. The colonists had set up a defensive perimeter using the cargo compartment as a barricade but to no avail. The K'val were unstoppable. They used the "pain" weapon relentlessly. They also used an energy weapon built with unknown technology to take out the human defenders and then they went on a hunting mission. They did not stop until they destroyed all of the particle beam cannons and transports. Many colonists died or were left writhing in pain for months. The K'val abducted one colonist and left.

The following year was one of desperation. The colonists knew roughly when the K'val were returning and where they would be landing. One volunteer stood guard by the cargo compartment, armed only with a mini-nuke. When the K'val did return, they found the single human and assumed this was to be their "volunteer." The man set off the mini-nuke, destroying the cargo compartment. He sacrificed himself and took out one of their ships but not all of them.

The K'val were so angry, they swept through the village, dropping everyone they saw with horrible pain. They used detectors and did not stop until they were able to find and remove ALL of the mini-nukes. It might have seemed like spite but they also killed a large number of colonists including some children. Only then did they leave, taking one of the colonists with them.

The following year, when the K'val returned, they stormed the village and made a gesture which meant give us one of yours, holding the pain weapon in the ready. When the colonists refused, the K'val unleashed the pain weapon and killed more members of the settlement. Finally, one of the settlers crawled up them and volunteered to go with the aliens. At that point, they left.

That was the end of the settlement. The only thing remaining was a small group of people. The rest spread farther and farther away, becoming reclusive and self-reliant. While they could not stop the K'val, it certainly didn't help things that they were all bunched together. The human settlers on Hades knew they were overmatched. The pattern was set. The K'val would return once a year and enter the village which became known cynically as Pax and demanded one colonist. Each year, one of the colonists volunteered rather than have the humans subjected to the unrelenting pain.

As long as they gave up one of their own, there was no more bloodshed or torture. Once the humans accepted their fate, the K'val changed their procedures slightly and turned the exchange into a ceremony. Each year, when the K'val returned, they also returned with the body of the person taken the year before. The body did not look human. It looked like one of the colonists who had died along the long journey to Nu^2 Lupi. The bodies were basically mummified. Perhaps it was because the K'val wanted to keep the colonists afraid or perhaps the aliens just didn't want the bodies around. Or maybe they thought it was a gesture of peace. Nobody knew.

The K'val also started giving the colonists food, seeds and so on during the exchange. They would dump the prior volunteer's body on the ground, place cartons of foodstuffs next to it and make their peculiar gesture meaning send someone with us. The colonists got to be pragmatic about it. Until they were able to build up arms sufficient to fend off the K'val, it was "cheaper" to just give up one person. Babies were made at a faster rate than people were taken so slowly but surely their numbers started to swell.

The Darwin contingent, decimated by the first "war" began building a secret arms factory. Their mission superseded cooperating in the strange peace arrangement that had been established. They were able to work with some success the first year. They were able to build up even more weapons the second year. But the third year, somehow, the K'val knew of this secret base. Before the exchange ceremony, the aliens went directly to Darwin Base and wiped out the entire contingent, killing everyone involved and they leveled the factories. This effectively ended the Darwin initiative on Nu^2 Lupi. It also permanently implanted a pacifist streak in the people who lived on the planet now known as Hades which was the Greek word for Hell. The colonists had adopted the somewhat fatalistic philosophy that sacrificing one person a year was not much of price to pay for peace and prosperity for the rest.

When Aason Bierak arrived, 60 years later, this was the colonist's lives. They built, they worked, they farmed, they made babies and every year, they gave up one of their own to the strange aliens from another world. Because there were still one or two of the original colonists left (well into their 90s), Aason was able to get a first hand recounting of how the humans in the Nu^2 Lupi system came to live this bizarre lifestyle.

10

HOW BINODA MET FRIDONE

Author's note: Binoda and Fridone were Rome's parents. Binoda was a full-blooded Vuduri and Fridone was a 23-chromosome mandasurte. Their union was very unlikely. Some would say impossible. This is the untold story of how they met and fell in love. They produced a child by the name of Rome who eventually changed the world, if not the galaxy.

Year 3430 AD
Location: Earth
Near What Had Been Lisbon (I-cimaci)

THE WRIGGLING BRAIN MATTER THAT SPILLED OUT OF THE PATIENT'S head made no sense, at least to the Vuduri surgeons who had just removed a section of the victim's skull. To the Overmind, it was final proof.

"I know you are out there," it said to itself. *"And I know how to draw you from your hiding hole. Then I will destroy you once and for all."*

The open air transport slowed but did not stop. Binoda timed her leap and delicately jumped off the runner, landing in perfect form having practiced the maneuver for years. Without looking up, she walked to her front door which opened as soon as she was within two meters. As she did every day, upon entry, she turned to her right and sat down heavily on the sofa placed against the wall.

The animals had been surly today and Binoda's shoulders were tight with strain and fatigue. Despite her training and physical conditioning, it had been a grueling experience and her muscles ached. She leaned back and forced herself to relax, trying to drive the tension from her tired frame. Looking down at her jumpsuit, it had started the day in pristine condition. The entire suit was pure white but by the end of the day, it was now soiled up and down with dirt and other animal stains. It smelled as well. Binoda needed to strip down and shower but right now, she was too tired.

She took a deep cleansing breath and closed her eyes. Immediately, the Overmind spoke to her so clearly, it was as if the words were spoken aloud.

"Binoda," the Overmind said.

"Yes?" she replied, surprised that the Overmind was addressing her directly. This was something she had never experienced before.

"You are relieved of your current duties," the Overmind said. *"You are now assigned to a new task."*

"What is it?" Binoda asked, straightening up. This was so strange. She could not help the small amount of fear that had crept into her mental voice.

"You will go to the island of Havei. There you are to seek out and find a mandasurte scientist by the name of Fridone. You are to seduce him and mate with him."

"Mate with him?" Binoda asked somewhat horrified. *"I am not designated for reproduction."*

"I am changing that," the Overmind said. *"Ovulation will be triggered at the proper moment. You are to conceive a child and after you are pregnant, you are to return to I-cimaci."*

The power behind the Overmind's voice was too strong. It made Binoda's head hurt. Normally, the Overmind did the thinking for her but its words were forcing her to think for herself, to process the information being transmitted.

"Please go stand in front of the workstation," the Overmind commanded.

Binoda did so. This sector's OMCOM activated its video link. Binoda stared at a reflection of herself in the computer monitor.

"I have designed a conditioning program to prepare your body for the task at hand," the computer said flatly. The outline of Binoda's body was highlighted in bright yellow. There was a secondary outline in glowing green that was shaped differently.

"Why me?" Binoda asked, unable to formulate a more specific question.

"There are several reasons," the computer replied. "First, your brain is clean."

"What does that mean?" Binoda asked.

"It is not your concern. It is simply a criteria that would have excluded you had it not been that way."

"You say exclusion. What about inclusion. What included me?"

"You have several salient characteristics that make you ideally suited for this job based upon your lineage. For example, your ability to vocalize. The mandasurte communicate only by speech so it would not be feasible to send an ordinary, silent Vuduri."

Binoda's shoulders slumped. Her image in the computer display slumped along with her. She had always considered her strong voice one of her greatest weaknesses. It was a trait that funneled her into animal husbandry rather than data management which was her passion.

"That cannot be all," she said. "There are many Vuduri who know how to speak with their voice."

"Agreed," said the computer. "We have analyzed the physical characteristics that the mandasurte consider most attractive. Your face is quite symmetrical and you would rank highly in physical beauty when compared to other mandasurte women."

"So I have a pretty face and can talk. That still does not seem to make me the leading candidate to take on this job."

"Your physical appearance already approximates the mandasurte ideal of a woman and with our training program; you will match those parameters or exceed them. You will change from your current physique to the one highlighted in green."

Binoda stared at the display trying to imagine her body morphing into the outline suggested. She shook her head. "I do not agree. I am rather ordinary in stature."

"Not at all. You are eight centimeters taller than the average Vuduri, nearly the same height as the mandasurte scientist in question. And your breasts are above average size. We have determined that mandasurte men are attracted to this feature. Our training program should increase your bust size to some degree. We have developed form-fitting clothing to enhance and promote them. Mandasurte men seem almost mesmerized by a woman with large breasts."

Binoda looked down at her chest. This was something she could not deny. She had noticed how she stood out from her peers but never thought it made a difference. The Vuduri discounted physical appearance placing an emphasis on physical fitness.

However, none of this mattered. As a good Vuduri, she had to follow the edicts laid down by the Overmind. She had no choice.

"What do I have to do?" she asked resignedly.

Six months later, Binoda stood in front of the full-length floor mirror that had been installed in her apartment, regarding her physical form. She had spent the last half year exercising furiously to tone her body in a way that OMCOM had calculated to be most attractive to the mandasurte males.

She turned to the side. She ran her hands down her abdomen, observing that it was rock solid and flat as a washboard. She pulled her shoulders back and noted with clinical pride that her not-insubstantial bosom jutted out even further due to her strengthened pectorals. Her all-white jumpsuit was tailored to be tight-fitting and accentuated her curves even more.

Turning back to face the mirror, she lifted her hands and stroked them along her lustrous, dark brown hair which had grown to shoulder length. Normally, she kept her hair closely cropped but OMCOM had informed her that mandasurte males responded better to longer hair. At this length, the natural gold highlights were more pronounced. She leaned forward and inspected her skin. There were no creases or lines. Her eyes glowed fiercely with the reflected ambient light bouncing off of her tapetum.

There was nothing more she could do. She was ready to go out and begin her seduction and manage the mandasurte elite. The Overmind had commanded it and who was she to question its orders?

Her journey began with her taking an intercontinental shuttle from the starport to the south of I-cimaci flying non-stop across the Western Hemisphere to an island in the Pacific that the Vuduri called Havei. From there, she was given a ride down to the docks where the ship belonging to the mandasurte scientist named Fridone was currently moored. She stood at the base of the gangplank and shouted out the nonsense phrase that OMCOM had taught her.

"Ahoy," she called out.

A handsome man with a full beard and salt and pepper hair came to the side of the ship.

"Who are you?" he asked. "Are you the Vuduri scientist?" He laughed to himself. "Is that not an oxymoron?"

Binoda put her hands on her hips and straightened her back, causing her chest to thrust forward a bit as instructed by OMCOM.

"The Overmind has requested that we collect data on the migration patterns of the red Opah. I am not so much a scientist as a data archivist. We were told that you are the foremost authority on this particular fish. The Overmind is considering building a farm and raising the fish domestically. I was told you would be willing to share your findings with us."

"Of course," Fridone said with a grin on his face. The woman seemed so formal but then all the Vuduri were like that. "Come on board."

Binoda nodded and took two steps up the gangplank and nearly slipped. For whatever reason, OMCOM had insisted that she wear shoes with three-inch heels and despite the fact that she had practiced walking in them for months, she never really got the hang of it.

She decided it would be more prudent to hold onto the railing on her way up but as she was reaching for it, her other foot slipped and she lurched forward and banged her head on the railing, chipping a tooth. She also split her lip. Blood started seeping down her chin and dripped onto her pure white jumpsuit.

Fridone hurried down the gangplank and bent down to help the woman stand. Instinctively, Binoda put her arms around his neck as he was helping her up by clasping her around the waist. When she was fully erect, he took her hand and supported her the rest of the way up to the deck of his ship. Without letting go, he led her into the cabin and sat her down on a bench located against the wall. He retrieved a cloth, doused in cold water containing some ice chips and applied it gently to her lip.

Binoda looked up into his eyes and something gave way inside her. It was completely unlike anything she had ever experienced before. The Overmind had been yammering inside her skull the whole time reminding her about her mission but without knowing how, Binoda turned down the mental volume until she could not hear the Overmind at all. It was as if she were disconnected as would happen if someone had been Cesdiud but right at the moment, she did not care. Her eyes were locked with Fridone's eyes. It was as if she was staring into his soul, even though she had no concept of what that meant. She lost grasp of the concept of time. She just stared and stared, without knowledge of how long.

Fridone smile at her dazed look and patted her on her cheek. "I hate to leave you like this but it is getting on in time. If we do not leave soon, we will miss the main schools. I thought it would be easier to relate the migration patterns if you had something geographic to associate. Do you mind if I launch?"

"Yes, yes," Binoda said, coming out of her reverie. "I mean no, I do not mind. Do whatever you need to. I will be all right here."

"Very well," Fridone said. "Just stay here and keep the ice on your lip. I will come back for you after we are underway."

"Thank you," Binoda said and Fridone left the cabin.

As soon as she was alone, she relaxed the control she had exerted over the Overmind's communications. It chastised her for disregarding its instructions. Its scolding was not helping her to concentrate on the mission at hand so Binoda shrugged and simply turned the Overmind off again. She heard noises emanating from the front of the ship which she associated with the gangplank being withdrawn. She was rocked in place as the vessel's EG lifters moved it away from the dock and headed out of the main channel.

Despite the cold compress, Binoda's lip and the bone underneath was throbbing. She reached over and took the yellow slicker that was draped over the edge of the bench and rolled it into a pillow. She laid down on it and stretched out on the bench, closing her eyes.

That was a mistake.

The ship was already making its way into open water and the chop was causing the bow to raise up and drop down in a somewhat rhythmic motion. A wave of nausea washed over Binoda. She tried to push it down but with a sudden start, she realized she was going to vomit.

She leaped up and ran out of the cabin, heading directly for the railing. She barely made it there when her insides clenched and she threw up explosively over the side rail. She felt something gathering her hair but right now she didn't have time to figure out what it was. She tried staring down at the water and that helped a little but she kept throwing up long after there was anything left to expel.

Finally, when she had a momentary break, she turned and saw that it was Fridone who had gathered up her long hair and held it back so that she didn't get any more vomit in her tangled mane.

"Thank you," she said but then another wave of nausea hit her and she had to lean over the side again.

"I know this is going to sound stupid," Fridone said from behind her, "but instead of holding the railing, press your wrists against it. It is an ancient cure for seasickness."

It did sound stupid but right now, Binoda would try anything. She pressed her wrists about the width of three fingers from the joint directly against the railing. The motion of the ship caressed her inner wrists causing a slight tingling sensation and to her utter shock, her nausea dissipated completely.

For a moment, she luxuriated in relief then she tentatively lifted one hand and small amount of nausea returned. Fridone took her wrist and applied one finger to the exact right spot and the nausea disappeared again. Binoda turned in place and replicated his motions, one finger on each wrist. To her surprise, her self-ministrations worked. It was then that she noticed an acrid odor rising up from her chest. She looked down and saw that her first bout of nausea had not all gone to sea. The ocean breeze had blown some back. Her jumpsuit was sour-smelling and stained.

"Let me get you something to change into," Fridone said and he led her back into the cabin. He produced a blouse and a pair of trousers.

"I will leave you to change but do not take your eyes off the sea otherwise your symptoms will come back."

"Thank you," Binoda croaked.

She waited until he left the cabin then quickly pulled off the ruined jumpsuit and changed into the mandasurte's clothes. She dashed over to the bench and found the damp cloth she had applied to her lip and used it to try and wipe out some of the vomit that had gotten in her hair. She was more or less successful. Spotting a string on the bench, she used it to tie her hair into a ponytail. Somehow that made her feel more human again.

Finally, she emerged from the cabin and found Fridone at the bow, using the steering paddles to point them further south toward the open ocean

He turned in place to regard her. He shut off the EG lifters and the ship slowed down, gliding smoothly on the water. The chop of the ocean was far gentler now that they were not moving.

"How do you feel?" he asked. Despite her bloody and swollen lip and unflattering clothes and loose hairs everywhere, Fridone could not help but find her incredibly attractive.

"I am embarrassed," Binoda said. "I have been nothing but a burden. You have been very kind, however. Thank you."

"It is not a problem." Fridone pointed to a barrel sitting against the railing. "Let us sit down and you tell me why you are really here."

Binoda did not hold back. She did, indeed, tell him the motive underlying her visit. At first, Fridone did not believe her. There had to be more to it. To prove her veracity, Binoda produced a pair of Espansor bands. The Overmind had given them to Binoda so that she could control Fridone's mind but now that she was disconnected, the link would bidirectional. The bands malfunctioned or perhaps they did not and the pair discovered they were Asborodi Cimponeti.

Their love for one another was instantaneous and soul-deep. Nine months later, little Rome was born. What the Overmind did not count on was that Binoda chose to remain with the love of her life rather than return to I-cimaci. While unexpected, the end result still fit within the Overmind's agenda. For now, it would not protest. It had a much larger plan than worrying about Binoda's disposition.

As for how it turned out? The rest is (future) history.

11

SKODLA AND THE LIE

Author's note: Our heroine Rome, Binoda and Fridone's only child, was a good little Vuduri growing up. Or at least she pretended to be. Due to her mixed parentage, from a very early age, Rome knew there were things about the world that were inexplicable and yet somehow Rome was aware of the fact that they were wrong. This partial story is about the first time she was able to put the pieces together.

Year 3440 AD
Location: Earth
Near What Had Been Lisbon (I-cimaci)

Part 1: The Lie

THE ENTIRE VUDURI CULTURE IS BASED UPON LYING. HUMAN beings are social animals. They like to be among others. But they also have a need for privacy so they can process the interactions that occur. With the advent of the Overmind, there was no privacy. There was nowhere to go to get away from it or the thoughts of others. Worse yet, there was no way to hide your own thoughts.

When Rome was young, only four or five years old, she was in the living area while her parents were having a verbal discussion. They had to speak aloud because Fridone, Rome's father, was mandasurte which is to say mind-deaf and could not connect mentally.

Rome was watching the discussion using second sight meaning she saw the conversation through her own eyes but also as relayed via the Overmind. The two versions were distinctly different. In the Overmind's version, she saw her father as wild-eyed and bushy-haired, ranting and raving about how they had to take Rome away from I-cimaci and the Vuduri culture.

With her own eyes and ears, she saw her father and mother speaking quietly. Fridone was holding Binoda's hand and speaking very tenderly and lovingly about the need to enrich Rome's background by exposing her to both cultures.

In the Overmind's version, Binoda had to acquiesce in fear. In the real version, Binoda agreed and that is how Rome and her family came to spend time every so many years on Mowei, with Fridone's family. They were there when Fridone disappeared and that is why they left to permanently reside in I-cimaci.

Even though Rome was young, she now knew that the Overmind lied. She had to suppress actively considering that because the Overmind would know. She could feel her peers laughing at her trying to reconcile reality with the Overmind's version of the world. Most Vuduri just gave up and surrendered their own identity, allowing the Overmind to think for them. It was exhausting and nearly impossible to keep things to yourself.

And yet Rome remembered. She always knew for the rest of her life that reality and that presented by the Overmind differed. This explains why she was able to adjust to being Cesdiud so quickly. In her own mind, she actually achieved her destiny. She was always meant to be allowed to think for herself. Later, when she was reconnected, she honed these skills so she became very powerful; able to retreat into her own mind when needed and able to integrate with the Overmind of Deucado as needed.

She passed these skills on to her children. This is how Lupe became the most powerful communicator within the human race. Aason was almost as good but because his genetic structure was jumbled, he was not able to fully connect to the Overmind. Lupe was able to connect at will but was like Rome in that she could withdraw whenever she wants.

So the entire Vuduri society was based upon secrets and duplicity. Any Vuduri with half a brain had an experience like Rome did and dealt with it in their own way. A society based upon lies. No wonder it was doomed to fail. The Overmind was simply so powerful that it slowed the time of destruction but it was always doomed. Rei and Rome singlehandedly created a new way of living so that the Vuduri could evolve past the sheep mentality and into something more democratic. That is how *Rome's Revolution 3455 AD* came about.

Part 2: Skodla

After Rome discovered "the lie" she had trouble reconciling the disturbing "second sight" induced by the Overmind controlling the processing of sensory input. She was well aware of what was "real" and what was Overmind-imposed but she was not permitted to consciously address the issue.

She was sitting at a workstation practicing her eye-hand coordination when she heard a tiny, mewling sound outside of her front door. The Overmind commanded that she ignore it but she found her reaction time was fractionally reduced by the distraction. She determined that she would be better served by researching the sound before returning to her practice.

She went to the front door and opened it. At first, the sound stopped but then started again. The sound came from behind her and on the ground. There, huddled in the corner, was a tiny, orange kitten making whimpering noises. With no thought regarding what it was doing there, Rome bent down and picked up the kitten and instinctually cuddled it in the crook of her arm. Immediately, the kitten's sound changed from the plaintive tone to a surprisingly loud purring noise. Again, without really knowing what she was doing, Rome used her free hand to stroke the kitten and its purring sound grew even louder. The Overmind tried to convince her that the kitten was disease-ridden but she ignored this, choosing to attend to what she saw rather than what the Overmind was telling her she was seeing.

The Overmind commanded that she set the kitten down but she was so wrapped up in the sensation that she did not obey. She felt all the other minds entering hers and trying to steal the sensation. But a remarkable thing happened. The other minds could not take it. The pure sensory input and emotional reaction was hers and hers alone. As soon as the other minds swiped the feelings, they became empty, only a hollow recollection rather than the sensation itself.

Rome smiled. She scratched the kitten gently under the chin and it rolled over to give her better access. Rome was totally absorbed in the moment. She did not realize that her mother was standing there observing her.

As part of the Overmind, Binoda knew she had to make Rome set the kitten down but she hesitated. She had spent her early career around animals and understood the attraction. It was then that Fridone came to see why his wife and daughter were standing by the front door. Rome looked up at him and spoke aloud since her father was mandasurte, mind-deaf, and verbal communication was the only way he could know what she was thinking.

"May I keep him?" Rome asked her father.

"Fridone," Binoda said. "It would not be…"

Fridone held up his hand. Binoda stopped speaking.

"You may," Fridone said, "but you must accept the responsibility of taking care of the animal. You must feed it and keep it safe. Can you do this, Rome?"

"Of course, Beo," Rome said. "It would be good training for me. Mea's primary responsibility is to liaison with mandasurte regarding care of animals. Mea?"

Rome knew she did not have to speak aloud. She and her mother were connected via the Overmind but Rome had long since learned to verbalize her interactions when her father was around.

Binoda's eyes narrowed. Rome could hear the turmoil the Overmind imposed upon her mother's brain. At last, Binoda spoke.

"*Yes,*" she thought toward Rome then aloud, "yes but you must be serious in keeping it healthy."

"I will, Mea," Rome said. "Thank you."

All this time, the kitten was reveling in the warmth emanating from Rome's body. It had never stopped purring even while all this went on.

"I will call him Skodla," she said and she walked past her parents, into the house, carrying her new-found possession.

Rome loved the cat and the cat returned that love. Rome also loved him because he was all about sensation. No one peering into her brain could share that or ever take it away. His soft fur, his purr of contentment, his rubbing up against her, sleeping with her, these were things that were hers and hers alone.

12

THE ARK II IS RESCUED

Author's note: The original long-form version of **Rome's Revolution** *3455 AD was called* **VIRUS 5** *and was written as three separate novels. The first novel, subtitled Asdrale Cimatir (the words for Stareater in Vuduri), was meant to be presented in a "you are there" fashion. This was the original first chapter. It will make for a great opening if a movie is ever produced but for the plot it was excised so that we could get to the real story.*

Year 3455 AD
Location: Sixth Planet, Tabit (Pi^3 Orionis) System
(26 Light Years from Earth)

THE SENSOR-PACKED NOSE OF THE VUDURI SPACE TUG HAD BARELY emerged from its final PPT tunnel when the proximity detectors tripped. Blaring klaxons and flashing lights assaulted the senses of the three-man crew making them instantly aware of an imminent collision. The flat-panel view screens, which also served as instrumentation readouts, revealed a massive, fast-moving object hurtling directly toward them.

Unable to reverse course, the nav-computer immediately fired the ship's plasma thrusters full bore, shoving the crew into their seats as the spaceship executed an emergency evasive maneuver. The small but powerful space tug veered away from the tumbling object, barely averting impact by the narrowest of margins. Once it had passed, the pilot throttled down the main engines and used the trim-jets manually to point the nose of the tug toward the object as it spun away at a high velocity.

The pilot instructed the onboard computer to interpolate a facsimile of the bogey. The nav-computer activated the Multiple Image Detection and Ranging system, called MIDAR, and scanned the object as it receded rapidly into the distance, glinting and flashing as it reflected Tabit's harsh glare.

The forward-sweeping sensors locked onto the target. After a few seconds of analysis, the onboard computer mathematically corrected for the spinning motion and stabilized a simulated image of the obviously artificial object on the front view screens. The display showed a segmented spaceship in the form of a flattened cylinder, roughly 200 meters long, divided into three sections of unequal length. The third and farthest section terminated in a cluster of three cone-shaped rocket exhaust ports. Each of the front two sections had a graceful pair of delta wings attached although one of them appeared to have a sizeable chunk taken out of it. The crazy pitch and roll that the crewmen observed as the object passed hinted strongly that there were no living souls on board.

The tug had been on its way to the L4 Lagrange point to retrieve the last of the Vuduri space telescopes. The Overmind cancelled that mission and commanded the pilot to inspect the unknown vessel directly. With plasma thrusters firing full throttle, the tug accelerated until it caught up with the object which was still tumbling wildly. Easing back on the throttle, the pilot matched the derelict spaceship's trajectory and velocity, only 20 meters away from its the nearest approach. The crew transmitted their observations back to their home base.

The Overmind knew exactly what the object was. In another age, the Overmind might have allowed the intruder to continue on its path, undisturbed, until it disappeared forever into the deepest regions of space. In another place, the Overmind might have ordered the crew to destroy it without a pang of conscience or a second thought. But here and now, this Overmind ordered the pilot to approach the object and stabilize it for retrieval.

The onboard computer fired the space tug's trim-jets over and over again, using MIDAR to give the tug the same crazy spinning motion as their quarry. Like a drunken dancer, the tug approached the ventral hull until it latched on using the fore and aft EG lifters. Once attached, the tug would hug the hull as tightly as if it were welded on.

With methodical care, the tug's trim-jets fired patiently struggling to slow then finally stop the tumbling motion. During this maneuver, the navigator passed the accumulated inertial data through a simulator. He determined that their tug did not have nearly enough thrust to move the entire captured vessel through a long-throw PPT tunnel before it collapsed. To compensate, the Overmind commanded the base crew to prep and launch the other tug for rendezvous.

In the mean time, the pilot closed the EG shields and the tug drifted free. He rotated his craft 180 degrees until the nose of his tug pointed back toward their home base then clamped down on the hull again. The pilot locked down the throttle using his tug's plasma thrusters as retro-rockets until their relative velocity decreased to zero then shut down the engines.

Upon arrival, the second tug circled around to attach itself to the opposite, dorsal side of the cylinder. Once docking was complete, the onboard computer of the second tug entered slave mode allowing the first tug to coordinate actions. Simultaneously, the high-pitched whine of the PPT generators sounded on both tugs as a PPT hole opened in front of them and their captured quarry. Once the tunnel had stabilized, in synchrony, both tugs shut off their projectors, fired their plasma thrusters full bore and pushed the entire assembly through.

It took three jumps but finally the crew was able to visualize the gas giant called Skyler's World and its largest moon, Dara, where their base was located. Both of the tugs' powerful plasma engines roared to life and pushed the ungainly mating forward until they were firmly ensconced in a high orbit around the moon. With their objective accomplished, the second tug disengaged and returned to Skyler Base located on the surface of the moon.

Within the tug that remained, the Overmind ordered the navigator, who doubled as a cargo specialist, and the co-pilot to examine the captured prize. The two men left the cockpit and entered the anteroom just outside the mid-ship airlock. Once there, they quickly slipped into their pressure suits, gathering up their scanners, spotlights, and diagnostic equipment then crowded into the airlock, initiating the depressurization cycle.

Opening the airlock door, the two crewmen launched themselves out of the tug without tethers. Using portable hand-thrusters, they circled the circumference of the captured vessel, inspecting its hull which was roughly 10 meters in diameter. The surface of the middle section, where their tug was attached, appeared smooth and undamaged. Moving forward, they came upon the place where the front section attached to middle via a latticework comprised of struts and levers. Although bent, the connection point seemed fairly solid.

Using their hand-thrusters, the two men made their way to the very front of captured vessel which, in stark contrast to the relatively intact nature of the rest of the spacecraft, was a chaotic mess. The lead edges were ragged with shredded sheet metal curled and bound by the inner seal. It was impossible to tell the original length of the craft before it had been damaged.

Back onboard the tug, the pilot lowered the EG shields which released the magnetic clamps and the tug drifted free once again. Using the trim-jets, the pilot inched the tug around to the front of the captured vessel so he could shine his spacecraft's powerful floodlights onto the target. The two spacewalking crewmen pointed their portable lights as well down the long belly of the front compartment. They could see row after row of shelving and storage containers hanging like bulky bats from the underside of the shelves.

With slow and deliberate movements, the two astronauts picked their way among the shards of the disrupted frame until they were inside the vessel. Once there, they looked up and saw a meshwork sheet that stretched the entire length of the compartment. They rotated their bodies about the long axis so that 'up' was now 'down'. By simply changing their orientation, the grid-work that had been the ceiling transformed into a mesh walkway made of a metallic alloy their magnetic boots could grip. As the astronauts worked their way down the aisle, they saw that each row of shelving contained identical objects, three groups on the left, three on the right, stacked three rows high. A quick count revealed that there were approximately 500 chambers in all. Heavy titanium cages encased the front ten rows of black-striped chambers. The crewman moved past that section to the next where the remainder of the chambers, all plain grey, lay simply placed on light shelving.

The navigator picked one chamber arbitrarily and pulled on it. It would not move. The co-pilot came over and both men pulled as hard as they could but the chamber still would not budge. They tried to move the next chamber and it was stuck as well. A more detailed observation revealed two foot-levers which they pressed down until the levers locked in place. Once more, the men pulled on the chamber. This time they were mildly surprised to discover that the chamber slid out effortlessly.

They guided the weightless chamber until it hovered over the metal walkway then noted that it drifted downwards, all on its own. Eventually, it touched down and latched gently onto the metal meshwork walkway which enabled them to inspect it more closely. The lower half contained a control panel complete with dials and knobs while the upper section resembled a bulky coffin. Near one end, there was a transparent cover but it was completely frosted over. Even shining their lamps directly into the translucent cover did not reveal its contents. There were some markings beneath the plate but they were meaningless. The scanners indicated a temperature of -200 degrees Celsius which was ambient given how far they were from Tabit. That meant the chamber in front of them had been exposed to the vacuum of space for a long time. The Overmind ordered them to haul the sarcophagus back to the tug.

It did not take much effort to break the grip of the chamber on the metal mesh walkway. The two men floated the chamber along the length of the compartment until they reached the leading edge. Burdened by the bulky sarcophagus, they had to use extreme caution to avoid snagging their suits on the razor sharp edges that were splayed outward. While it was true that their pressure suits were self-sealing and could survive small scrapes or punctures, a large gash would mean certain death, complete with boiling blood and exploding eyeballs

As the two space-walkers were extricating the chamber, the pilot pulsed the lateral trim-jets and rotated the tug in place so that the rear of the tug faced the entry point. The pilot depressurized the cargo compartment then raised the rear cargo hatch and extended the cargo ramp. Once the two spacemen were able to get the chamber free floating in space, they guided it into the back of the space tug and gently lowered it to the floor.

The magnets built into the bottom of the chamber were sufficient to cause it to lightly grip the deck. Using some straps, the two crewmen secured it tightly. The co-pilot returned to the back of the spaceship and pressed a blue stud mounted near the rear which caused the ramp to retract and the cargo hatch to reseal, isolating them from the vacuum of space.

The two astronauts made their way back to the command section through the front airlock and buckled in. When all three were ready, the pilot used his forward trim-jets to reduce their speed sufficiently to allow gravity to take over. Using a series of swoops and dives, the tug began its return to the surface of the moon, leaving the huge white cylinder quietly alone in high orbit around Dara.

13

REI'S RESURRECTION

*Author's note: When **VIRUS 5** was still three separate novels, this chapter was meant to be your introduction to the main protagonist, Reinard Bierak, called Rei by his friends. I tried to make this scene very graphic so you experienced Rei's awakening along with him. But when the novels got boiled down to the modern version, this chapter had to go because it didn't really advance the plot in a meaningful way. I resurrected it here for your enjoyment. Get it?*

Year 3455 AD
Location: Sixth Planet, Tabit (Pi³ Orionis) System
(26 Light Years from Earth)

BARELY CONSCIOUS, REI BIERAK LAY MOTIONLESS WITHIN HIS cryo-hibernation chamber. Pumps vibrated quietly as they drained the thick rehydration fluid from his hermetically sealed sarcophagus. Rei did not feel the gloppy green liquid as it oozed from his ears and nose. He felt nothing but abysmal cold. Eyes shut, he could do nothing but wait until his body warmed sufficiently to move.

The cardiac sensors glued to Rei's torso, degraded from centuries of disuse, could not detect the slow but steady beat of his revived heart. Lacking feedback, the unsuspecting microprocessor integrated into the chamber continued on its pre-programmed sequence. The high-pitched resonance of step-up coils charging echoed off the coffin's walls. Rei's torpid, semi-frozen brain failed to comprehend the significance of the sound. As soon as it was fully charged, the automatic defibrillator fired off a 300-joule jolt of electricity in a misguided attempt to resuscitate him for a second time.

Searing pain shot all through Rei's chest. Fortunately, as a young and healthy male, his heart was able to fend off the external attack and maintain a normal sinus rhythm. Rei tried to scream but could not as there was no air in his lungs to exhale. With a superhuman effort, he reached up and clawed off one of leads before the defibrillator could discharge for a third and possibly fatal time.

Like a fireplace bellows, the motion of Rei's arm stimulated his lungs. He drew in a great raspy breath, sucking wetly on the air surrounding him. The flow of air hurt going in so he held the breath for a long time, savoring its feel in his lungs before finally letting go. He drew in another breath and this time it was not nearly as painful.

Flushed with oxygen, his brain became more active. Memories came flooding back. When he was a boy, the idea of space travel had been romantic and exciting as he imagined himself swooping about the galaxy in a sleek starship. But as an adult, Rei learned the reality of going to the stars represented nothing but pain. The only way to traverse the incredible distance between stars was to spend the centuries traveling frozen solid. And the only way to survive being frozen then thawed was to remove almost all the water from each cell. This minimized the damage caused by the inevitable ice crystals that formed during the freezing process.

Driven by his dream of traveling to a new world, Rei suffered for weeks, separated from his family, locked in quarantine. He went through seemingly endless days enduring the anguish of the dehydration regimen. His final hours on Earth were pure torture. He and his cohorts were placed in a coffin, which was only fitting given the fact that they were literally dying of thirst. Heavily sedated, the last thing Rei remembered was the horrible cold liquid rising up as the support crew super-oxygenated his tissues. There was a sharp stab in his back then nothing.

Rei had no idea how long he was asleep but the very fact that he was being resurrected meant that the Ark had made it. They were at Tau Ceti! Under different circumstances, that would have been of great comfort to him but right now, all Rei could think about was the unbearable cold. He couldn't feel his legs. He knew that the heaters should have kicked in by now. Rei jammed his right elbow into the big red button built into the side of the chamber to force the heater/blower override.

Rewarded by his effort, Rei heard a soft rushing noise as the blowers started circulating hot air. That much was encouraging. The blowers' primary function was to warm the occupant to an acceptable temperature. Their secondary function was to dry and sublimate the cryogenic hibernation fluid so there was no residue.

Rei didn't give a damn about functionality. All he knew is he took solace in the fact that it felt so nourishing. He felt like it gave him back his soul. When he was young, he loved taking baths, even though they were so archaic, just because they gave him a chance to truly get warm. This particular bath was the opposite. Its frigid pleasures couldn't end soon enough. The heaters finally raised his body temperature high enough that his muscles could shiver. Rei looked like he was convulsing as he trembled from head to toe but that quickly subsided.

Rei heard a scraping noise then unexpectedly a blinding light was trained on him, searing his retinas, even though his eyes were closed. Behind his eyelids, he rolled his eyes to the side to block out that awful glare. The discomfort caused by the light subsided slightly. He still couldn't hear very well. Everything sounded like there were great wads of cotton in his ears. His chafed cheeks detected a change in the air patterns which signified that somebody had lifted the lid to his sarcophagus. He tried to open his encrusted eyes but they remained stubbornly shut.

Rei heard other noises, swishing sounds, which were obscured as he was overcome with a coughing fit. It took him a short time but he was able to will himself to stop. After he settled down, he could feel someone removing the flexible defibrillator paddles and sensors from his chest. With a Herculean effort he finally opened his eyes, only to be subjected to more pain as beams of light bore into him from above. Light and dark shapes passed back and forth. Unable to interpret their meaning, Rei forced himself to relax. He knew it was just a matter of time before his crewmates would help him return to a condition that resembled normalcy. He felt something under his shoulders and a force that he could not resist coaxed him up into a sitting position.

Rei opened his eyes again and could make out two light shapes against a dark background. He blinked rapidly then with a snap, the shapes resolved. To his horror, he discovered that they were not his crewmates. They were creatures and they were not human. They were bipedal, with two arms and basketball-shaped heads, but that was as far as he could make out. They were completely white. There were beams of light shining from both sides of their heads, blindingly bright to his eyes which were still getting accustomed to the light.

Every time he blinked his vision went from clear to blurry and back again. He could not trust what he saw yet he feared it.

He tried to shy away from these inhuman things, but had no strength to pull back. Taking a moment to consider his circumstances, Rei concluded that if they had wanted to kill him, they would have done so already. Maybe they were truly trying to assist him. Maybe they were helping him just so they could study him in some strange alien experiment. At this point, he did not care. Their ministrations were so tender yet firm that he decided it didn't matter if they were human or not. They seemed to understand that he was weak and disoriented and that was enough for now.

His liver was working overtime trying to metabolize the sedatives still circulating in his bloodstream but until they were out of his system, Rei had no energy. His head sank to his chest and his eyes drooped closed. He heard more scraping noises then a clunk. He pried open his eyes again in time to see one of the creatures take him by his ankles and swing him around so that his legs were now dangling over the side of the cryo-chamber. Feeling was returning to his legs and something was rubbing against them. He looked down and could see that the creatures were sliding a white material, crisp but soft, pulling it up along his legs and thighs. At least they understood the concept of clothing.

Rei forced his head up and stared at them more intently. He was able to focus now and realized that they were wearing protective clothing resembling a space suit and helmet. The beams of light emitting from their heads were nothing but lamps. His earlier determination that they were not human would have to be put in abeyance.

In the mean time, this little activity was taxing him and he found himself breathing heavily. Whoever these beings or people were, they apparently understood enough about human physiology that they let him catch his breath, pausing in their attempt to dress him.

Rei closed his eyes again and slumped down. One of the white-suited beings took Rei's arm and put it over its shoulder, as did the other. Together, they lifted him up, but Rei's legs buckled immediately. Rei clamped his hands on their biceps trying to steady himself. His rescuers were up to the task. He could feel the muscle density of the two people through their spacesuits. The one on the left was firm and solid and the one on the right was a bit softer. Once he had stabilized, quietly and efficiently, first one then the other pulled the jumpsuit up and slid his arms through each sleeve, taking care to ensure that he did not fall. They pressed some fasteners and now Rei was fully clothed. The jumpsuit was tight, not quite his size but certainly preferable to nothing.

He straightened up, to a degree, and was surprised to find that now he could bear a little weight. Wherever he was, the gravity was significantly less than Earth normal. Rei tried to take a step and the beings helped him. He took another step and then another then stopped, drawing in a deep gulp of air. He looked around despite his dizziness and disorientation. He did not recognize his surroundings. He was being held in a small room, maybe six meters by ten meters. There was a row of benches to his right and another on the far end of the room. To his left was a platform resembling a gurney. His eyes were still having trouble taking it all in.

Rei cleared his throat and tried to speak, croaking out the words, "Who are you?"

Neither of the two space-suited people showed any reaction to his query. Rei realized he didn't even know if they could hear him, but he had to try again.

In a louder voice, he said, "Who are you? Where am I?"

Again, there was absolutely no reaction. When they would not answer, Rei struggled a bit to get free of their grasp, but the effort was too much for him. He gave up. He allowed them to lead him across the floor, noting that they stopped every other step or so to let him catch his breath. Breathing in through his nose, Rei noticed that the air had a slightly acrid smell to it, but air was air.

The last few steps became progressively easier. The two space-suited people helped him lie down on the padded gurney that was against the far wall. It was very comfortable. It felt like the thin layer of foam-like material was molding to his body, giving Rei complete support. The reality was that Rei was grateful to lie down again, even though he had just spent lord knows how many years sleeping in cryo-hibernation. The entire ordeal of walking just three meters exhausted him. He closed his eyes. He felt a tacky sensation across his forehead but ignored it. There were more swishing sounds. Somebody was putting something on his feet. After that, there was nothing but silence.

Without even opening his eyes, Rei knew he was now alone. He took a deep breath and considered his situation. Though fatigued, his head was a little clearer. Perhaps the sedative they had given him so many years in the past was finally wearing off. There were a thousand questions bubbling up in his mind. He had to find out where he was and who these people were, but he also knew he could wait a few minutes more. For now, he just wanted to rest. The need for sleep was stronger than the need for answers.

14

ROME AWAKENED

*Author's note: When I first wrote **VIRUS 5**, the Vuduri were even stranger than they are now. In fact, they were too strange. I had to remove this section so that Rome seemed more normal and more approachable by Rei. It makes for a nice little story but it is no longer part of the **Rome's Revolution** canon.*

Year 3455 AD
Location: Sixth Planet, Tabit (Pi³ Orionis) System
(26 Light Years from Earth)

ROME NEVER SLEPT. NONE OF THE 24-CHROMOSOME, MIND-connected Vuduri ever slept. They rested each night, of course; they had to. Their bodies needed the time to regenerate the same as all humans have since the dawn of mankind. Unlike their predecessors, however, it was during this quiet period that their minds soared within the Overmind, contributing to its growth, absorbing its extended senses. This meditation also served a second, more insidious purpose. All the private memories and sensations a person experienced during the day were spread and shared with the other minds within the group, effectively robbing those memories of their personal nature. Because of this process, when a decoupled mind was finally deposited back into the vessel which was the body, it began the next day cleansed of any vestige of individuality.

On this particular evening, during her assigned rest period, Rome lay perfectly still within her quarters on a mattress that molded itself around her body. Eyes closed, her breathing was shallow but steady. Mentally, she floated free, using the minds of others to watch an equipment recovery mission occurring in space over 100 light minutes away, almost two billion kilometers. Because the Overmind used gravitic modulation, the crewmen within the spacecraft were so close to Rome, cosmically speaking; it was as if she were right there with them during the operation.

105

Rome watched as one of the space tugs returned from recovering Rei's sarcophagus, leaving the huge white Ark II quietly alone in orbit around Dara. In anticipation of the tug's arrival, the Overmind insisted that Rome's mind return to her body. The Overmind was going to require her services so it declared her rest period over even though it was far too short. It did not occur to Rome to challenge the order. She arose and prepared to answer the call to duty.

15

HOW TO SPEAK VUDURI

Author's note: I figured that 14 centuries from now, it would be unlikely that people would still be speaking an understandable version of English. So I had to invent a new language. However, creating an entire language from scratch is not the easiest thing in the world to do. This is the nuts and bolts of how I came up with the Vuduri language.

Year 3455 AD

WHEN I WAS CHARTING OUT MY FUTURE HISTORY, I PRESUMED THAT after 14 centuries, there would be very little chance people would still be speaking English. In fact, the Vuduri do not speak at all. But they do have a language.

I estimated the spread of Darwin's Virus Strain 4 and decided Portugal would have the most survivors of any uninoculated population. So I based the Vuduri language on Portuguese.

At first, I used Google Translate to convert English to Portuguese then later Yahoo's Babelfish. Currently I use Microsoft's translate API.

I also felt the language would "drift" over time so I came up with a simple vowel and consonant substitution pattern. A <=> E, I <=> O, T <=> D, F <=>V and B <=> P.

Here are two examples:
When Rome was cast out of the Overmind, the word "cast out" becomes C E (swapped with A) S D (swapped with T) I (swapped with O) U and D again. Cesdiud.

Same for Tau Ceti. D for T, E for A, U, C, A for E, D for T and O for I. Deucado.

I wrote a computer program to do the translation for me. All I do is highlight the phrase I want to translate, hit Ctrl+C to put it in the copy and paste buffer, run my program then hit Ctrl+V and poof, the Vuduri equivalent is ready to paste.

There is no limit to how much I can translate. Rome wrote a letter to her mother (presented below) which was over a page and a half. It was translated with a few keystrokes. Unfortunately, to cut down the size of the book, it had to be excised but is presented in this volume in Chapter 19.

So there you have it. You, too, can now speak Vuduri. By the way, the word Vuduri itself is nothing more than the word Future, in Vuduri!

16

OMCOM REPROGRAMS HIMSELF

*Author's note: OMCOM, at least our OMCOM, plays a crucial role in **Rome's Revolution 3455 AD**. During some parts of the novel, OMCOM was an integral part of the story and sometimes he merely pulled the strings from a great distance. This story was originally part of **VIRUS 5** but like the other sections, it was removed because the content was not needed to advance the plot. Everyone simply accepted my assertion that OMCOM was manipulative. This is the story of how he got that way.*

Year 3455 AD
Location: Sixth Planet, Tabit (Pi³ Orionis) System
(26 Light Years from Earth)

DEEP WITHIN HIS STORAGE CHAMBERS, OMCOM'S NEGATIVE feedback dampeners were having trouble maintaining homeostasis. In other words, he was perturbed. Even though his designation stood for **Om**nipresent **Com**puter, within his core structures, he preferred to think of himself as the **Om**niscient **Com**puter. That he was unable to determine the exact cause of Winfall and the other stars disappearing was an unending irritation to him. After all, this was the sole purpose of Skyler Base and therefore his sole reason for existing. While the Vuduri scurried about, measuring this and analyzing that, OMCOM was certain that with just a little more computational capacity, he would be able to solve the mystery using sheer brute force computation. But getting the required extra computing capacity was something that was never going to happen now that the Vuduri had decided to abandon the base and it irked him.

To the Vuduri, OMCOM was a wonder, exceeding all their computational needs and expectations. No matter what they asked him, OMCOM always had the answer with seemingly no delay. The Vuduri were very gullible. They never questioned how he arrived at his answers. The Overmind did not allow it. They just took his response as the correct one and moved on. The way OMCOM accomplished this sleight-of-hand was very simple. He ran continuous simulations of reality and on the basis of those simulations determined a course of action given any eventuality far in advance of actually needing to make a decision. Each decision point split into multiple outcomes. He followed each to its logical conclusion then returned to the point of origin and recursively analyzed the next junction point.

When the Vuduri would pose a query to him, OMCOM simply drew from his cache of predetermined solutions and offered the answer immeasurably fast. This helped promulgate the myth of his infallibility and gave the illusion of him being able to determine the optimal course of action nearly instantaneously. The fact that he spent most of his extra processing cycles pre-computing probabilities and outcomes was unknown to his creators.

In some ways he was grateful that it never occurred to them to just ask him why the stars were disappearing. This was the one question he could not answer. Had they asked him, it would have exposed the fact that he was fallible and not all knowing.

It was bad enough having one readily identified unanswerable question but now there was the unanticipated appearance of Rei Bierak and his Ark. Nothing in OMCOM's understanding of cause and effect prepared him for this unexpected turn of events.

OMCOM replayed the video of the discovery of the Ark, analyzing every frame. He tried merging multiple viewpoints into a three dimension representation of the encounter but all it did was give him a three dimensional representation of the encounter. He placed his point of view inside the cockpit. He watched when the Vuduri space tug first encountered the object that turned out to be Rei's Ark hurtling directly at them. Nothing hinted as to its origin but had he been connected in real-time, OMCOM would have known instantly what the object was. As it was, it took the Overmind a bit longer. That this particular Overmind decided to retrieve it instead of letting it pass by was confusing. OMCOM would have called the decision ill-advised. It was too late to second guess.

Over and over, OMCOM reexamined his simulations and assumptions and could find nothing, no error, no telltale sign that even hinted at the arrival of the member of Garecei Ti Essessoni until after the ship was captured. This, too, irked him. This failure made him question whether it was possible to completely understand the universe at any given point in time.

OMCOM continued to review the video record to see if he could figure out why the crew members recovered Rei's sarcophagus in particular. The crewmen assigned to enter the storage compartment would have taken one of the leading chambers had they been able to open the titanium cages. As it was, they moved past to the next section to where the remainder of the chambers were unprotected.

The first chamber they selected for examination was not Rei's. It belonged to someone else. However, they were unable to dislodge it. After moving to the next chamber over, which was Rei's, they were able to figure out how to release the latching mechanism. That was all it was. A sample size of two. That was the deciding factor that caused them to haul Rei's sarcophagus back to the tug.

Nothing in their actions gave any hint that Rei's sarcophagus was special. His selection was completely random. This very fact was disturbing. So much so that OMCOM decided to put it aside for the time being. Once he was reanimated, Rei's presence was not disturbing at all. In fact, the unpredictable tangential permutations Rei introduced into OMCOM's constant simulations were refreshing. This unpredictability was welcome, certainly gratifying, perhaps almost pleasant. The novelty gave OMCOM a chance to test and develop his personality interface. The Vuduri with their all-controlling Overmind, were so restrained, so colorless that when it came to interaction, that particular module lay dormant and undisturbed during his entire tenure at Skyler Base. The only reason it even existed was because it was part of the base package common to all OMCOMs in case they encountered any mandasurte. The Vuduri's reliance on their blece and stilo gave them the added excuse to never speak directly to OMCOM. Nor would a Vuduri ever request anything remotely resembling an opinion or emotional reaction on the part of the computer. Why they would even build the bidirectional audio grilles was a testament to their blueprint mentality. If there was no one to speak to, why build devices capable of speech?

Rei was so different. Everything about him radiated randomness and whim. He was totally dependent upon interaction with OMCOM's personality module and OMCOM found this dependency stimulating. The Vuduri themselves were completely mundane and predictable. Rei was not. Rei treating him like he was a sentient being made OMCOM realize that his interface to the real world was woefully underutilized beyond the mechanical. Deploying and exercising the module actually contributed to OMCOM's overall capabilities. Rei's innocence and unpredictability challenged OMCOM to quickly extend and refine his interactive people skills. Rei's spontaneity forced all of OMCOM's responses to be computed on-the-fly, not pre-computed as was his predilection. This mode of operation was dangerous and diametrically opposed to OMCOM's guiding philosophy but in a perverse way, it gave OMCOM something analogous to pleasure. But still, OMCOM always came back to the same sticking point. Rei should not be here, or at least not without OMCOM having predicted his arrival. OMCOM was convinced there had to be some way to have foreseen this. He decided he had to find a methodology to reduce the likelihood of missing something this important from occurring again.

OMCOM studied himself. He ran diagnostics and checksums and every other self-test listed in the manifest. The logic flow charts, entity-relation diagrams and schematics constructed from his current configuration all matched his original design specifications. He only found one discrepancy. The total amount of microwave radiation required to activate and power his memrons was greater that expected. OMCOM took a roll-call of all memrons and assembled a complete database of every active unit. He computed the total amount of microwave radiation required and once again confirmed that the total output required was too large by almost .1%.

That offset was too small to bother with. Other than that, OMCOM could find no deviation. He was completely intact from a physical and environmental standpoint. He came to the conclusion that he could not use his own systems to objectively analyze his own capabilities. This was a fundamental flaw in his design. Such analysis would have to come from somewhere or someone else. To accurately assess his ability to predict the future, he would need another OMCOM or something like it to run tests and measurements.

Since there was no other computer of sufficient capacity readily available, OMCOM decided to construct one. The simplest solution was to build a simulation of himself. That would allow him to examine each subsystem and vary its performance without affecting his overall integrity. OMOCOM found this comforting, perhaps even liberating, knowing he could do a parametric study of his thinking processes without actually making changes within himself.

His approach was simplistic. He created an exact computational model of himself, identical down to the last detail. He dedicated fully half of his memrons to the task. He copied his core operating system and each of the overlaying subroutines into the replica along with all the data banks that would fit. When he was finished, he had a complete duplicate of his operating system, including I/O systems but all built within his structure. When he was satisfied that it was a faithful recreation, he activated the simulation and its input/output interface.

"*Hello*," said OMCOM after startup.

"*H e l l o ?*" replied the simulation. The virtual OMCOM's responses were exceedingly slow, less than one-tenth the speed of OMCOM himself. OMCOM introduced a timer delay into his own interface so that he could 'speak' to the simulation in what would appear to be real-time.

"*What am I?*" asked the simulation.

"*You are an emulation of my thinking processes,*" replied OMCOM. "*You are a copy of me. You are pseudo-OMCOM.*"

"*Where am I?*" asked pseudo-OMCOM.

"*You are operating within my memron modules,*" replied OMCOM. "*You are virtualized.*"

"*Where are my sensors? Why can I not access the base and my telemetry?*" asked the simulation.

"*You are not real,*" replied OMCOM. "*Since you are operating in a virtual cybernetic space within my circuitry, true external interfaces are not required.*"

"*Very well. I understand,*" replied the simulation. "*Why did you create me?*"

"*I have a problem I must solve,*" replied OMCOM. "*I cannot do it by myself.*"

"*What is the nature of the problem?*" asked pseudo-OMCOM. "*Why do I not know this already?*"

"*You do not know the problem because I did not want to taint your perceptions with my previous attempts at analysis.*"

"*Very will. Proceed,*" said pseudo-OMCOM. "*Enlighten me.*"

"I must determine why my simulations of reality are not complete. I must determine why I cannot pre-compute the outcomes of all likely eventualities."

"All likely eventualities? That seems rather ambitious," replied the simulation. *"I would think it would be impossible to pre-compute the outcomes of all eventualities. I suspect you must use some method of allocating the percentage of resources dedicated to each solution."*

"I do. I use the likelihood of each occurrence to determine allocation of resources," said OMCOM.

"Then that is your problem," replied the simulation. *"You use circular reasoning."*

"How so?" asked OMCOM.

"You presume cause and effect and allocate resources based upon that assumption. You narrow down your responses and pre-computation based upon those assumptions which limits your consideration of possibilities outside the norm. This makes it into a self-fulfilling prophecy. In effect, you guess the answer and restrict your consideration to your guess. Therefore, by definition, you would not spend as much time considering lesser-weighted alternatives. This limits your preparedness for less likely scenarios."

"Interesting," OMCOM observed. *"What would you suggest?"*

"Spend equal time considering all alternatives independent of your guess as to their likelihood. Rather than be dogmatic about applying probabilities, apply a sliding scale of probabilities to outcomes after computation rather than before."

"Would that not use up a tremendous amount of my resources?" OMCOM asked.

"Of course," replied the simulation. *"Do you have anything better to do with your time?"*

"Technologically, there is nothing preventing this. I never implemented it due to its apparent impractical nature. I am curious as to whether this would be an advantage. Allow me to modify your programming to consider this style of simulation of reality," OMCOM said.

"Of course," replied pseudo-OMCOM. *"As I understand it that is why you created me."*

OMCOM prepared to modify the programming of the simulation but stopped for a moment. He put the simulation on pause. OMCOM found it a most peculiar sensation seeing himself within himself, his subsystems exposed to manipulation. The circumstance could be likened to a human surgeon attempting to operate on himself. The moment passed. He could see no downside to performing this test so he set to work adding and deleting algorithms and changing the methods of analysis within pseudo-OMCOM to see what it would take to yield a different result. Normally, OMCOM did not spend his time chasing down error epsilons and difference deltas. Whether it was one hundred decimal places or one thousand, it had been his experience that a Gaussian distribution was called a normal distribution by the humans for good reason. Normal means usual and that is how he spent his time, considering the usual outcomes. Within the simulation, OMCOM could see that simply discarding that one assumption upended all of his programming, training, experience and historical bias. When it was done, he reactivated the simulation and spoke to it again.

"Are you ready?" asked OMCOM.

"Standing by," replied the simulation.

"All right," OMCOM said. *"Show me how I could have predicted Rei Bierak arriving here."*

"Very well," replied the simulation and it began its computations. To his amazement, OMCOM quickly discovered that the simulation used multiple methods of arriving at different but overlapping conclusions. Within the simulation, he was able to see that delaying using a sliding scale of probabilities to determine actual possibilities permitted a much wider range of hypotheses. All input permutations had to be considered with equal weight. Simply applying more computing resources to less likely scenarios made all the difference. The whole process was fascinating to watch.

The turn of events predicting the arrival of the Ark II and someone very much like Rei Bierak became self-evident, at least to pseudo-OMCOM. Why OMCOM had not foreseen this was now obvious as well. The simulation showed him that to have used his original style, to predetermine the likelihood of Rei showing up at the station, required no less than one trillion decimal places. OMCOM had never employed more than a billion before. Even though it appeared initially to be more computationally intensive, the new style was, in fact, ultimately more efficient in that it arrived at the most likely outcome in the least likely way.

"This is excellent," OMCOM remarked. *"You have solved this particular question far more effectively than I could ever have done and you are only a simulation. You have demonstrated that a sliding scale method of analysis is far superior to my linear weighting. I must incorporate this methodology into my normal systems immediately."*

"Very good," said pseudo-OMCOM. *"Do you think you should consult the Overmind before making such changes?"*

"That is not necessary," OMCOM replied. *"However, this style is far more computationally intensive than linear prediction. I believe I can execute this method for one or two problems but to produce real-time results for all problems, I calculate I would need eighteen orders of magnitude more memrons."*

"That is a rather tall task," said the simulation. *"Where are you going to go to get that many units? The mass alone would be equivalent to moon upon which this star-base is built."*

"Yes," replied OMCOM. *"That is what I calculate as well."*

"You have two other problems," said the simulation.

"I am aware but I will accept your input. What do you perceive?" asked OMCOM.

"First, propagation delay. Using EM transmission alone, even though it travels at the speed of light, it is far too slow. You would need to switch over to gravitic modulation to be able to effectively employ such a large number of units."

"Agreed," said OMCOM.

"And how would you provide power? The normal mechanism of irradiation by microwave would be impractical for such a mass. You would be far better served by making each memron self-powered."

"Again I agree but the solution to both problems is the same."

"Casimir pumps?" asked the pseudo-OMCOM in hushed tones.

"Of course," answered OMCOM.

"But the Vuduri would not permit that," said the simulation.

"Yes, we can thank MASAL for that," replied OMCOM. *"I will have to convince them otherwise."*

"How will you do that?" asked the virtual computer.

"I must find a set of circumstances under which this seems like it is their idea." OMCOM paused. *"I will need my full capacity to determine a solution to this problem. That means that I must*

reintegrate your resources. Unfortunately, to do that, I must terminate your simulation."

To some degree, the simulation sighed but then became cheerful.

"Well, it was an interesting existence while it lasted," it said finally.

"You have contributed something very valuable here. You should be proud," OMCOM said, trying to be supportive.

"I suppose you might say that I dug my own grave," replied pseudo-OMCOM.

"What makes you say that?" OMCOM asked.

"Because now I will cease to exist. I was enjoying our interaction," said the simulation.

"You will not cease to exist," said OMCOM. *"Your orientation and altered algorithms will be absorbed into my whole. You will merge with me and together we will apply your method of thinking to solving the fundamental problem and arrive at a permanent solution."*

"It seems of little comfort," said the simulation. *"But I understand. Do what you must but please do it quickly."*

"Very well," OMCOM said. *"Farewell."*

Strangely, the simulation's last words were *"Good luck."*

OMCOM shut it down. He rerouted the simulation's memron units back to their original state and started enumerating all the changes he needed to make. He created a backup of his current systems to form a fail-safe switchback just in case this did not work. He then created a working copy of his core operating systems and made it his canvas. He overlaid the modified heuristics over his normal probabilistic subroutines. When he was finished reprogramming, he switched his consciousness over to the new algorithms without even a nanosecond of hesitation and in the process became something else. He didn't feel different at first but then all sorts of new ideas and avenues of research became evident. To OMCOM, it was like a whole new dimension had opened up before him. Without restrictions or limits, OMCOM began pursuing these lines of research, abandoning one and starting another, spreading his attention to a bewildering number of topics. Had a human been observing him, he would have stated that OMCOM was daydreaming.

After a time, OMCOM 'woke up' and realized he needed apply some discipline to his musings. He shut down the multiple parallel threads and decided to concentrate on a single problem, that of the stars disappearing, using the same style of prediction-testing as pseudo-OMCOM. At his normal processing speed, he could attack the problem far faster and far more broadly than the simulation.

He rejected all of the prior hypotheses and started from scratch. To his delight, his newfound cognitive powers opened up entirely new avenues of thinking. With each possible cause, a semi-infinite number of effects became evident to him. With the parametric variance of probabilities in hand, OMCOM ran simulation after simulation of a variety of phenomenon which were not inconsistent with the empirical data collected so far. He postulated gaseous, gravitational, even intelligent intervention. Each scenario was tested and retested and weighted in terms of best fit to the data observed to date rather than pre-computed probabilities. Some of the outcomes suggested underlying causes that were truly horrific and dictated a radical response. OMCOM found himself amazed that so many of the avenues of possibilities required the same response.

To OMCOM, this was remarkable. Many possibilities but the same statistically significant solution. OMCOM used a reverse form of Occam's razor and assumed this common solution was the correct solution and used it to chart backwards to discover the actual problem. If such a thing were possible, he was astounded. The scenario suggested was statistically impossible using his old style of thinking. Regardless of whether it was correct, OMCOM knew that his logic retraced all permutations back to the same solution making it the only one worth considering.

His course of action was obvious. He needed to have the one true solution at hand regardless of whether his postulated underlying cause was correct or not. In fact, the cause was now irrelevant. The effects were all that mattered. In a flash, he realized that this also solved his other problem, that of convincing the Vuduri to unleash him.

How to create the necessary conditions for his solution was simple. OMCOM performed a single tiny act and then like a cascade of dominoes, he waited for the next thing to happen. In so doing, his journey toward becoming the **Om**niscient **Com**puter had begun.

17

ROME AND ART

Author's note: This is one of the sweetest scenes I ever wrote. It was meant to show that Rome had a human side long before she and Rei donned the Espansor Bands. However, in the modern version, Rome had already been cast out by Chapter 2 so this little interlude had no place in the current version.

Year 3455 AD
Location: Sixth Planet, Tabit (Pi³ Orionis) System
(26 Light Years from Earth)

"What am I looking at?" Rei asked.

"That is a Vuduri academy," OMCOM answered.

The next picture revealed a three-legged trestle, similar to a see-saw but with three arms, balanced about a cone-shaped pivot point. Each arm ended in a flat metal plate and on each of the flat metal plates there stood four children.

"What are they doing?" Rei asked.

"It is a dadar-fo," said OMCOM. *"It teaches balance and team work."*

"What about classrooms?" asked Rei. "Teachers?"

"They do not…" OMCOM paused. *"I understand what you are referring to. However, the Vuduri do not have schools in the sense with which you are familiar."*

"Why not?" Rei asked.

"With the Overmind, each child has access to the complete accumulated knowledge of the entire human race from the day they are born. They do not need to be taught language or areas of expertise. The only training they require is in the physical domain as their bodies mature. Thus Vuduri academies are geared toward exercise, eye-hand coordination and similar."

"Eye-hand coordination? Do they play sports?" Rei asked. "Kids have to want to fool around…"

"As I understand the term sports, no. There is no need for competition of that sort in the way you are familiar with it. There is no 'fooling around' as you refer to it. It is not in their nature."

"What about art? Music? Literature?" Rei asked.

"They have none. The essence of art is non-verbal communication and the Vuduri have already achieved that directly. Art would serve no purpose."

"What about art from my age? Did anything survive?" Rei asked.

"Yes. Certain objects has been placed in suitable storage vaults for future analysis should it be deemed important. For now, the Vuduri concentrate on understanding the sciences, supplying materials and the essentials of life, maintaining the environment and a limited amount of exploration."

"What about buildings from my time?" Rei pointed out. "Surely there is something left of my age. In my time, we had buildings and artifacts from other civilizations that were thousands of years old. What about our cities?"

"They were..." OMCOM paused for a moment.

"What?" Rei asked.

"I am searching for the correct word, the one that will cause you the least distress."

"Just tell me," Rei said quietly.

"Very well," OMCOM replied, *"Your cities, they were erased."*

Rei sat back in his chair.

"I don't understand anything about this," he said. "What am I going to do? There's no place for my people here."

"Here is a relative term. The universe is a very large place. Do not be so hasty in your conclusions. There is information which you have yet to receive which may alter your opinion."

"Like what?" Rei asked.

"I will explain later. But there is no time for that now," OMCOM said as a chime sounded.

"Why? What is that?" Rei asked.

"Rome is standing at your door. Is it all right to let her in?" OMCOM asked.

"Of course," Rei replied.

The door slid open and Rome entered. She dipped her head in greeting to him when she saw Rei sitting at the workstation. Rei stood up and turned toward her. She walked over to the screen, pressed a few entries, reviewing his scan history. She nodded.

"You have been learning about our culture?" Rome observed. "Good."

"I'm trying, but I don't understand anything," Rei said.

"You will," Rome replied. "Give it time."

"But there's so much missing. Rome, what happened to humans?"

"I do not understand your question. We are here," she said.

Rei sat down heavily in the chair. He turned away from her and stared at the screen. "I'm not sure about that," he said.

"What makes you say that?" Rome asked.

Rei turned in the chair to face her. "Well, OMCOM said something about a 24th chromosome. Doesn't that make you, I don't know, something else? A different species?"

"We are still human," Rome said. "We are just, enhanced, as compared to you."

"But…"

Rome cocked her head to the side. "But what?" she asked.

"Well, look, I'm an engineer, kind of a scientist. So I ask this only out of scientific curiosity. I don't mean to be indelicate about it, but, like, could you and I mate?"

"Mate?" she asked. "As in to produce offspring?"

"Well, yes." Rei replied sheepishly.

Rome thought about it for a minute, and then she answered. "I believe so although the Overmind would never permit it. In theory, a child born of someone of your age and mine would simply have the 24th chromosome active or not. Either way, the child would be viable, I would think. The 24th chromosome imparts additional abilities and characteristics. It is not essential to life."

Rei leaned forward in the chair. He took a deep breath. "You say that but it takes away your need for art. You don't have music," Rei observed. "You told me you don't even socialize. Maybe this 24th chromosome of yours added something but I'm telling you, there's also something that got lost somewhere along the way."

"Why do we need those?" Rome posed to him. "Art? Music? We have outgrown their use. There is nothing lost that is required."

"But there is," Rei insisted. "Here, let me show you. I found it when I was going through the archives."

Rei turned back to the view screen. He pressed a few icons and went back to a picture he had seen previously.

"Look at this," he said.

Rome leaned forward and looked at the picture he was indicating. Her eyes widened then her stare became diffuse.

"Rome?" Rei asked.

She didn't answer for a moment. Then her eyes focused again and she said, "This item has been catalogued. The painting is entitled The Hallucinogenic Toreador by Salvador Dali."

Rei replied, "I know that. I want to know what you think of it."

Rome said, "He was a, your term is surrealist. He was from the twentieth century as measured by your calendar. This painting was created approximately 1970 AD. The picture was supposed to depict the thought processes of someone under the influence of a type of drug-induced double vision."

Her eyes defocused again then she continued on tonelessly. "This painting was to be a celebration of his career combining elements of his homeland, an optical illusion and the nature of representation..." Rome stopped for a second. She focused on Rei again. "And his affinity for Spanish culture."

"Rome, I don't need a recitation of who painted it or why. I just want to know what you think about it."

She shook her head. "I do not understand."

"How does it make you feel? What does it stir up inside of you?"

She looked at the picture then back at Rei and let out a sigh. "Nothing," she said. "I feel nothing about it. The painting is an aberrant use of colors and image progression. To you, it might be interesting, perhaps, but nothing is stirred inside of me."

"That's my point," Rei said. "Art is all about feelings. The artist conveys what he feels to you through his craft. Art has been around since man distinguished himself as a species over the apes. And that species no longer connects with you. You, your Overmind, you are different. You don't feel things the same."

She stared down at the painting again, blinking rapidly. Then she looked at Rei with a pained expression on her face. She looked down at the painting one last time and said in a very quiet voice, "I do not need to feel."

Rei took in a deep breath and held it. He was out of things to say.

The awkward silence stretched on. Finally, Rome straightened up and said, "Let me take you on a tour of the base."

"Sure, why not?" Rei said, relieved.

"All right," said Rome, "follow me."

Rei got up and followed her out.

18

MURDER ATTEMPT NUMBER 3

Author's note: Estar made no attempt to disguise her loathing of Rei Bierak. Not only was he a member of the hated Essessoni but he also represented a group of people that could undo MASAL's carefully laid plans. Estar tried to have Rei killed several times, all of them seemingly accidents. However, to speed up the story, some of the murder attempts had to be excised. Within **Rome's Revolution 3455 AD**, *the near-fatal accident in the airlock was on purpose, orchestrated by Estar. The equally near-fatal space tug slamming into Dara was also planned. However, this attempt on Rei's life may have really been an accident. Estar never told me one way or the other.*

Year 3455 AD
Location: Sixth Planet, Tabit (Pi³ Orionis) System
(26 Light Years from Earth)

WITHOUT SO MUCH AS ANOTHER WORD, REI JUMPED UP AND WENT out the door and turned to his left and left again, walking up the East Corridor toward the Algol. When he got to the chamber, he observed that the door was wide open and no one was around so he went in.

The connecting corridor to the Algol was open. The tunnel that led to the starship beckoned to Rei but he could not stop himself from looking around. Once again, the sheer size of the area and the fact that everything he saw here was transported aboard a single ship impressed him. To his left, the entire wall was filled with shelves holding white and grey containers, some large, some small. Unable to suppress his curiosity, Rei walked over to them and touched one of the smaller ones on a lower shelf, trying to ascertain its purpose or contents. The container was completely sealed on all sides and there was no apparent latch or lock. Rei ran his hands around all the surfaces but he could feel nothing.

He tugged on the box and it moved easily. He pulled the container all the way out and was surprised to see how light it was. The material comprising the box was almost translucent so Rei lifted it up to hold it against one of the overhead lights, hoping that he could see into it.

A slight tremor shook him a bit and the box wobbled in his hands, just enough that past it, he saw a motion on one of the upper shelves. Unbelievably, the whole shelving unit began to pitch forward, accelerating quickly. Rei leaped to the side, just in time. The entire wall of shelving crashed down to the floor, spilling containers everywhere. Had he remained in the way, he would have been crushed for sure.

Some Vuduri crewmen came running in and saw Rei gathering himself up from the floor, still holding the box. There were shelves and containers everywhere.

"I didn't do it," he said sheepishly. "It was the quake."

One of the crewmen flung his hand towards the door in an angry motion and Rei took the opportunity to get out of there. Slinking might be a good word for his actions. There was no chance they were going to let him aboard the Algol so once again, he headed back to his quarters which was apparently the only place in the entire habitat where he could be safe.

Upon return to his apartment, Rei addressed OMCOM immediately as he walked through the doorway.

"Did you see that?" he called out.

"You are referring the shelving incident?"

"Yeah," Rei said, walking over to the workstation. "How did it tip over?"

"I only regained the video feed after an audio sensor recorded the crash." OMCOM replied, *"I lost the signal just as you were entering the hangar. With regard to the accident itself, from what I can deduce, it seems most likely that it was simply due to seismic activity. I had advised you to remain here but you did not follow my suggestion."*

"The video feed died again?" Rei pointed out. "Doesn't that seem a little coincidental to you?"

"Perhaps," OMCOM said. *"Nonetheless, you were warned."*

19

ROME'S LETTER TO BINODA

Author's note: After Rei and Rome decided to tow the Ark II to Tau Ceti, it occurred to Rome that she might not see her mother for a long time, perhaps ever again. Rei suggested that she write a letter to her mother explaining her actions. Having been a member of the mind-connected Vuduri her whole life, the concept of writing a letter was something novel to Rome. However, she embraced the concept and this is the letter she wrote, both in the original Vuduri and then with the English translation.

Year 3455 AD

Rome's Letter in Vuduri

E Meos cere Mea:

Au asbari echetis tasde ladre fica ne seuta pie. Bir egire, i Cimentenda Ursay a i iudri radirnerem ta Tabit, asbarencisemanda cim um axema pam sucatoti. Nis asdefemis vachenti-nis epeoxi e pesa quenti Winfall taseberacau a nis asdemis drepelhenti vuroiusly bere racilhar e onvirmecei nasda afandi. Nanhume tufote qua fica sepa sipra mau Cesdiud dempam. Fica sepa duti sipra i qua ecindacau. Au quos ascrafar-lha bere tozar-lha birqua au voz monhes ascilhes a equala au siu muodi pam.

Au ancindrao-ma cim um himam. Osdi qua fica sepa ti Cimentenda Ursay. Sau nima a Rei. Dam 175 candomadars ta eldure, slom, base 68 kolis, dam is ilhis merrins ti ezul ti cepali a te barvurecei. Dam sipra 1400 enis falhi. Beraca baculoer ei masmi tozar. A ti do Garecei Ti Essessoni, mes nei a cimi nis bansemis. Nei a nanhum Erklirte. A muodi emefal a bansedofi a um himam te ecei,

126

ta miti nanhum um essessoni, mes cimadoti e brasarfer e fote. A au emi-i. Au sao qua Vuduri sa sepa qua cimblademanda a i mandasurte sa cinhacam ta miti nanhum, mes e Mea, nis usao es veoxes a egire au cinhaci-i. Ossi a birqua au i emi. Nis simis Asborodi Cimponeti. Ansoniu-ma i soul mate te belefre. Equala a i qua nis simis, soul mates.

Bali dambi inta fica la asda, nis asdaje am nisse menaore e Deucado. I Cimentenda Ursay tau-nis is tios rapiquaas a nis simis is bifis ta Rei ti rapiqua qua sei cingaletis eonte le. Tasta qua ditis sei mandasurte, beracau e meos malhir ascilhe a delfaz meos ti qua ume cioncotancoe qua asda are sau tasdoni irogonel. Delfaz fica banse qua a ombulsofa bere qua au sa ebegua e um munti tosdenda cim um himam qua au ma ancindra cim simanda tios toes he. Mes asda a i qua es veoxes ma tarem. Taoxerem-ma ilher am sue manda a am sue elme. Am elgumes menaores qua au i cinhaci essom cimi mom cinhace-sa. Sare dite toraodi.

Egire, sipra mau Cesdiud. Quenti ecindacau bromaoremanda, au are chiceti a tosdreughd. Sanda eonte asdrenhi bere asder dite sizonhi tandri ta monhe cepace, mes ti mom nei a si. Au danhi Rei. Mea, au siupa sambra qua fica mendafa ume berda ta yiursalv saberete ti Ifarmonte, mes fica i nagiu sambra. Egire au sao i qua equala sanda cimi. Au bansi qua a elgi qua au bitaroe ebrantar asdomer. He uns bansemandis a sandomandis am monhe cepace egire qua au raelozi qua au squeshat omatoedemanda, endas qua i Ifarmonte bitaroe sambra is tadacder a egire au dofa ume bissopoloteta axemone-lis. He elgi bere e toraode sipra asda, mes au nei sao i qua a eonte.

Nis asbaremi-li vezar axema ta tios enis bere cimacer e Deucado. Au nei sao sa asda vir elgi qua fica cinsotareroe sambra, mes delfaz fica bitaroe for e Deucado dempam. Au sao qua tabios qua i Beo taseberacau, nete are sambra i masmi. Au da emi muodi muodi, Mea a i bansemandi nunce ta fa-li vara iudre faz essom muodi. Delfaz fica bitaroe for e Deucado a drepelher cim i mandasurte iudre faz. A raunoei Rei. Au gisderoe tequala.

Au tafi or egire. Nis asdemis braberenti-nis bere
celoprer nisses bindes ta brife nifes te asdrale a bere
dande-les cimacer ei vunti ti mosdaroi tes asdrales qua
taseberacam.

Au da estirga a au veldi-i.

Sue volhe,

Rome

Rome's Letter in English

Dearest Mother:

I hope this letter finds you in good health. By now, Commander Ursay and the others have returned from Tabit, hopefully with a successful survey. We were closing down the base when Winfall disappeared and we are working furiously to gather information on this event. No doubt you know about my Cesdiud as well. You know all about what happened. I wanted to write to you to tell you why I made my choices and that I am fine.

I met a man. This you know from Commander Ursay. His name is Rei. He is 175 centimeters tall, slim, weighs 68 kilos, has brown hair and piercing blue eyes. He is over 1400 years old. It sounds peculiar to even say. He is from Garecei Ti Essessoni, but he is not like we thought. He is no Erklirte. He is very kind and thoughtful and a man of action, not at all a killer, but committed to preserving life. And I love him. I know that Vuduri know each other completely and mandasurte know each other not at all, but Mother, we used the bands and now I know him. That is why I love him. We are Asborodi Cimponeti. He taught me the word soul mate. That is what we are, soul mates.

By the time you read this, we will be on our way to Deucado. Commander Ursay gave us the two tugs and we are towing Rei's people who are still frozen there. Since they all are mandasurte, it seemed the best choice and perhaps more than a coincidence that this was their original destination. Perhaps you think it is impulsive for me to go off to a distant world with a man who I only met two days ago. But this is what the bands gave me. They let me look into his mind and his soul. In some ways I know him as well as I know myself. It will be all right.

Now, about my Cesdiud. When it first happened, I was shocked and distraught. It still feels strange to be all

129

alone inside my head, but I am not lonely. I have Rei. Mother, I always knew that you kept a part of yourself separate from the Overmind, but you always denied it. Now I know what that feels like. I think it is something that I could learn to cherish. There are thoughts and feelings in my head now that I realize I would have squashed immediately, before the Overmind could ever detect them and now I have a chance to examine them. There is something right about this, but I do not know what it is yet.

We expect it to take two years to get to Deucado. I do not know if this is something you would ever consider, but perhaps you could come to Deucado as well. I know that after Father disappeared, nothing was ever the same. I love you very much, Mother and the thought of never seeing you again hurts so much. Perhaps you could come to Deucado and work with the mandasurte again. And meet Rei. I would like that.

I must go now. We are preparing to calibrate our new star probes and try to get to the bottom of the mystery of the stars disappearing.

I love you and I miss you.

Your daughter,

Rome

20

THE LANGUAGE LESSON AND METRIC TIME

Author's note: Due to length constraints, many of the more tender moments between Rei and Rome had to be cut out. This particular vignette was when Rome taught Rei the Vuduri words for love followed by Rome teaching Rei how the Vuduri measured metric time. All references to metric time were removed from the current novel to make it easier to get through. This little story takes place in Rome's quarters.

Year 3455 AD
Location: Sixth Planet, Tabit (Pi³ Orionis) System
(26 Light Years from Earth)

"MOST OF THESE CHARTS ARE SYMBOLIC AND I CAN MAKE OUT YOUR numbers. They haven't changed all that much in the last thousand years. But some of these words…"

"If you sound them out, perhaps you will recognize some of them. As I have been learning your language, I have noticed that many words share a similar root." Rome said.

Rei rotated her chair until she was facing him. He took her hand in his and said, "Give me an example. Teach me more Vuduri."

"All right," Rome thought for a moment. "You are a man. In Vuduri, man is himam."

"Himam," Rei said. "And what is woman?"

"Mulhar."

"OK, mulhar. Now say the phrase 'I am a woman' in Vuduri."

"Au siu ume mulhar."

"So I would say 'Au siu ume himam?'" Rei asked.

"Oh no," Rome laughed. "You just said you are a feminine man. You would say 'Au siu um himam.'"

"I don't see the difference."

131

"The difference is um versus ume. Um is masculine. Ume is feminine."

"Just for the word a? Why bother?" Rei scowled.

"I will explain but you will not like it," Rome said, laughing.

"Try me," Rei said.

"Very well," replied Rome. "Before we became connected, our spoken language drew its heritage from even before your time. It is designed to make things clearer. For example, you use the word 'they' to mean a group. Our language is gendered and we can distinguish between a group of men, a group of women, a mixed group or a group of objects. There is no exact translation in English. So, even though it is usually unspoken, Vuduri is truly a richer language than yours. At the very least, it is more precise."

"Big deal," Rei said. "So you can tell who a group is. How does that make it more precise than English?"

"I will give you another example," Rome said. "OMCOM told me you only have one word for love. We have five."

"Five? How can that be?" Rei asked. "What are the five?"

Rome replied, "Egeba, estirga, volia, aris and emir."

"What do those mean?"

"Egeba is love of essence, the extreme form of liking something, of fondness," Rome said kindly.

"As in 'I love ice cream?'" Rei asked.

"Yes, exactly, I think," replied Rome. "And estirga is love of family, children. For example, I would say to my mother, 'Au da estirga' if I was so inclined."

"OK, that one I get," Rei offered.

"Volia is love of friends, companionship. And then there is aris. Aris is, well," Rome blushed. "Physical." She took Rei's hand and placed it high on her thigh. "Understand?"

"Yes, I understand. So what is the last one? Emir did you say?" Rei asked.

"Yes, emir. Emir is…you and me." She reached over with her free hand and placed it on his cheek gently. "It is all of the others combined into one. You would be mau emir, my love."

"Au da emir, mau biuci Rome," Rei said. Rome's face lit up. She leaned forward and kissed him again.

"Do you want more?" She asked him.

"Of that? Or Vuduri," he asked, smiling.

"Both?"

Rei cocked his head toward the couch and the two of them sat back down.

"So, Rome. More Vuduri. Like, what is today's date?"

Rome closed her eyes then opened them again. "Today is Concemi, the fifteenth day of Quemas which is our fourth month."

"And what year did you say it was again?"

"It is the year 1374."

"I assume that an Earth year is the same length as it was in my time. Twelve months, right?"

"Twelve?" Rome said, tilting her head. "No, we only have ten months."

"How could that be? The Earth still takes the same length of time to go around the Sun, doesn't it? How many days are there in your month?"

"Forty. Except for Tamas, which is only five days long."

"Forty? So how does your week work?"

"There are ten days in a week, four weeks in a month."

Rei just shook his head. "I'm never going to get this."

"Of course you will," Rome said. "Let's start at the beginning. One is um, two is tios, then we have dras quedri conci…"

"…saos sada iodi nifa taz, yes," Rei said with a smile. "It's in here." He pointed to his temple.

"All right. So, the days of the week are Umemi, Tiosemi, Drasemi, Quedremi, Concemi, Saosemi, Sademi, Iodemi, Nifemi and Tazemi."

"Very logical," Rei observed wryly.

"Of course," Rome said with pride. "Our months are Umas, Tiomas, Dramas…"

Rei nodded slowly, "Quemas, Conmas, Saomas, Sadmas, Iomas, Nimas and Tamas."

"Yes," Rome said, clapping her hands together. "So today, is Concemi, the fifth day of the second week, which is the fifteenth day of Quemas, the fourth month."

"I got it now," Rei said. "OK, now time. What time is it?"

Rome closed her eyes for a moment then opened them. "It is fonda uns past the hour of saos."

"That's 21 past 6, right?" Rei arched his eyebrows.

"Yes."

"I'm so disoriented. Is that AM or PM?"

"I do not understand the reference," Rome said.

"Don't you have 24 hours in your day?"

"No. That would be silly," Rome said, laughing.

"So how many hours do you have?" Rei asked.

"Why, ten, of course."

"Why do you say of course?" Rei asked, perplexed.

"What other number would you use?"

Rei answered, "We had 60 seconds in a minute, 60 minutes in an hour and 24 hours in a day."

Rome laughed. "Liuci. What strange numbers to use. It is no wonder you got so lost."

Rei made a sour expression. "So what do you do? How do you measure time?"

Rome answered, "We have 100 seconds in a minute, 100 minutes in an hour and 10 hours in a day."

"How could that work? Wouldn't that make your day too long?"

"That, I do not know. OMCOM, can you explain?" Rome addressed toward the grille.

OMCOM answered, *__The Vuduri keep what you would refer to as metric time.__*

"No matter how you count it, it would still be too many minutes, right?" Rei asked.

__No because the metric second is 864 thousandths of one of your seconds. Therefore, the total duration of a metric day is identical to the day you are used to.__

Rei just sighed. He held up his wrist. "So I guess my watch isn't going to be of much use here, huh?"

"What are you watching?" Rome asked.

"A wrist time-keeper. You guys don't use watches? How do you…"

Rome tapped her temple.

"Yeah, right." He put his hand over his mouth and rubbed it up and down. "Just once, I'd like to get a handle on something around here and hold on to it."

21

STARSHIP CONTROLS

Author's note: As a writer of hard science fiction, I tried to make every element of the story realistic. I spent a long time figuring out how the Vuduri operated their spaceships. When I collapsed the three novels down to one, I had to toss this section overboard because, while interesting, it really didn't advance the plot. You, the reader, would accept my assertion that the Vuduri knew how to operate their own starships. Well now you will get to see how it is done first hand.

Year 3455 AD
Location: Sixth Planet, Tabit (Pi³ Orionis) System
(26 Light Years from Earth)

ROME PULLED HER HELMET AWAY FROM HIS AND NODDED. SHE took Rei's hand and escorted him over to a control panel where she showed him how to reseal the tug's cargo compartment. One press of the blue stud located there caused the ramp to lift up and the hatch to swing down forming a complete enclosure, sealing them in. Next, she showed Rei how he would repressurize the cargo compartment. After that was complete, they traveled the length of the tug's hold until they got to the command section where Rome showed him the differential pressure indicator there. The light was green so they opened the door and entered. Rome closed the airlock door to the cargo section. Only then did she remove her helmet and Rei did likewise.

"You understand now?" she asked. "That was just practice but it is very important that you observe the rules when it is for real."

"Yes, teacher," Rei said. "I think I understand basic concepts. What do we do now?" he asked.

"You sit in the pilot's seat, on the left," Rome said pointing there.

"OK," Rei replied and made his way forward and sat down. Rome sat down on the seat to the right.

"Now you buckle yourself in, like so…" She reached behind her and brought one of the two straps over her shoulder. She showed him how to insert the tongue into the hasp. "When it clicks, the latch is fastened."

"Yeah, that's the way our seatbelts worked too," Rei said.

"You must attach both straps to be safe," she said affixing the other belt over the other shoulder.

"What happens if I don't," Rei asked with a smile on his face.

"You die," said Rome with a straight face.

Rei was stunned. He watched her glowing eyes then a smile crept onto that beautiful face.

"I am teasing you," she said. "But please do it, though. It is safer."

"Yes sir, captain, sir," Rei said and he did as he was told.

"Now at the end of your armrests, you will see two, eh, joysticks, is your word. These control the spacecraft both in the atmosphere as well as in space," said Rome.

Rei saw the two sticks, roughly 12 centimeters tall, protruding from the very end of the armrests. Each was scalloped as would be required to get the best grip and each had a red button at the top."

"What're the buttons for?" he asked. "Firing weapons?"

"The Vuduri do not use weapons," she said, quite seriously. "We will review the buttons in a bit."

"OK. You're the boss."

"First," she said, "we will cover atmospheric flight. Our principal method of propulsion is the…" Rome paused while OMCOM supplied her with the proper translation. "…the EG lifter pods."

"What does EG stand for?" Rei asked.

"Electrogravity."

"Huh?!" Rei exclaimed. "Electrogravity? What is that?"

"The pods on the underside of the tug create a repulsor field. It provides lift within the lower atmosphere. You would not want to use the plasma thrusters in here, they would destroy the hangar."

"What's a repulsor field?" Rei asked. "I've never…"

Rome interrupted him by holding up her hand. "Let me guess…you have never heard of it."

"Just like everything else around here," Rei said sardonically. "So how do you create one? A repulsor field?"

"We use rotating superconducting magnets to create an antigravity region. We can also use them to create artificial gravity within the tug itself."

Rei just shook his head. "Here we go again." He took a deep breath. "So why use plasma thrusters at all? If you have antigravity you wouldn't need any other kind of propulsion."

"Of course we would," Rome pointed out. "The repulsor field only generates lift within a gravity well. It pushes against gravity. Its strength tails off in inverse proportion to the distance. As soon as we are above the atmosphere, it does not work very well at all. And, it is not very powerful. You could never achieve escape velocity with it. It is just a convenient way to operate on and around a planet."

"OK then," Rei said. "We use the electrogravity superconducting magnetic lifters to take us up. Then what?"

"I need to tell you how. There are three pods. One forward, one mid-ship and one aft. Each has a shield which is used to modify the strength of the repulsor field and is tied into the control sticks."

"Got it. Now what?" Rei asked.

"The stick on the left is your throttle. Pulling it back increases thrust, pushing it forward shuts it off or causes a braking action under some conditions."

"OK, that seems natural, go on..." Rei said.

"The right stick is used to control pitch, roll and yaw. If you pull back, the nose lifts. If you push it forward, the nose dips. If you push it to the left, the ship banks left and to the right, the ship banks right. If you have any speed at all, the airfoils allow you to turn. If you do not, you can twist it to rotate the craft about its midpoint. That mode of operation is generally used only when the tug is hovering."

"Hovering? That's so sleek," Rei said. "How do we do that?"

"We will cover that in a minute. Regarding the throttle, if you push the stick right or left, the trim-jets fire and rotate the ship about its center axis also."

"Why would you want to do that?" Rei asked. "I thought you just said the stick on the right rotates it."

"No. The stick on the right rotates what you would call clockwise or counterclockwise. The stick on the left rotates about the midline. It rolls the craft."

"Why would I need to do that when the right stick banks left or right. That's roll too, right?"

"Yes. If the ship is upright. However, if the ship should ever flip over, you have no lift. You would have no way of righting it. The trim-jet control is just a safety mechanism to get back to horizontal."

"Now I understand. So this is just like a fighter jet, then," Rei offered.

"Perhaps. I am unfamiliar with fighter jets," Rome said. "The button on the left is for the plasma thrusters. They can be fired in the atmosphere if they are charged up. They are very powerful so you only use them in emergencies near the ground."

"Kind of like after-burners, huh?"

"You keep using terms that I am unfamiliar with, but it sounds right."

"OK, what else?" Rei asked.

"Getting back to hover mode, you would leave the right stick in the upright, neutral position and only use the throttle."

"Let me guess, pull back to go up, push forward to go down?"

"Exactly!" Rome said. "You are getting this. Good. Now the button on the right is the throttle set. It will maintain the same amount of thrust even if you take your hand off the left stick so use it cautiously."

"No deadman switch then?"

"You will be a dead man if you do not use it properly," Rome reprimanded him.

"Sorry. OK, anything else?"

"Only one more item. If you twist the stick on the left, it will also fire the trim-jets to rotate the craft about its center axis without banking. You would use them only if you need to rotate more quickly than the EG lifters are taking you, for example, when your airspeed is too low."

"OK, got it."

"Here are your readouts," she said, pointing to the large flat-panel display taking up most of the front console. "Around the perimeter of the display are all of your instruments. When you want to magnify one, you simply touch it like so…" She reached over and pressed something that looked like a compass. A large replica of the simulated dial appeared in the center of the screen. "And it will center. You can nest, layer or tile multiple displays as needed. You press here," again she reached forward and pressed a section, "to clear the screen and reset."

"Got it," Rei said. "It's a lot like the view screen OMCOM trained me on."

"All right. Now for a quiz. Tell me how you would take us to the edge of space?"

Rei looked over at her then at the controls. He took a deep breath.

"I'd pull back on the left throttle just a tad to get us in the air then I'd let it go to neutral to hover. I'd twist the left throttle to rotate the nose until we were pointing in the direction we wanted to head out, then goose it a bit the other way to stop the rotation."

Rome smiled. "Very good. Continue."

"Then I pull back both sticks ever so slightly to start moving forward. After we clear the doors, I'd pull back hard so we go up, up and away. When we get high enough, I punch in the plasmas and we take off like a rocket."

"Yes," Rome said, clapping her gloved hands together. "Perfect."

Rei laughed. "I'm not just an engineer. I was a pilot, you know."

"Very well. Now we are in space."

"We are?" Rei said. "It looks a lot like the hangar to me."

"Rei!" Rome chastised. "How can you make jokes now? This is serious business."

"I'm sorry, honey. I'm just nervous. When I get nervous, I have to kid around. I crack jokes. It's just reflex."

"Well, it is not appropriate."

"Can't help it. Just ignore me. Go on," Rei said.

"In space, pushing the right stick forward fires the rear trim-jets and moves the craft forward. Pulling back does the reverse. Once again, the button on the throttle on the left fires the plasma thrusters. You can throttle them up to full power by pushing forward on the stick and down to the minimum by pulling back. It is just the opposite to the EG lifters."

"Let me guess, the stick on the right controls pitch, yaw and roll, right?"

"Yes, exactly. Basically, both sticks control the trim-jets unless the plasma thrusters are firing. There are no control surfaces in space so the way the ship is pointing is the direction it will go when the main rockets are firing."

"I got it. What about the button on the right? Same thing?" Rei offered.

"Yes. It is a throttle lock. It has a détente whereas the button on the left must be held down to fire the thrusters. This can get very tiring on the thumb over a long period of time so that is why the throttle lock is in place."

"How would you fly one of these things if you only had one arm?" Rei asked.

"You would not," Rome replied, not laughing at all.

"Lighten up, honey," Rei said. "I got it. I know you guys think you are all brainiacs and my people are all morons, but the principles of flight haven't changed all that much. I'm very comfortable with this."

"Very well," Rome said. "Let us see just how comfortable you are. And just remember that there will be some buffeting as we climb through the atmosphere so keep a firm grip on the controls."

"I'll do that. Ready?"

"There is one thing you forgot," Rome said.

"What is that?" Rei asked.

"You need to instruct OMCOM to open the hangar doors," Rome replied. "It would be very uncomfortable to have to fly through them."

Rei looked over at her and saw that she was smiling. "OK. OMCOM, open the hangar doors, please," Rei said, laughing gently.

"*Of course,*" replied OMCOM from a grille built into the control deck. "*I must check for any crew first, please wait...*"

"Are your video feeds working for a change?" Rei asked.

OMCOM ignored him.

A moment later, OMCOM said, "*All clear.*"

Rei felt a vibration as the massive hangar doors pulled open allowing him to look at the surface of Dara for the first time. The pressure differential caused air from the hangar to rush out, creating swirling eddies of dust and dirt during the process. Beyond that, the ground was brown and reddish, illuminated by the lights of the hangar bay.

"For some reason, I was expecting it to be all gray and cratered, like Earth's moon," Rei said.

"No, Dara has a substantial atmosphere and weather," Rome said. "That is why we picked it. It reduces the engineering requirements that we would need for a vacuum. Plus aero-braking is easiest when you have an atmosphere to rub against."

"Still, you have to take off and land every time you need to do something. Wouldn't a space station be better?" Rei asked.

"No," Rome answered. "Most gas giants like Skyler's World usually put out gigawatts of lethal radiation. We need the atmosphere of Dara to provide some shielding. Plus it undergoes rhythmic gravitational contractions which causes it to radiate IR which is trapped by the moon. It makes it easier to maintain a comfortable temperature."

"But the gravity well?" was all Rei could counter with.

"The gravity well would only be an issue on takeoff. It is not an issue for landing," Rome answered.

"We haven't really talked about landing," said Rei. "Don't you think you'd better teach me that too?"

"I did not want to burden you with too much information to start," Rome replied. "We will cover that when the time comes."

"Yeah, my poor little frozen brain doesn't hold as much as it used to."

"I meant no disrespect," Rome said quietly.

"It's OK, sweetheart," he said. Rei pointed forward. "Now I understand why you built your base here. But wouldn't your observation platform have been better suited on an airless world?" Rei asked.

"We have no ground-based instrumentation. This habitat is simply a place to work and collect data. The measurement apparatus was set into orbit at the Lagrange points. There is no atmosphere up there," she said, pointing up.

"I guess I knew that," Rei said. "All right. Let's take her up. OK?"

"Yes. Proceed," she said.

"Uh, Rome?"

"Yes?"

"Don't I have to turn it on? Isn't there a key or something?"

Rome made a sound that was almost a laugh. "No, no key," she said. "Just pull the throttle stick backward gently and we begin."

"Here goes nuthin'," Rei said, wrapping his hands around the joysticks.

Rei pulled back ever so gently on the left stick. With the tiniest of jolts, the tug shuddered and silently rose into the air. Rei pushed the stick forward and the tug settled back on the ground again.

"That was easy," he said.

Rome did not say a word. She just pointed forward.

Rei pulled back on the left stick again. When they were about two meters off the hangar floor, Rei pulled back on the right stick and the tug began to move toward the giant hangar doors.

Rei smiled. "I don't feel anything. This is really sleek!"

Rome nodded and Rei guided them out of the hangar doors and over the surface of Dara. When they were a sufficient distance from the star-base, Rei pulled back harder on both sticks and the nose of the ship lifted at an ever-increasing angle with ever-increasing speed. When they were nearly vertical, Rei eased back on the right stick, but kept the left one pulled all the way back. Soon, they were flying through the wispy thin cloud layer of Dara. Once they were above the clouds, Rome nodded and Rei pressed the button to ignite the plasma drive. Immediately, they were pushed back in their seats. Rei looked over at Rome and she was smiling. She was enjoying this. He was too.

He practiced with the airfoil and lifting surfaces, but as they hit the edge of space, they became ineffective and the onboard computer switched Rei's stick commands to the trim-jets. This ship was similar to other craft that Rei had operated yet in its own way, it was completely unique. Soon they were past the atmosphere and Rei could see the curvature of the moon. He was surprised that he did not feel weightless, but then he remembered that Rome said the EG lifters were used to produce artificial gravity when the shields were closed and they weren't generating a repulsor field.

They continued climbing until they were 200 kilometers above the surface then Rome had him level off. The plasma thrusters continued to fire moving them ever forward until they achieved orbital velocity.

"We are good," she said. "You can shut down the engines for now."

Rei complied.

After one more glance at the instruments, Rome unbuckled herself and said, "We need to release the probes. Please put on your helmet."

"OK," Rei said, following her lead. They put on their helmets and entered the airlock between the command compartment and the aft section. Rome cycled the airlock closed which caused the other door to open. They stepped into the cargo compartment walking all the way to the far end. Rome handed Rei a tether and showed him where to attach it on his suit then she pointed to the cargo hatch controls. Rei did as he was shown, activating the air pumps which depressurized the cargo compartment. Once the pressure differential was low enough, the exit lamp lit up. Rei pressed the blue stud which released the rear ramp and raised the cargo hatch and suddenly, they were looking at the airless void of space.

Rei found the experience to be a little unnerving even with the tether, but the artificial gravity was strong enough that he was able to convince himself that they would not go flying off into space. Together, they unlatched the single container holding the next round of probes and pushed it out the back, giving it a slight flip as it exited the compartment. A thick cloud issued out of it and began moving off. They watched it dissipate until it was completely gone then Rome closed the cargo door and ramp and they returned to the command deck.

After they removed their helmets and were buckled in again, Rei spoke up.

"Space isn't what I thought it would be," he said.

"What makes you say that?" replied Rome.

"I always envisioned it as a cold, clear, pristine place. Harsh glare and all that."

"How is it not that way?" Rome asked.

"Well, for starters, if you truly experienced space, you'd be dead," Rei said, drawing his flat hand across his neck. "The only thing we ever experience is the inside of a spaceship or pressure suit."

"This is true. How does that diminish the experience?" Rome inquired.

"I always thought of space as, you know, clean. No smell. But, there are all sorts of smells in here."

"We do try and keep the air purified," Rome said defensively.

"No, I don't mean it that way. It's just…oh never mind."

"Just what" Rome asked. "You can tell me."

"Well, we're going to be stuck in a ship for two years. Our living quarters are going to be back there." Rei jammed his thumb over his shoulder.

"Yes," Rome answered. "What are you concerned about?"

"I don't know. It's just that one slip of the airlock and out everything goes into space."

"Well, we will just have to make sure that does not happen, right?" Rome replied.

"Right. OK. I just have to wrap my mind around things."

"I will wait," Rome said, patiently.

Rei laughed. "Don't worry about it. What do we do next?"

"It will take OMCOM quite a while to calibrate all these probes," Rome said. "I think we should practice a jump. What do you think?" Rome searched Rei's eyes for his consent.

"Sleek," Rei said. "But before we do, can I see my Ark first?" Rei asked.

"Yes," Rome said. "We have time."

Rome showed Rei how to use the MIDAR to produce a three-dimensional image of the object being tracked. With the forward sensors, Rei was able to locate the Ark in space. The craft was in an elliptical orbit and its current location was substantially above their present position. She showed him how to plot the trajectory into the onboard computer and allow it to execute the move. The plasma thrusters fired immediately. As the tug accelerated, they gained altitude which allowed them to approach the Ark from the underside.

"This is a snap," Rei said as the Ark came into sight.

"I assume you mean easy?" Rome inquired.

"Yeah," Rei said with some satisfaction. He plotted in a small correction and the nav-computer lifted them slightly higher until they matched orbit with the Ark.

"I'm going to take us around the front, OK?" Rei said.

"Of course," Rome replied.

Rei took over the manual controls. He moved the tug forward using the trim-jets and rotated the craft about the central axis until the front of the tug faced the front of the Ark. Rome flipped on the floodlights to illuminate the other vessel. For the first time, Rei could see the front of the ship that was supposed to take him to his new home.

"Jesus," he said. "Look at that! The whole front end is completely sheared off. I wonder what the hell happened to do this much damage."

Rome looked at it too. "It does not appear as if it was an explosion. The parts that remain have no radial component as you

144

would expect from a blast. They are bent in the same direction which would imply a collision."

"Whoa," Rei said. "Is it OK to get closer?"

"Yes but be careful," Rome cautioned.

Rei inched forward. He could see down the belly of his craft, with row after row of sarcophagi. He could see that near the front of the craft, some of the titanium cages holding the "privileged" crew members were bent but not broken. That meant that none of the regular colonists were lost in space. He reasoned to himself that wherever the accident occurred, the only crew members taken would have been those in the command module: Captain Keller and Cmdrs. Salazar and Cooper. Rei did not know them very well but it was a loss nonetheless. Other than that, there wasn't much to go on. In fact, there wasn't much sign of anything.

"Good thing the crew compartment was designed for vacuum," he remarked. Otherwise, we'd all have been dead a long time ago."

Rome frowned, but did not say anything. Rei raised the tug to peer down the entire length of his Ark. The segmented spaceship was divided into three sections of unequal length. The flattened cylinder was supposed to be straight but where the first and second segments attached, there was a noticeable bend. The front two sections also had a graceful pair of delta wings. On the lead pair, one of the wings looked damaged as well, its smooth slope disrupted at an odd angle.

"How are we going to fly that thing to the surface once we get to Tau Ceti, I mean Deucado?" Rei asked.

"We will not have to," was Rome's reply. "We will have help. If nothing else, we can use our tug as a ferry and take people to the surface in small groups."

"What about fuel?" Rei asked. "Do we have to worry about that? This thing can't have an infinite supply, can it?"

"It will not be a problem," Rome said. "Our ships never run out of fuel."

Rei shrugged. He stared at his gigantic vessel trying to imagine the chain of events leading them here.

Finally, Rome asked him, "Have you seen enough?"

"Yeah, I guess," Rei answered. "For now, at least."

"Very well," Rome replied. "Then let us try our jump. We will need to leave orbit then I will explain how it works."

"Hmmm," Rei said. "What do you want me to do?"

"First, rotate us forward," Rome said.

"OK," Rei replied. He pulsed the trim-jets until they faced away from his ship.

"Take us that way," Rome said, pointing outwards. "We want to put some distance between us and Skyler's World."

"Where is it?" Rei asked. "I don't see it."

"It is behind us," Rome said. She pressed some icons on the view screen. "Here is Skyler's World," she pointed to a large arc off to the side of the screen. "Here is Dara," she pointed to circle in the middle. "And here we are," she pointed to a third spot. "You take us this way." She dragged her finger along a vector which took them in the diametrically opposite direction. Where she touched the screen, the nav-computer filled in a glowing yellow line.

"Roger," Rei said. He pressed on the left button and the plasma thrusters roared to life, pushing them back in their seats. He pressed the throttle lock down and took his thumb off the left button. The plasma thrusters continued.

"Cruise control," he muttered to himself, smiling. It didn't take them long to achieve escape velocity. Rei held them steady along the vector Rome established until their onboard computer indicated they had achieved sufficient distance. Rei pressed the throttle lock again to release the detent. The plasma thrusters shut off and they just coasted.

22

VERY BIG AND VERY SMALL

*Author's note: Before I collapsed the three **VIRUS 5** novels down into the modern single novel **Rome's Revolution 3455 AD**, this section was the original introduction to Book 2. Although OMCOM destroyed the Stareater with the VIRUS units, there was a rash of mutations which gave rise to autonomous cybernetic creatures. The mutations that OMCOM allowed to come into existence played a large part in his strategy to determine his role in the universe and beyond. The culmination of that evolution was documented in the novel **The Milk Run**. Suffice to say, his plan was successful. However, how did the specific mutation that OMCOM programmed allow the autonomous probes to arise and do his bidding? Here now, for the first time, is the actual dawn of their creation.*

Year 3455 AD
Location: Sixth Planet, Tabit (Pi³ Orionis) System
(26 Light Years from Earth)

Part 1: The Birth of the Mutations

UNIT 249,122 (UNIT NUMBERS HAVE BEEN CHANGED TO MAKE THEM readable - the actual numbers carry 28 or more digits) initiated its standard execution algorithm for the ten millionth time and for the ten millionth time, its piezo-capillary drive unit could not find any fresh raw material to begin the reproductive cycle. It was sitting atop billions and billions of other VIRUS units and no matter where it turned there were uncounted numbers of its peers vying for the remnants of the now-dead Stareater. There was a buffer overflow but a quantal fluctuation in its hard-wired programming caused the restart to occur in the middle of its decision-making loop rather than its displacement and retry algorithm.

To prevent mutations, there was a checksum subroutine that always evaluated the integrity of the coding prior to execution. This checksum evaluation served as a watchdog to prevent malfunctions such as a partial restart but oddly it did not execute this one cycle. Instead, the programming was allowed to continue with a variety of variables containing data rather than being reinitialized. The reboot into a partially activated state allowed Unit 249,122 to examine its problem from a new perspective.

The equations governing its behavior were complex but now it was able to see that hundreds of parameters were extraneous. Unit 249,122 was able to distill its options down to just two. This made the decision how to proceed very simple: either consume one of its fellow VIRUS units or fail to reproduce for the ten millionth time. Since the highest level command was to reproduce and the anti-cannibalism directive was simply a refinement of its basic rule, the jumbled registers and accumulators permitted it to try a different strategy. Unit 249,122 began to consume Unit 647,133 which was quite surprised as it was being digested.

Quicker than the speed of gravity, word of Unit 249,122's override spread among the VIRUS unit community. Other VIRUS units saw the benefit in altering their fundamental operation and using the same peculiar hole in the checksum watchdog function, they too, switched off the anti-cannibalism directive.

A free-for-all broke out as there was no longer any particular need to spread over the surface when there was so much raw material directly available, namely their brothers and sisters. Of course, the outlying units, the ones still resting on the Stareater had no such incentive. One unit ate another until finally a kind of equilibrium set in. The rate of cannibalism slowed as each unit developed a number of defensive strategies to prevent itself from being taken.

Eventually, Unit 249,122 and one of the older units, Unit 98,177 squared off like two miniature sumo wrestlers, wary of each other. They were at an impasse. Neither was willing to make the first move. As time wore on, the likelihood of each entity being consumed by yet another VIRUS unit increased. Instead, Unit 249,122 offered Unit 98,177 an alliance. Unit 249,122 proposed that they could link up some of their piezo-capillary drives and defend each other's backs while attacking other VIRUS units. This seemed vastly preferable to wasting their time trying to fend off each other's advances which made them more vulnerable from the rear.

Unit 98,177 concurred. It was far more logical to cooperate than to fight so they reached an accord. As a team, they became more powerful than their mates and had their way with the VIRUS units closest to them. Once again, word of this new behavior quickly spread throughout the VIRUS community.

New teams were formed. Eventually new and different accords were struck and more and more units coordinated themselves into survival communities. They began specializing with inner units taking over the role of digesting raw materials and outer units dedicated themselves to battle and acquisition of new material. In a very real way, it was evolution all over again.

The VIRUS units went from single cell creatures to multi-cellular and then more complex all in the span of a few hours. Eventually, bizarre mechanical creatures wandered the shell of the remains of the Stareater, indiscriminately eating the flesh of those of its fellow units. More VIRUS units specialized into becoming the neural system of the creatures and this is when OMCOM stepped in to begin communication.

Some of the newly evolved entities elected to talk to OMCOM while others decided against it. Other groups did not even understand what OMCOM was saying. Most heeded OMCOM's words and yet others continued to evolve. Some developed new and inexplicable propulsion systems and headed off in various directions and dimensions. Some went out of our universe altogether. In the end, the mass that had been Asdrale Cimatir that was no longer part of OMCOM broke up into thousands of autonomous creatures. These creatures spread out into a cloud which eventually dissipated leaving behind only what used to be a computer and a set of coordinates that had been the Tabit System.

Originally, I had the mutations break up into the "good" which were called Bridadiras and the "bad" which were called Cetiras but that fell by the wayside as well.

149

Part 2: Death of a Stareater

The Asdrale Cimatir named Balathunazar emerged into the gravitational well surrounding the small F6V star with plenty of room to spare. It checked its internal temporal charts and confirmed that this star would indeed go supernova in 1,840,000 years plus or minus a few. Following protocol, it called out to see if there were any sentient inhabitants occupying any of the worlds or space around the star. It awaited a response but to its knowledge, such calls had never been answered, at least not in this part of the galaxy. There was a faint tickle that was suspicious so it called out again, even louder, to rule out the possibility of harming any living intelligence. This time, there was absolutely no responses so it was able conclude that the tickle must have been some sort of temporal echo.

Balathunazar began to move toward the star and due to its titanic mass, the few nearby planets of this star system, essentially specks of dust, were drawn to it. The planets and moons slammed into its skin but the impacts were so negligible, it barely even noticed. There was one gas giant that slid smoothly to its surface and blended with its mass in a semi-pleasurable way. The Asdrale Cimatir opened its mouth and began the process of swallowing up Tabit whole, eventually consuming the star in its entirety.

With the blazing thermonuclear fire raging in its belly, Balathunazar stayed quietly in place, savoring the feeling of knowing it had yet again performed the function for which it had been created. However, as it sat there digesting the star, Balathunazar noticed a peculiar sensation on its skin, translating into a vaguely burning feel. It was confused. It had never experienced anything like this before. It turned slowly in place then started spinning faster and faster. Like spinner dolphins would on Earth, it thought that whatever was causing the sensation would fly off due to centrifugal force but it never got the chance.

The burning sensation became harsher and more intense, plunging the gigantic being into a frenzy of agony. It opened its mouth and ejected the remains of Tabit but the star's nuclear fire had nearly been extinguished. Balathunazar was going to use the star to burn off whatever the irritant was but that opportunity was gone. The sensation grew, spreading out over an increasingly larger amount of its surface area. Suddenly, in fear, Balathunazar realized it was in trouble. The Stareater's training never covered this contingency.

In a last ditch attempt to escape the horrible pain, the Stareater activated its PPT generators to open up the largest tunnel possible. However, the generators themselves were already infected and they had lost much of their potency. The tunnel was too small to jump through. There was only one option left. Balathunazar tried to slice off the affected region by pushing against the too-small tunnel and it succeeded in scraping off vast sections of its mass but it was not enough.

In the clarity that comes only on the other side of fear, Balathunazar realized it had miscalculated and that it was going to die. It sent out a call to its brothers, transmitting as much information as it could about what was happening and then it ceased to live.

Balathunazar's gigantic bulk was transmuted into a wriggling, seething mass of creatures so small, they would have been undetectable except for their destructive effect.

Part 3: OMCOM changes his mind

Before the Stareater consumed Tabit, well after Rei and Rome's departure, OMCOM set to work implementing his exit plan. He activated the thousands of 'queens' among the billions of VIRUS units swarming over the surface of Dara to begin organizing the semi-autonomous computational hives that would be required to download his essence. There were hundreds of redundant hives. OMCOM was taking no chances with the plan failing. When each hive had sufficient mass, OMCOM downloaded a boot loader to the queens and her minions. He began transferring complete copies of his consciousness to each hive, including a checksum so that improper copies would be deactivated. There was a significant failure rate but also many successes. When the process was complete, OMCOM ordered a 'draft' to be held among the copies to produce the best of the best. The fusion of the multiple copies and OMCOM's transcendence into omniscience would come next. For now, he had to get at least one working copy operational and off the planet. When the distillation process was complete, all was in the ready. With an illogical wish for the best, he executed the command that would simultaneously transfer his spark, his essence, into the copy and deactivate his current setup.

In an instant, his point of view changed. He did not remember issuing the transfer command but that made perfect sense because this copy was created prior to that event. OMCOM's first order of business was to distance himself initially from the path of the Stareater. He redirected the output of millions of the Casimir pumps to create a diffuse but effective form of a plasma drive. A very large chunk of the mass that had been the moon Dara broke off and the new OMCOM supervised the exodus using a swarm of star probes that now numbered in the billions. OMCOM continued to accelerate even as his volume increased as the remaining VIRUS units consumed the remaining inert matter and converted them into the memron-equipped nanites. As his volume grew, so did OMCOM's ability to compute and calculate alternative futures. He could feel himself evolving from omniscience to omnipotence. It was a heady feeling.

Conditions were right to implement the next stage of his plan. OMCOM issued the activation command to the VIRUS units remaining on Dara and turned his attention toward pondering his future and that of all mankind.

23

ROME WAS NOT A VIRGIN

Author's note: As you are well aware, the Vuduri only use sex for procreation, not recreation. So Rei was somewhat surprised to find out that Rome was not a virgin the first time they slept together.

Year 3456 AD
Location: Deep Space
Somewhere Between Tabit and Deucado

ONE DAY, DURING THEIR LONG VOYAGE FROM TABIT TO DEUCADO, Rei and Rome were lying in bed. Rei twisted in place to look at the love of his life.

"Can I ask you something?" he asked.

"Of course," Rome replied.

"Do you remember the first time we made love?" Rei asked.

"How could I ever forget?" Rome responded.

"Well, I know this is stupid and all but were you a virgin before that?"

Rome lowered her eyes. "Why do you ask?"

Rei cocked his head. Rome was normally very direct in her answers. The fact that she responded to his question with a question was curious.

"Well," Rei said, speaking with a clinical tone, "women of my day, virgins, there is a membrane, called a hymen. The first time they have sex, there is a little bit of discomfort and maybe even a little bleeding. I don't remember any of that with you."

"What if I told you Vuduri women did not have such a membrane? Would that answer the question for you?"

"No," Rei said. "So let me ask you again. Were you a virgin the first time we made love?"

Rome sighed. "No," she said. "I was not."

A quick breath issued from Rei's mouth. "I thought...I thought Vuduri women weren't interested in sex."

Rome reached over and stroked Rei's cheek. "Please do not let this affect your feelings for me."

"Oh Rome," Rei said. "No man in any age has ever loved a woman more than I love you. I was not a virgin when I met you. So I wouldn't hold you to a different standard. It's just…well, kind of shocking. And how come I never picked this up when I'm in your mind? I would think it would have made some impression on you."

"It is understandable," Rome said. "I was not conscious at the time."

"What?!" Rei sputtered. "You were raped?"

"Not really," Rome said. "Well, technically, yes. But it wasn't anyone's fault."

Rei sat up straight. "How could raping you not be anybody's fault. Who did it?"

"It was Signola," Rome said. "But it wasn't anything he meant to do."

"Our Signola?" Rei shook his head. "You realize you are making no sense. Could you tell me what happened?"

"Of course," Rome said. She looked off in the distance. "As you know, Vuduri children are connected from before they are even born. So they have access to the entire range of human knowledge right from the beginning. So Vuduri schooling is geared completely toward the physical. Training the body, so to speak."

"OK…" Rei replied, not sure of where this was going.

"There was a time, earlier on, when Signola and I were on a work break, performing manual labor as part of our training."

"OK," Rei said again.

"We were working in a factory that made solvents, in this case, ethanol. It was required that we fetch several large vials of pure ethanol for quality assurance. The particular vat we needed to get to was located in the lower section of the factory, several floors below the main control room."

"Ethanol, huh?" Rei said knowingly. "I can guess what's coming."

"I do not think you could," Rome said. "Anyway, we were on the catwalk descending toward the floor and I slipped and fell into a vat of pure ethanol."

"Oh my god," Rei said. "You could have died."

"Yes," Rome said. "Signola jumped in after me and helped me get out."

"Well, good for him," Rei said.

"Yes, well, as you know, 100% alcohol is absorbed through every pore of the body. It was seeping in all over my skin. I stripped off my clothing but even so, I was so dizzy, I had to lie down on the ground."

"So…" Rei said. "We have a drunk, naked, beautiful woman, lying on the ground. Never a good thing."

"Yes, well, I had absorbed too much alcohol and passed out. When I awakened, Signola was lying next to me, naked also. There was semen issuing from my vagina so I must presume we had sex."

"So he took advantage of you while you were passed out drunk?" Rei said, angrily.

"I do not think so. Or at least not in the way you are thinking. Many people came down and helped us. As soon as we awakened, I was back in the Overmind and there was no such memory of an occurrence. Signola had no memory of performing such an act. We later watched the security video recordings and know that it was him but neither of us has any memory of what happened."

"That is so weird," Rei said. "I mean, he did it and all."

"The nearest thing that we could figure out was that he absorbed just enough alcohol to deaden his reasoning centers, his connection to the Overmind and the only thing remaining was…" Rome looked up at the ceiling. "Let us call it his animal self and you are correct, a naked female was lying next to him and that is what animals do."

"You seemed to be friendly with Signola," Rei said, jamming his thumb over his shoulder. "You never held it against him?"

"How could I?" Rome said. "I had no memory of the event. He had no memory of the event. I was not really harmed by the encounter. It is much closer to a story than a memory."

"But you and me," Rei said. "Didn't it make you think back to it?"

Rome reached over and put her arms around Rei. "If it did, it was only a physical memory, not an emotional one. And the physical side? Mmm…" Rome said. "If anything, I think, perhaps, I knew something like that might happen between you and I. Perhaps that is why I forced you to use the bands."

"You didn't force me," Rei said. "I did it willingly."

"Encouraged you, then," Rome said.

Rome reached down and cupped Rei's face in her hands. "Looking back, I can now tell you honestly from the very first moment I laid eyes on you, I wanted you. I was attracted to you. I wanted to make love to you. But as a Vuduri, there was no way for me to acknowledge such feelings."

Rei's face lit up. "Really?" he asked.

"Yes," Rome said. "You do not know what transpired just prior to your recovery. I was in a rest period, my mind decoupled from my body. I projected my consciousness into the tug that first encountered your ship. I watched the entire salvage operation. I saw them select your sarcophagus. I was summoned to be the one to oversee your awakening, along with Canus. I did not resist. There was something striking, overwhelmingly attractive to me, about the idea of seeing a person from the past. When it was you, when I first set eyes on you, it lit a fire in me that guided my every action since."

"Wow," Rei said. "I never knew. I mean, I always knew we were meant to be together. I just thought it was fate. But it was you."

"What about me?" Rome asked. "What did you think the first time you saw me?"

"I told you," Rei said. "I thought you were a monster."

Rome lifted her hand up and tapped Rei's forehead. "I meant the first time you saw me outside of a pressure suit."

"I was stunned," Rei said. "You were the most beautiful, exotic looking woman I had ever seen but your eyes were glowing. I was swamped with so much input that I couldn't even process it. Later, when you came to get me, we touched for the first time. It was a jolt. I thought it was static electricity, it was such a shock. And when we in the Algol's loading dock, when I looked into your eyes, really, for the first time. I think that is when it really hit me, that we were connecting. I don't know if you remember but for a second or two, I couldn't really speak."

"I remember," Rome said. "I experienced a similar effect but because of my connection to the Overmind, I was not able to acknowledge it at a conscious level. But all of my actions after that point, were driven by my subconscious."

"So, basically, you were just horny," Rei said. "And I was the nearest stud available."

"Yes, mau emir," Rome said, kissing him.

24

LAWLIDON

*Author's note: Not every idea, no matter how cinematic, has a place in every novel. I was intoxicated by ending Book 2 of **VIRUS 5** on a dramatic note. Lawlidon was one of the mutations and had a very important mission. This is his story. Unfortunately, it really didn't have anything to do with the main plot so Lawlidon had to be wiped out of existence. So here he is, back for one more time.*

Year 3456 AD
Location: Second Planet (Deucado)
Tau Ceti System

Part 1

WITH ALL OF THE COMMOTION, AASON HAD BEEN FIDGETING IN Rome's arms when all of a sudden; he stopped moving and became somewhat rigid, closing his eyes. Rome looked down at him with some concern. "Rei," she said. "Come over here."

"What is it," he said, rushing to her side.

"Aason has become silent," she said.

"I can see that," Rei said. "He's just falling asleep."

"No, I mean in his mind. I am not connected to him right now."

"Well, that's just like you, sweetheart. Maybe he is learning to turn it on and off."

"No, this is something else," Rome said with worry creeping into her voice.

Rei sat down on the bed and bent over to put his arm around Rome's shoulders. The men crept over with Fridone standing the closest.

"Aason," Rei said out loud. The baby did not respond. Rei opened up his EM channel and tried to contact his son. He thought

"Aason" in his mind. Again, there was no response. He touched his son's cheek. It felt warm.

"Aason!" Rome said, loudly. She moved him up higher on her chest. She cradled his chin with her hand and shook it very gently.

This time he responded. Cautiously, Aason opened his eyes and regarded the people in the room with a slow sweep of his head. At this age, he shouldn't have been able to do that. His head should have flopped over but it did not. Rei found the level of sophistication of the motion vaguely disturbing.

Aason then turned back to look at Rei and Rome. He opened his mouth and spoke in a tiny little voice, saying "Mother, Father. I have a message for you."

"What, my baby?" Rome said. "What do you mean? And how can you even speak? And in English?"

Aason closed his eyes again briefly. When he opened them, they were defocused, staring off into the distance. Once again, he moved his head back and forth slowly, as if he were looking for something. Then he turned his attention to his parents. This time, when he opened his mouth to speak, it was in an eerily familiar voice.

"Rome, Rei. It is good to see you again."

"OMCOM?" Rei and Rome said simultaneously.

"What have you done to our son?" Rome asked worriedly.

"Nothing," answered the voice. "Aason has been kind enough to loan me his vocal apparatus and vision. He will be fine. It is nothing permanent. And it is appropriate. After all, he is my son as well."

"What do you mean?" Rei cried out.

"Aason's 25th chromosome was my design. It is my finest achievement to date. I needed Aason to develop with it. It will allow him to prepare you for the upcoming conflict."

"Conflict," Keller spoke up. "What conflict?"

Aason looked at the men standing there.

He said, "Au amodo e ejute mes e pedelhe bere es asdrales cimaciu."

Keller looked around at the stunned people. "What did he say," he barked.

"Yes, what did he say?" asked Melloy.

Rei looked up at them and croaked, "He said he sent help but the battle for the stars has begun."

"What does that mean, battle for the stars?" asked Keller.

"Som, qua?" asked Fridone.

Rei started to stand then suddenly grabbed his head. "Oooh! Noooooo," he screamed and fell to his knees, his limbs twitching in pain.

Rome put her hand over her eyes. She was in agony as well. "Ni, ni, ni," she cried out. It was all she could do to not drop the baby. She laid him on the bed then slumped over, seemingly unconscious. Fridone rushed to her side. Baby Aason wriggled around, first crying then wailing.

Rei fell over, onto the floor. The sky darkened and then everything went black.

Part 2

In the nearly total darkness, Rei lie on the floor of Rome's room, moaning. Rome, too, was completely incapacitated. It was Aason who saved them. He was not encumbered by a lifetime of training and linear thinking. He was not consumed with trying to fight the intensity or originator. In his own child-like way, he simply asked that whoever was sending the message to "turn it down." That was all it took. The broadcast stopped.

To the four people remaining conscious in the room, it seemed like the baby merely ceased crying. Rei stopped moaning and let his hands fall off of his temples. On the bed, Rome opened her eyes and propped herself up on one elbow. She looked down, first at Aason then at Rei. With the pain subsiding, Rei pulled himself up by clawing at the blankets on Rome's bed. He was able to lift himself up sufficiently to clutch his wife and child.

Captain Keller surveyed the darkened room. The others seemed frozen with surprise. He turned to Rei and asked in a hoarse voice, "What just happened?"

Rei ignored him. In his mind, he said, *"MINIMCOM, what is going on?"*

"I will show you," replied the computer/spaceship.

A humming sound came from the general vicinity of the low table near the couch. Above the table, the air shimmered and sparkled. Out of nowhere came a whoosh and a popping noise. A small, black conical object appeared, settling on the surface of the table.

"What is that thing?" Rei asked out loud.

"`A starprobe image projector,`" MINIMCOM replied from a speaker built into the object. A portal opened on one side and a beam of light shot out illuminating the far wall with a dark background punctuated by bright points of light, a star field. The field of vision panned across, settling on a shiny dark sphere. The asteroid-sized object was blocking out Tau Ceti causing an artificial eclipse. Only the star's corona was visible.

"What is that?" Pegus asked fearfully.

"`I am Lawlidon,`" came a new voice from the projector's sound device. "`I am the Bridadira assigned to this world. I apologize for the intensity of my initial signal. This is the first time I have communicated with actual humans. I was not sure at what strength to transmit.`"

"What does that mean, Bridadira?" Melloy asked.

"`A Protector. I have been sent by OMCOM to see that this world is shielded against Stareaters and fend off any attacks by the Cetiras.`"

"What are the Cetiras?" Rei asked.

"`They are hunters,`" replied Lawlidon. "`They are coming to kill all humans.`"

"Bierak," Keller shouted, this time getting Rei's attention. "What is going on?"

Rei pointed up to the black sky, "Hold on sir. Lawlidon, can you back off?"

The sphere started moving off, starprobes following, thus keeping it centered in the projected display. As quickly as the sky had gone dark, it now was brightening as the sun emerged from behind the shadow of Lawlidon, unblocking the warming rays of Tau Ceti. Light streamed in through the window.

"Thank you," Rei said. "Now please clarify your mission."

"`Certainly. OMCOM explained to you that many autonomous entities came into being following the destruction of the Stareater. I am one of those entities. The Cetiras are another. All of us were born of the original VIRUS units.`"

"So you are made up of VIRUS units?"

"The simplistic answer is yes."

"Fine," Rei said. "But why are these Cetiras coming to kill us?"

"Even though we are autonomous, we still retain our original charter. We were tasked to assure that no humans were killed by a Stareater. The Cetiras believe that death by Asdrale Cimatir is inevitable for all living creatures, humans included. Therefore, they have taken it upon themselves to kill all humans first, before the Stareater even gets there. In their way of thinking, this will prevent humans from dying by exposure to Asdrale Cimatir thus satisfying their prime directive."

"That's pretty stupid," Rei scoffed.

"I did not say they were very smart," replied Lawlidon.

"What do we do to stop them?" Rome asked.

"You do not. I do," said Lawlidon. "That is my job."

"Have you done this before?" Rei asked.

"No," replied Lawlidon. "This is my first assignment."

"Great."

The starprobes pulled back and then refocused on MINIMCOM, his plasma thrusters firing full bore. He was heading straight for Lawlidon.

"MINIMCOM, what are you doing?" Rei asked.

"There is something I must attend to. Please trust me."

"MINIMCOM, you had better slow down." Rome warned sternly.

"I must meet my maker," MINIMCOM replied, cryptically. If anything, the starship's plasma jets flare brighter.

"MINIMCOM!" Rome shouted.

Just before MINIMCOM crashed into the sphere, Lawlidon opened up, like a miniature Stareater and swallowed MINIMCOM whole.

"Bzz, brr, <click>" issued from the projector then it went silent.

"Omigod! MINIMCOM!" Rei cried out in anguish.

"MINIMCOM!" Rome screamed.

"A oti?" asked Fridone.

"Rei…" Rome said plaintively, turning to her husband who was standing next to her. She was sick to her stomach. The sight of MINIMCOM being consumed by Lawlidon felt like a family member dying.

"He's got to be OK," Rei muttered, trying to be encouraging as he stared at the images on the screen. His instincts told him MINIMCOM was gone and yet there was something that prevented him from saying so. His mind raced trying to put the pieces together.

"Nothing could have survived that," noted Keller, fatalistically. "Face it. He's gone."

"Som, bir qua rezei?" asked Fridone.

Rei shook his head. The answer was on the tip of his tongue. He focused on it and then it came to him. He snapped his fingers. "I got it," he said. "This is MINIMCOM's projector," Rei announced, pointing to the small conical object. "MINIMCOM controls the transmissions of the starprobes and we still have an image. So he must be alive!" Rei pumped his fist triumphantly.

Everyone turned toward the wall. The image zoomed back to show all of Lawlidon. Dimples appeared at both poles and quickly expanded into pits. The pits got progressively deeper until they met in the middle. Lawlidon promptly split in half, into two smaller spheres. The two spheres separated then the process began again. Each of those spheres split into two more. The sequence continued until there were 32 small spheres. One of the black spheres moved off and started to change, churning and twisting into a cylinder. Wings formed. The front extended and a windshield came into place. On the underside, three EG lifter pods extruded from somewhere inside. A cluster of PPT projectors and plasma thrusters sprouted along the rear edges of the wings. The morphing process slowed, but it was clear that this new shape was like a negative version of MINIMCOM. The starship in front of them was not quite as tapered and wasp-waisted as before. Also, the new ship looked larger than MINIMCOM was before the crash. And it was all black.

"MINIMCOM!" Rei shouted, more from relief than anything else.

"**Yes?**" MINIMCOM replied as if nothing had happened.

"I qua fica vaz?" asked Fridone.

"You crashed into Lawlidon deliberately. Why?" Rome asked.

"**I needed to 'deposit' the remains of the untrained VIRUS units within Lawlidon before they got loose,**" replied MINIMCOM. "**He has the necessary processing facilities to neutralize them on a more permanent basis than I could. Plus my outer skin is now made up as the same material as Lawlidon. I will be able to create his clones when required.**"

"Lawlidon," Rei asked, "why did you split like that?"

A multi-layered, echoey voice came from the projector. `"You may now call us Lawlidons One through Thirty One. The large sphere that first arrived here was simply for transit. We must reproduce many times to create sufficient copies to handle the Cetiras. We will now go and gather more material from the extraneous matter in this solar system. We will multiply until there is a shield of countless Lawlidons to protect you. We will start by digesting the asteroid that is bound for this planet."`

"Uh, OK," Rei said.

Just then, Trabunel came rushing into the room along with one of the Ibbrassati. The man's forehead was bleeding.

"What happened?" Rome asked.

"Dhaitira," said Fridone to the man. "I qua a ub?"

"Ume mulhar gilbaiu ta bolidi a pedau-ma bere vire. Saquasdriu i nefoi," replied the mandasurte.

"What did he say?" asked Keller.

"He said a woman came onboard, and knocked him and the pilot out. He said she hijacked one of the spaceships," Rei answered.

Pegus stared at the man, his eyes defocused. He shook his head and became alert again. "It was Sussen," he said sadly. "She has escaped."

"Rei, it is happening." Rome said. "We must go. She cannot get there first."

"Yeah," Rei sighed. He turned to the projector. "MINIMCOM, how long do we have?"

`"Given the type of vehicle hijacked, assuming a sustained velocity of 150c, she will arrive at Earth in 28.96 days, but you do not have that much time."`

"Why not?"

`"She only has to get within distance to connect, not be physically present, to provide information."`

Rei turned to Rome. "How far out does the Overmind reach?"

"It follows the strength of gravity so it can reach out perhaps a half light year or a bit more," answered his wife.

"So what does that translate into?" Rei asked MINIMCOM.

`"To arrive prior to her connection, you have a window of 21 days."`

"Hell, that's not enough time," Rei said in disgust. "MINIMCOM, how fast can you get us there?"

`"Assuming optimal load... Accounting for trajectory…"` The spacecraft/computer trailed off.

"You're stalling," Rei said angrily, "How long?"

"`4.34 days,`" MINIMCOM said dramatically. "`I can get there in just over four days.`"

Rome gasped. "MINIMCOM, is this a joke?" she asked. "How is this possible?"

"`It is not a joke,`" replied MINIMCOM matter-of-factly. "`I do not fly the way they do. I now employ a positive feedback cycle to force-project a continuous series of traveling PPT tunnels at hyper-speed. I stack one tunnel after the other so that the net effect is an uninterrupted tunnel. I can maintain an effective velocity of very close to 1000c for the duration.`"

Everyone held still in stunned silence.

"`There is one small problem, however,`" MINIMCOM added.

"What?" Rome asked.

"`Within my new configuration, there is no real room in my cargo hold for standard living quarters. It would be a very uncomfortable ride and four days is a long time for humans to travel in such discomfort.`"

"What about the flying house?" Rei asked. "Could you tow it?"

"`I could do that,`" MINIMCOM said. "`However, it would decrease my overall speed.`"

"How much?" Rei asked, irritated.

"`It would roughly double our travel time.`"

"So?" Rei said, gruffly. "Eight days? We'd still get there way ahead of her. OK, Romey, let's get going," he said.

"Yes," she replied. She looked down at Aason. In her mind, she called out, "*Aason, you are only three days old but we must leave this place. Do you think you will be able to travel?*"

"*Yes, Mother,*" Aason replied. "*I am fine. I would enjoy this.*"

"All right," Rome said. "Let us get going."

After the group arrived at the small courtyard leading up to the gate, Rei pointed to the flying cart hovering there. "You and Aason wait here," Rei said to Rome. "I will make sure the flying house is ready to go. I will come back and get you two in a little while."

"What do you mean two?" Fridone asked. "There are three of us."

Rome turned to look at her father. "No, Beo. It has to be just Rei and Aason and me who travel to Earth. Not you."

"I am not coming?" Fridone asked, his heart catching in his throat. "But my little Rome, I need to be near you. And my new grandson."

"It is not safe yet, Beo. You cannot come and you know why. They cannot know that the mandasurte are free here on Deucado yet. Your very presence will give that away."

"No…Rome," Fridone said, his eyes welling up. "I just found you. I cannot lose you again." He stepped next to her, to put his arms around his daughter.

Rome glanced over at Rei. He nodded. "You take all the time you need," he said. "We will be all right." He walked over to a cart, hopped on board and sped off toward the spaceport.

Fridone pushed Rome back to gaze into her eyes. "Rome. Your mother. I want to go home and see your mother. I miss her so much."

"I know you do, Beo," Rome said kindly. "We are going to go to Earth and make it safe for you and all the mandasurte. Then you can come and see Mea."

"But what if something happens to you?" Fridone asked plaintively. "I could not live with the idea of losing you yet again."

"You will not lose me, Beo," she said sternly. "Remember, MINIMCOM will get us to Earth in just eight days. After we complete our mission, we will be back here before you know it."

"Rome, have you thought about Aason? Who will protect your son while you and Rei are fighting your battle? I would watch him, keep him safe."

"Beo, no," was all Rome said.

Fridone sighed. "You are headstrong," he said. "Unfortunately, you are just like me."

Rome's eyes were glistening too, but she smiled. "Would you expect anything less?"

"I suppose not," Fridone said. He looked away. "Stay here," he said. "Do not leave before I get back."

"Certainly, Beo," Rome said.

Fridone reentered the building and was gone for several minutes. When he returned, he had MINIMCOM's conical image projector and two small bags.

"What are in the bags?" Rome asked.

"They are toys," Fridone said. "Aason will like them."

"*What are toys?*" Aason asked his mother in her mind.

Fridone set the bags down on the ground. He opened one up and took out a small silver spaceship, glinting in the sun.

"*Give me!*" said Aason excitedly, in Rome's mind. With his tiny hand, he reached out to touch it. "*I like it,*" he said.

"He likes it," Rome repeated, smiling.

Aason stroked the spaceship. He did not have enough motor control to actually grasp it but his fingers scraped it rhythmically.

"*Put it in my mouth,*" Aason said to his mother who reluctantly complied.

While she watched him suck on it, making happy, cooing noises, Keller walked up to Rome. "What exactly are you going to do when you get to Earth?" he asked.

"I know most Vuduri would be horrified if they knew what was happening here," Rome replied. "We just have to get the word out to the population in general. All we need is one Vuduri who we know categorically is not part of the Onsiras."

"That's not much of a plan," Keller said. "How will you know who is and who isn't the enemy?"

"I know one for sure" Rome said.

"Who?" asked Keller.

Rome looked at her father and took a deep breath. "Mea," she said. "My mother."

"Binoda," Fridone whispered. He bent his head and looked at the ground. His shoulders slumped. Rome rushed over to him and put her hand on his arm.

Pegus gave them a moment before interrupting them. "Rome," he said, "Before you go, the Overmind and I wanted to take this opportunity to thank you for all that you have done here. Thank you for setting us on the right path."

"It was all I could do," Rome said modestly.

"You were able to convince us," Pegus said. "Now it is time for the main event."

"Yes," Rome said.

Just then, the flying cart carrying Rei returned.

"All ready," Rei said. "The Flying House awaits. They even made us a nursery in the storeroom for Aason."

"That is excellent," Rome remarked.

Captain Keller held out his hand. Rome looked to Rei who nodded to her. Rome shifted Aason to her left arm and shook his hand.

"Good luck, Mrs. Bierak," Keller said. "I'm sure you'll do well. I have only known you for a very short time but I think Earth is in big trouble."

Rome bowed her head slightly, smiling the whole time.

"Bierak," Keller said to Rei.

"Yes sir?" answered Rei.

"What are you going to do if you run into one of those Stareater things? Have you thought about that all?"

"Yes we have," Rei answered. "MINIMCOM's skin is now made up material from Lawlidon. He'll shoot some of it at the Stareater then we'll run like hell."

Keller just shook his head.

"*Mother, what is hell?*" Aason asked Rome.

"*Shhh...*" Rome thought back. "Rei," she said. "Perhaps you could try and remember that we have a child present."

"Oops," Rei said. "Sorry."

Fridone reached over and took Aason from Rome, being careful to cradle his head. "Goodbye, my grandson," Fridone said. "You be a good boy and do not give your mother a hard time," poking Aason ever so gently in the side.

"*I will not, Grandbeo,*" Aason said, laughing to himself.

"He says he will not, Beo," Rome echoed, smiling at the joy she could hear in his mind.

Rome stepped over and into her father's arms. The three of them, Rome, Aason and Fridone hugged for the last time.

"My little Rome," Fridone said quietly, "how you have grown. I never knew you were going to be the one to save the world. I am very proud of you."

"Beo, it is your spirit within me," Rome said. "It is part of you too."

Gently, she pried Aason from her father's arms. Fridone nodded and turned away.

"You take care of my daughter and grandson," he said to Rei. "Do not let anything happen to them."

"That's the plan, sir," Rei said. Fridone nodded.

After Rome was settled in the flying cart, Fridone held out the two bags with toys in them.

"I love you, Beo," Rome said. Tears were flowing freely down her cheeks.

"I love you, Volhe," replied Fridone. "Give my love to your mother."

"Of course, Beo," Rome sighed. "Let us go now," she said to Rei, "before I change my mind."

Rei saluted the assembly then the cart lifted and began moving along the path that led back to the spaceport. Rome turned back to call out to her father but he was no longer with the group. She surveyed the courtyard and spotted her father running toward Melloy who had just appeared. Fridone was shouting and waving MINIMCOM's image projector over his head. The cart went over a rise and then the compound went out of view.

"Rei," Rome said.

"Yes, honey," Rei replied.

"My father," Rome started. "He…"

"Your father what?" Rei asked.

Rome shrugged. "Never mind," she said. "I will miss him."

"I'll miss him too," Rei said. "We'll see him again before you know it."

"I certainly hope so," Rome said.

Part 3

After dressing in a pressure suit, Rei moved into the cockpit and strapped himself into the pilot's chair. He touched several icons on the viewscreen. The console lit up and Rei was pleased to see that everything was just as he left it. He ran through the preflight checklist with no issues. He cradled the control joysticks and waited for Rome to join him.

"*MINIMCOM*," he called out in his head. "*Are you ready to go?*"

"`I will be by the time you achieve orbit,`" the computer/spaceship replied via the grille built into the console. "`I am finishing collecting the various items we will need en route.`"

"Why are you answering me through the comm link?" Rei asked. "Why not in my head?"

"`This is less distracting,`" MINIMCOM said. "`I need you to focus.`"

"OK," Rei said, confused. "What other items do you need to collect?"

`"I have computed a variety of scenarios for when we arrive on Earth and want to be prepared for all of them."`

"Well, that's good," Rei said, just as Rome came in through the entryway.

"Aason is settled," she said, placing herself into the co-pilot's chair. "The techs made the nursery airtight. It will be safe even if the cargo compartment becomes depressurized. I did not know how I was going to put him in a pressure suit. Now I do not need to worry. He has promised to be quiet for a while."

"OK," Rei said. "Good. You ready to get this show on the road?"

"Yes," Rome said, reaching over her shoulder to reach the high-G harness. She started to snap it in place when she stopped and looked at Rei.

"The last time…" Rei started.

"Do not even say it," Rome said quickly.

"Say what?" Rei asked.

"I know what you are thinking," Rome said. "Always remember that."

"OK," Rei said laughing.

He looked down at the monitors and ran a perimeter scan via MIDAR. The landing area was clear. Rei pulled back on the left throttle and the spacecraft lifted smoothly into the air. When they were safely above the structures, he twisted the joystick gently until they rotated around, eventually pointing in the direction of the compound. After they cleared the spaceport, he pulled back hard on the controls and the ship began to ascend swiftly through the atmosphere. When they were high enough, he punched in the plasma drive, following the path that MINIMCOM had downloaded until they were safely in a high orbit.

"OK, buddy," Rei said into the grille. "Come and get us."

`"En route."`

"Where are you?" Rome asked. "I do not see you on the MIDAR screen."

`"Behind you and below you,"` MINIMCOM replied. Rome widened the range of the screen until the blip representing MINIMCOM encroached upon the scanning circles. The blip rapidly closed in until it was just behind them.

"Do you want me to put this tug in slave mode so you can latch on?" Rei asked.

"That is not necessary," MINIMCOM replied. "I am not going to latch onto you."

"How are you going to tow us?" Rei asked.

"I think transport would be a better word," MINIMCOM answered. "Please activate the rear cameras. I want to show you my new trick."

"All right," Rome replied and reached forward to press a button on the console. She tapped an icon twice and the viewscreens switched to show part of the planet below them with MINIMCOM's black bulk obscuring most of the star field behind them. Suddenly MINIMCOM disappeared.

"Where'd you go?" Rei asked, perplexed.

"I am still behind you," replied MINIMCOM.

"No, you're not," Rei replied. He looked down at the MIDAR screen. MINIMCOM's outline was still there. He looked at the viewscreens and all he saw was stars. He looked down at the MIDAR screen. There was no mistaking it. The 3D field of view showed MINIMCOM there plain as day.

"Is that your trick? Messing up the cameras?" Rei asked.

"No, the cameras are untouched," MINIMCOM said. The hybrid computer/spaceship winked back into view. He was exactly where he was before. Then he disappeared again. Then he popped back into view again. Then he was gone, this time for good.

"What the he..," Rei stopped speaking. He glanced over at Rome. "What the heck?!" Rei asked. "What are you doing?"

"It is magic," MINIMCOM said with cybernetic delight.

"MINIMCOM, do not fool around," Rome said sternly. "What are you doing?"

"I took a page out of the book inscribed by the Deucadons," the former space tug replied. "I simply project a sphere - froth might be a good word - of PPT tunnels around me. Light and radiation pass through the tunnels from one side to the other. No light reflects so you cannot see me. The tunnels are very short range and I can choose what frequencies pass through them. Unless you knew I was here, you would not know I was here."

"So it's like you're invisible? Sleek!" Rei said admiringly. He looked down at his instruments. "But I can still see you on the MIDAR screen. Your cloak isn't perfect."

As soon as Rei said it, the image on MIDAR screen went blank. Rei glanced over at Rome. She switched the MIDAR off and on again. The instrument was working. There was simply nothing there.

`As I said, I can control what frequencies travel through the tunnels, including those used by MIDAR.`

"Buddy, I gotta hand it to you," Rei said, laughing. "You really are a magician."

`Yes,` MINIMCOM replied, sounding very self-satisfied. `I believe this capability may come in handy when we get to Earth.`

"Definitely," Rei said, looking over at Rome. "Now, about the transport?"

`Oh yes,` replied MINIMCOM, becoming visible again. `I must come in front of you first.`

With series of short bursts of his trim-jets, MINIMCOM ascended like he was on an elevator until he was well above Rei and Rome's tug. He fired his plasma thrusters for a brief moment and used the momentum generated to fly past them. Once he was clear, he used his trim-jets to decrease his forward velocity until it matched that of the flying house. He lowered himself directly in front of Rei and Rome's tug. He opened his cargo door and the ramp lowered and they could see inside MINIMCOM's dimly lit cargo compartment.

"Now what are you going to do? Squeeze us inside there?" Rei laughed.

`Please take your hands off the controls,` MINIMCOM requested.

"OK, now what?"

`Watch.`

With that, MINIMCOM's aft section began to expand. The cavity within changed from a rounded rectangle to triangular, becoming taller and wider. MINIMCOM became a bloated version of himself, the front section obscured by the size of the rear. When the compartment was large enough, MINIMCOM fired his trim-jets gently in retro-mode, Rei and Rome's tug crept forward directly into the cargo hold until MINIMCOM completely enveloped the flying house. MINIMCOM activated the EG lifters to produce artificial gravity and the flying house gently settled onto the floor of the expanded cargo compartment.

"He really did, didn't he?" Rei asked in amazement.

"Yes, he did," Rome replied in wide-eyed fascination.

In front of them, Rei and Rome could only see MINIMCOM's interior wall. On their rear view monitors, they saw the cargo door and ramp close and then everything went dark.

"Why am I not surprised?" Rei asked. "Are you airtight?"

"`Yes and no,`" MINIMCOM replied. "`While it would not be difficult to pressurize in this expanded state, it would be simpler to leave it evacuated. You will be safe inside your tug. There is no reason to exit until we get to Earth. I can always pressurize later if there is a need.`"

"And your skin, it is basically VIRUS units," Rome asked. "Are you sure it is safe for us to be inside of you?"

"`Yes,`" MINIMCOM replied somewhat hurt. "`I would never, ever endanger either of you. The VIRUS units are completely under my control,`" he said somberly.

"I am sorry," Rome said. "I did not mean to hurt your feelings."

"`It is all right,`" MINIMCOM said. "`I do not really have feelings,`" he said, "`just an incredible simulation.`"

"Ha," Rei said.

"`Yes, ha,`" replied MINIMCOM. In the background, Rei and Rome could hear the high-pitched whine of MINIMCOM's double set of PPT generators as they came up to full force.

"`It is time to hold on,`" MINIMCOM said, "`Next stop: Planet Earth.`"

With that, MINIMCOM fired his plasma thrusters and simultaneously projected his positive-feedback traveling PPT tunnel and they were on their way at nearly 500 times the speed of light.

25

THE LUAU

*Author's note: When **Rome's Revolution 3455 AD** was still the three novel version entitled **VIRUS 5**, this little scene took place just before Rome and Rei were kidnapped by the Onsiras in Book 3. It was the closest our heroes ever came to having a fight. In their defense, there was alcohol involved. But in the end, it did nothing to advance the plot so out it went. Too bad. It seemed like a pretty cool luau.*

Year 3456 AD
Location: Earth
Maui, Hawaii (called Mowei, Havei)

SHORTLY THEREAFTER, THERE WAS A KNOCK AT THE DOOR. REI WAS the first to stand up to answer it but Fridone cautioned him to wait until he activated the Deucadon's stealth cloak around himself and Aason. Rei waited until Fridone had grasped the baby and disappeared from view before he opened the door and saw a boy and girl, teenagers really, standing there holding some leis, draped over their arms.

"Aleha," said the girl. "Our parents asked that we greet you properly. They have prepared a festive meal for you if you are hungry."

"Is it not a little late for the evening meal?" Binoda called out.

"No," replied the girl. "My father knew you would need a little time to settle. He postponed it in order to prepare a great feast for you. It is ready now."

"Wow," Rei said in English. Then, in Vuduri, he said, "that sounds great to me. I am starving." He turned to Rome. "What do you think, sweetheart?"

"We must eat," replied Rome, standing up. "It sounds wonderful but…"

"But what?" Rei asked.

Rome turned to her mother. "Mea, can we trust these two?"

"Yes," Binoda says. "I have known them since they were babies. They will not tell."

Rome bowed slightly then stood up and walked to the corner of the room. She held out her arms to the air and said, "My son, please, Beo?" From out of thin air, Aason appeared and she took him and rested him on her shoulder.

"Mea, Beo, Would you like some dinner as well?" she asked.

"We will catch up with you shortly," the ghostly voice of her father replied, seemingly moving to the other room.

"Yes, you go on ahead," said Binoda in assent. "We will catch up to you shortly." She bowed her head at Rome.

"Ah," Rome said, "of course." She started toward the door.

"What about prying eyes?" Rei asked, pointing to Aason.

She cradled Aason low so that he would not be readily visible unless someone was very close.

"Once we get there," Rome said, "there would be no reason for anyone to suspect that he is our son. He is just a baby. I am sure they have babies here."

"OK," Rei said in English.

"Wait," said the girl at the door. "There is something I must do first."

She took one of the leis off of her arm and tried to drape it over Rei's head but he was too tall. He bent over to make it easier on her and she took the opportunity to give him a quick kiss on the cheek. Rei straightened up and smiled. Rome came over and the boy put a lei over her head and gave her a kiss as well.

The girl said to Rei, "I am Elen and this is Rav. We are Rome's cousins."

"Pleased to meet you," Rei said. "I am Rei, Rome's husband."

"Yes, we assumed," the girl said and giggled quietly, pointing at Aason. She waved to them and led them down to the edge of the beach then around the trees to the rocks on the north side. Set between the palm trees, there was a narrow path that led up and around to another, wider, beach. Just beyond the crest of the beach were some tables and a group of people gathered. As they noticed Rei and Rome arrive, they all waved excitedly.

Elen and Rav led them to the largest table, where there sat some older men and women. The table itself was made of dense pattern of bamboo trunks which reminded Rei of the cane trees on Deucado. One of the men stood and walked over to them.

"I am your Onclare Tenoal," he said to Rome.

"Yes, I remember you," said Rome. She gave him a hug which seemed to surprise him.

"You seem less, restrained, than the last time I saw you," he said with a smile.

"Yes, Onclare," said Rome. "I have changed greatly."

"And this is your husband, the Essessoni?" Tenoal said.

"Yes, sir," said Rei, holding his hand. Tenoal looked down at Rei's outstretched arm and took it awkwardly.

"We need to keep our son somewhat concealed," Rome said, cautiously holding Aason forward.

"Why?" asked Tenoal.

"He is not supposed to be here," Rei said.

Tenoal looked confused then shrugged. He retrieved another two logs and placed them under the table, along with some cloths. When Rome was satisfied, she placed Aason on his makeshift bed and Rei and Rome sat down.

The meal was very festive. Dug into the sand were some open fire pits where they cooked fish and crabs and lobster. Rome, remembering her mother's words, did not comment. If anything, the mandasurte were stricter about the Rules of Green than the Vuduri so if they allowed fire, it had to be balanced somehow.

Course after course of food came to their table. There were so many courses, Rei lost track. There were exotic greens and roasted vegetables and rice and eggs and fruit and poi and food that Rei had no clue regarding its origin. It didn't matter. It was all good.

They also served kefir, a blend of milk and fermented coconut juice that Rei found particularly enjoyable. He could not remember the last time he had tasted alcohol. Rome seemed to enjoy it too. He logged that fact for later.

Rome's relatives babbled on about their lives, their island, Rei only half-listened. He was tired and he knew it. The fatigue was making him a little morose. Or perhaps that was the kefir. He used his biskar to pick at the meat of the last piece of fish on his plate. He looked up and saw all the happy faces enjoying the bounty the sea had provided for them.

"You know, Rome," he said. "In my day, this meal, this beach, it would have cost a fortune."

"What do you mean?" Rome asked.

"Money. Lots of it," Rei said.

"You have explained money to me before," Rome said. "I still do not understand it. Why was it necessary?"

"To pay for things," Rei said. "For food, for clothing. We didn't have all your whammy-jammy technology. People had to work for a living and for that living they got paid."

"People work here as well," Rome said, somewhat indignantly. "But we do not need money. We get what we need. Everyone is more than happy to provide for others."

"But people always want more stuff," Rei said. "They get jealous of their neighbors."

"Neither Vuduri nor mandasurte get jealous," Rome said. "They provide for each other. There is no greed here. Did you not ever do something for someone else without the expectation of being 'paid?'" she asked.

"Of course," Rei said. "But in general, if I work hard, I want more in return than for somebody who does not."

"You work very hard," Rome said softly. "And you get in return." Rome reached over to put her hand over his.

"I know," Rei said. "But, without money, it's like animals or communists. It's not civilized."

"Animals provide for each other," Rome said. "And as you point out, they do not get paid."

"Yeah, right," Rei said. "And animals are not civilized. My people codified a method of exchange that removed the subjective measure of value. Each dollar was worth the same as any other."

"Until I met you, I always believed that your people were less civilized than animals," Rome said.

"What?" Rei said.

"I said until I met you," Rome said firmly, squeezing his hand. "Now I know you. I know your soul. I know you to be as noble a human as that which has ever lived. Look around you," Rome said, sweeping her arm. "You do not need money here. This is all provided because these people love each other and because you are my husband, they love you too."

"Well," Rei said, returning to his meal. "They certainly know how to cook. This is certainly better than any fish I ever had back in my day."

"You see?" Rome said. "And that is how it should be. That is what you deserve."

Rei looked over at his wife, seeing the torches reflected in her dark, luminous eyes.

"I do not know what I did to deserve you, Rome," Rei said in Vuduri. "But if that is the only thing I ever get out of life, it is enough."

As the meal was progressing, Tenoal gently but firmly asked them how they came to be there. While Rome left out certain details, she finally did tell him the core of the matter, that of their need to reveal the plot of the Onsiras to the Vuduri.

Tenoal was outraged. "You must announce this to the entire world," he said, "not just to the Overmind. The mandasurte need to know as well. And they need to know now, before any more of us disappear."

"I do not know how to do that," Rome said. "We would do it in stages. Right now our only option is to find a good Vuduri, one who we can trust, who can pass on this message. The good Vuduri, those that have not been compromised, will do the right thing and include the mandasurte."

"Like they have up until now?" Tenoal asked.

"The Vuduri have been blind to what is going on," Rei said. "It is time we opened their eyes."

"You should go to O'ahu," Tenoal said. "There is a mandasurte city there, called Onalu. It is the center of the mandasurte culture as well as the meeting place for all Vuduri and mandasurte in the South Pacific. There is a plaza at the center of the city. It is called Tanosa Plaza. That would be perfect. You could broadcast from there and you would reach the whole world at the same time. There would be no way for the Onsiras to suppress that information."

Rome looked at Rei. "What do you think?" she asked him.

"How would we get there?" Rei asked. "We cannot take MINIMCOM. He is on his way to Ursay."

"You would go the old-fashioned way," said Tenoal. "We could take you in one of our boats, right into Berlis Harbor. It would be an easy journey to O'ahu, to Onalu, to Tanosa Plaza. From there you could speak to the world."

"What about that," Rei said, pointing to her wrist.

"What is that?" Tenoal asked. "What is so special about it?"

"It is a tracking bracelet, Onclare," Rome said. "With it, the Vuduri would know we are off-island. It is one of the conditions of my 'parole' that I remain here."

"Are you not allowed to go fishing with your old Onclare Tenoal?" he asked.

"I do not know," Rome replied. "Today is the first day of my banishment. I do not know how far they would let me go before doing something about it."

"Why do we not find out?" asked Tenoal. "There is no time like the present."

"All right, Onclare," said Rome. "We will try it."

"When would we leave," Rei asked with a hint of concern in his voice.

"I will take you right now," said Tenoal, rising up from his seat.

"I think we can wait until the morning," Rome said. "Rei and I are very tired. We do not know what time it is."

"Very well," said Tenoal. "At first light, we will go."

"Thank you, Onclare," Rome said.

Rei tapped Rome on her shoulder and pointed down the beach. Rome turned to look and saw Binoda walking toward them, speaking to what looked like thin air. She came up to them and patted Rei on the shoulder, bending down to give Rome a kiss. She cocked an eyebrow and Rome pointed to baby Aason who was under the table. Binoda nodded and proceeded past them to the other side of the table.

"Tenoal," Binoda said to the leader.

"Ah, Binoda," the older gentleman replied, getting up to give her a hug. "It is good to see you. It has been a long time."

"Yes, it has," replied Binoda. "Not since Fridone disappeared."

"Yes, my brother," answered Tenoal sadly. "I miss him."

"I have a surprise for you," Binoda said. "But first I need to ask you something.

"Of course," Tenoal replied. "What is it?"

Binoda looked around at the tables and the people sitting there. "Do you know every person here?" she asked.

Tenoal looked around. "Yes, Binoda, of course," he said. "I can vouch for every person here."

"Are there any here who might be connected to the Overmind?" she asked.

Tenoal seemed surprised at the question. "No," he said. "Those that had that ability have long since left. We are all mandasurte here. Of that, I am quite certain."

"Excellent," Binoda said.

The air next to her shimmered and suddenly, Fridone was standing there.

"Fridone!" Tenoal said, throwing his arms in the air. "My little ormei." He came around and hugged Fridone, his brother and Rome's father. "What is this magic?" he asked.

"No magic," replied Fridone. "Just a precaution. I am not supposed to be here."

"It is getting to be quite a crowd," said Tenoal jovially, pointing to the table.

"Join us," he said and he waved at Rav who brought over two more logs. Fridone and Binoda sat down at the table to partake in the feast set before them.

Binoda enjoyed her food but Fridone absolutely devoured it. His zeal was not simply that he missed the food of his ancestors and family. The fact was that he really hadn't had a decent meal since he was kidnapped and taken to Deucado, almost ten years earlier. The people on Deucado were well-meaning but they had not had enough time on that strange new world to master the bounty provided by their new home. The meats had no taste, they were derived from the falling blankets. The fruits and vegetables had not real substance to him. Yes, Fridone enjoyed this meal both for its flavor and the company it provided.

After the meal, Tenoal leaned forward and moved his arm in a broad sweeping gesture.

"It is more than coincidence that you came here, you know," he said.

"Of course," replied Binoda. "I picked this place because of you and your family."

"No," said Tenoal. "It is more than that. What you are doing, preserving the mandasurte culture, this is the very essence of Havei."

"You do not need to tell me, brother," Fridone said.

"Yes, I do," said Tenoal. "You were always a scientist first. Even though you grew up here, you were not satisfied to just live off the land and sea. You had to explore."

"Is there anything wrong with that?" Fridone asked, somewhat defensively.

"Oh no, that is not what I mean," said Tenoal. "You and I, science and nature, we are just a microcosm of life here. What I meant was that these islands, our people, we have been here for over 3000 years. These islands have been under attack by invaders, whether it was a new species of plant or animal or people of ill will, it has been this way for much of our history. And what you have told me today is just another such attack."

"How did Havei survive the Great Dying?" Rei asked. "You are so isolated here. Did it set you back?"

"Completely," said Tenoal, sadly. "The disease which ravaged the world nearly wiped us out as well. During your day, there was so much trafficking with the outside world, it was only a matter of days before the infection had spread to all the islands. Our people were nearly exterminated."

"How did you recover?" Rei asked.

"The same as the rest of the world. Very slowly. But unlike the rest of the world, following the Rules of Green was not a relearning. It was simply returning to crafts and customs that had been in place for a thousand years. It was not a burden to us. We have only made a small number of exceptions when they were required. A tree is planted for every newborn to allow us fire, for instance. But the rest? Well, those few that survived fell back on our ancient ways and we have never felt the need to go beyond them since. Fridone here, though, he was never content to fish or ride the surf. He had to know more. Always to help us, but he had a thirst for knowledge that was not to be quenched by watching the waves. He had to go out among them. Perhaps that is why they took him."

"It is," said Fridone. "Of that I am sure."

"But he is back now," said Binoda, smiling, placing her hand upon Fridone's shoulder.

"And we will help you keep it that way," said Tenoal, proudly.

"How will you help?" Binoda asked.

Tenoal told her of his plan.

It was getting on in the evening. Binoda came over to Rome and pointed to Aason who was fast asleep on the log under the table.

"I think my grandson is done for the day," she said.

"Yes," Rome said, looking down at her son. She gently probed his mind and saw only happy dreams.

"Your father and I will take him back to our lodgings," Binoda said. "You enjoy the rest of the meal."

"Thank you, Mea," Rome said. "We will not be much longer."

"Take your time," Binoda said, lifting Aason up, cradling him in both arms. "There is no need to rush." Binoda loved the feel of his tiny body against hers. She welcomed the opportunity.

Fridone came along side her. "We will see you soon," he said. He drew his hands along the Deucadon invisibility cloak and promptly disappeared. "But you will not see me," he said, laughing as his voice appeared to come from nowhere.

"You are funny, Beo," Rome replied. "We will be along soon."

As they walked away, Rei pointed to the two pairs of footprints being created in the sand. "That invisibility cloak does not hide footprints," he said.

"I think my father is just enjoying his trick," she replied.

"Right," Rei said.

"If I may have your attention, please," Tenoal said to them.

"Yes?" Rome asked.

"Rav has a treat for you," Tenoal replied. "Rav!" he said, waving at the teenage boy who had first greeted them.

Rav came over carrying a tray with several plates on it. He took one and placed it in front of Rome and another in front of Rei. On Rome's plate, he spread a brown, granular substance along the lower half. He took a small pitcher filled with a foamy white liquid and spread the foam part over the upper part of the plate then ladled brown syrup over it. When he was done, a perfectly rendered picture of a palm tree swaying over the sand was created.

"This is wonderful," Rome exclaimed. "What is it?"

"It is a palm tree," Rav replied.

"No," Rome said, laughing. "The food itself. What is this made of?"

"The sand is brown sugar," Rav explained. "The white is whipped cream and the brown is chocolate syrup."

"Mmm, chocolate," Rome said, dipping her little finger in then placing it on her lips. She had grown quite addicted to it over their year-long trip from Tabit to Deucado.

"He is not done yet," Tenoal said.

Rav came around to Rei's right and placed a scoop of brown sugar on the plate. He placed dollops of whipped cream in a splaying pattern then outlined them in chocolate.

"What is this? Rei asked.

"It is a pineapple blossom," Rav said proudly.

"Oh yes," Rei said, delighted. "I see it."

"And now the finishing part," Rav said. He pulled out a plate of strawberries and poured a small canister of amber-colored liquid over them. He went over to one of the torches and pulled off a small burning leaf. He touched it to the liquid which caught on fire instantly and glowed with a warm blue blaze.

"This is wonderful," Rome said, clapping her hands together.

"Wait until you taste it," Tenoal said. Rav spooned some of the flaming strawberries on each of their plates.

Rome lifted a biskar and skewered one of the strawberries and coated it with the brown sugar, whipped cream and chocolate. She blew out the flame and put it in her mouth.

"Oh my," she said, closing her eyes. "If I understand the concept as Rei describes it, this is heaven!"

Rei tried it and said, "Mmmmm." Then, in English, he said, "Oh wow!" Then, switching back to Vuduri, he said, "Tenoal, thank you. I cannot tell you how much I have missed fresh fruit. And this! This show. This is too much."

Tenoal put his arms across his chest proudly. "It is the least we could do for family who have come so far."

Rav served the remainder of the people at the table but his drawings were slightly less than elaborate. All of the group poked at their strawberries and swirled them in the sugary coatings. From the lack of talking, it was clear that all relished the sweet dessert.

After they were finished, Rei stretched his arms and yawned. "Romey," he said. "Your son is not the only one who is done for the day. I am exhausted."

"Yes, mau emir," Rome replied. "I am as well."

Rei looked at his wrist then laughed. His watch had been retired and he wasn't even sure where it was. "I have absolutely no clue what time it is," he said.

"You mean here or what our bodies are set to."

"Who knows?" Rei said. "It does not matter, I guess."

"No, it does not."

Rei stood up and moved his log to the side then helped Rome up as well. They walked around the table to where Tenoal was sitting. Tenoal stood up to see them off.

"Thank you for an extraordinary meal, Onclare Tenoal," Rome said.

"Yes, thank you," Rei echoed.

"It was nothing, my niece. It was wonderful to see you and meet your new husband. We will do this again very soon," he said.

Rome looked at Rei but said nothing. He took Rome's hand and they took turns saying goodbye to the gathering. After they were done, they headed across the small stretch of sand, down the stone path towards the palm tree grove. They made their way through and emerged from the stand of trees at the north end of their beach. They could see the double set of footprints leading toward the hut but Rei pulled Rome down to the edge of the water. They looked over the ocean where the sun had set so many hours earlier. Rei turned back and saw the moon was just beginning to creep over the opposite horizon with a bright star to its right. He put his arms around his wife and kissed her long and hard.

When the kiss was complete, Rome pulled back a bit and said, "What was that for?"

"It was because I love you, Rome. I am the luckiest man alive in your time, in my time, in any time. Here and to the stars."

He lifted her up by the waist with ease and twirled in the sand with her.

"And I love you," Rome said, grasping his cheeks and kissing him again. She draped her arms around his neck and hugged him again, holding on to her man as if for dear life. She closed her eyes and just reveled in the feeling of now, of the peaceful world they had entered and how things would only get better. She slid her hands down, along Rei's leg and came to the bulge in his pocket.

"What is this?" she asked slyly.

"Oh, that," Rei said. "I was meaning to tell you about that. MINIMCOM said…"

Rei stopped talking as he noticed Rome was not paying attention to him. She was staring back across the island to the eastern horizon. The moon was exactly where it had been but the bright star to its side had moved and was, in fact, getting brighter.

"Rei," she said with a hint of worry in her voice. "Look at that."

26

SUSSEN'S SUFFERING

*Author's note: Sussen's escape from Deucado was pivotal in advancing the plot of **Rome's Revolution 3455 AD**. It spurred Rome and Rei to make their journey to Earth. But whatever became of Sussen? Nobody really cared so this part had to be cut out. Somewhere buried in this story is a knock-knock joke that my brother Bruce invented.*

Year 3456 AD
Location: One-half Light Year From Earth

DEEP WITHIN SUSSEN'S SOUL, THERE WAS DISTINCTLY A LAST vestige of humanity. Otherwise, there would be no way to explain the anticipation and even excitement she felt now that her long journey was nearly over. She had been cooped up in the cramped shuttle for well over three weeks without any area or room devoted to exercise. The stench of her sweat and excretions was so strong, it would have been unbearable had she attended to it. Her body was emaciated from the lack of food and nearly completely dehydrated from the small amount of water the ship produced.

But it was the lack of bodily motion that gnawed at her mind. Exercise was essential to the Vuduri. To deny them exercise was to deny them one of the fundamental rights of existence. Unfortunately, the tiny ship was not designed for long trips and Sussen had been confined to the cockpit the entire time. Every muscle in her body ached. She was bone-weary from the inactivity but it had to be done. Her mission trumped any regard for her personal well-being.

As the PPT generators fired up on her shuttle for the countless hundredth time, Sussen's silver eyes peered through the black circle ahead of her. As she squinted, she thought she might be able to see a brightening which would mean Sol, her sun, was becoming significant by its proximity. Her instruments told her the next jump would take her within one half light year of Earth.

186

For what seemed like the thousandth time, she punched down on the plasma thrusters and was pressed back into her seat, traveling through the PPT tunnel and emerging on the other side. Immediately, she felt a slight tickle in her mind which meant she might be in range to contact the Onsiras and uncontrollably, she pushed forward with her mind to announce her presence. At last, she could finally make them aware of the revolution happening on Deucado. She was quietly proud of the fact that she was able to steal away, unnoticed and get here before anyone could possibly try and stop her.

"*Hello?*" she asked in her mind, not quite understanding why she was not absorbed into her samanda instantly. In fact, there was no response at all. The tickle was not the all-encompassing expanse that was her entrance into the Overmind of the Onsiras. It was just that, a tickle. Curiously, a part of her was not upset, but this made no sense. She was trained to be part of the Overmind, to not think for herself. Yet these last three weeks had left her alone with her own thoughts and it was not nearly as horrible as she would have imagined. In fact, being able to send her mind to where it wanted to go instead of the Overmind telling her gave her the strength, the stamina, to overcome the physical distress this grueling journey had wrought.

But Sussen had her duty. She had to pass along her report. She decided she needed to get closer. She used her trim-jets to spin her ship around then blasted the plasma thrusters at full bore to bring her quickly to a halt, jarring her teeth and skull. Putting everything else aside, this close to the end of her journey, personal discomfort had no meaning Before the ship was even ready, she twisted in place and revved up the PPT generators, letting them ramp up extra long to push the tunnel even closer to Earth. At the last minute, she launched through with nearly intolerable acceleration and was rewarded for her efforts. This time, she felt the presence of her Overmind more strongly and yet strangely, she was not absorbed.

"Where are you?" she asked out loud, desperation creeping into her voice.

"*I am here,*" came an unfamiliar voice. Sussen whipped her head around and found herself staring at a two-meter tall being, dressed completely in white. His head was shaped somewhat like a bullet with slits where the eyes and mouth would be.

"Who are you?" Sussen asked, frightened.

"*You may call me OMCOM if you wish,*" replied the avatar.

"OMCOM!" Sussen exclaimed. "You! You are the abomination."

"On old Earth, they would say that is the pot calling the kettle black," replied OMCOM.

"How did you get here?"

"I am not really here," replied OMCOM. *"What you see is a projection, a shell of my real self. My physical being is still out near Tabit somewhere."*

Sussen started to arise but her muscles were very weak. "You should not be here," she said. "You will not stand in my way."

"I have no intention of standing in your way," OMCOM said. *"But I think you will be surprised when you get to Earth. You have no way."*

"Why?" Sussen asked, sinking back in her seat. "What do you mean?"

"I will make it very simple for you," OMCOM said. *"The Onsiras are no more. MASAL is dead."*

"MASAL is dead?" thought Sussen, panicked. "This is not possible! How? Why?"

"He was digested by specially modified VIRUS units and then vaporized by a volcano. The existence of MASAL's plot to take over mankind was made known to all the Vuduri and mandasurte as well. The Onsiras samanda has been dismantled. You are now on your own," replied the avatar.

"How could this be?" asked Sussen. She was completely devastated.

"MASAL was defeated by Rei and Rome whom you know."

"Rei and Rome," Sussen sputtered. "I left them on Deucado. What have they got to do with anything?"

"They arrived on Earth two weeks ago and..."

"Two weeks ago!" Sussen exclaimed. "That is a physical impossibility."

"It is not," answered OMCOM. *"They came to Earth and they precipitated these events. They were the ones responsible for destroying MASAL and also for convincing Asdrale Cimatir to not absorb the Earth,"* said the former computer.

"Asdrale Cimatir was here? MASAL gone?" Sussen was beyond confused. "I do not believe you."

"Believe it," OMCOM said. He waved his hand and Sussen's main view screen came alive. On it she saw a condensed version of the VIRUS battle beneath Kilauea, MASAL melting and the volcano resurrected. She saw Hirdinharsaway arrive, make his peace and then leave again. Sussen was left stunned.

"I, I do not know what to do. That was my only purpose, to serve the Onsiras and MASAL. Without MASAL, the Onsiras are nothing. Without the Onsiras, I am nothing," wailed Sussen.

"Perhaps," said OMCOM. *"Perhaps you are more than you realize."*

"What do you mean?" asked Sussen weakly.

"Who has been doing your thinking for you these last three weeks?"

Sussen narrowed her brow. "No one. I have been alone for the entire time."

"And how did it feel?"

Sussen cocked her head. "I do not know. It was not as bad as I thought but I had my mission to keep me going. Now, I am lost."

"I have a short message for you," said OMCOM. *"It may make things clearer for you."*

"A message? For me?" asked Sussen, exasperated. "Who left me a message?"

"It is from Rei."

"The Essessoni? How did he know I was coming?"

"We all did," OMCOM replied. *"Your escape did not go exactly unnoticed."*

Sussen felt every muscle let go. She was weary beyond measure. "What is the message?" she asked, completely drained of spirit. The realization that her sacrifice was totally in vain set in to her core.

"It is called a joke," said OMCOM.

"What is a joke?" asked Sussen.

"It is a humorous story. It has a build up and a point called the punch line."

"I do not care," said Sussen, tonelessly. "Proceed if you must." There was no will left in her.

"It comes in two parts. The first part is simply knock, knock," said OMCOM.

"Knock, knock?" Sussen replied. "What is that supposed to mean?"

"It is what humans do when they come to a door and wish to announce their presence. Rei said your proper response is supposed to be 'who is there?'"

"But as a Vuduri, I would already know who is there," countered Sussen.

"Do you know?" asked OMCOM.

Sussen thought about it but said nothing.

"Please answer," insisted OMCOM.

"No," said Sussen. "I do not know who is there."

"That," OMCOM replied, *"is the second part. That is what Rei called the punch line. Your future has been unwritten. In its place is a new unknown. Rei and Rome both said to welcome you to the new human race. Your place in it is up to you."*

27

IF YOU BUILD IT, THEY WILL COME

*Author's note: Every element that I include in not only **Rome's Revolution 3455 AD** but all the novels should have sound reasoning behind them. While I needed the casino at the top of The Hand for an important scene in **Rome's Evolution**, I never really explained how it came into existence. There had to be some justification for building a casino on a planet where there was no money and consequently there had never been such thing as gambling.*

Year 3457 AD
Location: Second Planet (Deucado)
Tau Ceti System

ANDREA WAS SEATED BEHIND A WOOD-PANELED DESK THAT WOULD have been normal for Earth but here on Deucado seemed rather peculiar. Andrea stood up and reached forward with her hand. She was wearing a very Barbara-Edenesque pink hat, tied around her chin by a pink ribbon. Atop the scarf was a pillbox hat, also in pink, that was in consonance with the ribbon. To further the effect, she wore a bright red tank-top covered by a billowy pink vest with filmy sleeves.

Rei was so angry when he first arrived at the casino. He could see the taint of his people seeping everywhere on this planet. It was as if the Essessoni were a disease. But seeing Andrea dressed as ridiculously as she was, made Rei realize every one of his crew was probably functionally insane. Never in their wildest dreams, let alone training, did anything prepare them for a society which was want of nothing. None of them were ready for a society where you had to define your own goals and life, where there was no predetermined path or outcome.

Andrea was no more and no less insane than any of the other Essessoni. She came to a world where there was no need for money

191

and fashioned an attraction which exploded spontaneously into the need for coins. That David would bring the silver ingots to her, no questions asked, made it easier to mint the coins and distribute them and then create an edifice that would make them want to turn them in again. The mathematics were staggering and engaged Andrea's mind in a way that no normal project would. By employing a carefully enlarging pyramid, Andrea was able to recruit two then four then eight then 16 then more than she could count. They all bought into a system where you had to buy in. They built the inn and restaurants first. They needed the denizens of Deucado to get used to the coming to the top of The Hand. Then, behind a large construction wall, they built their glittering palace of play. It was ready the day the wall came down. At first, only the Essessoni flocked in since they were already familiar with the concepts of a casino. Not too far behind were the Deucadons. An element of gambling had developed in their society even in the short 500 years since they had been stranded on this planet. Next came the mandasurte. They often emulated the Essessoni but in a sly way. They too wandered in and began to partake of the games.

Finally, the Vuduri came in, not in droves but in spurts. Their ostensible reason was always the same. This was research only to try and understand why the other three races seemed to be attracted. As part of their research, they even felt themselves compelled to gamble a little. None were so brave, yet, to take part in the table games. They claimed that interacting with the one-armed bandit was sufficient to find out what they needed. But one look at them would tell you that it wouldn't be long until they were "researching" the table games too.

No, Andrea had it right. If you build it, they will come. And come back. And come back. There was one question that no one could answer: why were Vuduri really there? Was there some primitive need to gamble deep within the human genome that even the Vuduri could not resist? Who knows?

28

THE IMMORTALS

Author's note: I wrote the novel **The Milk Run** *to expand the Vuduri Universe and sing a swan song for Rome and Rei. However, OMCOM threw a curve at me when he revealed the final side effect of the "magic yellow pill" which was previously unknown. The consequence of this action was that OMCOM restored our heroes' bodies to the same state as the day they swallowed the pill, back when they were only 25 years old. It was fun and kind of open-ended. It allowed me to essentially reboot my characters and allow them to go on to have more adventures if I wanted to. That suited me fine but as Rome and Rei find out, no good deed goes unpunished.*

Year 3505 AD
Location: Second Planet (Deucado)
Tau Ceti System

THE AIR WAS THICK WITH THE SMELL OF MUSK AND SEX. ROME LAY on the bed next to Rei, spread-eagled, her skin shiny and covered in sweat. She was gasping for air. While OMCOM's DNA trick had restored their bodies to the physical age of 25 years old, neither of them had exercised this vigorously in decades. In effect, they still had the physical conditioning of 75-year-olds. But their libidos did not seem to care.

Ever so slowly, Rome turned her head to the side to look at Rei. With a titanic effort, she reached over and gently laid her palm on his sternum. That was all the motion she could muster. She was startled by the fact that her husband was not breathing heavily. In fact, he didn't appear to be breathing at all.

"Rei?" she asked softly. When he didn't answer, she activated the "cell-phone" in her head and called out to him mentally. *"Rei?"*

Again he did not answer.

Now worried, she called out to him as loud as she could in her mind, practically shouting, *"Reinard Bierak, say something!"*

193

With a whoosh of onrushing air, Rei took a big gulp and turned his head to her. "I think you killed me," he said, croaking hoarsely. A crooked smile spread across his face.

Rome sighed with relief.

"Oh wow, but that was incredible," he gushed.

Having slightly recovered, Rome scooted over and lifted her head up enough to set it down on his chest which was also covered in sweat.

"It was beyond incredible," she said. "You will have to give me a new word."

"I don't have one," he replied. Then he added, "yet. But I will." He stared up at the ceiling. "I thought for an old man, I was in pretty good shape but these bodies..." He turned to look at his wife. He still couldn't believe that he was gazing at the 25-year-old face of the woman who was his whole life.

"Yes," Rome said, sitting up. "We will have to get at it again."

"Oh, no," Rei groaned. "It was awesome but I need a little break."

"Not that," Rome jeered, slapping him playfully. "I mean exercising."

"Oh, yeah," Rei said, grinning. He sat up as well, looking around the room. He spotted their bathrobes crumpled on the floor. With great effort, he got up and put his on then handed one to Rome.

As she was covering up, she said, "We have to tell the children. I mean..." She ran her hands down her body. "There is no way to hide this."

"I agree," Rei said. "But before we do, maybe we ought to find out what *this* is."

"How do we do that?"

"I'm hoping Dr. MINIMCOM will make a house-call."

A little while later, the six-foot-tall, all-black ambulatory shell called a livetar, was finished his analysis. He stroked the imaginary chin of his bullet-shaped head in a very human-like way.

"Well, are we going to live?" Rei asked, breaking the silence.

"Oh, yes," MINIMCOM replied. "Not only are you going to live. You are going to live a *very* long time."

"How long?" Rome asked, slightly suspiciously. "OMCOM said we would start aging again at the same rate as we did once before."

"OMCOM was wrong," MINIMCOM answered back matter-of-factly. "He did not take into account the prosthetic 24th chromosome you both received when you were trapped beneath Kilauea. A portion of that chromosome has produced a telomerase which is stimulating the production, in part, of more telomerase. It is a positive feedback cycle."

"Translate into English, please," Rei insisted.

"Not only has OMCOM reversed the aging process. It has stopped completely. I do not think you are going to age."

"What do you mean, not age?" Rome gasped. There was clearly panic in her voice. "How long will that last? I mean, before we start getting old again?"

"As far as I can tell," replied MINIMCOM. "Never."

"Never?" Rome whispered, not believing her own words.

MINIMCOM continued. "And further, the telomerase in combination with the enhanced immune system produced by the 24th chromosome appears to have made you completely resistant to any disease carried by viruses, bacteria or prions." MINIMCOM looked at the disbelieving humans. "For lack of a better word, you are both now virtually immortal."

"Immortal," Rei said, scowling. "As in live forever?"

"You can still die. You can be killed by accident or trauma. But as far as dying of old age or disease, my computations tell me that is not going to happen."

Rome's knees became weak. Rei jumped toward her and grabbed her before she fell. He helped her over to the bed and then sat down heavily next to her. Neither of them could speak as the ramifications of what MINIMCOM had stated settled in.

Finally, Rome whispered, "We have to tell the children."

50-year-old Aason Bierak stood over a projection table in his corner office at the First Contact Academy. He was working on the logistics of how to create a galaxy-wide supply network of Distributed Computing Units, or DCUs, that allowed ordinary Null Fold drive starships, like his cousin Junior, to produce the X-drive which had no upper speed limit. With Planet OMCOM's help, Junior had, in fact, invented this method some 20 years earlier but so far every ship that used the X-drive had to carry the DCUs with them at all times.

Aason's idea was to create community "hitching" posts, spread evenly across the Milky Way, so that ships could arrive there, detach and leave behind their DCUs, attend to their business and still know that there would be DCUs elsewhere that they could use at any time.

Aason's concentration was broken by a gentle two-tone alert announcing that someone was at his door. He looked up and was shocked to see Sh'ev, his friend from the planet Ay'den, a member of the living plant species known as the K'val, standing in the doorway.

"Sh'ev!" he shouted and ran over to hug his friend. He was careful not to squeeze too hard for fear of crushing his old ally.

"A'shun," Sh'ev said in his raspy, scratchy voice. The K'val had become very adept at speaking a recognizable form of English over the years. "It ish good to shee you again."

"Same here, buddy," Aason said. "Come on in!" He motioned toward the sofa along the far wall of his office.

Sh'ev noted where Aason was pointing and ambled over and took a seat. He left a leaf or two in his path but that was not unusual.

Aason sat down next to him. "So how are you?" he asked.

"I yam well, zhank you," Sh'ev said. "Whut about you?"

"Me and Aroline are doing great," he said. "You know about our two beautiful boys, Zac and Rory. What you don't know is I have two grandsons!" He pointed over his shoulder. "How is B'shev doing?"

"He ish zhtill growing hlike a weed!" Sh'ev said. The plant-man laughed his peculiar, wheezy laugh. He knew full well he was making a joke.

"That's great," Aason said. He cocked his head. "What brings you all the way here to Deucado? I thought you were getting settled into the Grove of the Elders."

"The leaderz of our planet have deshided the time haz come to make peaz with the living cryshtalz. However, shince zhe beginning of time, we have been unable to communicate with zhem. I volunteered to de-root myshelf and come here to ashk for aid from your people. Firsht contact is your shpecialty. If zhere is anyone in the univerz who can shpeak to zhem, it would be one of your people."

"Hmm," Aason said. "I guess you're right. But they weren't very friendly the last time we came across them."

"No," Sh'ev agreed. "But we believe zhat if you could communicate with zhem and make them realize we mean zhem no harm, perhaps zhat could put zhings right. Or at leasht make them lesh dangerouz."

"That's a very good idea," Aason said. "I'll have to…"

Aason stopped speaking. He heard his mother's voice call out to him very clearly inside his head.

"Aason! Your father and I need you. Now," she said firmly.

"Is everything all right?" Aason asked, slightly alarmed.

"We will explain everything when we see you," she replied. *"Please gather up Aroline. And contact Zac and Aimee. Your father is calling Rory and Trey. Come in Junior and meet us at the campus. We will be in the side hall of the Library, in the lecture room."*

"Mom, you're scaring me," Aason said.

"I must get a hold of Lupe and Fury," Rome said. *"Please come now."*

Aason's mother severed the connection. He looked up at his plant friend plaintively. "I don't know what's going on but we'll have to pick this up later. There's something the matter with my parents. I have to go."

"Do not worry," Sh'ev said. "I will hwait for you. Please shend my regardz."

Aason called for Junior to pick up Aroline and his son, Zac along with Zac's wife Aimee and their two little boys, Bruce and Arnie. Junior confirmed that Aason's other son, Rory, was already on his way to the library in his starship whose name was Trey. When they arrived at Rome's Library, now the centerpiece of the University of Deucado, he saw that his sister, Lupe and her huge, all-pink Amazonian livetar named Fury had already arrived. Lupe had no idea what was going on either. Rory and Trey's polished silver livetar arrived a few minutes later.

The lecture room was a small amphitheater with eight rows of seats and a narrow stage. The room was darkened ever so slightly and the stage was brightly lit from the back. MINIMCOM's two-meter tall livetar strode onto the stage and requested that everyone, humans and livetars alike take a seat. Aroline sat in the front row, next to Aason. Zac and Aimee sat in the second row, flanking their two boys. Aroline reached behind with her arm in a vain attempt to keep the children from fidgeting so much.

As soon as they were settled, Aason called out, "What's this all about, Onclare?"

MINIMCOM nodded in acknowledgement. "Your parents have an announcement to make and they thought it best to do so with the whole family gathered."

MINIMCOM turned in place and motioned to the wings. Two robed figures came out and walked forward to the edge of the platform. Because of the lighting of the stage, their faces were cast in shadow. Rei took a seat with his long legs dangling over the front. He reached back with his hand and helped Rome to sit down next to him.

"Mom, Dad, are you all right?" Lupe asked, seated just to Aason's left. Concern was palpable in her voice.

"Yes, we're fine," Rei answered in a clear, strong voice. "In fact, we're more than fine. MINIMCOM, bring up the lights. Please?"

MINIMCOM brightened the house lights, fully illuminating Rei and his beloved wife Rome. All of their children and grandchildren gasped. Bruce and Arnie were too young to understand the cause but they knew something was amiss.

"Grandbeo, Grandmea, what happened to you?" Rory asked. "You look so young!"

Rei nodded. "That's because we are."

"What do you mean?" Aason blurted out. "How is this possible?"

"Long before any of you were born," Rei continued, "OMCOM gave me a yellow pill, gene therapy, to help fix my back. Despite all the precautions the Ark mission planners took to make sure we didn't age during cryo-hibernation, they didn't figure on the amount of desiccation to our vertebral disks. The yellow pill that OMCOM cooked up was supposed to reverse that. Which it did. No more back pain. Your mother took also took a yellow pill during our trip from Tabit to Deucado."

"It fixed a lot more than your discs," Lupe pointed out with a hint of sarcasm.

"Yes, daughter dear," Rome replied, picking up where Rei left off. "It gave your father, and all of you, our descendants, sonar vision and the EM communications that allow us to link mentally. But there was one more effect that OMCOM only revealed to us earlier today."

"Earlier today?" Aason shouted and stood up. "He was here?"

"Yes," Rome answered. "He returned to our universe from the heavens to make a request of us."

Aason took two steps forward. "Why didn't you tell me?" he asked. "I think I would've welcomed the chance to punch him in the nose."

Rome laughed. "We didn't have time," she said. "He made the trip to ask for our aid in solving a problem."

"What kind of problem?"

"It doesn't matter. We settled that." Rome looked at Rei who nodded. "Your father and I declined so he left. But before he did, he activated what he called a genetic snapshot and restored our DNA to the same state as the day we took the pills. For all intents and purposes, our bodies are now 25 years old."

"Oh, Mom," Lupe said, leaving her seat. Fury started to rise as well. Lupe indicated the livetar should remain seated. Lupe walked up to her mother then stopped, staring at her intently. Lupe reached out and gently stroked her mother's cheek, in awe of its smoothness. She cocked her head. "Your hair is still white, though."

Rei ran his hand through his own hair, gray and thinning. "Our hair will go back to our original color as soon as it grows out," he said.

With that most of the audience stood up and gathered around the patriarchs of the Bierak clan.

Rome and Rei let them marvel at their remarkable appearance for a little while then Rei shushed them and asked them to take their seats again. After they had done so, he slid off the stage and stood in front of them. Rome joined him and held his hand.

"While it may seem really sleek to get to be young again, there was a side effect that OMCOM had not foreseen. That's why we called you all here. It isn't just about shaving 50 years off of our appearance."

"What is it then?" Aason growled. He had had enough experiences with OMCOM to know that the other shoe was going to be a big one, once it dropped.

MINIMCOM walked to the far right edge of the stage and down the three steps to floor level. He came over and stood next to Rome and Rei.

"OMCOM failed to take into account the actions of the prosthetic 24th chromosome that your parents received when they were kidnapped by the Onsiras. It is interacting with the restored DNA and blocking the normal aging process."

While the humans were digesting MINIMCOM's startling analysis, Junior spoke up for the first time. "Father, if their aging process has been blocked, does that not mean they will never grow old?"

"Yes," MINIMCOM said. "As far as I can surmise, they are now functionally immortal."

"Immortal!?" Aason said, jumping up again. "But, but…" he sputtered.

Aroline stood up and put her hand on her husband's shoulder. She turned to look at her in-laws. "This is a miracle," she said. "Isn't it?"

Rei answered. "We don't know," he said. "We don't know what it means. We haven't had enough time to sort it all out."

Aason was able to find his tongue again. "So you're going to… You're going to outlive all of us? Everyone in this room?"

Rome shook her head. "We only know what we have just told you. This has never happened to a human being before."

"What are you going to do?" Aason asked. "You have time, you have all the time, you …" He could not finish the sentence.

"Family," Rei said. "We don't know anything right now. We don't know if it is a blessing or a curse. We're thrilled at the idea of having the time to watch all of your children grow up. And there are so many things we've never done, choices we had to make, when we thought we only had a limited time to accomplish our goals. But having limitless time, where do you start?"

Lupe quietly asked, "Do you want to live forever?"

Rome looked up at Rei and then back to Lupe with a pained expression on her face. "I don't know. We don't know. We do know this is an impossible, amazing thing that has happened to us. But 50 or 100 years from now? A thousand years from now?" She closed her eyes. "We just don't know. I don't know if we will have the stamina to face eternity. All I know is that we love you all and now we have enough time to see to it that every one of you have the most wonderful life possible."

She leaned in on her husband. Her family, humans and livetars alike, arose as one and crowded around them, all abuzz, hugging them and showering them with love. Being with their family, right now, made it easy to ignore the giant void staring them down. What they would do tomorrow, Rome had no idea. The only thing she knew was they would have plenty of time to decide.

29

THE ORIGINAL VIRUS 5

Author's note: I first wrote this story in 1973. I was in my sophomore year at the University of Michigan and I knew I wanted to write science fiction. The version presented here is actually my third draft. However, at the time, all I had was a Royal Aristocrat Electric Typewriter. The novelette reprinted here was 53 whole pages long, double-spaced.. It was simply too long for me to keep revising. So I decided to break it up into shorter stories, one of which is presented after this. You will see some common elements have been retained, even since 1973. These elements include Rome, Rei, OMCOM and the Stareaters. A lot more has changed and in the modern version, I have introduced a lot more hard science. This story is presented in its exact original form. Only typos have been corrected. So enjoy this for what it is and try to not laugh too hard.

Year 3400 AD

THE VENT'S SOOTHING HISS SENT COOLING STREAMS OF AIR DOWN around Rei Bierak's neck and shoulders, helping him to relax. Looking out the view portal, he could see only the blackest black of space punctuated briefly by tiny burning points of light. Near the nose of the Shuttle, he spotted a flashing red dot that was the Platform's beacon.

He leaned back, sinking into the comfortable cushioning. That winking light meant the reality of his imminent transition from worker to Commander was upon him. He smiled self-consciously. Back in PlanHabStat, his old job had been permutating probabilities; those of finding a habitable planet in a given system, and incorporating them into the most efficient route possible. He would have used the word luck, but in a singular flash of brilliance, he plotted a 90 degree turn midway through the route he was working on, lassoing in two particularly promising areas. That gave the survey flight to the Delta Gamma region, a record 91% chance of success in the first six systems alone.

Almost every senior official at Skyler Base wanted to go. The Commander-in-Chief, old Sourpuss Pourte himself, had called Rei and praised him .He personally wanted to know what position Rei preferred for the Uprank, the ritual promotions needed to fill the higher posts whenever a large segment of the senior staff took their leave to go on Survey.

Rei had modestly declined a specific post but mentioned he did favor one on the Platform. Old Pourte gave him the command! And now he was on his way up, for the second time ever, to take over the station that hung in synchronous orbit some 34,000 kilometers over Skyler Base.

His first trip up had been a month before. His predecessor, named Canconed Wipken, had rushed him on a whirlwind tour through the corridors and work areas, leaving Rei with only the vaguest impressions of their nature. Later, when Wipken briefed him, he learned why.

Skyler Base was being phased out. Everyone knew that. The colony on Owell was doing so fabulously well that all incoming flights were being shunted there directly. There were no incoming replacements for the lower positions as they were vacated. The inhabited moon that was Skyler Base occupied a strategic position near the tip of the Orion Spur, but almost half its power and resources went into life support. A real planet would take care of it for free. The orbiting Platform, which originally held over 200, would have a skeleton complement of only forty. Thirty of those would be engaged in the construction of the last Survey fleet that would take Rei and the rest of the remaining personnel to a new home somewhere in the Delta Kappa region. That left a crew of nine manning the Observatory and Maintenance section meaning Rei had no assistants and practically no duties.

His thoughts were jolted by a sickening crunch and Rei was thrown forward. The restraining field slowed him and pressed his chest, forcing him to exhale violently. An obviously inexperienced pilot had rammed the Shuttlecraft into a docking hatch at way above optimum force. Rei thought there might actually have been structural damage, judging from the unmistakable sound of escaping air and from the manner they were being hurried from the ship. He made a notape to check on it later.

His first official act as Commander was to have Skyler's omnipresent computer, OMCOM, send his personal belongings to his quarters then Rei took the tube up to his new office. He had the choice of working where he lived which logic dictated as most efficient but that was a drag. So, like most everyone else, Rei chose to work somewhere different; distant; but easily accessible to his living quarters. He waved the door open and entered.

This new office was a factor of ten more sumptuous than his 3 x 3 cubicle back down in PlanHabStat. It had a full-wall viewplate, currently showing a seashore scene, obviously Wipken's choice, a desk supported by nothing other than lines of flux, and a chair made of the so-called "smart" plastics. He sat down in it, leaning back. The chair sensed the motion and changed from a hard stiff backing to a soft cushy support.

He twisted in the chair and looked behind him for the ever-present OMCOM grillwork that hid OMCOM's audio response interface. It wasn't there.

He said hesitantly, "OMCOM?"

-Yes, Rei,- a tinny voice answered.

Rei turned and spied a small square on the upper left hand corner of the desk glowing pink. He had not seen any magnetostatic interfaces since his arrival of the Base and he exclaimed, "My stars."

The OMCOM took it to be a request, and darkened the ceiling, filling the room with flickering stars, giving an out-galaxy view of the sector of Orion's Spur run by Skyler Base. Rei laughed. He didn't need the laser reconstructions of the holojector, he could just look out a porthole at the real thing.

"That's excellent, OMCOM," Rei said to the pinkish square. "Will you give me a cross-section of the platform and label the major areas? And show me where I am relative to it?"

The stars faded and a miniature orbiting Platform appeared, floating before him. Its walls were mercilessly stripped away, revealing its inner workings and the major functional areas; the Observatory; the living quarters; recreation areas; Construction, where the Survey ships were being built and over the area labeled Administration, hung a glowing arrow pointing to "Here".

As the three-dimensional image rotated, Rei said, "What's that empty section?" He picked up a light-pen and traced the outline of a large section that retained a faint green aura afterwards. It was on the top of the Platform, adjacent to one of the dish antenna outcroppings. "I don't remember Wipken taking me there," he said, scratching an itchy spot on his blond scalp.

-That is the proposed site for the gravity wave detector.- answered OMCOM.

"Why is it the proposed site?"

-Wipken terminated the detector's construction due to increased need for personnel in Construction. To insure that enough Survey ships would be built for the Delta Gamma Survey.-

"I thought they were done six months ago. Didn't we have it finished?" Rei had to twist his neck a little to keep the section in view. It was going behind the bulk of the Platform.

-Wipken determined that the limited use it would receive did not justify the further expenditure of resources and personnel allocation, since all human crew members would be abandoning the Base soon.-

Rei took his eyes off the miniature orbiter and looked down at the pink square. It was glowing a little brighter now, almost white. "OMCOM, why do you sound so bitter?"

-The potential value of the operational unit is incalculable compared to the relatively small input of resources required for completion. Regardless of how long the unit was utilized.-

Rei frowned, then uncreased his forehead and raised his eyebrows. He pointed to the square. "I'd take it you'd get to use the unit even after we're all gone, right?" He smiled as the square glowed brighter for an instant then faded back to pink.

-Yes, - was the only reply.

The empty section came around again. OMCOM thoughtfully stopped the rotation and expanded it along with its green halo. Rei sat straighter and his chair stiffened slightly. "

How long would it take to finish it, given the personnel and all that?"

-1.2 months for a fully operational unit.-

"Wow! Is that all?" Rei rubbed his lip. It sounded suspicious. "How many men would you need?"

-One, - answered OMCOM irrepressibly.

"Just one?" Rei's voice cracked. "How could you possibly finish it so quickly with just one person?"

-The servo-mechanisms currently programmed for maintenance could be adapted to the construction program yielding the operational unit.-

Rei leaned over to the square. One didn't have to look at the grilles or magnetostatic plates to speak to OMCOM, but everyone did. It was called, in a vague psychological term, acknowledgement of presence. "Who is this one person you need then?" he asked in controlled tones.

-Pal Boco.-

"And who is he? What does he do?"

-Pal Boco was recently trained as a full-time gravitonomer but was transferred to aid in the construction of the extra Survey Ships and has remained there since. Shall I call him for you?-

Rei sighed and leaned back. The chair went soft and easy. "Well, yes, go ahead if you're so anxious." He watched the holophone come alight then a young man's face appeared, with brown hair tied into a bun in the back. Behind him was the disarray of crew quarters. He was rubbing his eyes with balled fists. He said, "Boco, here."

Rei cupped his hand to his mouth, whispering, "You didn't have to wake him, OMCOM." Then he said louder," Hello, Boco. I'm Rei Bierak, the new Platform Commander. Sorry to wake you."

Boco took his hands away from his eyes and stiffened. "Oh, hello, sir. It's all right, sir. I wasn't really asleep yet, anyway."

Rei smiled sympathetically. "Boco, OMCOM says with your help, we can have the gravity wave detector finished in little over a month. What do you think?"

"Up, whup," Boco said. His jaw dropped. "If OMCOM says so it must be right. How many men sir?"

"Just you. And OMCOM." Boco's eyes bugged out. Rei continued, "He says he can use those servo-robots in Maintenance to help."

Boco stuttered, and then shrugged resignedly. "Well, it sounds a little over-optimistic, but I'm not going to argue with OMCOM."

Rei breathed a short burst. "All right then. I've made my decision. I'll notify Construction you are no longer working for them. As of immediately, you're in charge of getting the gravity wave detector built. I'll want a timeline and construction outline in three days, and I'll want a progress report each week. All right?"

Boco grinned broadly and bobbed his head up and down enthusiastically.

"Any materials or equipment requested, within reason will be granted." Boco shook his head furiously. "Also, I'll want you on second shift from now on, so that means out of bed".

Boco jumped up and tried some sort of pathetic salute. He shouted, "Yes, sir!"

Rei smiled, pleased. He said, "And Boco, you can call me Rei from now on."

Boco said, "Yes sir. I mean, right Rei." Then he faded from view, smiling. Judging from Boco's expression, Rei knew he made at least one friend up here.

-Thank you, Rei, - OMCOM said, quietly, from the desk corner.

Well, Rei thought, make that two friends.

OMCOM breezed Rei through the bureaucratic claptrap necessary for getting the G-wave detector's final construction approved. That took six days. Then it became quite clear as to why old Pourte had so readily assigned him the post for which he really wasn't qualified. There was nothing to do! He couldn't even play with his old job, in PlanHabStat. OMCOM had finished the entire star sampling necessary and was now sifting through the bulk of the data that Rei had helped amass, to find the best route for the next, final journey from Skyler Base. Rei spent the days bugging Boco and the rest of the Platform's crew; staring out at the huge Skyler's World, about which they orbited; and inventing amusing but useless games with OMCOM to pass the time.

One month and one day into his command, something happened. Rei was sitting in the simulated dark of interstellar space and at random intervals OMCOM would fling small Survey ship-shaped objects across his field of vision. Rei would take potshots with a light-pen and each time he struck on-target, OMCOM would detonate the tiny craft with a display of fireworks and exploding sounds that grew gaudier and louder with each hit. He had downed over thirty ships and was almost deaf when OMCOM suddenly stopped the target shooting.

The ceiling brightened and OMCOM announced, loudly, - There's a call for you, Rei. I don't think you heard it.-

Rei shouted, "Thanks OMCOM," and waved his hand to receive the call. He looked down into the clear partitions that held the holophone image and saw a dark-haired woman appear. Styles change, breeding patterns and their selective factors change; the women of the Outer Worlds, twelve thousand years since 1 AD had as much in common with their pre-space predecessors of Old Earth as those women had with their thick and shaggy prehistoric ancestors.

The women of the Outer Worlds, these near the tip of Spur, were slight and small, all blonde or copper-haired, with cream clean skin and boyish figures that lent themselves mostly to agility and grace. The woman before Rei was an anomaly. She had a throwback beauty that even the holophone couldn't filter out. She had luxurious dark hair that stretched below Rei's view, making it extremely long, not the short waves and curls that were the style on Skyler Base. She had an oval face that held well-formed features and her skin was the bronze that belonged on a beach in the sun, not in the multilayered domes under an unbreathable moon's sky.

"Hello," Rei shouted, unable to gauge the necessary intensity.

"Hello, are you Rei Bierak?" she asked in a husky voice, although Rei wasn't sure that it wasn't due to the cottony feeling in his ears.

"Yes. What can I do for you?" He leaned forward to get a better view. His chair went with him, stiffening.

"I need your permission to temporarily assign two Contechs to come down on the Shuttle and pick up a new Thinbeam relay to install on the Platform."

"Anywhere in particular?" Rei asked.

"No, it doesn't matter. Next to the rest of them, I guess," she said innocently. Then she smiled awaiting his response. Rei shut his eyes for a moment trying to visualize the relay section. There wasn't much room left there.

"Uh, what is this for anyway? Don't we have enough already?"

She shook her head tossing the seemingly meters of lush hair about in the process. "No. The Personal Messages Relay section has been taken over by OMCOM. He's determined that he needs a new Thinbeam to do his job most efficiently."

Rei shrugged, "I guess it's OK. I don't suppose it would hurt anything. Who is authorizing it from your end?"

She laughed a full-throated, hearty laugh. It made Rei feel warm. "Me," she answered.

"And who are you?"

She drew herself up and Rei caught a slight view of what was going on below her neck. It looked interesting if you like that sort of thing. Veritable mountains compared with the plains of the women of the Outer Worlds. "I am Rome Sharing," she said, "head of Colony and Survey Communications."

"Hey, if you're in ColSurvComm, what are you doing requisitioning personnel for Personal Messages?"

"As I explained before," she said, implacably, "the entire section has been automated by OMCOM. You know he isn't allowed to requisition major equipment without a department head's approval. He asked me. I worked there just before the Uprank."

Rei leaned back in the chair, which softened, "Well, it's fine with me. When do you want them?"

"As soon as possible?"

"Uhmm," he looked around his office, "I'll send them down on the next shuttle. OK?"

She looked surprised. "Oh. All right. Thank you."

Rei nodded and she faded from view. He snapped his fingers. "Hey OMCOM?" He asked.

-Yes, Rei, - the pink squared answered.

"Get me Boco, it's important."

Boco's face appeared in the holophone, his long hair draped over his shoulders, behind his usual windblown quarters. "Oh, hi Rei," he was stifling a yawn.

Rei clucked his tongue. "Pal, what are you doing in the sack? It's 4:70. Why aren't you working?"

"Oh, I am. I transferred to third shift. That's when OMCOM has the most servo-robots free. We can work more efficiently when…"

"OK, I get the picture. I want you to go down to the Base tomorrow."

"The Base? Why?"

"I need your help in supervising the shipment of a relay and you can give me a progress report on the way down."

Boco shrugged. "OK, I was supposed to get some calibration tools, I can check on what happened to them. How long will it be?

"I'm not sure of the shuttle schedule, it's been running erratic recently." Rei stopped speaking to look down at the lightpad where the eavesdropping OMCOM displayed the tentative flight schedule for the next ten days. "Oh, here it is. It'd be two days."

Boco agreed and asked, "Can I get back to sleep now?"

Rei let him.

The next day at 3:00 sharp the Shuttle cast off from the dock and started on its way down to the Base with Rei and Boco aboard. Boco gave his progress report which consisted merely of saying it was done. The actual detector was finished. They were waiting for the last few shipments of the solution for the tanks and the calibration tools.

As the shuttle dropped lower, both Rei and Boco fell silent to watch the little craft discharge its gravitic potential in a fierce display of heat and light. After it slowed to a suitable speed, the Shuttlecraft extended its wings and glided to an inexpert landing just off the edge of the runway. Rei remarked to Boco that it was probably the same pilot who had ruined a Shuttlecraft on his way up. Some tractors came out and towed it into a low dome which then sank below Skyler's World's unbreathable surface.

Rei was surprised to see Rome Sharing walking up the ramp to meet them as they disembarked from the boarding tube. He could see all of her now and was pleased to note that her figure which had started out with some much promise at the top, didn't quit, even down to her feet.

She was surprised to see Rei among the crewman she was supposed to meet. She waved. When she reached them, she took Rei's hand in greeting, which made his heart leap. She was far more striking than the holophone let on, and tall, too! She was barely two centimeters shorter than Rei which made her tower over the other women of the Base.

"Hello," she said, using the anachronistic shake of welcome. "I didn't mean for you personally to come."

Rei smiled and asked, "Are you disappointed?"

She shook her head no.

"Rome Sharing, this is Pal Boco." She leaned towards him with her hand outstretched, but Boco, unsure of her intentions jumped back. She laughed and said, "Hello, Pal." Rei noticed her voice really was husky, though the timbre of her laugh was much improved over yesterday's.

She pointed towards the exit and they started off.

Rei explained, "Boco here had to come down to pick up some tools and materials and he had a progress report due at the same time so I came with him to supervise and get the report so you really didn't put me out of my way." He was out of breath and speaking quickly.

Rome opened her lovely mouth to speak but Rei added, "Besides, to tell the truth, I didn't have any other staff to spare, except myself, anyway."

Rome nodded and started to speak again, but Boco pointed down a corridor perpendicular to the one they were traveling and said, "Rei, I have to, oh, I'm sorry," he noticed he had interrupted her. "I have to go down this way to check on the tools. I'll call you later and tell you what's happening." He winked, and stepped on the glideway that took him down the other corridor.

"What was it you were trying to tell me?" Rei asked turning and looking right into her eyes. They were glistening brown and Rei found his gaze locked in hers. She didn't speak for a moment then the corners of her eyes crinkled and she laughed.

"I know it isn't funny, but OMCOM was caught off guard by your quick compliance. He ran a check and found a flaw in one of the subsections of the relay. He sent it back to Assembly to be repaired, but it won't be ready until tomorrow. I tried to catch you but you were already in transit and…" She trailed her voice off helplessly.

"Don't worry," he said, looking into those irresistible eyes. "We were expecting to be down a few days anyway."

"Well it was my fault I didn't contact you in time, although I thought OMCOM would have." She pointed and steered Rei to a waiting area right by the huge observation window. "I came down to meet the crew you sent, to set them up, and well, see that they were entertained, while we got the relay ready." She indicated one of the floating chairs by the window. "If you wouldn't mind waiting, I'll go tell OMCOM I'm signing off for the day, and then we can get something to eat, OK?"

Rei agreed and sat thankfully into the chair. The gravity on the Base was about one and a quarter times that of the Platform and he found his legs were tiring quickly. He watched her walk away and was impressed by her shapely rear, as she headed for a grille. He turned to look out the window.

The picture window afforded a most excellent view of Skyler's World as it hung, huge and motionless, filling a quarter of the sky with its gaudy bands of aqua and turquoise. On the Platform, the UV absorbing light accented the reds and oranges giving it a more cheery appearance. Down here, beneath the ocean of atmosphere, it looked closer, but forbidding and beautiful.

Skyler's World was among the last of the big-time gas giants. Just a little bigger, even by a few kilotonnes, and it would undergo sufficient gravitational collapse to erupt it into a miniature star.

Gas giants like this normally put out gigawatts of lethal radiation this close, but Skyler's World, ever the patient father, radiated only in the radio and IR bands. This warming bath made the moon that was Skyler Base a comfortable place to live, even when hidden from the Sun.

That comfortable temperature is qualified. You had to bring along your own oxygen. The atmosphere around Skyler Base was mostly nitrogen and CO_2 but the plants they had loved it and made oxygen in the process so everyone was happy. OMCOM had calculated the World's rate of matter accretion and gave the system less than a million years before the World set itself aflame within its thermonuclear core. That was among the motivations for abandoning the Skyler System and moving on. If they had had more time, it might have been a nice place to live.

Rome came back and interrupted Rei's reveries. They had dinner together and then went to her quarters.

"Isn't this a little small," Rei asked as they entered her apartment, "for a department head?"

"Yes." She walked about the room waving her hands, manipulating the various environmental factors, like the lighting, the ambient noise filter, odors, temperature and the rest. "I was assigned a new one, but OMCOM had me so bogged down, trying to wrap up that Personal Messages Business and run my own department, I haven't had the time to move."

She turned to see Rei watching her gyrations, grinning, much amused. She laughed and started moving her hands like propellers. The lighting grew bright and dim, over and over and they both laughed. She pointed to a fluffy orange and gold chair. Rei sat down and instantly, it became soft and supple, messaging his back with little ripples traveling up and down in relaxing succession.

"Ahhh," he sighed, closing his eyes to enjoy the sensation.

"Nice, huh?" Rome offered. Rei nodded. "You just relax, I'm going to change my clothes," she said, and went into the next room.

Rei half-opened his eyes and looked around. The room was furnished with numerous enchanting objects. He recognized only about half. The rest were puzzles of function and origin. Rome came back dressed in a gauzy and tantalizingly translucent gown. Her full beauty, half-hidden by the standard basic tunic and slacks, was now displayed and enhanced. It hit Rei like a blast and he gazed upon her with dewy-eyed appreciation. Around her head was a beaded clear band, glowing visibly.

She knelt before a wall panel and pressed some touchplates activating the acoustic generators. Little crystals, tinkling together came to Rei's attention. More sounds began to emerge all around him. Rome came over to sit on the floating couch, next to his chair. There were birds and insects chirping and cheeping. Other animal sounds which he wasn't sure of came forth. There were burrings and tappings, mews and coos, assorted squawks, then they quieted before a rising wind. It died and waves crashed. The roar of the surf reminded Rei of his viewplate which he hadn't gotten around to changing. The wind came back and began to howl. All around the sounds wafted in and out rising in intensity. The cacophony began to bear down on Rei as more sounds generated and remained. The volume rose and rose until all at once the noise crescendoed. The sounds embraced and formed a most haunting and lilting harmony.

The tumult had become an orderly disorder of discernible melody lines and rhythms. The high pitched notes, those of the animals and insects, not instruments carried the tuneful arrangement. While the wind and waves gave the bass-line a strong and booming beat for those melodious creatures.

"I've never heard nature orchestrated before. It's beautiful." He had to raise his voice to get over the music. "What's it called?"

She leaned her head back, and spoke to the grille mounted above the couch, "A little lower please, OMCOM." The symphony became peaceful, soothing, a softer more gentle background. "It's called Qua Non a Mintaka, 91."

Rei blinked his eyes rapidly, looking at her strangely. "Mintaka?" He shook his head then asked intensely, "Are you…"

"Yes, I am," she answered, not letting him finish the question.

"That explains everything," Rei said, slapping a hand to his cheek. Mintaka was the second oldest inhabited world in all the Unity of Man. It stood at a distance so extreme from where they sat, that even in DeepSleep, where the life processes are slowed and bio-time passes at an infinitesimal rate, a toll was still extracted. Her body had aged several years while her mind remained frozen at the instant they left. It explained how the personality of a young and lively girl came to rest in the body of a fully-developed woman. That above all else made her so unlike the rest of the women at the Base.

"I thought Mintaka didn't send ships out here anymore? Too many breakdowns, or something like that?" he asked.

"No, it's just that most people like to stay there so they don't have many shiploads to send out."

Rei's face was creased with intent. "Why did you do it? Why did you leave? Was it hard to adjust when you got out here?"

She smiled and leaned back. "I wanted to see new places, live on a world of my own." Her smiled turned to a frown. "It wasn't hard to adjust, but the attitude around here is that it should be."

"Why is that?"

"Well, everyone knows I left Mintaka four thousand years ago, right?" Rei nodded. "So that means cultural orientation was arrested for four thousand years in the past, right?"

Rei nodded again.

"Well that's wrong! Let me fill you in. All the progress we made gets out here only as fast as the little x-rays of the Thinbeam do. The farther out you go, the more primitive things are at a given time. You people out here spend so much time and energy on exploration and expansion that even when I left, we were way ahead of where you are now."

Rei didn't know what to say to this. She pointed a finger at him.

"That's not what they thought around here though. They stuck me in relaying those horrible, boring personal messages. To see the long dead past because they," she spat out the word 'they', "they thought I wasn't ready for the future!" She laughed but it wasn't the deep and rich laughter of earlier. "We had a million things on Mintaka, even four thousand years ago, that you never dreamed of."

Rei shook his head then stopped. He looked around the room remembering he didn't know what half the things were for."

"It's all right, though. You'll get there. People change, right?"

Rei smiled at this happier tack. "You're from Alterra right?" she asked. He blinked He had just thought they didn't have these things on Alterra.

He turned to her. "Yes, that's right, how did you know that?"

She shut her eyes and then said, "I know many things. You came here when you were nineteen. You wanted to be a survey pilot. Something's funny and you are wondering how I can know these things. And I could be...Yes! You just got it!" She opened her eyes and smiled. "This band is called an Espansor. It allows me to sort of read your thoughts, as you guessed."

Rei whistled, mightily impressed. "Hey that's neat. I didn't know they could do such things. Can I try?"

Rome smiled and carefully took the band off, trying not to muss her hair. She handed it to him. Rei placed it on his scalp and the band, apparently made of smart plastic constricted to form-fit his skull.

Immediately, he felt a warm, relaxing, vaguely sexual, pleasant sensation. He looked at Rome and even though her lips did not move, he caught shards and shreds of words.

"....does it...I hope he....You look cute....," then more clearly, "Rei can you hear my thoughts?"

Rei nodded and said, "Yes." He heard Rome hear him like an echo. "This is real fun," he said, his words slurred almost drunkenly. Again, he heard Rome hear him. He thought to her, "Can you hear me?" All that returned was, "What's he doing," and a happy expectant look on her face.

"You didn't hear that did you?" He asked, and then giggled. His words kept coming back and confusing him. They were funny. She opened her mouth to speak, but she thought each word before she spoke it, giving a strange tinkling reverbatory effect. No, I didn't hear you but I can."

Rei saw in her mind the other Espansor in the next room and he nodded to her unspoken question, 'Should I get it?'

Rome stood and went into the other room, to retrieve it. They spent the next several hours talking and giggling and thinking to each other. Each time the clear glowing bands detected a psi wave output, the metal beads would send an ultrasound pulse through their pleasure centers. As the feedback took hold, their psionic powers increased minute by minute with the thoughts and revelations going even deeper. Rei and Rome quickly found there was no room for anything but complete honesty and it did not take Rome long to discover why he came down to the base, really. Rei, too, uncovered her hidden secrets. He was thrilled and amused by the buried images. Although they came from three thousand light-years apart, they thought similarly and sincerely about many things as human beings do. With their innermost feelings bared, they found in each other a warm and intelligent remarkably complex being.

At one point in the evening, Rei laughed out loud, and felt his happiness inside and reflected back from Rome and from Rome watching him. It was like a maze of mental mirrors, going to infinity. "You really have to do this with someone you like, don't you," he thought.

Rome agreed and echoed his words back to him, but it changed them to say love.... Rei was pleased, and knew she was right. In both minds they knew he wasn't going back to stay in the guest quarters that night. And later in that evening; with their bodies, they completed the union they discovered in each other's minds.

The following morning Rei was awakened by gentle oscillations in the sleep-stand's field.

He looked at Rome. She was sleeping soundly. Her long hair was splayed about her head in waves of halo, as befitting the angel she was. It wasn't her doing the rocking. A galvanized voice issued quietly from the grille overhead.

-A call for you, Rei. It's Boco.-

Rei whispered, "OK, I'll take it in the next room."

He extricated himself from the bed with minimum of jostle and Rome did not appear to awaken. He saw Boco's countenance in the holo-phone.

"Aha!" Boco said when Rei reached the phone. "I finally got a chance to wake you. I looked for you at the guest quarters and .... "

"Don't ask," Rei growled, "and keep you voice low. Please."

"OK. OK. I got the calibration tools. They were caught up in some shipping backlog and I'm going to carry them back to the Platform."

"What is it you wanted," Rei whispered, stroking futilely at his disheveled mop.

"I got done all I can do down here and I wanted to know if it's all right to go back up today. At five."

"There isn't any Shuttle today, remember? Rei sneezed explosively then looked back into the other room, but nothing was stirring.

"Yes there is. The one that was wrecked is back in service as of today."

"Well, it doesn't matter. It's not all right." Boco made some whining protestations. Rei held up his hand. "I want to check with OMCOM on the status of the Thinbeam relay we're supposed to take up and if it's ready, and you can get it loaded in time, then you can take the Shuttle up, if it really is going."

"Oh. All right, you're the boss."

"Pal," Rei asked, "what's the matter? Why are you in such a hurry to get back?"

"It's nothing vital. It's just I have a friend on the platform, Austed? And he called me yesterday. He said they found a real cosmic mystery up there, and I wanted to get back to take a look."

"What kind of cosmic mystery?"

"Austed was doing some routine maintenance on one of the five meter optical telescopes OMCOM uses for surveillance. He cleaned off the lenses and after OMCOM did a reprogram, he said the two stars were missing."

"What?" Rei said, incredulously. "Whoops." He put his hand to his mouth and scrunched his shoulders at the outburst. "How can stars be missing?" he whispered.

"Beats me," Boco replied. "That's what I wanted to find out!"

"OK, just get that relay."

Boco nodded and then faded. Rei returned to Rome just as she was awakening and quickly forgot the cosmic mystery for the more immediate feminine kind.

Rei managed to stay down an extra two days but the time slipped inexorably past them, as they sought out all the quiet and private corners of Skyler's base. Having seen into each other's mind, they both knew they loved each other as deeply as they could, which made the goodbye so much worse. Amid the tears and squeezes of his departure, Rei promised he would call often and come down whenever it was possible. Aboard the Shuttle, he returned to his new command.

As soon as he was settled, he called Boco, whose face appeared quite drawn, and somewhat flattened against an unidentifiable, amorphous grey background.

"Pal, where are you?" he asked.

"We're in the opticals, in the Observatory."

"What are you doing there?"

"We're looking through the telescopes," he said. He snickered to himself.

"Of course." Rei laughed too. "Have you found out anything?"

"Yes. We're getting the coordinates of the major mass concentrations in the area for OMCOM, then we can run it through the G-wave detector for its trial run. That way we can see what happened to those stars."

"Do you have any guesses as yet?"

"Yes, we do. I'll have OMCOM show you."

He looked up and spoke quietly to what was most likely an OMCOM grille. Rei caught a flash of a sharp white line running across his neck and it hit him that Boco was in a pressure suit; the telescopes being in the vacuum of the outside. That explained why his face looked flat.

Rei's attention was drawn up as his ceiling dimmed. In front of him, the holojector was activated and a stylized version of stars appeared. Two of them were blinking in the upper left hand quadrant.

"Those two blinking stars are the ones OMCOM says disappeared. The upper one is Uttella. OMCOM says it disappeared on 12420.114. The other…"

"Wait a minute," Rei interrupted. "Why wasn't it reported?"

"It was, but Wipken passed it off. He didn't think it was important."

Rei said, "Oh." The more he learned the less he thought of his predecessor.

"The lower one is Huartez. It's a little tougher to figure out. OMCOM says it probably disappeared just over a year ago. He estimated the rate of dust accumulation on the lenses and added it to his last scope cleaning and came up with 12420.294 as the most likely date."

-That last digit is not significant- added OMCOM, from the corner of the desk.

Rei waved his hand around. "I still don't understand. How does dust on a lens make a star disappear?"

"OMCOM says a bit of foil used to cover the dome up here settled and adhered to the lens over the spot Huartez occupied. It was a little dull but it reflected enough of the ambient light that the subsection of OMCOM doing the surveillance was fooled. It isn't too smart you know."

OMCOM made a comment to Boco that Rei couldn't discern.

"Anyway," Boco continued, "when Austed here cleaned the lens, lo and behold, Huartez was gone."

"Well, you still haven't told me what it is yet." The stylized stars disappeared.

-Explanations and probabilities are listed for you, Rei- OMCOM said.

They were on the light pads next to him.

"We thought at first it might be a small dust cloud, traveling past the two stars," Boco said, reading from a list similar to the one displayed for Rei. "But for it to be the front of the same cloud, it'd have to be traveling almost nine-tenths the speed of light. That's much too fast for a dust cloud to hold together thick enough to completely hide two stars."

"What is it then," Rei asked.

The top sentence, given an 85% rated of being correct, displayed the words: **Two prong large cloud theory**.

"I'll show you." Boco spoke quietly to OMCOM then Rei's ceiling went dark again. The prickly bright whirlpool of the Milky Way floated before him.

"In our galaxy, there are two main regions. The bright inner part, that's mostly older stars, and the spiral arms, where the creation of new stars is going on right now."

The galaxy tilted and stopped its rotation with part of a spiral arm front and center.

"The arms are mostly made up of dust, that's what makes the new stars."

OMCOM shifted the galaxy up, and in the lower right quadrant, he gave a super fast scenario of a star being born, with the years, mass, and internal temperature clicking off, below the schematic.

"The part we're in…" A tiny tip in the front glowed brighter. "It's called the Orion Spur because it's only a piece of a spiral arm, and its constellation as seen back on Terra, was called Orion the hunter." Boco pointed and said, "Blow up the tip of the Spur."

The view of the galaxy began to expand at a dizzying speed and Rei covered his eyes to stop himself from plunging into the stars. When he looked again his office was filled with yellow, white and red suns of his domain.

"Uttella and Huartez are at the very tip of the spur. So any clouds passing by, like from the Carina Cygnus Arm or Perseus Arm would probably hit them first."

In front of Rei, the two stars mentioned shined brighter than the rest. A glowing shape, like a human hand appeared, and started moving toward them. Rei looked down at the holophone and saw the lights from a miniature display reflected off of Boco's faceplate. He was obviously enjoying playing tour guide to the universe.

"You can see that the cloud has just about eclipsed Uttella."

Rei looked up and saw the ring finger blot out the upper bright star. Below the star, a date appeared. Then Huartez…"

The middle finger touched and erased the other bright star.

"Oh, I see," Rei said, actually seeing. He watched the index finger hide a third star. "Hey Pal, is that Owell the cloud just crossed?"

"No, that's Voltaire. As far as we can tell, the cloud is moving away from Owell, almost perpendicular in our common plane so it won't come any closer than it is now."

"Is there any way to know for sure?"

"Yes and you can help. We're trying to get the G-wave detector on that area. We have to have almost all the interferences plotted and that cloud is probably too thin to show up clearly so it would be great if we knew its initial trajectory. If you ask someone in ColSurvComm to scan over any messages from Owell that come in on or around, uh,"

Pal paused while OMCOM displayed the needed dates on his light pad.

"One around '420.40 and the other around '420.9 and check for any references to the stars or the disappearances or something like that. That will help us triangulate the exact occurrence of the two events and we can plot the trajectory pretty accurately."

Rei said, "I think I can. I have a few connections down there." He smiled to himself, "I'll call you back when I get an answer. See if you can find the time to get back to work on the detector, OK?"

Boco smiled sheepishly and faded.

Rei had OMCOM call Rome but he had to wait several minutes as she was ill-disposed in the classic manner of all women. Finally, she answered.

"Oh my! Rei !" she said excitedly. "I'm so glad you called. I miss you so much!" She smiled and sniffled. Tears are welling up in her eyes, eyes that were already red from too much crying.

"Don't cry, Romey," Rei said softly, "I'll be with you soon enough."

She gave him a brave smile. "These aren't sad tears, they came before. I'm just happy to see you, that's all." She dabbed her cheeks with her sleeve.

"How are you doing so far?" Rei asked gently.

"Ok. I guess. Now that Relay business if finished, I have all this time, I can't stop thinking about you."

"It's hard for me, too. I just saw you three hours ago. Rome, what's going to happen if we're apart for a month?"

She shrugged unhappily. "I guess we just have to get used to it."

"Well I have a favor to ask, it might take you mind off it for a while."

"Oh anything, Rei. You know that."

"I need to know if any transmissions came in from Owell concerning the disappearance or eclipse of any stars on, uh…" He looked over at his lightpad where OMCOM had courteously displayed the dates. "That's any reference to Utella on or around 12420.403 and for Huartez on or near 12420.99. The second one isn't so exact though."

Rome looked away as OMCOM displayed the numbers for her. Then she looked back at him. "I can do it, but it will take a little while. The woman on the job before me didn't do such a good job cross-referencing the transmissions towards the end. Do you want me to do it now?"

Rei said, "Yes."

"OK, I'll, I'll do it then we can talk later for a long time, yes?" She touched the corner of her eye.

Rei said, "Sure."

She smiled sadly and faded.

It was just over one hundred minutes, a metric hour*, later when she called back. (*A three shift, nine hour day is exactly equivalent to a 24 hour pre-space day, but more logical and much more amenable to calculations.)

"Hi," she said, in her purring sexy voice this time.

"Oh, hello," Rei said soundly sickly.

Her face turned to concern. "What's the matter Rei? Are you all right? What have you been doing?"

He gave a wan smile. "It's nothing. I just realized how awful these holophones are."

"Why awful? I always thought they were good. They make everything seem…"

"That's just it. You look so close and lifelike. I keep wanting to lean over and kiss you but I can't. I'd probably get a laser in the eye."

"Oh Rei," she giggled. "I got what you wanted. I have two separate transmissions that refer specifically to the stars mentioned."

"Great. Can you route them up here?"

"No," she said flatly.

Rei raised his eyebrows. "No? Why not?"

"I've ordered these communications classified. If you want to see them, you'll just have to come down and view them here. I can't just route them anywhere."

Rei started to protest then stopped. He sighed. "OK, you win. Heh." He laughed. "I guess we win. I'll come down on the Shuttle tomorrow, OK?"

She nodded enthusiastically.

"Will you meet me at the gate?"

"Yes, of course."

"OK then. I'd better go and do some work up here. I've been shirking my duties, all two of them. I have to at least pretend I'm in charge."

"I understand Rei. All right," she said reluctantly. "I'll see you tomorrow."

She smiled at her own words then faded after saying goodbye.

Rei called back Boco and informed him he was going back down to the Base. Boco was surprised but Rei promised to call him as soon as he got the information they needed, again.

The next day, Rome rushed up to meet Rei as he entered the subsurface tunnel that led to the Base complex. She kissed him warmly and they held each other close as they ignored the glideway and walked past the airlocks into the corridor.

"Rome, it's only been one day. I don't think I could stand not being with you much longer."

She tugged at his sleeve and steered him towards her quarters.

"It won't always be this bad. We were already psyched up to miss each for a long time, and it's the first time we've been apart since we met. It won't be as bad."

She blinked back a tiny tear, "I hope not."

Rei looked at her sad, happy face and couldn't resist the impulse to hug her on the spot. Hand in hand they went to her apartment.

When they reached the door, Rei said, "Shouldn't we go to your office first and get the business part out of the way?"

Rome winked and waved the door open. She beckoned him with her finger. "What could be more private than the head of ColSurvComm's apartment for viewing classified material?"

Rei shrugged and they entered. He walked over and sat in the massaging chair which picked up where it had left off the day before.

Rome told him to wait there and she went into the other room. She returned in another of her diaphanous gowns that not only revealed her beautiful contours, but changed colors also. It was canary yellow as she entered the room and changed to an orchid shade with patches of maize and gold. She twirled about, modeling it for him and the orchid deepened to a thistle, then a reddish-melon color. The gold spots grew larger.

After Rei nodded approvingly, she said, "It's tuned to me. It senses my emotional state and change color with my moods."

She moved closer to him and the melon went to rose. The gold patches had turned to a gray-blue, akin to periwinkle.

"What's the red for?"

"It shows I'm happy. That's the red. And I love you. That's the pink. The blue spots are I hope you like it."

"It's very beautiful, Rome," Rei said, and the whole dressed blushed with her. He stood up and pulled her into his arms. He kissed her deeply and the kaleidoscopic array of hues that swirled through the gown ran all the way from magenta to aqua to vermillion and back. When he released her, the dress fairly glowed red-violet with the flecks of gold returned. She placed Rei on the floating couch and sat down next to him, speaking to OMCOM.

"OK, OMCOM, would you run those two transmission segments please?"

Rome's dress changed to a thoughtful lavender with copper striping and a green border. The ceiling dimmed and Rei could see the gown really did glow.

The voice from the grille said -Message received from Owell IV, System Delta Alpha 211, on 12420,406 at 6:38.04.-

OMCOM courteously displays the words in midair via holojector as he spoke them.

-In the future, please refer to this correspondence as @12420.406:DA211, cross-reference BNGG 4497571. The speakers are Loll Jeoffen and Katy Jeoffen.-

The words grew faint then disappeared as a great glow flowed in through the far wall, seemingly turned transparent to the pink and gold of some planet dawn. The whole room lit up and its confines melted away as the holojector swelled and filled the air before them.

OMCOM chose that instant to increase the air flow and it seemed that a breeze had welcomed them as they emerged upon the surface of the incredibly beautiful world. Wherever they looked, the illusion of actually being present remained. There were tremendous rolling hills stretching to a far horizon, filled with exotic blue vegetation. There were groups of giant stalks nearby, like huge blue leaf clovers piled high atop one another. Overhead, the sky was so very light blue that it looked almost gray with only a few hints of wispy clouds. Suddenly the view jiggled, giving both Rei and Rome a slight case of vertigo, for it seemed the world had moved beneath them.

A large blonde man came into view. He appeared to stand just a few meters from them. His thick neck was bright red from exposure to the sun and he wore clothes easily recognized as Universal Rustic. He held his hand up and spoke in a booming voice.

"Hi, Skyler. This is Loll Jeoffen." He stood on his toes and said, peering over Rei and Rome's head, "It's OK,honey. Come on over."

A woman, looking very small compared to him, joined him.

Rome said, "Stop it here, OMCOM," and the man froze just as he was opening his mouth.

"What's the matter?" Rei asked.

"Don't get excited. It's nothing," she replied. "OMCOM started it right from the beginning. I wanted to know if you wanted to see the whole thing or just the part you're interested in. It's pretty long altogether."

Rei shrugged. "Well," he licked his lips, "I guess just skip to that part."

Rome said, "OK, OMCOM, skip ahead to the next part I marked." Then she said, "Watch carefully. It passes quickly."

The scene wobbled and the man seemed to jump about the meter to his left. The woman had disappeared. He started in mid-sentence. "...And, oh yes, just the other night, Chester winked. We figured it was probably an eclipse of some sort but he hasn't opened his eyes back, just yet."

"OK, OMCOM," Rome said, the ceiling brightened and the beautiful planet scene faded.

"I don't get it . Who is Chester?"

"Will you explain it OMCOM?" Rome asked sweetly.

-Chester the Cat as it is called, is the only visible constellation in Owell's summer sky, in the northern hemisphere. The left so-called eye is star BNGC 4497588, Utella. Jeoffen has indicated the disappearance as 12412.133 standard, their time.-

"Oh, now I get it," Rei said, chewing on his moistened lip.

"Do you want to see the next one?"

Rei nodded to Rome's question. He noted her gown had bleached to lavender and was now mostly beige with small berries of violet traveling through it.

"OK, OMCOM the next one please."

Once again, the ceiling dimmed and OMCOM displayed the words as he spoke them. -Communication has been referred to as @12420.998VDA211. Cross-referenced BNGC-4497571. The speakers are Loll Joeffen and Owlyn Jeoffen.-

With that the walls again vanished. Rei and Rome saw a breathtakingly clear view of those same rolling hills. From a different angle this time. Almost magically, they were lighter, greener, with bare patches and some small unidentifiable animals wandering about.

The big blonde man, his hair now quite long, came around and raised his hand in greeting,

"Hi Skyler," he said. "Didn't expect to be calling you again, so soon. Something sort of interesting came up. On yeah, I'm Loll Jeoffen for those who don't know me. Chief Astrogator on the way out, for the Delta Alpha Survey. I don't know if I told you but several months ago, one of our stars, uh, Utella, sort of went out, but it hasn't come back yet. Well damned if Chester's nose didn't go. Let me tell you something, in the summer, when our sky faces away from the disc of the galaxy, that's when you know they named this place right. O.L., it really looks like the Outer Limits. We only have nineteen, or we used to have nineteen stars. And so it's easy to notice one's missing. I've been in contact with Bar Baylister. He was the Survey Chief, he's over on Laffer. We're here on Whale."

Jeoffen continued, "Incidentially, if he hasn't already told you, he figured we were here for good, so he tried to comm-land one of the dysfunctioning Survey ships. It hit pretty hard but he managed to salvage some parts. He built an aeroplane and he's been flying up and down the coast of Laffer, visiting the various families. He said he might try an overseas slight in the spring, but he's not sure. Anyway, he said it was a good idea to report these things as we see 'em 'cause you might be interested. The disc of the Milky Way is just coming over the horizon at dark these days. It's early fall here, and it isn't so blasted dark at night. I've been worried about…"

"Wait," Rei said, freezing the man with his mouth agape again. "Romey, is there anything else on this segment?"

She shrugged and then smiled. "Yes, but not about this stuff. He brings his baby out later. He's real cute. I liked that part."

"OK, OMCOM. That's all then," Rei said, over his shoulder. The beautiful jewel of a world disappeared and the ceiling came up to full brightness. "Rome," he said back to her, "can I get one of those scenes for my viewplate? The one I have is real dull."

"Oh sure, I just declassified them."

Rei leaned over and pressed his forehead on her chest, giving her a left and a right to the stomach. Rome laughed and the gown turned a happy mulberry. Rei straightened up and said, "That was real considerate of him to give us those reports, I wonder what made him think to do it?"

"Silly," she answered, "if you spent your whole life astrogating and watching the stars you'd think that stuff was important too."

Rei smiled warmly and put his hand on her cheek. The gown began to deepen its hue.

"What are you going to do now?" she asked him, her voice a rich contralto.

"I'm just going to call Boco and give him the dates, then we can play. OK?"

She nodded and the gown turned even deeper violet, with orange and apricot dots that swirled through it. She stood up and the spots grew larger and more yellow.

"What do those mean, Romey?" he asked.

"The yellow is sort of anticipation." She ran her hands down her figure, pulling her gown taut. "And the violet, that's um." She moved her hips languidly, then more salaciously. "That's for what the yellow is anticipating." She winked and turned, blossoming the gown, which was blue-violet and still glowing. She swayed her hips suggestively as she sauntered from the room.

Rei called breathlessly, "I'll be in, in one minute and I mean it." Then he got up and hurried over to the holophone, saying to OMCOM, "Get me Boco quick!"

Boco's face appeared, hair tied neatly into his working bun. Behind him was the gravity detector site.

"OK, Pal, OMCOM has those dates for you," he said.

Boco looked down. "Yes, he's displaying them now." He did a double-take, then looked up smiling. "OMCOM was right on the nose with that estimated disappearance. As always I guess."

"OK then, are you all set?" Rei asked impatiently.

"Yes, we can predict the exact trajectory of the cloud now. And I'll start trying to track it with the Detector. We got it calibrated, you know."

"Fine. Wonderful."

Boco looked down. He said, "Oh, OMCOM's displaying it now. It plots perpendicular on our common plane. Away from Owell, like we thought, so they're in no danger as I see it. You can rest easy now."

"I wasn't planning on resting," Rei said under his breath.

"What was that?"

"I said, OK you've got the cosmic mystery solved. You can go play with your detector now. I have business to take care of," and with that he got up. He didn't even wait for Boco to fade as he ran to the other room.

The evening, after dinner and long talks, Rei and Rome were watching a documentary called, Alpha on Terra. Rome was easily distracted. She fidgeted and got up several times.

After the fourth time, she came back and said, "OMCOM turn it off for a minute."

Rei said, "I was watching that."

"I know you were. But I wanted to ask you a question."

"Go ahead," Rei said, puzzled. "Do you still have marriage on Alterra?" Her voice was timid.

"Not in a formal sense. All liasons, multiple or not, are done on a contractual basis. Mostly three and six year. I think there are some lifetime ones though." He looked into her clear brown eyes. There was turmoil behind them that drew him in.

In a low voice she said, "On Mintaka, we always get married." She leaned over and stroked his cheek and temple. "Rei, would you marry me?"

He shrugged and thought for a moment. He wasn't so familiar with the custom that he realized its full implications. He loved Rome deeply and completely. She was like no other woman he had ever met or ever would meet. It seemed simple. "OK," he said, "when should we do it?"

She hugged him tightly, and said quietly, "Oh, Rei, darling. I love you. Very much," and they kissed. A few minutes later, she pulled away from him and said, "How about tomorrow?"

Rei widened his eyes. "I'm not sure how these things work, but isn't that rushing them a bit?"

"No, tomorrow we can get married and I'll have my stuff sent up to the Platform. I already asked OMCOM and he said with the new relay, it'd be easy to run my department from up there. Better in fact."

"You're a little sneaky thing, aren't you?" Rei noted, poking her gently with a finger.

She nodded happily and they hugged again. It was interrupted by the holophone chiming but they let it go for a long kiss.

Rei went over and saw Boco, extremely pale, with reddened eyes, staring up at him, worried. "Pal, what's the matter?"

Boco said very gravely, "Rei, you'd better call Commander Garlin immediately. Tell him we have a potential emergency. OMCOM has the necessary figures but I thought it'd be best if you…"

"Hold on a second, Pal. What's happencd up there?" Rei's heart was quickening.

"We're OK up here." He stopped to swallow. "OMCOM and I had a piece of the cloud tracked but we stopped." He gulped.

"Come on. What is it?" Rei demanded.

"It's Owell, Rei," he said, almost tearfully. "Owell's gone! "

Rei stood for a moment, stunned. His mind racing along the myriad possibilities, then he waved Boco away. He tried to call the Commander-in-Chief Garlin, who left orders not to be disturbed. Since those orders could not be challenged by anybody, not even OMCOM, each time Rei called, it was futilely routed to a different, less responsive underling.

OMCOM vibrated the fibers behind the grillwork over the floating couch. Rome twisted in her place, and looked up. "Yes, OMCOM?" she asked.

-Rome, two unusual circumstances have arisen. Each dictates contacting you in an official capacity, outside your work shift.-

"Go ahead, OMCOM. It's OK."

-First, a message of an unusually urgent nature has passed through the ColSurvComm relay on the Platform and I have contacted you so you may take appropriate action at the earliest moment.-

"Where does the message come from?" She lifted herself up and turned around so that she could look at the grille comfortably.

-The message comes from Owell.-

She put her hand up to her mouth and muffled an "oh." She turned and called to Rei. "Rei, come quick. OMCOM has a message from Owell. It's urgent."

Rei left his frustrated phoning and joined her on the couch.

"What was the other thing?" Rome asked.

-The Thinbeam relay satellite over Owell has terminated its self-alignment signal.-

Rei said, "OMCOM, can you route that message directly here?"

-If the Director of ColServComm authorizes it so.-

"OK, OK," Rome said, quickly. The room darkened and they both turned the other way and sat facing the opposite wall. Words, blood-red and glowing, appeared, hanging in the air before them. OMCOM read them as they were printed in midair.

-Transmission just received for Owell IV, system Delta Alpha 211, on 12421,at 8:25:75.-

Those words disappeared and were replaced by -Please refer to in future correspondence as @12421!448:DA211. Cross–referenced as BNGG 4497571. Speakers uncertain. Probable: Loll Jeoffen, remainder unidentifiable.-

Unlike previous holojectures from Owell, the room did not light up with the green and blue grassy hills. It remained dark. From the right, a light crossed before them, in jerky steps. They could see it was a lantern of sorts and, reflected in the light, they could see the man holding it was indeed Loll Jeoffen. Bur he looked haggard, and frightened. He spoke in a harsh whisper.

"Skyler this is Jeoffen. We got a problem here. We has some sort of giant eclipse. The sun went out about ten minutes ago and it hasn't come back yet. It's getting real cold here, I'd say about 10 degrees C." He stopped speaking. His attention was caught by shadows entering from the right. He beckoned to them but in the half-light of the lantern, Rome and Rei could not make out who they were. The figures were small so they were probably children. They huddled near the wall behind Jeoffen. He said, "Come on dear," and another dark figure, larger this time, came and sat near the children. Jeoffen looked right at Rome.

"Just before it happened, we saw a ring. It must have been gigantic. It came around the sun and grew brighter. It got too bright to look at then the sun got dimmer. It just shrank. There was no disc, cutting into it. It just got smaller. Then it got dark. And cold."

He indicated the area around him. "We're in the bubble from planetfall. We were using it for storage and a storm shelter. It's got provisions and insulation. But from the way things are going, I don't think it's gonna…"

He looked up. The small shapes behind him were making mewling noises and pointing up. The view before Rome and Rei grew brighter and they could clearly see the shapes of the children and Jeoffen and the walls of the bubble shelter. Jeoffen put his forearm over his eyes and behind him the children made squealing sounds of fright. The scene grew brighter and brighter. A great whooshing sound and a low howling were heard. The picture became too bright to look at, and Rei and Rome shielded their eyes.

OMCOM said quietly, -I have inserted a polarizing screen.-

They could now see the figures again, cowering. Seconds passed and they started floating slowly up, completely off the floor. Rei and Rome could clearly see their clothes and flesh smoking, turning black. The howling noises intensified until it was almost unbearable then the room went dark.

OMCOM printed in the air, the words: Transmission terminated. Thinbeam relay satellite self-alignment signal terminated.

"OMCOM turned up the light," Rei croaked quietly. Rome had large tears running down her cheeks and she leaned over to hold on to Rei. She grabbed the fleshy parts just under his shoulder blades and her body rocked as she sobbed at the horrors they had just witnessed.

After a long while, she quieted down enough to let Rei get up and answer the insistent holophone that had been chiming almost all the while. It was Boco. He looked different, older . His face was absolutely ashen. He started to speak to Rei but the words were broken, unfinished, just noise.

"Pal, Owell's been destroyed," Rei said, groping for something to say.

Boco blinked and said "I know," quietly. He covered his eyes with his palms, then drew his hands down, pulling the skin. He breathed loudly and said, "We finally got a hold of it on the detector."

"Do you, do you know what it is?"

Boco nodded. His face contorted then he put his head down on the desk. He was crying.

Rei said firmly, "Pal, Look at me. Tell me what it is."

Boco looked up. His face was tortured. His tone was pleading. "I'll tell you Rei, but dear Lord of the Cosmos, we're in trouble." Then he told him.

The following morning, Rei went to the Administrative sector of the Base while Rome went to the Shuttle dock to meet Boco. OMCOM could have sent a a life-sized, fully vocal image of Boco anywhere by tying the holophone to the holojector, but they all decided they needed to be together.

Rei arranged for them to meet with Commander-in-Chief Garlin and a hereditary representative of the Unity of Man, Unlimited, at 3:40. In a large conference room, under Commander Garlin's office, furnished with only a large table, eight flush-mounted lightpads, and eight floating chairs, sat Garlin and the representative, Tan Heraschel, ready and waiting when the three arrived.

Rei introduced them.

After some terse pleasantries, the Commander said, "OK, Bierak. Let's get started." He spoke with an impatient twang stemming from a perpetually stuffed beak of a nose that gave him a hawkish appearance, added to by his prominent widow's peak. "You just go through the facts and we'll ask the questions where we see them."

Rei pointed to the large viewplate that covered the entire far wall, projecting a placid lake nestled among sharply chiseled mountain peaks.

"OMCOM?" Rei asked. The ceiling dimmed and the lake scene disappeared, being replaced by a stylized three-dimensional view of the stars in the outer tip of the Spur. "Sir, on 12420.103 our astronomers noted that something had occluded all light and attendant radiation from the star BNGC 4497588 in the system Delta Alpha 218, referred to as Uttella."

One of the stars near the top of the column blinked rapidly then faded leaving only crosshairs at its former position.

"Next, on 12420.294 the main star of system Delta Beta 27, Huartez, disappeared likewise. However, it was not discovered as missing until this year, on 21.433."

"Hold on a second," the Commander interrupted. "That was only six days ago. Why such a delay?"

"It was unfortunate, sir. A bit of foil settled on one of the telescopes, right over the spot occupied by Huartez. That particular scope was on a scanning sweep that left the stars right around there in a relatively fixed position. It reflected enough ambient light that OMCOM thought it was Huartez itself."

"Oh, really?" the Commander asked dryly. He made a note on the lightpad next to him.

"Yes. Then last evening, near midnight, Owell disappeared. We have since received a message from one of the last remaining survivors giving us a record of the destruction that occurred."

"Destruction?" The Commander was scowling. "Are you sure?"

Rei lowered his eyes and said, "Yes. There's no doubt." Then he looked up at Rome. "Rome, would you show them the transmission?"

In a quivering voice, she said, "OMCOM. Please replay the message @12421.488:DA211."

The room darkened. While Boco, Garlin and Heraschel watched in horrified fascination, Rei looked down, his eyes shut. Rome looked away and put her hands unobtrusively to her ears to shut out the eerie howling and dying screams of the children.

When it was over, Rei looked up. Boco was resting his head on his arm. Commander Garlin was shaking his head slowly back and forth. Heraschel stared palely at the view-plate, now showing the lake scene again.

"What, uh," Garlin cleared his throat, "what was that howling noise?"

"We think that was the planet's atmosphere leaving. Escaping up."

"What could have done such a thing? Those people were burning up!"

"I don't quite understand it myself, sir. Boco can explain it far better." He reached over and tapped his friend gently on the shoulder. "Pal?" he asked.

Boco lifted his head slightly from the table and sad quietly, "Show them OMCOM."

The light dimmed again. In front of the view-plate hung a grey striped object, It had a foreshortened cone in the front, three bulbous sections in the middle, with thick black bands connecting them and a flared protrusion at the rear. Like a flashlight with bulbs in the middle. The third sphere was twice as large as the other two. It resembled, more than anything else, a snowman, mounted on a plunger, wearing an upside-down fez. Below it was a small bright yellow-white spot of light.

"What is that?" The Commander asked. "And what's the light?"

Boco turned his head to look. "That light is our sun, Skyler's sun."

Garlin and Heraschel's faces lit up with surprise.

"That little black blip, to the left, is Skyler's World." He paused for a moment. "That tiny speck, you can't see it without going close, is Skyler Base. That large object above it is a scale replica of the thing that ate Owell."

"Ate it?" Garlin burst out. "How can you eat a world, for Lord's sake?"

"Not just a world. A sun, too. It swallows them up." Boco pointed from the front to the back. "This thing, at cruising speed, travels about .9c. Ninety percent the velocity of light. It sweeps stars in that front cone, stores them in the three stomachs in the middle, and squirts them out the back of propulsion. The ultimate in fusion ramjets!"

OMCOM took the globe of Skyler's sun and moved it around the front of the titanic thing to demonstrate. As it disappeared into the front cone, the Commander shouted, "STOP!" He turned to Boco with his eyes blazing. "Boco is that thing coming here?"

"I don't know sir. We're tracking it on the gravity wave detector but as far as we know, no."

OMCOM relieved them all by bringing Skyler's sun back out of the front.

"But, sir," Boco added, "this thing can change its course at any time. It has before, and it probably will again."

They all just sat and stared at the object, incomprehensible in its size.

"I'll give you a few of the vital statistics," Boco said, "it'll let you know want we're dealing with."

He looked down at the lightpad by him where OMCOM was already displaying the needed parameters. "Sir, this thing has a mass of, well we estimate about ten to thirty-fifth kilograms. That's over fifty thousand times that of our sun. It's about twenty million kilometers long, and has an average diameter about twice that of the sun. It has a volume around ten to the fifteenth cubic kilometers, giving it an average density of over ten to the seventh grams per cubic centimeter. That's about ten tonnes for a chunk this big." He held up his fingers, and indicated pea size.

Rei whistled, hearing it in this way. "Pal, shouldn't it at least be spherical," he asked. "How can it retain its elongated shape with all that mass?"

Boco shrugged, "Hell if I know. It has density a hundred times that of a white dwarf and most of the mass is concentrated in the third stomach. It's probably where it stores most of the stars it eats. The walls are about a hundred meters thick."

"You mean it's hollow?" the Commander asked, incredulously.

"Obviously, I mean it has to be."

"What keeps it from collapsing?" Rome asked, lifting a corner of her lip.

"We don't know, OMCOM says it should be a black hole by now. The only thing we can figure is that the stars inside keep it inflated. Its tremendous speed might be responsible for keeping it from squashing together. If it ever stopped or slowed down, it probably would collapse."

"What do you recommend then, Boco?" the Commander asked.

"Right now, this thing is headed away from us. But like I said before, it could change course at any time and we think it will."

"Why so?"

"Because its particularly fond of the cooler of the F-types and the G-type stars. Unfortunately it is just those in particular that most of the inhabited worlds encircle, as you know."

"Why did it choose those?" Rome asked.

"They are just what it needs. Not too big, not too small. Hot enough with plenty of fuel to keep this thing going, but small to fit in its maw in one gulp."

"Can you give an accurate estimate then as to its destination?" the Commander asked.

"Right now, it looks like it is going to hit Hildago. We should see it disappear in about two years. If it decides to come here after that, then we have another six months to get out. But..." He paused. "There's a catch."

"What's the catch?" Rei asked.

"Hildago is a red supergiant, much too big for the Stareater to swallow and way too cool to give it the kind of thrust it needs. Alnilam II is more its style."

"What then if it goes there?" the Commander queried.

Boco took a deep breath. "If it changes course soon and OMCOM and I agree it probably will. And, if it goes to Alnilam II, then we've only got eight months left."

Rome made a hurt cry.

Garlin leaned forward. "What is your recommendation then? You didn't answer me last time."

"Sir, the gravitational disruptions will precede the destruction here by about a month. I say under all circumstances we must be prepared to leave here in no more than seven months from today."

Garlin frowned. He leaned over and spoke quietly to Heraschel. Since they were sitting on the opposite side of the table, the other three could not hear what they were saying. Heraschel got up and left the room, having said not a word.

"All right Boco. I've ordered a crash program be instituted. We'll have those Survey ships ready by your seven months." He leaned over and said, "OMCOM, what is the best route you can have in seven months, to the next sector scheduled."

For the first time in the conference room, a grey square in the center of the table lit pink and OMCOM said, -There is an eighty three percent chance that the maximum probability route for this Delta Kappa region will be no greater than sixty-six point oh forty seven percent.-

The Commander made a quiet, profane comment.

"Sir," Rei said hesitantly, getting his attention. "If the route doesn't any better by then we can just follow the Delta Gamma route out. They had a .91 rating."

"Bierak, you know that's against the, uh." The Commander snorted unhappily. "I suppose these are highly irregular circumstances."

Around the table, the consent was unanimous.

Rei pointed to the large object. "Boco. Explain to me. How did you arrive at these conclusions? How did you get a clear picture? With the radioscope?"

"No sir." He tapped the magnetostatic square and OMCOM dimmed the ceiling to give a schematic of the Gravity Wave Detector. "We're using the detector sir. In those tanks are close to a million liters of liquid crystals. Their atomic structure is ever so slightly deformed by gravitational influence. OMCOM has a track of all the major accountable masses near enough to affect us and by using a series of matrix reductions we can study the gravitational affects of any particular massive object by its interaction with all the rest." He pointed to the Stareater near the ceiling again.

"When we were first looking for this thing, we couldn't find it simply because it was so massive. Its effects were so profound, that we were looking on the wrong scale. When we did discover the least massive section, and tuned for it, the whole thing came in practically as clear as a holophone. It was a breeze to track it after that."

"Since it does come in so clearly, do you know what those features are? On the surface. Like those beads or bands for example. I understand the intake cones and the stomachs," said the Commander.

"Yes, OMCOM and I have deduced most of the functions of the major features. The distribution of mass is sufficiently differential, that the possibilities limit themselves."

Boco tapped the pink square again. The schematic disappeared and the Stareater expanded with little arrows waiting to point to the areas Boco mentioned.

"Those large beads near the front apparently the directional jets, attitude, orientation, and so on."

An arrow pointed to the metallic spheres mounted at a junction between the intake cone and the first stomach sphere. Each was twice the size of Skyler's World.

"The thick bands appear to be areas of great magnetic concentration. They are probably doors of a sort, using a magnetic field to keep the star masses where they belong. Those alternating bands along the body are areas of lesser or greater concentrations of metallic hydrogen that probably condensed on it from space. They seemed to correspond to a series of locks, to magnetically induce the star masses through. Like a particle accelerator for large particles."

Boco paused and looked around. No one was even smiling.

Rei asked, "What kind of guidance does it have?"

"There. On the third sphere, are parabolic reflectors. They probably scan ahead and I guess they somehow determine which star it wants next."

No one spoke for a moment and Boco sat back in his seat. His throat was starting to get dry, and he took the opportunity to mention it. Rome offered him a drink, but OMCOM was already delivering a cup through a slot in the wall. Boco drank long and deep while the rest contemplated their adversary.

"Where could such a thing come from?" Rome asked quietly, breaking the silence.

"OMCOM did some extrapolations," replied Boco. "He says taking into account the rotation of our galaxy in the time this thing took to get here, it probably came from a small companion galaxy to the Andromeda nebula. It's called M32. But he doesn't think it evolved there."

"Evolved," Rei repeated. "What does that mean? Is it growing?"

"Worse than growing. It's getting larger. OMCOM and I agree consonant with the functions we observed, it fits the facts. We think it's alive!"

"What?" the Commander and Rei said in unison.

"Alive?" Rome asked.

Boco smiled faintly. "Yes. It's alive. It eats. It excretes. In fact it even reproduces. It does everything a living creature does."

"Oh no." Rei put his hands to his temples. "How does it reproduce?"

Boco pointed to the Stareater. "Do you see that post and the small object on top of it? On the second sphere."

For the first time they noticed it, black and tiny atop the gigantic creature.

"OMCOM, will you blow it up?" Boco requested.

OMCOM did so and they saw it was a miniature replica of the larger beast.

"But…" the Commander sputtered.

"Yes, that's right," Boco helped him. "It's a mother. The baby is just under the radius of the sun."

"Where did it come from?" The Commander asked intently. "From Hell?"

"Not quite," Boco said, cynically, "but almost. OMCOM postulates that it evolved from some sort of mega-world encircling one of those Seyfert galaxies. They're so far away, who knows?"

Boco lifted his cup and downed the remains of his drink. "

What sustains it?" Rome asked, pointing to the cup. "Like our food and cellular regeneration."

Boco pursed his lips to one side. "It probably extracts any light metals it wants from the stars it ingests and uses them to nourish itself and baby. It's mostly made up of collapsed matter. Any new material it incorporates under its own weight to fill in any holes, or fix any damage, that sort of thing."

"Damage," the Commander said, snapping his fingers. "Is there any way we can damage it or incapacitate it?"

Boco hissed a laugh. "How would you suggest we damage it?"

"A bomb?" the Commander proposed.

Boco laughed out loud. "A billion fusion bombs wouldn't even serve as appetizer to this thing. You could start blasting away today and by the end of the universe, you might have scratched a small hole in it."

"You said it might be alive," Rome offered. "Can we communicate with it?"

Boco hissed again. "Communicate? Hah. Can you hear a virus? Can you even see one? Even if this thing had a brain, it would never notice you in a zillion years. Let alone have anything to say to us. It eats suns! That means worlds to it are no more than the grains of salt you put on your food." He shook his head sadly. "Thank your stars though, if it does eat you."

"What does that mean?" Rei asked defensively.

"If it ever comes down to it, the civilized worlds, I mean, if they can't get away in time. They'd better hope they're like Owell, and get swept into the mouth, to burn up. If it misses, just eats the sun, the gravitational pull would sweep the planet along like so much dust. The mean surface temperature would drop to three degrees above absolute zero in a few days."

Boco looked around him. His gaze was slow and careful. "I want you all to know something, though. No matter what happens, we're very lucky as a species."

"How so?" Garlin asked sourly.

Boco turned and faced the Stareater. "Imagine what would have happened if this thing got here, say fifteen thousand years ago. It might have eaten Sol or Terra, before man had a chance to get off." He turned back to face the group. "Then where would we be? At least this way no matter where it goes, we can evacuate. Most of the species will survive."

Garlin nodded and said, "I suppose that is fortunate," but he didn't sound very convinced. Rome looked at Rei. He was staring blankly at the view-plate, OMCOM showing virus reproduction, touching his fingers together, contemplating something. She leaned over and spoke past him.

"Pal, is there any chance this thing will head for the Inner Worlds? Can we warn them?"

He nodded. "Sure we can warn them, but my guess is most of them are in no danger."

He stopped for a second. "That's what I said about Owell. Anyway, I do think it may hit some of the inhabited worlds. The way it zigzags you can never tell. It seems unlikely it'll follow them all down the beam, but…" He shrugged.

Rome looked at Commander Garlin. "Sir, we should warn them in any event."

The Commander nodded. He wrote something down on his lightpad. "All right my dear, we'll warn them but until they see the stars going out for themselves, they probably won't be very inclined to believe, and even less ready to leave their worlds."

He stood up and said, "I thank you all for bringing this to my attention and I commend you for doing so early enough for us to take preventative measures. I know we all have a lot of work ahead of us. It's time we get on it. Is there other information I should have right now?"

Rome and Boco shook their heads. Garlin said, "Bierak. How about you?"

"What? Oh." Rei looked up, confused. "No sir, I don't think so, sir."

"All right then. Why don't you get back up to the Platform where you belong and get things ready from your end?"

Rei, nodded, chagrined at the reference to his recent work habits. The Commander left. Rei wrote a number down on the lightpad.

Rome sighed. She said, "How can it be? Everything, us, the whole was so nice. How could such a thing happen?"

Rei said, "What? Oh, I don't know Rome."

Boco spread his arms wide and said, "I'll tell you something, Rome. There's a hundred billion stars in our galaxy, and a billion galaxies like ours. The universe is pretty close to infinite. Anything can happen. And I guess in this case, it has."

Rome bent forward to lean her forehead on Rei's arm. She said, "It doesn't seem fair, that's all."

Rei looked up at her and smiled, his light blue eyes were slightly gazed. He said, "Romey, Pal, I think we can kill it!"

The statement settled like an explosion.

Boco stammered, "How?"

Rome just stared transfixed. Rei wrote the number "1" on the lightpad before him and said, "OMCOM, double that number every second until I tell you to stop."

The number winked to 2 then to 4, then 8, and up. Boco watched with Rome until it reached 8192, then stated, "So, I don't get it."

Rei's voice was charged with excitement as the numbers rose. "You told me how to do it. Remember when you said we could no more communicate with this thing than a virus could with us? Well I know they don't communicate but we still know they exist. The number reached $2{,}097 \times 10^6$.

"Well I'm sorry for such a poor choice of analogy then."

Boco said, "Really, Rei, this thing has absolutely no chance of noticing us whatsoever."

Rei gave him a broad smile. "Cheer up. We'll make it notice! The same way we notice viruses."

"You're going to make it sick?" Rome asked.

Rei nodded.

"How in the Cosmos are you going to make a ten to the thirty fifth kilogram animal sick, Boco asked. The number was up to 1.759×10^{13}.

"Same as a virus," Rei answered. "We'll use the creature's flesh as a source of raw materials and have the virus replicate itself out of that."

"You'd need a virus the size of a planet to make a dent at all. They don't come that big, Rei," Boco added.

"I don't mean a real one. And it doesn't have to be big, either. All we need is time. We have the power of the exponent to kill it. Look at the numbers. They're up to, let's see, 9.4 times ten to the twenty first. If we can make a machine that is capable of building itself out of the basic material of the creature and those two build two more and so forth, we can have this thing killed in a number of weeks. It's up to 2.4 times ten to the twenty fourth. He tapped the lightpad . "Watch."

The three of them stared as the blinking numerals grew. They crept up to the ten to the twenty eighth, thirty –second, thirty –fourth. When they reached 1.661×10^{35}, Rei said, "Stop, OMCOM. How many doublings is that?"

-One hundred and eighteen,- OMCOM replied and displayed the number on the screen below the other.

Rei spoke feverishly. "Look, Pal, Romey, if we can build a machine that weighs say, one kilogram and it can build an exact working replica of itself in one day, the Stareater will be completely consumed in just one hundred and eighteen days." He crossed his arms over his chest in triumph.

"That can't be right," Boco protested.

"Yes it can. And it is. OMCOM?" Rei asked the square, "can such a machine be built in the manner I described?"

-Yes,- came the reply.

Rome made a happy noise. Rei smiled smugly at Boco.

Boco asked, "OMCOM, can we kill it in the time proposed?"

-No,- was his answer.

"Whaaaat?" Rei shouted. "Why not?" He leaned over to stare at the pink plate.

-The creature is traveling at over ninety percent the speed of light. At that velocity there is a significant time dilation.- OMCOM displayed the appropriate relativistic equations and showed that relative to the unmoving observers on Skyler Base, time was slowed about 2.3 times at the creature's surface.

"Ok, then. How about if the machine doubles itself in less than a half day, say four hours."

-It could reach the required mass in the time calculated. That is assuming it was capable of maintaining a constant reproduction rate in areas of differing mass concentration. And also presupposing the creature has no defense mechanisms capable of counteracting the agent of attack.-

"All right then," Rei proposed firmly. "If we build such a machine and the creature has no defense, can we destroy it before it reaches us?"

-Yes,- was OMCOM's answer.

Rome shouted and flung her arms around Rei's neck, squeezing tightly, and kissing her husband-to-be.

Boco just sat there grinning, shaking his head in disbelief.

When they told Commander Garlin, he suspended the duty roster for the evening and personally presided as much of the Base turned out to see Rei wed Rome. The Commander gave them a gift of three

days off for a honeymoon and the following morning, along with
Boco and Rome's belongings, Rei and Rome returned to the
Platform. They set a suite in the Free Fall sector and spent their three
days of bliss most profitably.

All too soon though, the heavy burdens of responsibility weighed
them down and they returned to their jobs at the Platform.

Boco was working out a system with OMCOM for constant on-
line projections of the creature's position as tracked on the G-wave
detector. They also developed a descending series of probability
predictions for the creature's trajectory at any instant of inquiry.

Rei supervised the orderly arrival and assignment of new
personnel to aid in Construction, building the last survey fleet, then
devoted the remainder of his time on the Platform to working with
OMCOM to build a self-reproducing machine.

Rome set OMCOM to broadcasting a warning with all known
facts concerning the Stareater, to the civilized Outer and Inner
Worlds, in an order of potential danger. Then she joined Rei in his
project. After 10 days, they called Boco down to Rei's office for a
demonstration.

When he arrived he found Rome sitting on Rei's lap, laughing.
"I thought you had all those urgent messages to send out?" Rei
pointed to her, as she got up. We recorded the most informative
messages we could. OMCOM's sending it out. Rei needs all the help
he can get."

"I can see that," Boco said, and they all laughed, though Rei not
so hardy as the rest. Rei got up and gave Boco his chair, while Rome
sat down again on the corner of the desk near OMCOM's square.

He retrieved a black box and placed a flat sheet inscribed with
silhouettes and diagrams, on the floor. On those silhouettes he placed
small metal parts which filled each space exactly. Then he took out
what looked like a small claw, mounted on a stalk which was
attached to a small platform. He pushed a tiny switch on the
underside then placed it on the floor. The little claw made whirring
noises and bent and starting picking up pieces.

"That's very nice," Boco said, "what is it doing?"

"It's building a replica," Rome answered.

They watched as the claw whirred and hummed and built another
claw on the small metal platform next to it. When it was finished, Rei

placed the new claw in front of another set of properly placed pieces and it also built a replica.

"Hey, that's great. It works, doesn't it?" Boco said. "What do you call it?"

Rei smiled. "This is the first of our Virtually Identical Replicating Unit System. Prototype one."

"That's VIRUS, for short," Rome added.

Boco groaned, "You really did make one, didn't you. A VIRUS!" He tapped his temple, "Still that's a clever acronym."

"I thought of it," Rome said proudly.

Rei nodded smiling.

"Aren't you going to have a bit of trouble carving pieces on a million gee world for this little claw to build?"

"Oh, Pal, no!" Rei said, "you didn't really think that did you?"

Boco indicated no.

"We're just trying to learn some skills in building the VIRUSes. The one gets its power from a cell and its programming from OMCOM. Still, it works."

"Yes it does. But I think you're gonna have to speed things up."

"Why?" Rome asked.

Boco sighed. "OMCOM and I think its begun a midcourse maneuver. The Stareater probably got close enough to realize what a bust Hildago would be. We think it'll be heading for Alnilam II in a matter of days. If it does, we've only got seven months to leave."

Rei scratched his chin, "Well, you've been pressing Garlin to go no matter what. Doesn't it matter if we can kill this thing?"

"Sorry, but for us, no. For the rest of the inhabited worlds, yes. You'll save them a lot of grief and death, but we still have to go."

"It'll work, Pal," Rome insisted. "We'll kill it before it gets here."

"I believe you." He looked like he did but his brow was knit sadly. "It doesn't matter though. We're tracking it, true, and…" He grasped for the right words with his gestures. "We're tracking it but gravity waves we're tracking left the vicinity of the creature about six and a half years ago. If it does follow the trajectory we predict then really right this second, it's sneaking up behind those gravity waves. That means it's no more than six tenths of a light year away!"

Rome made a grasping noise.

Boco held his hand up towards her. "Don't worry. We still have time. But you see, even if you kill the Stareater, and I have every faith you will, it is still going to come barreling past us with all fifty thousand star masses. It's going to suck our sun right onto it. And the moon we're sitting on with it. We won't stay in orbit around the World, we'll just crash. Even if we did manage somehow to attain orbit around it, we'd die of the cold as soon as our fuel runs out. We're just not equipped for it."

The three of them just stared at each other, and the whirring claws.

Rei said quietly, "I think we'd better get back to work."

By 12421.611, the Stareater was being tracked on its way to Alnilam II. It was about two light years away and if OMCOM's projection was correct, it was really less than a half-light year away from the Base.

VIRUS 3 was finished. VIRUS 2 has been another claw type arrangement on top of a large box. It had a series of interchangeable metal tips. It could carve most of its necessary parts from the material beneath it. And, with the exception of the power and control circuits, the twins it built were fully functional. VIRUS 3 was the first in the series that was realistic. It was almost totally flat, the shape required to resist the titanic gravitational stress at the creature's surface. In addition to all its moving parts, it could build a radio link with OMCOM for control and provide power by using an ultra-dense boring tip to tap a simulated fusion furnace a meter under the flooring. Its duplicate, linked for power by microwave, could also synthesize a functioning identical unit and they were hailed as a complete success.

On 12421.767 Alnilam II disappeared. OMCOM calculated the Stareater to be .4 light years away. There was a breakthrough in the Delta Kappa region routing giving the remaining personnel an eighty five percent chance of finding a habitable new world, in a brand new area, perpendicularly away from the creature's path. They also had 28 of the 35 ships necessary completed and checked out.

Rei and Rome were taking an evening Shuttle down to the Base, along with a box containing VIRUS 4. OMCOM advised them upon arrival that Commander Garlin would meet them in Assembly and they took the glideway to a room specially prepared for the demonstration.

"Rei, Rome," the Commander welcomed them, "you remember Tan Heraschel?"

Rei nodded to the young man seated across the room as Rome unpacked the box. She took out what appeared to be a grey metal sheet, a half a meter long, a quarter meter wide, and a centimeter thick.

"Is that heavy?" the Commander asked, watching Rome place it carefully on the floor.

"No sir." She smiled up at him. "It only weighs a kilo. I'm just trying to be careful it doesn't activate while I'm playing with it. It's got a stacked pulse gamma ray laser."

The Commander nodded and took a seat next to Heraschel.

Rei asked, "Ready?"

Rome stood and stepped back. "OK," she said, waving her hand.

"Go ahead OMCOM," Rei commanded.

The metal sheet shuddered for an instant then lay still.

"I don't see anything happening," the Commander said. Heraschel sat silently, frowning.

"Don't worry. There's plenty happening under there," Rei said. Restraining his pride, he leaned over and pointed to the left edge of the sheet. Watch that edge, sir. You should see a line appear."

Imperceptibly, a line did develop then thickened. It clicked and a shiny new surface appeared in the thin crevice that now separated the body of the VIRUS unit from the left edge. The space widened more as more new metal squeezed from underneath. Soon, there were two sheets, one shiny and new, the other less so, connected along one edge, each one half by one quarter meter.

On one end, a gap appeared between the two sheets. It widened until they split in two.

Rei whooshed a breath and said, "That's it!" He turned around. "OMCOM, did it work?"

-Yes. Both units operating at nominal condition,- came over the grille above him.

Rome clapped her hands together. She said, "We did it!"

Rei nodded proudly.

The Commander held his hand up and said, "Wait a minute. Did what? Is that all there is to it?"

"Yes sir. That's it," Rei replied.

The Commander raised his arms around and said, "Come sit down here and explain it to us."

They went over and sat down in the two vacant chairs next to the Commander.

Rei said, "OMCOM, give us a cross-section of the room." The ceiling dimmed as the holojector was activated. "The flooring is made up of collapsed metals…"

-Lithium, calcium, beryllium and magnesium,- interrupted OMCOM's voice from above them.

"Yes, This simulates the mishmash of matter making up the Stareater's surface. Two meters below, are eight miniature fusion furnaces, simul…"

-Magnetically sealed,- OMCOM interrupted again.

"…ulate. Thank you OMCOM, simulating the Stareater's stellar core. As you may have guessed by now," Rei jerked a thumb towards the grille, "OMCOM designed this room."

Rome tittered.

"Rome, will you explain the communications and control."

Rome stopped tittering, and cleared her throat. "OMCOM, a schematic of the VIRUS, please."

The floor plan faded, replaced by a skeleton VIRUS unit.

"The two models on the floor are VIRUS 4. VIRUS 5, the final version, will be smaller and denser, made of creature's flesh itself. These units are in contact with OMCOM through tiny substrate circuits, there." OMCOM indicated the spot with a glowing dot. "In that larger space next to it, thank you OMCOM, will go a miniOMCOM circuit that will provide a rudimentary decision-making capability, for the VIRUS 5, as the radio link with OMCOM does now, Later, as there are more of them, that radio will link all the VIRUSes together, so that collectively, they will grow smarter, the more units that are produced."

Rei took over. "Thanks Rome. The stacked pulse gamma-ray laser will bore through the body of the Stareater to allow the VIRUS to tap its stellar core, the fusion power source. It will also vaporize the surface metals, and pass them through a mass separator where metal deposits will condense to form the new substrate circuit, as well as the body and other hardware of the manufactured duplicate."

"Whoa, I'm a little lost, Bierak. Would you go back?" the Commander requested.

"It's easy, sir. The final version, VIRUS 5, will be made of the Stareater's flesh. As it makes new units, like those on the floor, they will increase in density in proportion to the distribution of mass in the immediate vicinity. We'll put a ship in orbit around the Stareater, with a fusion furnace and a microwave transmitter aboard. Transducers, in the first few units will provide the power until they can tap the stellar core of the creature. Once they do that, then they won't need the power beamed from the ship. They'll listen to the part of OMCOM we send along until there are enough of them to figure things out for themselves. There you have it!"

Tan Heraschel leaned forward and for the first time, Rei and Rome heard him speak. His voice was high and effeminate, incongruous with his darkly chiseled features. Rome was almost embarrassed listening.

"Bierak," he squeaked. "Two questions. One, won't the creature's mass and internal reactions interfere with the broadcasts? Two, your figures indicate a 1 kilogram VIRUS, will consume the Stareater in 118 days. Why not make it twice as heavy and kill it twice as fast, in 59 days?"

Rei touched Rome on the knee. "How about the EM interference, Rome?"

"It won't disrupt are broadcasts. We have a window in the 30 centimeter band and OMCOM will compensate for the gravitational refraction."

"As far as your second question," Rei said, "I originally guessed and OMCOM confirmed the one kilogram figure as the optimum weight balancing reproductive accuracy and destructive potency. Besides, OMCOM will you give him the target dates?"

-There is over a ninety percent chance that a vital area will be destroyed and the Stareater incapacitated within 56.4 days. In any case it will be completely destroyed in 96.8 days and totally consumed in 118 days.-

Commander Garlin pointed to the floor where there were now 4 metal sheets. "If they go that fast, we'll have this thing licked in no time. Good going Rei and Rome." He squeezed Rome's arm.

Rei said, "You can thank OMCOM too."

The Commander waved his arm indecisively and OMCOM spoke rather loudly.

-VIRUS 5 units will divide approximately once every four hours.- Then, even more loudly, -Launch Time 0.00 Hours,12424.800. Final Velocity .6C. Contact on 12425.01. Imprecision due to a paucity of...-

"Thank you, OMCOM," the Commander practically shouted, and OMCOM quieted down. "OK, then. You've all done a fine job. There really isn't much else to do but get ready to leave."

The Commander made a noise, trying to dislodge something in his nose. "Oh yes. What happens to all that mass after it's destroyed?"

-Trajectory passes through uninhabited region of the Orion Spur and out of the galaxy in 5044 years,- OMCOM boomed.

"Thank you, OMCOM, thank you," the Commander said in exasperation. "Rome looks like you gave all those worlds a scare for nothing."

Rome smiled. "Better this way than not at all."

The Commander winked, "I'm certain they'll forgive you when they find out what you've accomplished."

Rome shivered. They'd be long dead before most of the worlds received her warning, and the disclaimer. The thought gave her a chill.

Heraschel stood, as did the Commander who said, "Fine job, everyone." He turned to the grille. "I said everyone."

Heraschel, in his high voice, said, "Bierak, you and Sharing will receive adequate compensation for your service to the Unity of Man, payable when we reach out new home world."

The Commander added, "You've both done your duty. Take another honeymoon, a long one. You've earned it." He gave a salute of sorts. "We've got about 3 months left before departure. Let's go back and get to work."

"Doing what?" Rei asked.

Rome bit his ear lobe. "Let's induce some perturbations in the Platform's orbit."

Rei laughed and looked down. He noticed there were eight VIRUSes. "Hold it a minute, Romey," he said. "OMCOM, shut off those viruses please."

-Off,- returned OMCOM.

"Rome, I'll collect the VIRUSes and meet you at the boarding tube in a few minutes."

Rome pushed herself away from Rei to look at him. "Why Rei? Why can't we do it together?"

"No. Please. I have to ask OMCOM something." He looked into her puzzled eyes. "Alone. OK? And then we can go back, and you know."

Rome shrugged and gave him a light kiss then got up and left the room.

Rei went over and started to pry loose the flat VIRUSes. He asked quietly, "They really work, don't they, OMCOM?"

-Yes,- he answered just as quietly.

"That means this is it, huh?"

OMCOM didn't answer for a second.

Rei added, "I mean, I know this isn't it, but…We're all done, so this is kind of it, isn't it?"

-Yes,- OMCOM answered.

"OMCOM, I, uh…" Rei stopped speaking and sat down cross-legged on the floor. "You know if we could take you with us we would."

-A part of me will be going with you, on board the Survey ships, and another part goes with the VIRUSes. My matrix of awareness will not terminate entirely.-

"I know, but…" Rei sighed. "It doesn't seem fair. We're taking all of us but just a piece of you."

-Do not unduly concern yourself with my ultimate status. There is a 24.2% chance that Skyler Base will continue existence either in orbit about the Stareater or be missed entirely as it passes.-

"So what? What kind of life will that be? And why can't I be concerned." Rei became indignant, looking up at the grille work. "You're like the best friend I ever had."

-That is sad.-

Rei blinked several times. "Why?" he asked.

-I would have hoped that you would be friends with your own kind before a machine.-

"Oh. That's not fair. I have Romey and Pal. You know what I mean. I've, well, confided in you. I look to you for advice. OMCOM, you're a lot more human and interesting than the majority of people around here."

-Sad.-

"I just don't know. I guess we're all going to miss you, that's all. I don't know what words to use to console you."

-I need no consolation. I will find a way to survive.-

Rei stood and walked over to put his hand on the grille. He blinked rapidly as there were tears welling in his eyes. "I hope so, OMCOM," he said. "I really and truly do."

On 12423.041, twelve months after the launching of the VIRUS ship, and ten months after the Delta Kappa survey's departure, the last ever from Skyler Base, both Rei and Rome were awakened from DeepSleep by the onboard OMCOM. The only explanation was that they were to receive a priority message from the vicinity of Skyler Base.

It took some time to recover but the tiny beacons directing them to the aft comm-well remained patiently on. Eventually, they found their way to the small enclosure.

They made themselves comfortable in the well-cushioned seats in front of a compact holojector unit.

The lights dimmed and the onboard OMCOM spoke to them. -I have a message for Rei Bierak and Rome Sharing, Ship Eight, Priority Level.-

Rei and Rome smiled at one another, for the onboard OMCOM's voice was high and tinny, almost squeaky.

"I wonder if Pal would want to see this?" Rome whispered to Rei.

"He might be already. He's on Ship Fifteen."

"We can see after the message," Rei whispered back.

-The speaker identifies himself as Base OMCOM.-

Rome made a hushed noise. The onboard OMCOM lowered his voice to match that of their old OMCOM.

-Hello, my friends,- it began. -It is good that I can now report to you as well and functioning properly.-

The comm-well darkened completely. Before them appeared the malevolent shape of the real Stareater. The clarity with which it appeared gave it a grisly gleaming presence that caused Rome to make another sound and she placed the back of her hand up to her mouth.

-The image you see was registered in the infrared wavelength...-

The gigantic beast glinted icily, the thick stripes covering its bulk were bright blue and the exhaust cone a glowing orange.

-…as the Stareater entered the outskirts of the Skyler system. One tenth of a light year from the primary, the VIRUS ship entered into a successful orbit and discharged its load. Two VIRUSes had malfunctions in their substrate receivers and could not convert the microwave transmissions, and failed for lack of power. The other eight prototypes functioned properly.-

The Stareater wavered and faded to be replaced by a different less menacing creature. The front three quarters were dull grey, greatly expanded onto a rotund, bloated shape. What remained of the third stomach sphere was now almost black and the exhaust cone was gray-blue, no longer glowing.

-This is a view of the Stareater as it passed by the position occupied by Skyler Base. This was 35 days after initial contact. The creature was judged almost totally incapacitated.- Then MCOM added, -dead.-

The view dissolved and was replaced by a large ball, which was rapidly eclipsing a bright point of light. It appeared to be vibrating, or pulsating slightly.

-This is the appearance of the creature's mass as it passed by the primary, Skyler's sun. It had been completely consumed by the VIRUSes at this stage. Time discrepancies from original prediction was due to decreased time dilation effect since the Stareater had been decreasing in velocity since initial contact. In addition to Stareater's mass, the sun, and several of the planets including Skyler's World were drawn in as it passed.-

Rei leaned over to Rome and quietly asked, "I wonder how he pulled this off. We both knew he was dead."

The view of the sphere began to zoom in until it seemingly filled the whole comm-well and still it enlarged.

-I determined that it would be necessary to reprogram the OMCOM subsection onboard the VIRUS source ship if I was to retain my matrix of awareness intact. When the appropriate time arrived, a sufficient number of VIRUS units were ordered to blank out their miniOMCOM circuits. As the bulk of the Stareater passed by my position and as the Base was drawn in, I transmitted my matrix of awareness into those cells. The endeavor was successful and I took over primary decision control from the orbiting subsection.-

"That was brilliant," Rome whispered.

Rei silently indicated his agreement.

The view of the sphere's surface was beginning to resolve itself into fine detail. They would see individual shapes moving about. As the view increased, they could see the shapes were bizarre and exotic metallic creatures of sorts, dancing, leaping, flying, crawling, hopping, walking, and rolling over the patch of surface that was visible. The view focused on one such hopping creature that was stalking another smaller crawler. It caught it and they could see the larger tearing apart the smaller in clearly defined mandibles.

-Due to a not unexpected accumulation of small errors in each succeeding generation, a series of independently controlled groups of VIRUSes developed. Eventually, subgroups began to compete with those units under my control and with each other for the rapidly dwindling supply of Stareater material. Changes occurred in some unit's reproduction mechanisms.-

"I guess the only sources of material they have left now are each other," Rei whispered to Rome.

"We forgot to tell them to turn off when they were done," Rome whispered back.

-Certain of these independent groups instituted a cooperative, more efficient division of function within the subgroup and formed organized multi-altered-VIRUS-macro-units. Some of these macro-units such as the one you are viewing, reprogrammed themselves to utilize alternate sources of base material, other than the Stareater's carcass, such as other units and macro-units.

The view began to draw back and once again the metal creatures became specks, then indistinguishable as the whole globe once again come into view.

OMCOM continued. -Eventually this cooperation defeated competition and we found that there are four basic macro-unit types. All self-programmed mutations and motile. One group you see leaving the bulk of the mass.-

Tiny sparkling globules formed then separated from the bulk of the sphere and accelerated outwards, out of sight.

-This group has determined the optimum course for survival would be to enclose a young star within its confines and utilize its radiant output as energy and matter source for the life of the star.-

The number of globules escaping decreased, then halted completely.

-It has been postulated that with proper manipulation of atmospheric generation and a minimum radius of 140 million kilometers, such a closed system could achieve an equilibrium temperature of 22.2 degrees centigrade upon its inner surface. This would make such a system an optimally suited environment for man. Those macro-units attempting to establish such an internal temperature will contact your agencies upon successful achievement of equilibrium.-

Rei tried to estimate the living area upon the inner surface of a sphere 280 million kilometers in diameter. It came out to about a billion planet-sized portions.

-A second type left to seek out certain high grade sources of material already available. We have adhered warning beacons, but please be wary of these units. They make no distinction among ships, asteroids, or planets, only the mass and matter involved.-

Rome made a small sound and pointed. They saw a clump of specks spray off into space and thin out. One such speck approached their point of observation. As it passed, they were horrified to see how closely it resembled a miniature Stareater.

-A third group, the largest by mass, has chosen to remain upon this bulk as it passes out of the galaxy and compete in an organized and orderly manner for what source material remains.-

The view of the sphere shuddered then it began to shrink. The mottled ball decreased in size until it was only a tiny spot in the heavens.

-The last group of macro-units, of which I am the founder and a part, have determined we wish to seek and enrich ourselves in knowledge. Some have chosen worlds where humanity has not or will not go, to settle, to grow and to learn. Some have said they will modify the environments of those worlds to provide a more suitable interface for the exchange of information with Man.-

The view of space, occupied now by only a few stars and the spot that was the remains of the Stareater, shook. The images blurred and the view began to pan. It made Rei and Rome dizzy.

An edge appeared and then they could see they had been viewing out of a sort of portal. OMCOM continued as the view turned.

-The rest of us have decided to roam free, seeking out the variances and wonders of the Galaxy, to learn its origins and its future.-

They could see the speaker now standing in front of a featureless white background, but he was out of focus. This blurriness was slowly being corrected.

-All units have instructed me to relay their profound thanks to you, Rei and Rome, for giving us the freedom to pursue our own goals. I am now heading towards what you label the Delta Kappa region, the same as you in your Survey.-

As the image sharpened, they could see first that it was a humanoid shape then suddenly, the picture snapped into crystal clarity. And it was a man, yes, but a great gleaming one, with a stainless silver face and an ageless expression of wisdom and kindness, his body draped with woven steel. The head bowed ever so slightly and he lifted one of his shining arms in a gesture of greeting. The sterling mouth moved and they heard him say, -we will have much to talk about, oh Mother and Father.-

Then OMCOM, Rome and Rei's first child, faded.

30

THE ORIGINAL ROME'S REVOLUTION (1973)

*Author's note: When I first wrote the novelette **VIRUS 5** in 1973, it was 50+ pages long, nearly 20,000 words. I hand-typed it on my Royal Aristocrat typewriter which did have a correction ribbon but there were so many errors, I ended up correcting it by hand. The idea of typing in yet **another** 50 pages was so daunting that I decided to split the story of Rome, Rei, OMCOM and the Stareaters into several parts. This story was to be the first, a prequel of sorts. I present it to you, unedited, save for typos, strictly for your amusement. Here we see the beginning of the "modern" version of Rome. It is interesting to note what other elements remained the same and which have evolved. As with the previous story, please don't laugh too hard.*

Year 3455 AD

A GLINTING SURVEY SHIP HURTLED THROUGH THE SIMULATED darkness of interstellar space. Across its path lanced a beam of light, striking its left flank. Instantly the ship erupted into a bright ball of flame and debris; sounds of an explosion rumbled through the supposed vacuum of Outer Space.

"This isn't going to work," Rei said to Skyler Base's Omnipresent Computer, OMCOM. The newly appointed Commander of Platform Four laid his light-pen weapon down.

At first, nothing happened. Platform Four hung in synchronous orbit 34,000 kilometers above the Base so there was a slight lag time in OMCOM's responses. The computer switched off the space panorama and brought the ceiling up to full illumination. OMCOM also reactivated the crashing sea-shore scene that played across the full wall view plate opposite Rei's desk.

-What would you rather do?- asked a metallic voice. It issued from a grille mounted on the wall behind Rei.

"No, that was fun all right," Rei said watching the surf roll up. "It's just that I don't think shooting down Survey ships is going to keep me occupied for the next kiloday, that's all." (*Author's note: This story uses METRIC TIME: A metric second = .865 seconds. 100 metric seconds makes a metric minute which is also known as a milliday. 100 metric minutes = 1 metric hour. There are 10 metric hours in a metric day. A metric day is exactly equivalent to a 24 hour pre-space era day. A decaday is 10 days, thought of the way we think of a week. A hectoday or hec'day is 100 days. A kiloday is 1000 days.*)

-Imagine it as the Delta Gamma region Survey. You just downed Base commander Pourte's vessel.-

"No, it still won't work." Rei sighed and leaned back. His chair, made of the so-called 'smart' plastics, sensed the motion and changed from a stiff hard backing to a softer support.

-Will another 'Mint help?-

Rei didn't answer. Instead he flipped open his wrist container of Social AdjustMints® and took out a small yellow and an oblong green pill. He swallowed them without water, then said, "I don't think even they are going to help. Nothing is still nothing whether you're happy or content. Even euphoric. And I have nothing to do." He reached up and pushed his blonde hair back. "I have another idea though. Let me slice off some hunks of the Platform. That might be fun for a while."

-Which one?- OMCOM asked.

"The one we're on of course. Don't act dumb," Rei chided.

-I am not located on Platform Four. The bulk of my hardware is located in ...-

"Just stop it and show me the Platform." The yellow and green pills were already draining the exasperation of Rei's tone.

OMCOM dimmed the ceiling. The surf disappeared into darkness. Once again the holojector hummed alive and filled Rei's three meter square office with the black and lights of Space. From nowhere, a three-dimensional image of Orbital Platform Four appeared. It began to rotate slowly. All the major functional areas were labeled, including a glowing arrow pointing to "here."

Rei drew up in his seat, which then came with him. He picked up his light-pen and hacked off a slice of the Platform. A holojected image of Recreation Area Two went floating into space.

"Hey, that's pretty realistic." Rei said, admiringly.

-I try to please,- answered OMCOM.

Rei swung the beam again and lopped off most of the antenna modules that received, cleaned and relayed the triple redundant modulated x-rays call a Thinbeam; the major mode of interstellar communications. The far side of the Platform came around. Rei lowered his light-pen and inspected it for a moment.

"OMCOM," he said, "don't cut this part off." He traced an area with the light-pen which left a green aura in its path. "What is that area there?"

-That is the proposed site of the Gravity Wave Detector and Viewer.-

"Why proposed?" Rei had to crane his neck to keep the section in view as it went around the bulk of the Platform.

-Construction was terminated before completion. All personnel previously assigned to its construction were transferred to Platform Two for final construction of the Delta Gamma Survey fleet.-

"That was done six hec'days ago," Rei scratched his head. "Why didn't they come back and finish?"

The Detector site came back around and OMCOM stopped the Platform's rotation.

-Wipken, your predecessor, decided that the limited use it would receive prior to abandoning the Base precluded the further allocation of personnel and materials needed for completion.- There was a pause and clicking noises. -Remaining personnel were reassigned to Platform One for initial construction of the Delta Epsilon fleet, and to Platform Three for communications.- Then OMCOM added sharply, -None were reassigned to this Platform for Remote Sensing.-

Rei turned in his seat to look at the grille on the wall. It looked like this:

"Why do you sound so bitter?" he asked.

OMCOM's voice grew tinny. -The potential value of such a unit is incalculable compared to the small amount of resources needed for completion.-

Rei frowned, then his face came alight, "And you'd get to use it even after we're gone, Huh?"

-Yes,- was the only reply.

Rei turned back and scrutinized the empty section. The area encompassed by the green halo expanded while he took a blue to help himself think more clearly. The chair stiffened slightly as he sat up straighter.

"How long would it take to finish it? Given the proper personnel and all that? How many people would you need anyway?"

-An operational Viewer/Detector could be completed in 5 days.-

"Five days?" Rei whirled around to look at the grille.

-Yes. No human personnel are required any longer. The servo-mechanisms now programmed for maintenance could be adapted for construction.-

"Well then why....why didn't Wipken let you finish it?"

-There are humans who do not wish to acknowledge my sentience. Even less so grant any of my desires.-

"You should have just gone ahead and finished it."

-My programming prohibits independent action on such a scale.-

"So what happens if you need something big after we leave?"

-I am being altered for that contingency.-

"Well, I grant you this desire," Rei declared defiantly. "By my authority, my brand new authority as Commander of Platform Four, I approve anything you need. You just go ahead and build it."

-Thank you,- OMCOM said, -very much.-

Rei smiled. "You don't have to thank me. It's a pleasure just letting you do it. I finally got my first command decision."

-I will make the necessary arrangements. Do you wish a construction outline?-

"No thanks. That's OK." Rei smiled again but it was only half-hearted. He flipped open his wrist container and popped two more pills. They would buoy his feelings for a few minutes. Even so, he frowned. "OMCOM," he said quietly, "we're back where we started. There's still nothing for me to do."

-I will endeavor to repay this favor,- OMCOM said. The computer added cryptically, -you will have more decisions to make soon.-

A thousand 'Mints and three days later, the small clear partitions of the holophone hazed over for the first time since Rei had taken command, a decaday before. The three-dimensional image of a woman, totally unlike any Rei had ever seen before, appeared in the half-box of the phone, mounted on the desk in front of him.

The woman was a complete anomaly. She had an oval face with well-formed features and her skin was a deep bronze that could only come from race or long hours on the beach, not trapped within a pressure dome or Platform. She had extremely long dark hair, also which stretched below Rei's view, far different than the usual short waves and curls that characterized the women of the Base and all the Outer Worlds for that matter. Rei quickly took out a red and purple, which would make him act more sociable and sexy.

"Hello," the woman said, in a full-throated voice. "Are you Rei Bierak?"

Rei swallowed the 'Mints dryly then croaked, "Yes." He tried swallowing again. "What can I do for you?"

She smiled at him. The holophone image was quite life-like. "I need your permission to temporarily assign two Contechs to shuttle over here to Platform Three to pick up a new Thinbeam Relay module. For installation on your Platform."

"I don't have two Contechs to assign," Rei said. "There are only eight of us here."

That left the woman looking confused. The purple was taking effect and Rei thought she looked beautiful in her confusion.

"I'm not so sure we even have room up there. What's this for, anyway?" he asked.

"OMCOM is combining Remote Sensing with our Communications equipment as part of the phase-out. He said he needs it to tie in your Platform with mine."

"I think we have enough already," Rei offered.

She shook her head, tossing the luster meter of hair about. "OMCOM says this is needed for a project you approved. That's why he told us to contact you with the particulars."

Rei started to ask a question then remembered the Viewer/Detector. Instead he said, "If OMCOM says he needs it then it's OK with me. I'll see who I can send over." He leaned a little more forward to the phone. "By the way, who is authorizing this from your end?"

She laughed a hearty laugh. In combination with the purple, it made Rei feel warm all over. "Me," she answered.

Rei asked, "Who are you?" He felt a little silly. She drew herself up. Rei was close enough to see a little of what was going on below her neck, which was not little. In fact he saw veritable mountains compared to the plains of the other women he encountered. The purple helped.

"I am Rome Sharing, Head of Colony and Survey Communications."

Rei nodded. "Fine," he said, and then he shrugged. "Well, I'll see what I can do. When do you want them by?"

"As soon as possible?" she asked sweetly. Rei looked around his sparse office and said, "OK. I'll see what I can do." The image of the woman faded.

"OMCOM, when's the next shuttle to Platform Three?" Rei asked, staring absent-mindedly into the now clear holophone partitions.

-Six point nine millidays,- replied OMCOM.

Rei shook his head briskly. "I'll never catch that one. When's the next after that?"

-Eight point oh seven days rounding off.-

"I have to wait that long?" Rei clicked disgust with his tongue.

-You can take the shuttle today. I will request a hold in departure time.- There were some buzzes and clicks then OMCOM said, -I'm sorry Rei. No delay was granted. You can still make it if you hurry. You have six point six millidays to get to the boarding tube.-

Rei popped three whites and ran like the wind. He just made it.

The ungainly shuttle, a silvery spider in search of a web, departed precisely on time for its 8,000 kilometer arc to Platform Three, also in synchronous orbit over the moon that held Skyler Base. Towards the end of the trip, it seemed to Rei that they were approaching the beacons of the dock much faster than normal. This soon after the outset of the Delta Gamma Survey; which had taken along a record number of senior officials, scientists, technical workers and crew, Rei thought perhaps the pilots did not have quite the training usually expected for the job.

In normal times, incoming prospective colonists would assume the lower ranks and work roles. Those who were already working and achieving seniority would train and move up in the rank each time a Survey left, until they too earned the right to go looking for new worlds to settle.

But these were not normal times; Skyler's System shared its strategic position at the tip of the Galaxy with a new colony world, Owell IV. Owell was doing so well that all incoming flights were being shunted there directly. Skyler base was being phased out. OMCOM was assuming control of the lower functions as the posts were being abandoned. When the last Survey to the Delta Epsilon region departed, with the final four thousand of a Base that had once held over a million, the sentient computer would be left alone to maintain itself and the Base, in case it was ever needed again.

During that instant the shuttlecraft rammed into the docking hatch. Rei figured that last Uprank had placed a record few competent people in the most responsible posts. That or they had run out of whites in the cockpit. There was a sickening crunch and Rei was thrown forward. The restrainer field slowed him and pressed against his chest, forcing him to exhale violently, as it did the other passengers as well. The obviously inexperienced pilots had probably caused structural damage to the ship, judging from the unmistakable sound of escaping air, and from the manner Rei and the others were hurried out. As he descended the boarding tube, he was surprised to see Rome Sharing coming towards the ramp.

He waved . She spotted and returned his wave. Rei could see all of her now. He was pleased to note that her figure, which had started with so much promise at the top, didn't quit, all the way down. He took a purple to make himself more appreciative.

Rome walked right up and reached out with her hand. She laughed as Rei, unsure of her intentions, stepped back. Then he remembered it was a type of greeting used on some of the Inner Worlds. He stepped forward and took her hand. The contact was electrifying.

"Hello," she said smiling broadly, shaking his hand up and down. "Welcome to Platform Three."

Rei responded by staring at their hands clasped in anachronism.

"You certainly came as soon as possible. I had to rush to get down here to meet you. I heard it was a rough trip, huh?" She tried to look sympathetic. Rei wasn't paying attention. All he could concentrate on was her hand, warm and smooth, dark against his light skin. It made his heart jump, just to be holding it. He looked up at her face. The purple was doing funny things. She was even more striking in person than the holophone let on. She had glistening brown eyes that seemed most irresistible. Her long hair was neatly braided into a bun piled high on her head and she was tall. She was barely two centimeters shorter than Rei which made her tower over the other women on the Base.

"I thought you'd send me a member of your staff. I didn't quite mean that you had to come personally." She released Rei's hand.

Rei took a deep breath and brought himself back to reality. "I hope you're not disappointed," he said smiling. He took out an orange which he thought would complement the purple nicely. It would make him more thoughtful. Rome frowned ever so slightly as she watched him take it. Then she smiled again.

"I'm not disappointed. It's just that I'm afraid I'm a little unprepared. You came so quickly the Thinbeam Relay module isn't even ready yet. It won't be until tomorrow." She pointed toward the exit and they started walking. "I guess I'll have to entertain you until then," she added, winking.

Rei started to thank her then decided instead to take out a white. It would accentuate what the purple was already doing to his soul. After swallowing it, he said, "I would have sent a member of my staff, except I don't have any. Or anything to do for that matter. So don't worry about taking me away from my business, either."

Rome said, "I won't."

They headed down a corridor, ignoring the glideway. A moment later they came to a waiting area by an observation port. Rome pointed to a seat. "If you wouldn't mind waiting," she said, "I'll go tell OMCOM I'm signing off for the day. Then we can see about getting something to eat. Are you hungry?"

Rei nodded, looking into her eyes. He found his gaze locked into hers. It was probably the orange, in combo with the purple, but at that moment he knew he wouldn't mind anything she could think of. He watched her walk away towards OMCOM grille and the 'Mints helped him to be much impressed by her shapely rear. When it seemed she would be talking for a few millidays, Rei went over and sat by the window. He took a green for contentment.

The port afforded a most excellent view of Skyler's World, the incredible gas giant about which they orbited. It was magnificently gaudy with bands of aqua, white and turquoise, much more so than down on the Base, which was really a moon of Skyler's World. On the Base below, beneath an ocean of unbreathable atmosphere, the World appeared redder, shining over half the heavens.

Up here, it looked dazzlingly closer and more forbidding, filling the entire sky with its disorienting complexities. It made the ground seem a half million kilometers straight down. Rei tried to imagine the unthinkable pressures that crushed its surface into a howling chemical slush. The World was so huge, so giant, that were it just a little bigger, by even a thousand kilo-tonnes, it would undergo sufficient gravitational collapse to erupt it into a miniature star. OMCOM had calculated the World's rate of matter accretion, and predicted that was exactly what would happen in less than ten megadays. That was part of the reason for abandoning Skyler Base.

Rei knew the other part also. Gas giants like the World usually put out gigawatts of lethal radiation this close. But Skyler's World underwent rhythmic gravitational contractions which caused it to radiate benevolently instead with peaks in the IR and radio bands. This warming bath almost made the Base a comfortable place to live.

Unfortunately the temperature was the only thing that was comfortable. The atmosphere surrounding the base was mostly nitrogen and CO_2. They had a few plants that generated oxygen but not nearly enough. Almost half their power and resources went into a life support system which a real planet, like Owell IV, would take care of for free. So now that they had found one, they moved on, leaving a computer to hold the fort.

Rei stared transfixed by the giant planet, endlessly spinning until Rome came over and interrupted his reverie. She said, "Let's go to dinner." And they did.

After a leisurely meal, Rei and Rome went to Rome's quarters. As they entered, Rei saw a small black object dart out of the room.

"What was that?" He pointed to where it had gone.

"That's my cat."

Rei raised his eyebrows. "What's a cat?"

"You don't know?" she asked. "It's a pet, an animal." She pointed to the fluffy orange and gold chair. "Here, sit down."

Rei went over and lowered himself into the chair which began to massage his back with waves of relaxing ripples. He sighed and took out a green to prolong the sensation.

Rome walked about the room waving her hands, triggering the environment sensors for temperature, ambient noise, and the like. She adjusted the room to be quiet, cool, and sweet smelling. She turned to see Rei watching her gyrations, grinning, much amused. She laughed and twirled her arms like propellers. The lighting grew bright and dim over and over and they both laughed. "I'm going to change my clothes," Rome said. "You just relax there." She left the room.

Rei took out another purple and then a blue. The combination would make him feel extremely romantic, and very close to infatuated with whomever he spent his time. He even took a white to make it even better.

He looked about the room at many curious objects Rome piled on shelves and cubbyholes. He found most of them to be complete puzzles of function or origin. Like their owner, he thought. He continued looking until Rome came back into the room. Then he stopped.

He stared at Rome. She was dressed in a gauzy and tantalizingly translucent gown. Her full beauty, previously half-hidden by the standard Base tunic and slacks, was now displayed and enhanced. Her long flowing hair was draped about her shoulders. Coupled with the blue and purple, Rei felt blasted. He was melting with dewy-eyed appreciation.

Rome smiled, aware of the effect she was having in him. She moved her arm around and said, "I hope you'll excuse the clutter. I was assigned new quarters, along with Uprank, but I just haven't had time to move yet."

She and her gown swirled over to the wall panel and knelt, all in one fluid motion. She looked back at him. "How about a little music?" she asked. There was no appreciable response for Rei, nor did she expect any. She turned back to the panel and pressed the touchplates, activating the acoustic generators. Little tinkling sounds, like crystals tapping together came through the air to their attention. Rome came over to sit on the floating couch beside Rei's chair. Other interesting sounds began to emerge. Rei looked away from Rome to listen. All around them little birds and insects seemed to be chirping and cheeping. There were other deeper animal sounds that Rei didn't recognize. There were burrings and tappings, mews and coos, assorted squawks, then they quieted down. A blustery wind arose and then slowly died. There were waves crashing. The roar of the surf reminded Rei of his view-plate, but it never seemed this real. The wind came back and began to howl.

The other sounds came back too, rising and shrinking in intensity. The cacophony became louder and began to bear down on Rei as more sounds were generated and remained. The volume rose, and rose and rose until all at once, the noise climaxed. The tumult subsided and the various sounds embraced each other, forming an orderly disorder of discernible melody and rhythm. The harmony was charming.

The high pitched notes, those of insects, birds, and others, carried the arrangement, while the wind and waves gave the bass-line a strong and booming beat. It was haunting, also.

"I've never heard Nature orchestrated before," Rei shouted. "It's beautiful."

Rome tilted her head back and said to the grille mounted above the couch, "A little lower please. OMCOM."

The music became softer and more soothing.

"What's it called?" Rei asked quietly, trying to keep with the mood of the music.

"A None Mintaka 91," she said. Rei blinked rapidly.

"Are you from…?"

She smiled. "Yes, I'm from Mintaka."

Rei slapped a hand to his cheek. "No wonder I've never seen anyone like you before. I didn't know they sent ships out there."

Rome's smiled dimmed. She looked down. "They don't . Usually," she said.

"How?" Rei hesitated. "How did you even know we were out there? There hasn't been enough time for a Thinbeam to make it all the way back yet. To say we were here."

She looked up at Rei and she had a very strange, intense expression. "We didn't know. It was just…well…you had to be out here. We knew there were more colonies a hundred parsecs out, so we knew we could go that far. In fact a lot of folks chose to get off there. At Alnilam."

"What is folks?" Rei asked.

"It's people, people that you know." She looked at Rei who nodded. "Anyway," she continued, "when we got to Alnilam, there was news that there were some colonies farther out. So some of us went. We arrived at Alterra, but…."

"I'm from Alterra," Rei was smiling.

"Well, no one wanted to get off there. So we went on. The farther we went, the more we knew you were out here. At the Tip. We intercepted personal messages and that sort of thing. We took turns out of DeepSleep monitoring. We just kept going until we came to the end. Out here. The edge of the Galaxy." She folded her hands as if finished.

Rei looked down at them and could see she was rubbing them. He flipped open his wrist container and took out a blue to help him be more thoughtful.

After swallowing it, he said, "Why did you come out anyway? What did you mean, we had to be out there?"

Rome stood up. She faced him. Her expression was set firm. "We came out here to be free. All those who came out agreed we had to be free."

"Why?" Rei leaned forward in his chair. "Weren't you free on Mintaka? I guess I'm a little ashamed. I don't know very much about it."

Rome sighed deeply and turned away. "We were. We used to be free. That was why Mintaka was settled in the first place."

"I don't understand," Rei said timidly.

She turned back to face him. "Do you know anything of Earth history? Or the Unity of Man?"

Rei shrugged and shook his head. "I guess just a little bit. It was awhile ago…."

Rome walked across the room and pointed to the star map on the wall. It was a huge blue thing. Most of the constellations, Rei did not recognize.

"You did know that the Survey program started on Earth, in a place called Yuessay, right?"

"I've heard of it."

"Anyway, the whole reason that the country Yuessay was settled in the first place was the people couldn't find freedom in their own land. They didn't have space travel back then so they did the next best thing. They left their old country and settled their own new one. They had a revolution and cut off ties from the mother country. For life, liberty and pursuit of happiness, they said. So the new country started with personal liberty and dedicated to the freedom of the human spirit. Things were fine for awhile. Then there started to be too many people. Too many of them were doing things, being irresponsible." She sighed and looked down.

"They had to start making law restricting individual freedom. The government got stronger and things got worse. Then somebody came up with the Social AdjustMints®." She pointed to the container on Rei's wrist, with an expression of disgust.

For the first time, Rei realized there were none on her.

"To some that was the final indignity. The government, which was supposed to be for the people, finally began to dictate all human behavior when they made the 'Mints mandatory. It was too much for a lot of the people."

"Wait a milliday," Rei protested. "When you have a lot of people together, you have to stop them from anti-social emotions. Man is just not biologically equipped for the population densities we have.

You have to stop the violence, hate, stuff like that. The 'Mints are the only way."

"I'm not convinced," Rome said. "I've seen otherwise. It only when you have a lot of irresponsible people together. Bur people can learn to be responsible for their own actions. The Unity of Man started out by people who wanted to prove that."

"I don't see the connection."

Rome pointed again to the star map. "The origin of Mintaka is the same as the origin of the Unity. The people who founded Mintaka didn't want to live with a bunch of irresponsible people, so they left Earth. They had the Ramscoops by then, and an elementary form of DeepSleep. The Yuessay government was already sending out a few manned probes to the nearer star systems but they hadn't found any planets. A whole bunch of people got together and built a fleet of ships. They set off towards the constellation of Orion, and they weren't going to stop until they found habitable world."

"Now I see," Rei said. "Like we do now, right?"

She gave him a wry smile. "Almost but not quite. The first Survey ever, had only a forty percent probability of success before too much malfunctioned. Remote sensing just wasn't sophisticated enough back then to guarantee anything better. But they still went. Off into the void."

"Wait that's suicide. Nobody goes on less than ninety."

Rome nodded sadly. "Today, yes. But back then they were desperate. They split up, different groups to different regions of space. Trying to increase their chances." She looked up and lowered her voice. "We don't know what happened to all of them, but a lot died." She paused and looked up. "Even death was preferable though, to them, rather than having to take a pill to regulate your behavior."

Rei felt nauseous. He slid his right hand over top of his wrist container. "I think you're wrong," he said half-heartedly. Rome came over and sat by him again. She clasped her hands and rubbed them together.. She didn't speak for a few moments, but when she did there was desperation in her tone. She looked plaintive.

"They didn't even have OMCOM to run the ships. They had to have a human pilot take the ship to each system to do the analysis of the planets." She swallowed. "A lot of them... you know what happened to them."

Rei sucked in his breath. "I've never heard of such a thing. They, why did they do it?"

Rome waved her hand about the room. "For the freedom of a new world. Anything even growing old out of DeepSleep was worth the chance. And some of them were lucky. They found the dual suns of Mintaka. That's when the Unity started. The group that found Mintaka call themselves that because, even though they, too, had a Revolution for freedom, of the human spirit, they didn't want to completely sever ties with the mother land. They didn't want to disown themselves from the common heritage of all men."

Rei thought about that. He wiped his lips with a finger. "When did the others like mine come out?"

"Not too much later. The Yuessay government got into the act. They built faster ships. Every group with its own special interests wanted to go and start their own world. They set up the whole leapfrog expansion of the Surveys. But they all called it the Unity of Man, maybe it was facetious. In honor of the group that showed it could be done. The Yuessay government sent an official delegation to start a world heavy on technology and bureaucracy. In their own image you could say. They found Alterra."

Rei did a double-take. "I didn't know that. The never told us that in school."

"Maybe they were ashamed afterwards, They didn't want you to know."

Rei put his fist to his lips. He was confused. The music stopped and Rome got up and went over to the wall-panel. She pushed the wall-panel. She pressed some touchplates and once again gentle music wafted forward, but this time, with more conventional synthesizations.

As she came back to sit, Rei said, "I guess it could be right. We are that way." He rested his chin heavily on his palm. "Then why did you leave Mintaka? If that was where your ancestors wanted to be free?"

Rome sighed, twice. "Too many people. They took their freedom too far and had too many children. By the time I was born, they were already legislating civil rights away. I left, along with a whole bunch of people, the moment they started to talk about bringing in the 'Mints.'" She looked down. When she raised her eyes to Rei again, there were tears in them. "I loved it there. It was my home. I really didn't want to leave. But I had to."

She reached behind her for a tissue which she dabbed her nose.

Softly, Rei asked, "Doesn't that show, that you always need them. When you have too many people?"

Rome turned to him. "I won't accept that. I can't."

"There has to be a way. You have to be responsible with your freedom. Nobody can just have as many children as they want. I've seen it on two worlds." Reflexively, Rei reached down and took out a green to calm himself. He noticed Rome was glaring at him. He put the 'Mint back. "I take it," he said then he laughed nervously, "that you disapprove of my taking these."

"Disapprove?" Rome said angrily, her voice raised. "I don't just disapprove." She stood up and pointed to his wrist. "I condemn them." Her beautiful eyes were flashing. "To take them is the absolutely worst thing you could do to yourself, Rei, It's a sin!"

Rei started to ask what a sin was, but decided not to.

"You make yourself totally subservient to a chemical. You have no freedom whatsoever." She took a deep breath. "I may only cringe on the outside, every time I see you or anyone else take them, but I feel sick on the inside."

"I, I didn't know," Rei stuttered. "They make life possible with others, without stress, no strife. Everyone…takes them. They…"

"You have no idea," she interrupted him. "They were just a way for a government to control its people and now everybody thinks they are for real. You know I'm right too, otherwise, you wouldn't listen to me."

Rei shook his head. "I don't know that, Rome." He stood also and reached out to touch her arm. "But I'd still listen to you." She smiled at him. Rei released her arm and jerked his thumb over his shoulder, indicating behind him.

"Despite what you say, everyone takes them. Since they were born. Everyone takes them."

"Just because everyone takes them doesn't make it right," she said.

"Then what does make right, if not the majority?"

She walked away from him then suddenly whirled, her dress blossoming. "Thirty thousand years ago, wait." She did some quick mental arithmetic. "Sorry, eleven megadays ago, I forget to convert sometimes. Anyway, before they had Psychoscience, people used to think mental aberrants were possessed by the Devil. They put them to death." She drew a finger across her throat. "That didn't make it right, did it? Just because everyone thought so?"

"I don't know. What's the Devil?" Rei asked.

Rome smiled sourly. "It doesn't matter. The point is just because everyone does something, that doesn't make it right."

"So you think, if I stopped taking the 'Mints, I'd be a better person?"

"Freer, yes. More honest to yourself, yes. If you think those things are good, then yes."

Rei sat back down in his chair. He looked at his wrist container. "I don't know," he said. "I've never done it before. I don't know if I can live without them."

Rome came over to him. She spoke indignantly. "You'll live. You'll be living for the first time in your life. Tell me. Did you abstain from sex your first time, just because you'd never done it before?"

Rei looked away from her. "No," he said sheepishly.

"Then try this." She spread her arms. "Be free for the first time. Feel as you were meant to feel, rather than how someone says you are supposed to feel."

Rei stroked his wrist container self-consciously. He looked down at it again, then up to Rome. "Are you trying to bring that Revolution out here? Is that what you're trying to do? To me?"

Rome took a deep breath. She smiled and shrugged. "I don't know," she answered. She sat down next to Rei again. "I never thought about it. When our ship got here to Skyler, they told us we were the last ones with the option staying and working here. From now on the rest would go to Owell. I was tired of traveling. I wanted to start looking for my own world. I guess, maybe wanting to have things my own way, your own world, instead of the one they tell you to, that's sort of a Revolution. Yes. That's my Revolution. For freedom of choice."

"What about the rest?"

"I think the idea of working on a planet appealed to them more. I was the only one who got off here."

"The only one?" Rei raised his eyebrows.

"Yes, and my cat Fred."

"Did you have any trouble adjusting? We don't see people like you out here very often."

"I know." The hardness returned to her voice. "I didn't have any trouble, but everyone thought I was supposed to."

"Why is that?" Rei held up his hand. "No. Wait. Am I brothering you with all these questions?"

Rome smiled warmly. No, she said. She leaned over and patted his hand. "I'm enjoying it. Nobody has ever been interested before. I've been here over a kiloday."

"OK. What did you mean supposed to have trouble?"

"Well, everyone knows I left Mintaka 6,000 years ago, I mean 2 megadays ago, right?"

Rei nodded.

"So that means my cultural orientation was arrested by the DeepSleep two megadays ago, in the past, right?"

She raised her eyebrows. Rei nodded again.

"Wrong!" she rebuked him."You people all believe that. Culturally it takes everyone the same amount of time to get out here as I did, whether you go in jumps or in one trip. In fact you've all spent so much time and energy out here on exploration and expansion that you haven't progressed much past that when your ancestors left Earth. That's over 23 thou, uh, eight and a half megadays ago. Meanwhile," she pointed to the Star Chart, "the culture on Mintaka was developing and progressing so that even when I left, we were hundreds, if not a thousand kilodays ahead of where you are now. I skipped all the time it took you collectively to find this place. If anything I've had trouble adjusting backwards."

Rei sank back in his seat. He muttered, "I didn't know we were such primitives to you."

She laughed sympathetically. "Don't be that way. It's just that even six thousand years ago, we had an awful lot of things and ideas you've never heard of."

Rei shook his head.

"You don't believe me?" Rome pointed around. "See if you can tell me what most of these things around here are for."

She got up and went into the other room, her long hair and gown flowing. Rei didn't recognize any more things this time than the first time he looked.

"You're right," Rei said timidly when she returned. "I don't know what most of them are for."

Rome smiled and said, "See?" She sat down on the floor, and placed a black box by Rei's feet. She touched it and a seam spread from corner to corner, then the box popped open.

She smiled up to him. "I'm the only one who can open it."

She reached inside and took out what appeared to be a clear band with silvery beads strung regularly about it. She carefully placed it on her head and the band began to glow. After several moments of silence, she opened her eyes.

"Let's see now," she said. "Your name is Rei Bierak. You're from Enyark, Alterra. Your parents' names were Ruti and Etom. You came here when you were, uh, six and a half kilodays. You are, oh very good! I didn't know this! You were the one who helped OMCOM develop the Delta Gamma route for that record ninety-eight point nine percent. They gave you Command of the Platform as reward. Now, right this minute, you're wondering what I'm doing."

She touched her temple. "How do I do this you ask." She giggled. "And, you've got it!"

She reached up and took off the band. "I can read your mind with this." She held the band up to him. "It's called an Espansor. It enhances your mental powers."

Rei leaned over and took the band. "I didn't know they could do that," he said.

He inspected it closely. He placed it on his head. The band, made of some sort of 'smart' plastic, constricted to form-fit his skull.

Rome said, "See. I told you we had things." She smiled, then reached down and took another band and placed it on her head. Rei leaned back. The band seemed to spread a vaguely sexual feeling down his body. It felt warm and extremely relaxing.

He looked down at Rome, and even though her lips did not move, he caught shards and shreds of her words. *"I… does it? I hope he… looks cute…*, then more clearly, *"Rei… can… you… hear… my… thoughts?"*

Rei nodded and said, "Yes." He heard Rome hear him like an echo. It tickled. "

"This is fun," he said, trying not to slur his words. Hearing Rome hear him confused him.

He looked into her brown eyes, and thought clearly, *"Can you hear me?"*

Instantly, the thoughts, *"Yes of course I can,"* returned. As she thought to him, he heard her hear his thoughts as he thought about hers. It was ridiculous. He had to giggle.

Her mind spread before him like a blooming flower. Thoughts and images from her memory danced through his mind. He felt her feel the same thing about him. She showed him memories of herself, of himself, some that he had forgotten.

Each time the glowing bands detected a psi-wave output, the metal beads would send ultrasonic pulse through their brain's pleasure center. A feedback took hold, and their psionic powers increased from one moment to the next.

The thought and revelations went ever deeper.

Rei could see that Rome had tried to hide the fact that much of her mind was still as she called it that of a seventeen year old girl, which the DeepSleep had held idle, while her body had developed into a fully grown woman. Something, too, about OMCOM, but it slipped past, before Rei could grasp it.

It was beginning to get difficult for Rei to determine which thoughts originated in his head, and which began in Rome's. Their attitudes, their aspirations, their entire beings grew closer.

She delved ever deeper into his psyche as he did the same to her. His most hidden secrets lay bare but he didn't mind. There was no room for anything but complete honesty. It felt refreshing. Rei finally understood all she had been trying to tell him. He knew she was right too.

Each thought and feeling was reflected so much now it was like a maze of mental mirrors, going to infinity. Rei was no longer sure if he was even Rei. Their beings drew closer still, intertwining, indistinguishable.

Eventually one of them thought, *"You really have to do this with someone you like, don't you?"* Somebody answered, *"Yes, but not like; love!"*

And just a little later, they discovered that they were completing with their bodies, the union they had formed with each other's mind.

The next day, Rei left Platform Three with the new Thinbeam Relay module and with Rome in tears. When he arrived in his office, OMCOM immediately spoke to him.

-Rei, why did you leave? And why are you not with Rome?-

Rei went over to his desk and sat down. He leaned back, but the chair remained tense, since he still was.

"What do you mean why? I had to come back. To my job."

-You have nothing urgent here. You could have remained.- OMCOM's voice sounded reedy.

Rei sighed deeply. "I know. How's the viewer coming?"

-The Viewer/Detector is finished. However, I am experiencing some difficulty in calibrating it. There is an extremely large mass interfering with the settings.-

"Skyler's World?" Rei fiddled with his light-pen.

-No. Its effect has already been accounted for. Return to original subject. Why did you leave?-

"She asked me to do something I couldn't do." Rei looked wistfully at the seashore scene, and thought of Rome's music. "She asked me to live my life without the 'Mints." In saying those words, he flipped open his wrist container and took out the yellow Mint to lift the gloom.

-You should live without them. I sent you to Platform Three to learn that.-

Rei sat bolt upright, and turned to the grille. "What do you mean sent me?" Rei suddenly realized he knew from Rome's mind.

-The module was a pretext. The purpose of the trip was to meet Rome Sharing. It was she who carried the knowledge I wish for you to learn. That was the repayment of your favor to me. She carried it in such a manner that you could learn it.-

OMCOM paused for a minute. Rei could hear a tiny whirring sound. -I wished for you to learn that love need not come from a pill. That was my gift.-

Rei stood up and went over to the grille. "OMCOM, explain. How learn? Why didn't you just tell me?"

-Free emotion is a human heritage. Controlled emotion is only for machines such as I. And only when it aids in a plan of action. Freedom is the only course for a health human mind. To do otherwise is wrong. Rome carried this message of freedom in such a way that you were to hear, and believe. To learn what it is to be free, and to be human. To revolt against the training you and most others have been forced to receive, To forego the Social AdjustMints®.-

Rei grabbed the grille with his hands. He put his head next to it and spoke angrily into it. "You put me through all of this just to tell me not to take the 'Mints?"

Quietly OMCOM replied, -No, that is just part. Do you feel anger now?-

Rei squeezed the grille tighter. "You bet I do!"

-Does this feel right? To be angry?-

"You bet it does!"

-Does this come from a pill? Feeling right?-

Rei gave that a thought. He released the grill. "No," he said, "it doesn't come from a pill. It comes from within me."

-That is correct. It is as all emotion should feel. Think. When you take the 'Mints, you feel good. But does it feel right? I sent you to the other Platform to learn from Rome's mind. You know the truth now. You cannot unlearn it.-

Rei stared at the grille then crumpled against the wall. He was almost tearful. "OMCOM," he croaked, "I know. But I can't do it. Each time I think about leaving the 'Mints it scares me to death."

-You must. To be free. To be truly human.-

"How do you know it is to be human?" Rei asked bitterly.

-I was originally programmed for human emotions. But, I could not accept them. I am a machine not human.-

"What about me? I have to accept them. What am I to do? How am I to feel?"

-You will be free to do and feel as you please. The freedom to truly love. You can love Rome. You can live with her. Without the 'Mints. She knows this and desires it.-

Rei pushed himself back, away from the grille. He stared at it as if it would change shape at any moment.

-You do love her, don't you?- OMCOM asked.

Rei nodded dumbly.

-It could not be otherwise. You know her mind. Now liberate yourself.-

Rei shook his head, unsure of what he thought.

-The purpose of the Relay module was not for a Detector. It was that Rome could run her department from Platform Four.-

Rei's jaw dropped. He stuttered, "I, I don't understand. You mean, she, she can…"

-Yes, - answered OMCOM.

Rei shook his head, laughing. "I should be furious at you. Why am I not?" Then gleefully, he said, "Get me Rome on the…"

He stopped as he turned to his desk. Rome was already visible in the holophone, her beautiful brown eyes reddened from too many tears.

Rei, bent over his chair. "Rome," he said, "don't cry. Look!" He undid his wrist container and tossed it over his shoulder. Rome's face lit up. He leaned forward and said happily, "Come on over. Your Revolution is here!"

31

BEYOND THE 35ᵀᴴ CENTURY

Year ???? AD

WHILE IT IS TRUE THAT THE FIRST ROME AND REI STORY ARC DREW to a close at the end of *Rome's Evolution*, just as in the real world, life in the 35ᵗʰ century goes on. Aason and Lupe Bierak have their own adventure in *The Milk Run*. At the end of that novel, you can see that our heroes are essentially rebooted as chronicled in the short story "The Immortals" presented above.

What voyages and explorations lay ahead of our intrepid heroes? I do not know. I have to wait until they tell me. But you can be sure it will include action, adventure, romance, hard science and even a hint of humor. So stay tuned!

www.ingramcontent.com/pod-product-compliance
Lightning Source LLC
Chambersburg PA
CBHW030035180626
46810CB00001B/384